A QUIET BELIEF IN ANGELS

'*A Quiet Belief in Angels* is a beautiful and haunting book. This is a tour de force from R. J. Ellory'

Michael Connelly

'This is compelling, unputdownable thriller writing of the very highest order' *Guardian*

'Once again R. J. Ellory shows off his special talents . . . it confirms his place in the top flight of crime writing'

Sunday Telegraph

R. J. Ellory is the author of four other novels: *Ghostheart, A Quiet Vendetta, City of Lies* and *A Quiet Belief in Angels*. Twice shortlisted for the Crime Writers' Association Steel Dagger for Best Thriller, Ellory's books have been translated into Italian, German, Dutch and Swedish. Having originally studied graphics and photography, he intended to pursue a career in photojournalism, but for many reasons this never came to fruition. He started writing more than ten years ago and hasn't stopped since. He is married with one son, and currently resides in England. Visit his website at www.rjellory.com.

By R. J. Ellory

Candlemoth
Ghostheart
A Quiet Vendetta
City of Lies
A Quiet Belief in Angels

Candlemoth

R. J. ELLORY

An Orion paperback

First published in Great Britain in 2003
by Orion
This paperback edition published in 2004
by Orion Books Ltd,
Orion House, 5 Upper Saint Martin's Lane
London, WC2H 9EA

An Hachette Livre UK company

Reissued 2008

Typeset by Deltatype Limited, Birkenhead, Merseyside

Printed in Great Britain by Clays Ltd, St Ives plc

The Orion Publishing Group's policy is to use papers
that are natural, renewable and recyclable products and
made from wood grown in sustainable forests. The logging
and manufacturing processes are expected to conform to
the environmental regulations of the country of origin.

ONE

Four times I've been betrayed – twice by women, once by a better friend than any man might wish for, and lastly by a nation. And perhaps, truth be known, I betrayed myself. So that makes five.

But despite everything, all that happened back then, and all that is happening now, it was still a magic time.

A *magic* time.

I can recall it with a clarity and simplicity that surprises even myself. The names, the faces, the sounds, the smells.

All of them.

It seems almost unnatural to recall things with such a sharp level of perception, but then that is perhaps attributable to the present circumstances.

Present a man with the end of his life, place him somewhere such as Death Row, and perhaps God blesses him with some small mercy.

The mercy of remembrance.

As if the Almighty says:

Here, son, you done got yourself in one hell of a mess right now . . .

You ain't stayin' long, an' that'd be the truth . . .

You take a good look over all that's been an' gone, and you try an' figure out for yourself how you got yourself arrived where you are now . . .

You take that time now, son, you take that time and make some sense of it before you have to answer up to me . . .

Maybe.

Maybe not.

I have never believed myself to be anything other than a soul. A man is not an animal, not a physical thing, and where I go now I don't know.

Perhaps it is the last vestige of mercy afforded me, but I am not afraid.

No, I am not afraid.

The people here, the people around me, they seem more afraid than I. Almost as if they know what they are doing, this lawful and sanctioned killing of men, and know also that they are doing wrong, and they fear the consequences: not for me, but for themselves.

If they could perhaps convince themselves there is no God, or no hereafter, then they would be safe.

But they know there is a God.

They know there is something beyond.

There is a spirit to this place. The spirit of the dead. Men here will tell you that once you've killed a man, once you've seen the light fade from his eyes, he will always walk with you. Your shadow. Perhaps he will never speak again, never move close to feel the warmth from your skin, but he is there. And those men walk the same gantries as us, they eat the same food, they watch the lights go down and dream the same fractured dreams.

And then there are the sounds. Metal against metal, bolts sliding home, keys turning in locks . . . all reminders of the inevitability of eternity. Once you come down here you never come out. The corridors are wide enough for three abreast, a man in the middle, a warder on each side. These corridors are painted a vague shade between gray and green, and names and dates and final words are scratched through to the brickwork beneath. *Here we're all innocent. Out of Vietnam into Hell. Tell M I love her.* Other such things. Desperate thoughts from desperate men.

And lastly the smell. Never leaves you, no matter how long you've walked the walk and talked the talk. Assaults your nostrils whenever you wake, as if for the very first time. There is Lysol and cheap detergent, the smell of rotting food, the odors of sweat and shit and semen and, somewhere beneath all of these things, the smell of fear. Of futility. Of men giving up and consigning themselves to the justice of a nation. Crushed inside the hand of fate.

The men that watch us are cold and removed and distant. They have to be. Figure once you attach you can't detach. So they say. Who knows what they see when the lights go down, lying there beside their wives, darkness pressing against their eyes and their children sleeping the sleep of innocents. And then the cool half light of nascent dawn when they wake and remember who they are, and what they do, and where they will go once breakfast is done and the kids have gone to school. They kiss their wives, and their wives look back at them, and in their eyes is that numb and indifferent awareness that the bread and cereal and eggs they ate were paid for by killing men. Guilty men perhaps, but men all the same. Justice of a nation. Hope they're right. Lord knows, they hope they're right.

I watch Mr. Timmons. I watch him, and sometimes he sweats. He hides it, but I know he sweats. I see him watching me through the grille, his weasel eyes, his narrow pinched mouth, and I believe his wife comforts him in his guilt by telling him that really he is doing the work of the Lord. She feeds him sweet apple fritters and a white sauce she makes with a little honey and lemon, and she comforts him. He brought the fritters once, brought them right here in a brown paper bag, spots of grease creeping out towards its corners. And he let me see them, even let me smell one, but he couldn't let me taste. Told me if I was an honest man then I would find all the sweet apple fritters I could eat in Heaven. I smiled and nodded and said *Yessir, Mister Timmons*, and I felt bad for him. Here was something else he would feel guilty about come dawn.

But Clarence Timmons is not a bad man, not an evil

3

man. He doesn't carry the blackened heart of Mr. West. Mr. West seems to be an emissary of Lucifer. Mr. West is unmarried, this in itself is no surprise, and the bitterness and hate he carries inside his skin seem enough to burst a man. And yet everything about him is *tightened up*. Don't know how else to word it. Tightened up like Sunday-best shoelaces. His manner, his words, his dress, everything is precise and detailed. His pants carry a crease that could cut paper. Look down at his shoes and you look back at yourself. The whiteness of his collar is unearthly, a heavenly white, as if he walks back through town each night and buys a new shirt and, once home, scrubs it until morning with Lysol and baking soda. Perhaps he believes the whiteness of his collar compensates for the blackness of his heart.

First time I met Mr. West he spat at me. Spat right in my face. My hands were cuffed and shackled around my waist. My feet were shackled too. I couldn't even wipe my face. I could feel the warmth of his saliva as it hit my forehead, and then it started its slow progression over my eyelid and down my cheek. Later I could feel it drying, and it was as if I sensed the germs alive on my skin.

Mr. West possessed a single, simple purpose. That purpose manifested itself in many colors – humiliation, degradation, violence, an impassioned cruelty. But the purpose was the same: to demonstrate authority.

Here, in this place, Mr. West was God.

Until the time came, until you walked the walk and danced the dance, until your bare feet did the soft-shoe shuffle on the linoleum floor, until you actually did meet your Maker, then Mr. West was God and Jesus and all the disciples rolled into one unholy mess of madness that could come raining down on you like a thunderstorm, provocation or not.

Mr. West was Boss down here, and the other warders, despite their years of service, despite their experience and pledge of commitment to the United States government, the Federal Detention system and President Reagan, still acknowledged only one Boss.

They all called one another by their given names. All except Mr. West. To everyone, the Prison Warden included, he had always been, would always be, Mr. West.

If there was a Hell, well, that's where he'd come from, and that's where he'd return. I believed that. *Had* to believe that. To believe anything else would have tested my sanity.

I am thirty-six now. Thirty-six years back of me, thirty-six years of love and loss and laughter. If I weigh everything up it has been good. There have been times I couldn't have asked for better. It is only now, the last ten years or so, that have been tough. Too easy to ask myself what I could possibly have done to have arrived at this point. If there is in fact a balance in all things, then I have found my balance here. Like Zen, karma, whatever this stuff calls itself. What goes around comes around: you get the idea.

I feel sorry for the kids. The ones I never had. I feel sorry for Caroline Lanafeuille whom I loved from a distance for years, but never kissed enough, nor held for long enough. Sorry for the fact that I could not have been there for her through everything that happened with her father and how they left. And had I been there it perhaps would never have turned out the way it did. And for Linny Goldbourne, a girl I loved as much as ever I loved Caroline. Though in a different way. Sorry too for Sheryl Rose Bogazzi. She was too beautiful, too energetic and uninhibited, and had she never been crowned County Fair May Queen she would never have met the folks from San Francisco, and had she not met them she would never have believed she could captivate the world. But she was crowned, and she did meet them, and her mom let her go all the way out there to follow her star. A star which burned brightly then fell like a stone. Six months in San Francisco and she was dead from a methadone overdose in a filthy tenement room. She'd been pregnant too, no-one knew by whom. Apparently she'd fucked everyone on the block, and most of their relatives.

I feel sorry for my folks, even though they're not alive and weren't alive when all this happened. At least they were spared that much.

Feel sorry for Nathan's folks, because their son is dead and he should not have died the way he did, and never for that reason. Nathan's father, a Baptist minister, is a powerful man, a man of faith and strength and endless forgiveness. He knows the truth, always has done, but there is nothing he can do. Said to me one time that he believed his hands had been tied by God. Didn't know why. Didn't question why. Knew enough to believe there was a reason for everything. But despite his faith, his trust, his passion, I still saw him cry. Cry like a child. Tears running down his broad, black, forgiving face, and the way his wife held his hand until I felt their fingers might fuse together and never be separated.

And they stood there in the Commune Room, me behind the protective screen, my hands cuffed to the chain around my waist, and I saw Nathan's ma look at me, look right through me, and I knew she believed too. *I know you didn't kill Nathan*, her eyes said. *I know you didn't kill Nathan, and I know you shouldn't be here, and I know what they're doing to you is bad . . . but I can't help you now. No-one can help you now except the Governor or the Lord Jesus Himself*.

And I smiled and nodded at her, and I made it okay for her to feel she could do nothing more. They had done all they could, all they could dare to do, and I was grateful for that.

Grateful for small mercies.

It is hard to believe that all this time has passed since that day, but then again that day seems like yesterday, even Nathan's face, as alive in my mind now as if we had shared

6

breakfast together. I recall the sounds and colors, the rush of noise, the emotion, the horror. Everything intact, like a glass jigsaw puzzle, each piece reflecting some other angle of the same design.

It is hard to believe . . . well, just that. It is hard to *believe*.

Sometimes I take a moment to imagine I am elsewhere, even someone else. Mr. Timmons came down the other day with a transistor radio that played a song, something by The Byrds called 'California Dreamin'', and though his intent was nothing more than to lift my mood, to lighten my day a little with something different, it saddened me to hear such a song. I recall Hendrix and Janis and The Elevators and Mike Bloomfield playing the Fillmore. I remember Jerry Garcia, Tom Wolfe and Timothy Leary with The Merry Pranksters. I remember the Kool-Aid Acid Test. I remember talking with Nathan about Huddy Ledbetter and Mississippi Fred McDowell, and I remember the invasion from England of The Rolling Stones and The Animals . . . all of this as we perceived it then: a mad rush of passionate fury in our hands and heads and hearts.

Mr. Timmons never understood the culture. He understood JFK. He understood why it was so important to reach the moon first. He understood why the Vietnam War started and how communism had to be prevented. He understood this until his own son was killed out there and then he didn't speak of it again. He was passionate about baseball and Chrysler cars, and he loved his wife and his daughter with a sense of duty and integrity and pride. He watched the Zapruder film, and he cried for the fallen King, and he prayed for Jackie Bouvier, and if truth be known he prayed a little for Marilyn Monroe, whom he loved from afar just as I had loved Caroline Lanafeuille and Linny Goldbourne. Just as I had loved Sheryl Rose Bogazzi in 9th grade. Perhaps Mr. Timmons believed that had he been there he could have saved Marilyn just as I believed I could

7

have saved Sheryl Rose. We believe such small things, but believing them makes them important, and sometimes they have to be enough, carrying such things and believing perhaps that they will in some way carry us.

Mr. Timmons also believes I didn't kill Nathan Verney in South Carolina on some cool night in 1970. He believes this, but he would never say it. It is not Mr. Timmons' job to question such things, for there is the way of the law, the way of justice, the Federal and Circuit and State and Appellate Courts, and there are tall grave men with heavy books who look into such things in detail, and they make the laws, they *are* the law, and who is Mr. Timmons to question this?

Mr. Timmons is a Death Row warder down near Sumter, and he does what he does, as he abides by the code, and he leaves such matters as innocence and guilt to the Governor and the baby Jesus. He is neither expected nor paid to make such decisions. And so he does not.

Easier that way.

Mr. West is another story. Some of the guys down here believe he was not born of human parents. Some of the guys down here believe he was spawned in a culture dish at M.I.T. or somesuch, an experiment in running a body without a heart or a soul or much of anything else at all. He is a dark man. He has things to hide, many things it seems, and where he hides them is in the shadows that lurk back of his eyes and behind his words, and in the arc of his arm as he brings down his billy across your head or your fingers or your back. He hides those things also in the way his shoes creak as he walks down the corridor, and in the way he peers through the grille and watches your every move. He hides those things in the insectile expression that flickers across his face when the mood takes him. And in leaving the lights on when you want to sleep. And in forgetting exercise time. In dropping your food as it is

8

passed through the gate. In the sound of his breathing. In everything he is.

Before I came here, the brief time I'd spent in General Populace, a man called Robert Schembri had warned me of Mr. West, but what he'd said had been confused in among a great deal of things he'd told me.

No matter what had gone before, I could never have forgotten the first time we met, Mr. West and I. It went something like this:

'Gon' lose your hair there, boy. No hippy hair down here. What the fuck is this here? A ring? Take it off now 'fore we cut your goddam finger from your hand there.'

I remember nodding, saying nothing.

'Nothin' to say now, eh, boy? They got you by the C.O. Jones that's for sure. You done kill some nigger I hear, cut his goddam head clean off of his body and left it for the crows.'

That was the time I opened my mouth. The first and last.

His face was in mine. I remember the pressure of the floor behind my head, the feeling of that billy club across my throat like it would force my jaw up through my ears and into my brain. And then he was over me, right there in my face, and I could *feel* the words he spoke as he hissed so cruelly.

'You don't got nothin' to say, boy, you understand? You have no words, no name, no face, no identity down here. Here, you're just a poor dumb motherfucker who got fucked by the system whichever way you see it. You could be as innocent as the freakin' Lamb of God, as sweet as the cherubims and seraphims and all the Holy Angels rolled into one almighty bag of purity, but down here you are guilty – guilty as the black heart of the Devil himself. You understand that, you remember that, you don't ever forget that, an' you and me are gonna get along just fine. You are nothing, you have nothing, you never will be anything, and this is about as good as it's ever gonna get. Yo' gonna

9

be here a long time before they fry your brain, and hell if I ain't gonna be here long after you're gone, so understand that when you're in my house you abide by my rules, you mind your manners and say your prayers. Are we on the same wavelength now?'

I was unable to move my head, barely able to breathe.

'I will take your silence as an expression of understanding and compliance,' Mr. West said, and then he gave one last vicious dig of the billy and released me.

I came up gasping, half-suffocated, my eyes bursting from my head, the pressure behind my ears like a freight train.

It was Mr. Timmons who helped me back to the cell, helped me to lie down, brought me some water which I was unable to drink for a good twenty minutes.

And it was Mr. Timmons who told me to watch Mr. West, that Mr. West was a hard man, hard but fair, and I knew in his tone, from the look in his eyes, that he was all but lying to himself. Mr. West was an emissary of Lucifer, and they all knew it.

And that was eleven years ago, best part of. Arrested in 1970. A year in Charleston Pen. while the first wave of protests erupted, died, erupted once more. And the appeals, the TV debates, the questions that no-one wanted to answer. And then to Sumter, a year or so in General Populace while legal wrangles went back and forth in futile and meaningless circles, and then to Death Row. And now it's 1982, summer of '82, and Nathan would have been thirty-six as well. We'd have been somewhere together. Blood brothers an' all that, you know?

Well, maybe that ain't so far from the truth. Because if Mr. Timmons is right, and God knows who's guilty and who's innocent, and if there is some place we all go where sins are called to account and judgement is fair and just and equitable, then me and Nathan Verney look set to see each other once more.

Nathan knows the truth, he most of all, and though he'll look me dead square in the eye and hold his head high, just as he always did, I know he'll carry a heavy heart. Nathan never meant for it to be this way, but then Nathan was caught up in this thing more than all of us together.

Some folks say the death penalty's too easy, too fast by far. Folks say as how those who commit murder should suffer the same. Well, believe me, they do. Folks forget the years people like me spend down here, two floors up from Hell. They don't know of people like Mr. West and the way he feels the punishment should befit the crime whether you did the crime or not. Folks really have no idea how it feels to know that you're gonna die, and after the first few years that day could be any day now. They know nothing of the raised hopes that fall so fast, the appeals that go round in circles until they disappear up their own tailpipe. They know nothing of discovering that Judge so-and-so has reviewed your case and denied the hearing that you've waited on for the best part of three years. These things are the penalty. Gets so as how when the time comes you're almost grateful, and you wish away the days, the hours, the minutes . . . wish they all would fold into one single, simple heartbeat and the lights would go out forever. People talk of a reason to live, a reason to fight, a reason to go on. Well, if you know in your heart of hearts that all you're fighting for is someone else's satisfaction as you die, then there seems little to fight for. It is ironic, but most times it's the guy who's being executed who wants to be executed the most.

Mr. Timmons understands this, and he cares as best he can.

Mr. West understands this too, but the emotion he feels is one of gratification.

Mr. West wants us to die, wants to see us walk the long walk, wants to see us sit in the big chair. Knows that once one has gone another will come to take his place, and

11

there's nothing that pleases him more than *fresh meat*. Spend six months here and he calls you *dead meat*. Calls it out as you walk from your cell to the yard, or to the washroom, or to the gate.

Dead meat walking, he shouts, and even Mr. Timmons turns cool and loose inside.

How Mr. West ended up this way I can only guess from what I was told, what was inferred. I don't know, but seems to me he's the most dangerous and crazy of us all.

Down two cells from me there's a guy called Lyman Greeve. Shot his wife's lover and then cut out the woman's tongue so she couldn't go sweet-talking any more fellas. Crazy boy. Crazy, crazy boy. But hell, compared to Mr. West Lyman Greeve is the Archangel Gabriel come down with his trumpet to announce the Second Coming. Lyman told me Mr. West was a Federal agent in the Thirties and Forties, did the whole Prohibition thing, busting 'shiners and whores and bathtub gin-makers. Said as how he came up to Charleston when Prohibition was lifted and was employed by the government to keep track of the black movements, that he was down there in Montgomery and Birmingham for the Freedom Rides, cracked a few black skulls, instigated a few riots. Another day Lyman told me Mr. West raped a black girl, found out she got pregnant, so he went back down there and cut her throat and buried her in a field. No-one ever found her, or so he said, and I listened to the story with a sense of wonder and curiosity.

Seemed everyone had invented their own history for Mr. West. To me, well, to me he was just a mean, sadistic son-of-a-bitch who got his revs beating on some poor bastard who couldn't beat back. Few years before I came here someone made a noise about him, some kid called Frank Rayburn. Twenty-two years old, down here for killing a man for eighteen dollars in Myrtle Beach. Frank made a noise, people from the Penitentiary Review & Regulatory Board made a visit, asked questions, made some more noise, and then Frank withdrew his complaint and fell silent. Month later Frank hanged himself. Somehow he obtained a rope, a real honest-to-God rope, and he tied it up across the grille eleven and a half foot high. The bed was eight inches off the ground. Frank was five three. You do the math.

No-one had a mind to complain again it seemed.

And then there's Max Myers, seventy-eight years old, a trustee. Been here at Sumter for fifty-two years. Jailed in 1930 for robbing a liquor store. Liquor store guy had a heart attack the following day. That made the charge manslaughter. Max came here when he was twenty-six years old, same as me, and on his thirty-second birthday in 1936 he got a cake from his wife. Someone stole Max Myers' cake, stole it right out of his cell, and Max got mad, real mad. He argued with someone on the gantry, there was a scuffle, a man got pushed, fell, landed forty feet below like a watermelon on the sidewalk. Max got a First Degree. For the manslaughter he would've been out around 1950, would've seen another thirty years of American history unfold. But he got the real deal, the no-hope-of-parole beat, and here he was, pushing a broom along Death Row, delivering magazines once a week. When he was jailed his wife had been pregnant. She had borne a son, a bright and beautiful kid called Warren. Warren grew up only ever seeing his father through a plate glass window. They had never touched, never held each other, never spoken to one another save through a telephone.

Max's son went into the Army in 1952, got himself a wife and a home, a cat called Chuck and a dog called Indiana. Went to Vietnam in '65, was one of the first US soldiers killed out there. Killed in his third week. Warren Myers was buried in a small plot somewhere in Minnesota. Max was not permitted to attend.

Max's wife took two handfuls of sleepers and drank a bottle of Jack Daniels six months following. Max was all that was left of the Myers family line. He pushed his broom, he passed messages, he could get you a copy of *Playboy* for thirty cigarettes. He was part of Sumter, always had been, always would be, and he was the only inmate who had been here before Mr. West.

Penitentiary Warden John Hadfield was a politician, nothing more nor less than that. Hadfield had eyes on the Mayor's Office, on Congress, maybe even on the Senate. He did what was needed, he said what was required, he kissed ass and talked the talk and colored inside the lines. Hadfield ran the regular wings, the A, B and C Blocks, but D-Block, Death Row, he left that to Mr. West. Even Hadfield called him Mr. West. No-one, not even Max Myers, knew Mr. West's given name.

When there was trouble Mr. West would go see Warden Hadfield. The meeting would be short and sour, cut and dried, all business. Mr. West would leave having satisfied Warden Hadfield completely, and Hadfield – if required – would publish a statement that kept the Penitentiary Review & Regulatory Board happy. Sumter was a community, its own world within a world, and even those who lived in the town itself believed that Penitentiary business was Penitentiary business. There had been a prison here since the War of Secession, there probably would always be a prison here, and as long as inmates weren't off escaping and raping some nice folks' daughter, then that was just fine. Folks here believed people like Mr. West were a required element of society, for without discipline there would be no society at all. See no evil, hear no evil, 'cept if it's done to you, and then . . . well, then there's folks like Mr. West who take care of business.

But these things are now, and there is more than ample time to talk of now.

We were speaking of a magic time, back before all of this, back before everything soured like a bruised watermelon.

A thousand summers and winters and springs and falls, and they all fold out behind me like a patchwork quilt, and beneath this quilt are the lives we led, the people we were, and the reasons we came to be here.

Thirty-six years old, and there are days when I still feel like a child.

The child I was when I met Nathan Verney at the edge of Lake Marion outside of Greenleaf, South Carolina.

Walk with me now, for though I walk slowly I do not care to walk alone.

For me, at least for me, these oh-so-quiet steps will be the longest and the last.

TWO

Best as I can recall it all started with a baked ham.

I was six years old, it was summer and out there near the edge of Lake Marion the smell of the breeze off of the water was the most magical smell ever. Inside of that smell were the flowers and the fish and the trees, and summer mimosa down near Nine Mile Road, and something like pecan pie and vanilla soda all wrapped up in a basket of new-mown grass. It was all those things, and the feeling that came with them. A feeling of warmth and security and everything that was childhood in South Carolina.

I'd walk down there most every day, walk down there to the edge of the water, and sit and wait and watch the world. My ma would make sandwiches, roll them up in a piece of linen, and inside those sandwiches was the finest baked ham this side of the Georgia state line.

The little black kid that came down that Friday afternoon was the funniest kid I ever saw. Ears like jug handles, eyes like traffic lights, and a mouth that ran from ear to ear with no rest in between. He spoke first. I remember that vividly.

'What yo' doin'?' he asked.

'Mindin' my own business,' I replied, and turned away to look in another direction.

'What yo' eatin'?' the kid asked.

'Baked ham,' I said.

'Baked what?'

The kid was near me now, could've reached out and touched him.

'Baked ham,' I repeated.

Kid was so stupid he could've been run down by a parked car.

'Let me have some,' he said, and I turned, my eyes wide, so shocked he'd asked I couldn't get my breath.

'Shit me, you got some problem?' I said.

'Problem?' the kid said. 'What problem would that be then?'

I maneuvered myself off of the fallen tree where I'd been sitting and stood facing him. I clutched my sandwich in my hand.

'You don't just go up to folk who's eatin' an' ask for some of their food,' I said.

The funny-looking kid frowned. 'How come?'

''S bad manners,' I said.

'Hell, 's bad manners not to be sharin' your dinner with someone who's hungry,' the kid replied.

I shook my head. 'That'd be fine,' I replied. 'Be just fine if we weren't strangers.'

The funny-looking kid smiled, held out his hand. 'Nathan Verney,' he said.

I looked at him askance. He had one hell of a nerve, this boy.

'Nathan Verney,' he repeated. 'Please to meet you . . .'

'Daniel Ford,' I said, and even as I said it I wondered why I was telling him.

'So now we're not strangers no more you can gimme some sandwich.'

I shook my head. 'Knowing your name don't make us family,' I said.

Nathan Verney shrugged his shoulders. 'Fine,' he said. 'You go on eat your stoopid sandwich . . . sure it tastes like bad sowbelly anyhows.'

'Does not,' I replied. 'My ma makes the best baked ham in South Carolina.'

Nathan Verney laughed. 'And my ma sleeps with her eyes open and catches flies with her tongue.'

17

''Tis the best,' I said, defensive, irritated by this invasion of my lake.

Nathan Verney shook his head, and then he turned his mouth down at the sides in an expression of distaste. 'That there baked ham more 'an likely tastes like the sole of someone's shoe.'

And so he got the sandwich, more than half of it, because somehow he worked me on a gradient. He took a bite, he seemed non-committal, undecided, and so he took another, and then a third, and by the time he had his fourth bite of my baked ham sandwich we were both laughing, and the funny-looking black kid couldn't keep his mouth closed and he nearly choked.

Later, an hour, maybe two, he said something that would hold us together for the rest of our lives.

Six years old, ears like jug handles, eyes like traffic lights, mouth that ran from one ear to the other with no rest in between.

'Reckon yo' ma makes the best baked ham in South Carolina,' he said.

And I knew, I really knew, that me and Nathan Verney had connected on some crucial childlike wavelength where baked ham and Lake Marion and the smell of mimosa from Nine Mile Road were the greatest things in the world.

It was 1952, a year that would see many things that were beyond our ability to reason or comprehend, things that we would only barely understand years later. Truman was President, and in June of that year Congress would override his veto and pass the Immigration Bill. A man from Illinois called Adlai Stevenson would run as the Democratic candidate and promise equal employment rights for blacks if he was elected. Marlon Brando would mesmerize the nation as Stanley Kowalski in *A Streetcar Named Desire*. America was growing up, and in her growing pains she would feel the threat of riot and revolt skittering somewhere in the shadows, out there along the horizon like a storm on its way.

We were six years old, me and Nathan Verney, and the world we were walking towards would welcome us with open arms.

At least that's what we believed.

My father was a railroad engineer. A railroad engineer for the Carolina Company, and a just man. I can recall the number of times he switched me exactly. Four times. Just four times in all those years. And each time I deserved it.

There was a tacit consent between us, always had been, still would be today if he'd been alive. That consent was an understated agreement that certain things were done, certain things were not. You did not throw stones into the branches of the trees beside the church in order to knock down the fruit. You did not fill a canvas bag with mud and water and drop it off a bridge onto someone's car. You did not tie half a dozen tin cans to the neighbor's dog's tail and howl with laughter as he hurtled down the street. And you most certainly did not put a live fish in someone's mailbox.

The fish was Nathan's idea. We were eleven years old then, and summertime had crept around the world to meet us once again. Those first spring shoots, the run-offs melting and freshening the earth, the smell haunting down off the river, the geese and flamingo coming up from Florida . . . all these things were so much a part of the eternal magic that was summer near Lake Marion.

Nathan's daddy, a Baptist minister with his own church and congregation and solid silver collection plate, taught Nathan how to catch fish with a length of bamboo, a pin and a feather. Nathan's daddy believed that it was well enough to catch fish, sure well enough to eat them, but to kill another of God's creatures – namely a worm or a bug of some description – was just altogether unnecessary. Jesus performed a miracle with the fish, Jesus was a fisher of men, but he caught fish with nets, not worms. That was the way God wanted it, and so Nathan's daddy figured a feather would do just fine. Wet a feather it goes slim and curved, looks pretty much the same, and feathers could be found everywhere when the summer flocks came down and shed their winter plumes.

So that's what we did, me and Nathan Verney, with a length of bamboo, some string, a bent pin and a feather. Nathan said as how you sat still, sat like a stone, and even when your legs went numb you just had to keep on sitting there until something came along. If you moved they could see you, and if not you then they'd see your shadow, and these were no dumb fish, these were smart fish that came down from Albemarle Sound and Cape Hatteras on the coast.

So we sat there, Nathan perched like a small dark statue, the bamboo rod jutting from the middle of his body, the line trailing in the water, and every once in a while the silver flicker of something moving there beneath the surface.

When Nathan shouted he near scared me half to death.

My heart jumped into my mouth, and for a second I couldn't breathe.

'Yo! Yo!'

He sounded like some whooping bird, coming up suddenly and nearly losing his balance 'cause all the blood had been stopped from his knees down.

I could see him struggling with the rod, the line taut, so taut, and something at the end that pulled like a wild thing.

I got behind him, my arms around the sides of his torso to hold onto the rod as well. Between us we hauled at that line, hauled until I was sure it would bust right in half and whatever was on the other end would go catapulting down the river into a memory.

But hell, if we didn't land that sucker! Hauled that baby right in and up onto the rocks, and we watched as the silver monster flipped and flopped on the warm stones like someone had tossed him onto a griddle.

We were excited, more than excited, and the two of us squatted there and watched this fish as it jumped and skipped from side to side, its eyes wide, its tail going like a triphammer.

And it was Nathan who suggested the mailbox.

'Put the fish in her mailbox,' he whispered.

I looked at him askance. 'You what?'

'The witch . . . put the fish in the witch's mailbox.'

The witch of whom he spoke was Mrs. Chantry.

'Are you completely out of your tree?' I said.

'Scared huh?'

I frowned, stepped back. 'Scared? You wanna put a fish in her mailbox and you ask me if I'm scared?'

'You are, aren't you? Skeered like a jackrabbit caught in a billy-can.'

'No way, Nathan. There's no way on God's green earth that you're gettin' me to go put that in her mailbox.'

I would look back months, years, decades even, and still see the way his face looked, and how it sounded, and remember as if it were yesterday the way we laughed until we flip-flopped on the rocks like someone had caught us and was set to griddle us too.

Mrs. Chantry, Eve Chantry, was la grande dame, the matriarch of Greenleaf, the little town where Nathan Verney and I would spend what would seem like most of our lives.

Mrs. Chantry was a widow, and among the children that gathered and spoke in hushed tones on the boardwalk near the barber's shop she was widowed because she'd eaten her husband when he returned from the war. The fact that Jack Chantry was a hero who'd earned the Purple Heart and the Silver Star, a man who gave his life to save three young men he never even knew, a man who never did come back from the war in 1945, was hearsay and rumor and undoubtedly untrue. Eve Chantry was a witch and a cannibal and her house was a gateway to Hades. She appeared twice weekly, once for church, once to collect groceries, and it seemed that when she walked from her gate there was never a child to be seen from one side of the town to the next.

And Nathan worked on me, worked it good and proper, calling me scared, calling me chicken, and every once in a while looking at me like I was the one who'd lost the plot.

And so it was that Nathan Verney and me decided to put that fish in her mailbox.

I can honestly say that I don't ever recall being so scared. Scared is an understatement. I was terrified, stricken, aghast. I remember approaching that house, feeling all the color bleaching from my skin, as if my blood was sensing danger and withdrawing even as we neared it.

Nathan held the fish. We had wrapped it in the same piece of linen in which my ma wrapped my sandwiches. The fish had been out of the water for a good while. It was dazed and wriggled weakly every once in a while. But the fish was never the problem. It was what we intended to do with it that was the source of the difficulties.

If we had been caught by Mrs. Chantry we believed we would've been skinned alive and basted with maize oil and baked for ten minutes per pound. Perhaps served up with some corn and salad.

'You take the fish up there,' Nathan said.

'Hell, Nathan, it was your idea. You take it up there.'

'Yellabelly,' he sneered. 'No better 'an a girl.'

Had I felt any less terrified I would have slugged him upside the head.

'You gotta go,' he said.

'Why me? Why do I have to go?'

'Because it'll prove you ain't wearing a streak down your back.'

I stood there gaping at him, my mouth open, barely

breathing. I shook my head, shook it like it would snap off if I went any faster.

But Nathan persisted; that was Nathan's special quality, and for a further five minutes we stood at the bottom of Mrs. Chantry's drive and argued back and forth in this forced and unnatural whisper.

'You don't go then I'm gonna scratch your name with a stone on the side of her mailbox,' he eventually said, and there was a look in his eyes, a look of determination that turned me cold inside.

The idea that he would never ever do such a thing didn't seem to enter my mind, and it was only later that I realized that Nathan possessed another quality: he could convince you of anything, catch you up in the fever of the moment, and with those wide traffic-light eyes and the mouth that ran endlessly from one side of his face to the other, he could tell you a story that was all smoke and shadows and you'd think it gospel. Later, many times as I now recall, that quality would both help and harm us.

So I took the fish.

With my terror, with my tight stomach and Jell-O knees, with my heart in my mouth and my pulse racing like a bird-dog, I took one step at a time up that pathway towards the mailbox. If that fish had been anything other than coma-tose it would have wriggled from my grip without resist-ance. Seemed with every step I took my physical and mental co-ordination slipped away by degrees, and when I stood beneath the shadow of that tall wooden structure I could feel the coolness of the house. Despite the season, despite the bold sun and lack of breeze, despite the midday high that settled around eighty-five degrees, that house, the Chantry house, exuded a darkness and a dead chill that seemed to invade the street, seemed to creep through the earth beneath my feet and start up through my ankles.

I glanced back.

Nathan Verney stood on the sidewalk, and for the little

while I was there beside the mailbox he was as white as I was.

I could see him trembling. Trembling enough to wriggle out of his skin and run away.

I looked down.

My shoes seemed a million miles from me.

I felt the weight of the fish. Could feel the texture of the linen, and through that the smooth silver skin of the creature.

I looked up, raised my right hand, and with a flick of my thumb I released the catch and the front of the mailbox popped open. That little door seemed to spring quickly, and then slow down as it completed its arc. Seemed to slow down once more and then suddenly gain momentum, and as it approached the post upon which the mailbox sat it gathered velocity, gathered velocity at such a rate I believed it would snap right off its hinge.

But it didn't.

That door just came rocketing back until its rim connected with the post.

The sound was like a church bell at midnight.

Like a man going at a garbage can with a billy club.

The sound of two cars in a head-on up Nine Mile Road.

I dropped the fish.

Nathan screamed and started to move.

I felt like my bladder would bust right open and soak my shoes.

I looked down.

The piece of linen was there between my feet, and within it the fish, stunned now, suffering another degree of unconsciousness, and it moved ever so slightly from side to side.

Why I reached down and grabbed it, why I scooped up that fish, linen and all, and threw it into the mailbox I'll never know. It was as if a crime had already been committed. There was the evidence, right there on the

24

path. The evidence had to be hidden, had to be concealed, and the only place at hand was right there in Mrs. Chantry's mailbox.

And that's where it went.

And once that special delivery had been made I went too.

Like a comet with turbo-charged afterburners, we high-tailed it down the street until we arrived, gasping and sweating and laughing fit to bust wide open, at the edge of the Lake.

Nathan could barely breathe. He had to sit with his head between his knees, his hands gripping his ankles for a good five minutes before he could even speak. His face was streaked with tears, his eyes red and buggy, and when he tried to stand up he fell sideways like a plank and just lay there.

Never been so frightened.

Never laughed so much.

Never seen my father so angry as when he came home that night clutching a fish-smelling piece of linen that Mrs. Chantry had so kindly given to him with the message: *Pass that on to your son, Mister Ford, and tell him and his little negro friend that I did enjoy the fish.*

My pa switched me that time. Switched me good in the woodhouse.

Next day I stayed inside.

Nathan didn't come over. Nathan's daddy didn't switch him, didn't believe a child should be beaten. Believed the best discipline for a child was to have him stay indoors and copy out scriptures until his hand didn't work no more. *Write until you're wrong*, Nathan would tell me.

Later we spoke of Mrs. Chantry and the fish. Believed she ate it whole and raw and talked about how her neck swelled up as she almost inhaled the thing complete.

That was the way we saw it, and so that was the way it was.

*

Those years, as we approached our teens, were years that warned of things to come, like premonitions, portents, readings in sand.

Eisenhower became President in 1953, though Rocky Marciano's retained heavyweight title after he K.O.'d Jersey Joe Walcott seemed far more real and relevant and necessary to know. Jackie married JFK in the same year, and near Christmas something happened that only later, much later, would we even begin to comprehend. December of that year the U.S. Supreme Court took the banning of school segregation under advisement, and though another three years would pass before Nat King Cole was dragged off stage by a white mob in Birmingham, those mutterings of discontent and disaffection were so much the sign of Old America's death throes. Though folks seemed more occupied with Marilyn Monroe and Joe DiMaggio, Elvis Presley singing 'That's Alright Mama', James Dean in *Rebel Without a Cause* and someplace called Disneyland in Anaheim, Cal., there were things running their own agenda behind the scenes that carried so much more significance.

In March of '54 Eisenhower committed the U.S. to united action to prevent any communist takeover of South-East Asia. Seven months later Viet Minh troops began to occupy Hanoi. Tension was building. Out there in some unheard-of jungle a war was being born, a war that would take the minds and hearts of this nation and grind them together into one unholy regret for a million mothers and fathers.

Nathan Verney and I were children. We did not understand. We didn't want to understand.

In Montgomery, Alabama, the City Bus Lines ordered an end to segregated seating. Eisenhower told the schools down there to end their discrimination, and the Supreme Court ruled the segregation law invalid.

I was a white kid from South Carolina. Nathan was black. It was not until '57 and '58, when the Federal District Court ordered Little Rock, Arkansas to treat us all the same, when

Martin Luther King was arrested for loitering and cited police brutality and was fined $14 for refusing to obey a police officer, that the pains this country was experiencing started to creep into our lives in a way that actually touched us. February of 1960, Nathan and I were nearly fourteen years old, and someone put a bomb in someone's house. That house belonged to one of the first black students to enroll at Little Rock Central High. We heard about that, heard about it from Nathan's daddy, and he went down to Montgomery and marched with those thousand black students in March of the same year.

Martin Luther King spoke with Eisenhower, urged him to intervene to defuse the tension, but Eisenhower was a politician not a negotiator. Ten blacks were shot in Mississippi in April. They called it the worst ever race riot. They called it many things. Me and Nathan called it madness.

I recall Nathan's daddy back then, and twenty years later I would still remember the passion, the fury, the anger he lived inside for all those years. *Religion*, he said, *was unimportant*. Didn't matter what we called ourselves. Didn't matter what church we attended. Didn't matter what hymns we sang. And sure as hell, our color didn't matter. A man was a man, all men made in God's image, and all men equal at birth and equal in death. All men called to account for the same sins, no matter their race or belief.

Nathan's daddy came home one day with a bleeding head. Didn't want no bandage or dressing, and though Mrs. Verney fussed and clucked and hovered he sent her away while he talked to us. Said he would scar, and scar gladly. This was something he would wear for the rest of his life. He was a man of God. He was a minister of the faith. Yet to the police officer that hit him in Montgomery, Alabama he was another poor dumb nigger who'd forgotten his manners, his mouth and his place.

Nathan and I had never really seen a difference between us; not until then.

In January 1961 John Fitzgerald Kennedy was inaugurated as President of the United States. He walked into a minefield. Three months in office and armed Cuban exiles made a bid to overthrow Castro's Marxist government in Cuba. Khrushchev vowed to give Castro all the aid he needed. The following month the U.S. agreed to give more money and military aid to South Vietnam.

A week later white mobs attacked the freedom riders at the bus station in Birmingham, Alabama.

I was fifteen years old, and foremost in my mind were girls – girls like Sheryl Rose Bogazzi, Linny Goldbourne and Caroline Lanafeuille – but something out there told me that the trials and tribulations of a 9th-grader were the least of the world's concerns.

As I turned sixteen, Nathan there beside me, America seemed to hang on the edge of the abyss both at home and abroad.

We heard about someplace called the Bay of Pigs, and for thirteen days people honestly believed, I mean *really* believed, that the world would end. Like Dean Rusk said, 'We were eyeball to eyeball, and the other guy just blinked.'

More than eleven hundred Bay of Pigs invaders were jailed for thirty years and Castro tried to ransom them for $62,000,000. A month later, May '62, and JFK sent his Marines into Laos. In July, Martin Luther King was arrested for marching illegally in Georgia, a stone's throw across the state line from where I sat in Greenleaf Senior High.

In September the shit really hit the fan.

Whites stormed the University of Mississippi when James Meredith was scheduled to enter and enroll. Governor Ross Barnett ordered the State Troopers to stop the kid from getting in. JFK sent the Deputy Attorney General and seven hundred and fifty Federal Marshals down there to ensure that Meredith was given safe passage.

Later, Ross Barnett was urged to rebel against JFK by a vast crowd of whites in Jackson Stadium. The Ole Miss College Band, all decked out in Confederate uniform, brought that crowd to their feet for a rendition of 'Dixie'.

James Meredith would not attend his first classes until October, and even then two hundred arrests would be made.

In the same month JFK – a man who would be alive for only thirteen months more – imposed an arms blockade after telling the world that Russia possessed missile sites in Cuba. He lifted that blockade in November, and in December eleven hundred and thirteen of the original Bay of Pigs invaders were ransomed for $53,000,000.

Seemed the world had twisted on its axis. Seemed people had gotten their ideas all choked up with McCarthy and discrimination and Castro and how Marilyn might have been murdered because of who she loved.

These things were real, but not so real as to actually reach us where we lived.

Not until December, Christmas coming, and it was carried home so swiftly, so mercilessly, that there was nothing we could do but face the truth.

The world had gone mad, and finally, at last, that madness came to Greenleaf.

THREE

Ironically, it would have been Nathan's birthday today.

More ironically, Mr. West chose to speak to me. I could not remember the last time he had spoken directly to me. Perhaps two weeks, maybe a month. Down here in D-Block you lost track of time. Left without your exercise for forty-eight hours you didn't know if it was day or night. I'm sure they changed the times the lights were put off and on. Disorientating. You got confused.

Anyhows, Mr. West came down, he looked through the grille, and he said: *You're a fucking animal, Ford. What are you?*

And I said: *An animal, boss.*

And he said: *Sure as shit is shit you're an animal.*

And then he laughed.

I could see his legs through the spaces between the bars. Could have almost reached them from where I sat. Would never have made it. The man moved like a leopard. My hand would have been out through the bars and he would've broken my wrist with a billy club in a heartbeat. Less than a heartbeat.

Seems to me the only good thing you ever did was kill some nigra, he went on. *And now they gonna fry your ass for it. Fucking ironic or what, eh?*

And then he reached into his shirt pocket, took out a cigarette, lit it. He inhaled once and then, smiling through the grille, he dropped the cigarette to the floor and ground it to dust beneath the sole of his shoe. Did it on purpose.

Ground it so fine it could never have been retrieved and re-rolled.

And then he crouched on his haunches and peered through the bars at me. For a moment there was an expression of sympathy.

Some folks are here 'cause they deserve it, he started. *And then there's some folks that are here to pay for all of our sins. You're here 'cause you're just too fucking stupid to know better, Ford. That's the simplicity of it. Seems to me there was a time some way back when you did something you decided was worth buryin' yourself for, eh? Always the way. If you're not here for what they said you done, then sure as shit is brown and smells bad you're here for what you think you done. An' don't tell me I ain't right, 'cause I know I am.*

The sympathetic expression folded seamlessly into one of disgust and disdain.

Whatever the hell it was, boy, you felt bad enough to get yourself killed for it.

Mr. West, despite everything, knew when he'd caught a nerve, and once caught he'd twist it like some vicious and sadistic orthodontist. Some said he could read minds. Some said he could sense the tiniest tics and flinches in your expression and catch those like a frog catching flies. Never missed, always satisfied, always ready for more.

He stood up, the caustic sneer ever-present, and walked slowly away.

Mr. West's words had been timed perfectly, for he knew where I hurt, he knew where my wounds were, and he played at them ceaselessly.

Seemed to me Mr. West had chosen me as his *raison d'être*, at least for now, at least until I walked the walk and sat in the *Big Chair*. That's what he wanted; that's what would make him happy.

That was Nathan's birthday, and it was remembering this that made me think of Greenleaf once more. Made me think of a particular day; the day the world made it clear that Nathan Verney and I were not, and never would be, the same.

Seems to me now that all everyone wanted to do was fuck everyone else.

You could sense it in the atmosphere.

We were all the same age – sixteen, going on seventeen – and we hung around a soda shop called Benny's. Benny was Benny Amundsen, an immigrant from some place in Europe, a good man, an honest man, but a man who walked a fine line himself due to his own non-American status.

Benny's had a juke box, an ancient battered work of art. That juke box played maybe ten tunes, twelve on a good day, and though the records skipped and skidded, and sometimes you didn't hear a damned thing at all, it was still the center of the universe as far as the Greenleaf teenagers were concerned.

That day there were maybe twenty kids in all. Guys wearing skinny-legged pants and tee-shirts, girls wearing frocks, hair made up in beehives like Martha & The Vandellas or somesuch. They danced a little, they laughed, drank their sodas, and you could smell the tension in the air. Like I said, everyone wanted to fuck everyone else, though had they been presented with such an opportunity they more than likely would not have known what to do with it.

Nathan and I were seated near the window. Nathan had been folding a napkin into something like a bird. I had been watching him, amazed at how such large hands could do something so delicate and fragile.

I went for soda, stood there at the counter minding my own business, and it was in that moment, hesitating between straight cream or strawberry float, that I sensed a presence beside me.

I turned. She was there. Sheryl Rose Bogazzi. Long auburn

32

hair, eyelashes like the wings of a bird taking off into the sunset, her white blouse stretched tight across her breasts.

I felt myself blushing.

'Hi there, Daniel,' she purred, cat-like.

I felt a stirring somewhere beneath my stomach.

'Sheryl Rose,' I said, and sort of half-smiled as best I could. I think it came out like a pained grimace.

'What you getting?' she asked.

I shrugged, felt stupid for a moment. 'Some soda.'

She giggled, raised her hand to her mouth as if hiding her teeth. She needn't have done that. She had perfect teeth. 'I know soda,' she said, and sort of took a step towards me. 'Kinda soda?'

'Don't know,' I replied. 'Maybe cream, maybe strawberry float.'

She nodded as if understanding my dilemma. 'Got sick on strawberry float one time,' she said. She moved her head then, her hair flicking back over her shoulder. I wanted to touch her hair. Wanted to touch her face. I blushed again.

'Then it'll have to be cream then,' I said.

'Cream,' she purred, and I nearly died right there in my shoes.

'You want one?' I asked.

'You buying?'

I nodded. 'Sure I am.'

'Well thank you, Daniel Ford . . . I'll take a cream soda too.'

I paid for the sodas, she thanked me again, and then she smiled that smile that was all her own and I couldn't think of a word to say.

'I'll see y'around, Daniel Ford,' she said, and she leaned a little closer, and in the briefest of moments I felt her fingers graze my arm. I remember how cool they were, cool and a little moist from where she'd held the glass a moment before, and even as she walked away I watched those damp fingerprints evaporate from my skin.

I walked back to the table in slow-motion, my heart beating, my pulse racing. I sat down, I glanced across the room towards her, and even as I did I saw her glance back at me. My unsteady heart missed another beat.

'And where the hell's my soda?' Nathan asked.

I looked at him, I didn't hear a thing, and I smiled.

'Dumb-ass retard,' he said, and slid out from his chair to fetch his own drink.

It was an awkward situation already, there were jealousies brewing, things unspoken, things said that should have stayed private, and when Sheryl Rose Bogazzi felt a hand on her breast she slapped someone's face.

I turned first, saw Larry James and Marty Hooper standing there. Marty was red as a beet, the one side of his face bore the unmistakable imprint of a hand, and Larry, Marty's sidekick and consigliere, was already defending him.

Why I stood up I don't know.

Hell, yes I do.

I stood up because it was Sheryl Rose Bogazzi.

Had it been someone else, anyone else except maybe Caroline Lanafeuille, I would have stayed right where I was and kept my mouth shut.

But no, I was besotted and in love and, as such, certifiably insane.

And so I stood up, and Marty Hooper was immediately in my face, his expression one of challenge and self-defense. His manner was ugly and brutish, and I knew from previous experience that only folks who had something to hide became that mad that quickly.

Thus I knew he *had* touched Sheryl Rose Bogazzi.

He had committed a crime of immeasurable and unforgivable significance.

'What did you do?' I asked, my tone hostile and offensive.

Marty Hooper sneered. He sort of looked sideways

34

towards his friends as if to ask them who I was, what was I doing here.

I sensed Sheryl Rose to my left. I felt that unmistakable presence.

'I said what did you do, Marty?'

'And what the hell business is it of yours what I did?' he snapped back.

'You touched her,' I said. 'You damned well touched her, Marty.'

Marty bared his teeth in contempt. 'I'll damned well touch you, Daniel Ford,' he said.

I pushed Marty Hooper.

Marty Hooper laughed and pushed me back.

'Freakin' loser,' he hissed. 'Freakin' loser, Ford.'

The kids in the soda shop stepped away simultaneously, and suddenly there was an arena, a boxing ring, and I realized even in that moment that I was gonna get a pounding.

Marty Hooper was faster, taller, stronger, but more importantly he possessed greater confidence than me. I was defending Sheryl Rose's honor, perhaps the greatest and most powerful motivation for an all-out onslaught against this criminal of the heart. But Marty Hooper had done this before, and I had not.

The first roundhouse collided with my left ear.

I was sure I tasted blood. I saw thirty-five colors in stereo and howled like a stuck pig.

Larry James was laughing. 'Asshole,' he was saying. 'What an asshole this guy is.'

Sheryl Rose turned away, her expression one of terror and grief and panic and sympathy all rolled into one.

I came back then, came back like a rabid hound, and even as I started in on Marty Hooper I felt this hand on my collar, and suddenly I was jerked backwards, almost lifted wholesale from the ground.

Before I knew what had happened I was standing near

the window and Nathan was there ahead of Marty Hooper, his fists raised, his eyes wide, his teeth bared like a mad thing.

'You want some too?' Marty asked. He started laughing. 'This asshole wants some too ... come on then, asshole, come get a piece of me.'

When Nathan Verney hit Marty Hooper, Marty went down.

He didn't so much fall as *go down*.

It was hard to describe, harder to demonstrate when we spoke of it later.

Marty Hooper just flat-fuck fell.

Boom.

Down.

Like a stone.

And Marty didn't get up.

There was silence.

You could have heard a gnat's fart.

I stood there, jaw to the floor, eyes like a bug, hair on the nape of my neck standing to attention like a porcupine.

Larry James said it. No doubt about it. I even remember the way he said it. Like the smack of a baseball bat. Like a gunshot.

Nigger!

Marty Hooper stirred.

Someone came forward and helped him to his feet.

When he realized what had happened he was even more shocked and embarrassed than before. But now the source of his ridicule was neither Sheryl Rose nor me. It was the tall black teenager standing just three or four feet from him.

Nathan Verney had put him down with one punch, and he believed he could never live that down.

And then he said it too. 'Nigger! Damned nigger!'

And though he didn't say it the same, it sounded worse.

Now it was out there. Now it had been repeated by someone, and there were those among that crew who would have said or done anything to remain involved with these people.

And so someone else said it. I don't know who. It didn't matter.

Nigger!

By the time it had caught and become a chant Nathan Verney was already at the door.

I was beside him in a heartbeat, and we went out through that door quickly and quietly and hurried down the boardwalk towards the street.

'Go,' Nathan was saying. 'Go, Daniel . . . just go!' I could read a real sense of panic and terror in his eyes, something that I would see only years later when we were grown.

I remember the feeling of the sun. It was brutal. I felt naked.

I remember glancing back towards Sheryl and she was looking right at me. Her expression told me everything I needed to know. She felt for us, perhaps for me, but she could do nothing. She belonged here, Nathan did not, and if I was close with Nathan then I didn't belong here either. Hell, they were just honest white kids hanging out, having some fun, and Marty Hooper and Larry James had gotten a little overheated, granted, but no reason to go overboard.

I smiled at her, I remember that, but she didn't smile back. She looked away, looked towards the floor, anywhere but right back at me. And it was at that point she became something else, some*one* else. I felt a sense of loss, and yet again a sense of relief. For as long as I could recall I had been torn between her and Caroline, torn between the two of them like a man strung between two carts travelling in opposite directions. I could only have held out so long before feeling something give, before watching myself unravel at the seams and collapse inside. In that moment, the moment I turned towards her, she had betrayed me, she had become one of *them*. I believed it would have been impossible to ever forgive her. I let her go, I know I did. At that very moment I let her go, and even through those seconds of panic I found myself thanking some higher force that Caroline Lanafeuille had not been there to witness my bruised pride. Caroline retained her pedestal, while Sheryl Rose Bogazzi's crown slipped and rolled soundlessly to the gutter.

By the time we reached the street there must have been five or six behind us. The guys came out, the girls stayed inside, and I remember hearing Benny Amundsen's voice over the hubbub.

Take your trouble outside, he was saying. *You boys take your trouble outside.*

Benny knew what was happening, would have been the first to realize it, but he would do nothing. Benny could not be seen to side with a negro.

When the first stone came we started running. Nathan was taller than me, his legs longer, and had it been a race he would have outstripped me in a heartbeat.

But he didn't, he kept with me step for step, and when we reached the turning at the end of the street he actually hung back to let me turn first in case we collided.

Had he not done that he would never have been hit.

The stone caught him on the cheek, and to this day I can recall the sound as clearly as if it were but five seconds ago. A dull thud, like someone thumping a side of beef hanging in the shed. And even as he howled I saw blood, and in seeing blood everything changed.

Blood on the teeth is an expression I heard once. Once the animal has blood on its teeth it never loses that taste. Craves it. Lives for it.

The running gang behind us became crazy.

What had been a jog in our direction became a chase, and even as they chased us I felt stones whipping by my head, heard the sounds as they hit the sidewalk or the wooden front of a store.

Somewhere a window smashed.

I looked at Nathan. His eyes were wide with fear, the left side of his face covered with blood, and somewhere within me I found a reserve of passion and strength and stamina because I took off like a rocket and for a moment left Nathan behind.

How long we ran I can't remember, but suddenly there was someone ahead of us, and in a flash we were past them and I heard them shouting.

I slowed, came to a stop, Nathan alongside me, and when we turned we saw something that I would never forget.

Mrs. Chantry stood in the middle of the street, resolute, immovable.

Above her head she held a heavy-looking stick, and when she spoke it seemed like her voice came right up out of the earth and filled the street and every building along it.

'You stop right there!' she hollered.

I looked at Nathan.

Rock and a hard place, his eyes said.

The running gang behind us came to a staggered and surprised halt, bumping into one another, each jostling to see who was standing in their way.

'You boys stop right there! You see what you've done? You see what's happening here? Get back where you came from or I'll turn you into the lizards that you are!'

Mrs. Chantry's voice was commanding, like marshalling the forces in some Union-Confederate engagement.

And the gang of teenagers behind us was shocked.

Stunned.

Silent.

And then they went.

No question.

No hesitation.

One after the other they went, caterwauling down the street like a pack of whipped dogs.

Even at sixteen or seventeen you still remembered the

stories well enough, the eating of the husband, the gateway to Hell that lay right behind her porch door.

I remember Larry James' face in that moment. He glanced back towards us before he turned at the end of the street. He didn't know whether to feel angry he'd been cheated of the kill, or sympathetic because we had encountered what appeared to be a far worse fate.

And then *she* turned.

I saw myself at eleven years old, saw myself standing right there on her path with a fish in my hands, wrapped in a piece of linen that once held a baked ham sandwich, a baked ham sandwich just like the one Nathan Verney and I had shared a million years before.

And that moment seemed like yesterday, like an hour ago, like the fleeting second that had just passed by.

Possibly the last second of my life.

And then she spoke, and all I recall now is the sense of warmth in her tone, the timbre, the depth.

'You know, boys,' she started. 'I really did eat the fish.'

We were there for nigh on two hours.

Mrs. Chantry cleaned Nathan's face, she dressed it, put some gauze over it and held it with some tape.

She had homemade lemonade, some kind of dry cookie that tasted of nutmeg and sweet cherry and something else indescribable that made you want two or three more.

Her house did not have walls daubed with blood. She did not have the skull of her husband on the mantel over the fire. She had all her teeth, they were white, not black, and she smelled faintly of violets and peppermint.

She even showed us a picture of her husband, and when we told her of the stories we'd heard as children she told us she had in fact started most of the rumors.

'Get to my age,' she said, 'and you require a little peace and quiet. It was never the intention to frighten a soul, least of all a child, but you know how people are. They take

40

something and they embellish it, they twist it and exaggerate it, and when you hear that same tale come back it's twice as high and three times as wide, and you barely recognize it. That was all that happened, and now I'm kinda regretful folks took to such things in the first place.'

She smiled at Nathan.

'Like you,' she said. 'You saw something today that you were gonna have to deal with one time or other. You understand what I mean, right?'

'Dumb as milk white folks is what you mean,' Nathan said.

Mrs. Chantry smiled. 'Dumb-ass white folks, sure enough.'

'Trailer trash,' Nathan went on. 'All up and marryin' their sisters and eating three-day old leftovers out of a cooking pan.'

'Nathan,' I hissed, and he looked at me with this wide-eyed innocence.

Mrs. Chantry raised her hand. 'Ain't so far from the truth, Daniel.'

She turned and looked at Nathan. 'I know your daddy,' she went on. 'I know he knows all about what's happening in Alabama and Georgia. Never suspected it would do anything other than infect the whole country after a while. Figure there'll be a lot more shooting and rioting and marching and hollering before people come to their senses, you know?'

She looked at me and smiled. She turned once again to Nathan.

'You seem to have yourself a good friend here, Nathan Verney. Seems to me a white boy who'll stand up for a negro in this time is a man of spirit and backbone.'

She laughed, a tumbling infectious sound.

'But then you pair were always in a heap of trouble all by yourselves, weren't you?'

Nathan smiled, the first time since the street. 'Wouldn't

have been a pair, and wouldn't have been anywhere near as much trouble on my own,' he said, and I laughed with him, and for just a little while what had happened didn't matter.

Seemed to me we were laughing at the world from the gateway to Hell, and that was the funniest thing of all.

Later, after we left, left with an open invitation to return, Nathan walked with me towards the Lake. We always went this way, side by side, step for step, and then where the path separated fifty yards from the water's edge we would go our respective ways.

'We'll see this thing through together, Nathan,' I said.

He didn't reply. He knew what I meant.

He paused at the end of the path and turned towards me. He held out his hand.

I took his hand, and for an eternity we stood there without a word.

'Your choice, Danny Ford,' he eventually said.

'No choice, Nathan Verney,' I remember saying.

And then we went our different ways, back to our own homes, and later I sat at the window of my room and watched that slow Carolina blue skyline melt soundlessly into Lake Marion.

At sixteen years old it was not my job to understand why. That's what I believed.

The reason I ran with Nathan was because I was scared, because I had been unable to defend myself, because he had stepped in to protect me and I owed him the same.

Eleven years since the day we'd shared a sandwich by the Lake.

A little more than half of that again and Nathan Verney would be dead.

But that was the future, an unknown, and just as JFK would fall within the year, we had no idea of what was coming.

We lived for the present, a little for the past, but most of all it seemed we lived for one another.

And that, out of everything that was to come, was possibly the hardest thing of all.

FOUR

Back in Sumter, the year or so I spent there before being transferred to Death Row, I met a man called Robert Schembri. It was August of 1972, and by the time our paths coincided Robert was nearly seventy, and he walked with a stoop and a limp and the air of someone beaten. Beaten, however, he was not, for Robert Schembri possessed a spirit of unparalleled indomitability. Apparently he served thirteen years straight in solitary, a narrow cell, eight feet by eight, a metal-framed bed, a hole in the ground, fifty minutes of daylight every seventy-two hours. He went down there because of his stories, and his stories were wild and impossible and strangely fascinating. Folks were upset by his stories, the claims he made, the theories he presented, and though anyone in their right mind would have considered him far from the brightest light in the harbor, my experience of Robert Schembri remains lucid and clear. Schembri was a dangerously intelligent man.

I was the only person he ever told the reason for his imprisonment. Why I was chosen I never knew, for Schembri died of a heart attack, one of those special Federal Penitentiary kind of seizures, a month before I was transferred out of General Populace. And he was the one who gave me some kind of understanding of what had happened to me and, more importantly, why. It was he who'd warned me of a man called West, a man who walked the walk and talked the talk, and ran D-Block as if he was the last American God. I had not known at that time that Mr. West would figure so prominently in the latter years of my life, and had I known I would have paid a great deal more attention to what Robert Schembri told me of him. But I did not, and at the time it seemed unimportant, and Schembri had a way of making it clear what you should listen to and what you shouldn't.

What he did tell me took place over three days. We only ever met at meals, and after the first day I remember standing there in the line, craning my neck, looking at face after face after face, searching him out amidst the confusion of people. My trial and the subsequent months of legal and judicial wrangling were drawn out and complex. But that was another story, another story altogether. Until the case was concluded and the death sentence levied I was there with the rest of the innocents.

I found Robert Schembri in the corner of the hall, back and to the left. Apparently he always sat alone. People avoided him like a disease, a bio-hazard. Seems he'd sat alone for all the years he'd been there, and but for the few hours I shared with him he would sit alone for the rest of his life.

He possessed a strange manner. The way he would look at me I felt invisible, but that sensation did not disturb me, merely made me feel I was there to listen, to be a receipt point for whatever came tumbling from his lips. Schembri described himself as a channel from the gods. What that meant didn't matter.

'Tell ya something, kid,' he started. He said that each time he began. *Tell ya something.*

'It was a premeditated act, all of it. The Killing of the King. It was necessary as the second part of the trilogy. They had three goals to bring about the complete decay of matter, the total dissolution of society.'

Schembri smiled sardonically.

'Tell me you don't see society falling to pieces, going all to hell in a handbasket.'

'I see it,' I replied.

He nodded. 'What happened to you is a symptom of the disease.'

'A symptom? A symptom of what?' I leaned forward.

'All the shit and shenanigans you got yourself into down here.' He smiled wryly and winked. 'I know a little of this and a little of that, you see.'

I shook my head. 'You know about what happened to me?'

Schembri waved my question away. 'Got a question for you,' he said. 'You know why they killed John Fitzgerald Kennedy?'

He didn't wait for an answer; seemed he didn't really need to know that I was listening, only that I was there.

'The first part they called The Creation and Destruction of Primordial Matter. They had to make it sound complex so that people would take them seriously. They wanted the top people involved, all the Freemason Brotherhood, to bring about this mass-trauma, mind-control assault against the body politic of the U.S. They had a guy called Peter Kern, a Freemason himself, and they asked him to build a gate. The site of the gate was called The Trinity in Mexico, the thirty-third degree of the north parallel latitude. There's an old road down there called the Jornada del Muerto, The Journey of the Dead Man. So Kern built the gate, and they called it The Gate With A Thousand Doors, and once he'd completed it they ceremonially decapitated him. They did some other shit too, occult shit, all along that latitude through Truth Or Consequences, New Mexico.'

Schembri smiled and winked. He knew what he was talking about even if I didn't.

'I'll tell ya something else. These nuts believe in something called the Kundalini fire serpent. Say that it lives in the body of a man, and the serpent crosses the thirty-three segments of the human spine which they consider is the vehicle of fiery ascent. Thirty-three is also the highest degree in Freemasonry.'

He nodded and winked once more as if everything was now becoming clear.

'The second stage of the The Creation and Destruction of Primordial Matter also took place at The Trinity, the Place of Fire, with the detonation of the first atomic bomb.'

Schembri leaned back and smiled. He raised his spoon. 'They knew what they were doing, see? They knew exactly what they were doing.'

He lowered his spoon and used it to stir up the mess of food on his tray.

I wanted to ask him what he meant, what he knew of what had happened to me.

'The third stage was The Killing of the King,' he said, interrupting my thought. 'Ten miles south of the thirty-third degree of north parallel latitude between the Trinity River and the Triple Underpass in Dallas . . . and that was Dealey Plaza, the site of the first Masonic temple in Dallas. Used to be called Bloody Elm Street, and here they brought the King of Camelot, John Fitzgerald Kennedy, and they sacrificed him.'

Schembri was looking out towards the mass of people that surrounded us. He nodded his head slowly.

'They killed the King, you see? Killed him right there in front of the world. And that was the greatest trick of all.'

Schembri looked back at me.

'They had this picture from that day in Dallas. You've seen this picture, three bums, three hobos in custody. Hobos with good haircuts and clean shoes. Those three guys were just released without identification, though folks interested in what really happened have always believed that there was some significance to the presence of those men. I'll tell you who they were. They were symbols, Masonic symbols, because every time the Freemasons kill someone they have three unworthy craftsmen present, Jubela, Jubelo and Jubelum. They were there. They had to

47

be there. They were as much a part of the thing as anything else.'

Schembri smiled again, that same wry expression that said more than could ever be expressed in words.

'Kennedy wasn't killed for political reasons. They didn't kill him because he was trying to stop the Vietnam War or close down Bell Helicopters. It wasn't even because he was trying to stop the segregation of the blacks. They killed him because they could. They wanted the world to know they could take the most powerful man in the world and blow his head off on TV . . . and that no-one could do anything about it. Who actually shot him will never be known. Those details will die with the people that pulled the triggers and the folks who organized it. I should imagine the gunmen themselves were dead within an hour of the incident. Oswald was no more responsible than you were. Kennedy got caught in a triangulation of fire, a classic CIA strategy. The entire flood of disinformation that followed, the CIA-Mafia-Anti-Castro-Castro-KGB-Texas Right Wing theories . . . all of it was planned a year before the assassination. The people that put Kennedy there took him away again.'

Schembri looked away, for a moment an expression of sadness in his eyes.

'You see everything changed after November '63. The whole world changed. America started down the tubes. Quality of life deteriorated. Music got louder, drugs got into the mainstream culture, even down to the clothes people wore. No longer cotton and natural fabrics, but artificial, garish-colored, ugly. America realized that whoever could kill their President in broad daylight could do anything they wished. No longer was there one man, the Chief Executive of the nation, but some unelected invisible fraternity. And that same fraternity gave us LSD and psychiatry, free love, pornography, violence on the TV, everything that made it okay to be nuts.'

Schembri nodded his head.

'They took away the King of Camelot and gave us the Wizard of Oz. We exist in a palace of unreality, we are manipulated by invisible hands, and always in the distance is the awareness that somewhere there are people who know who we are, what we are doing, what we will do next, and when necessary they push the buttons and pull the strings and it all slots into place as it was designed.'

I opened my mouth to speak but Schembri went on.

My food was already cold.

'Kennedy was a visual leader, a man who won the hearts and minds of a nation through the TV set. People often said that Kennedy was elected because of how he looked – the all-American boy, the stand-up guy, the clean-cut military man. He was the personification of all our mothers' sons, the boy our fathers wanted us to be, and we identified with him. They killed him, they killed us, one and the same thing, and with that single, simple action they took away our identity and our vision. They managed to do to an entire nation what they had been doing to individuals for years. It was their greatest coup, a moment of sheer brilliance, and it made them feel bold and brave and committed to continuing their plan to introduce the New World Order. They even advertise themselves on the back of a dollar bill. The Eye In The Pyramid, the symbol of enclosed awareness, and beneath it those same words in Latin, New World Order. Even George Washington knew these people existed, and when he was asked about them he said they held diabolical tenets, and that their objective was a separation of the people from their government. Well, they succeeded, succeeded beyond their own wildest dreams, and the government behind the government is healthier and more robust than it ever was.'

Schembri leaned forward, his voice hushed. 'Ku Klux Klan, same shit you got yourself into, kid . . . they're inside it, all through that stuff.'

I felt my eyes widen. I attempted to ask a question, to elicit something further from him, but he just went on talking as if I wasn't there.

'And they hated Kennedy, hated him for speaking to Martin Luther King and Ralph Abernathy, for sending Federal Marshals down to the University of Mississippi back in September of '62. A man called Prescott Bush, Senator from Connecticut, best buddies with National Security Director Gordon Gray, he was straight out of the Order of Skull & Bones at Yale, both of them playing golf with Eisenhower. And Prescott's lawyer, John Foster Dulles, was Secretary of State, and Dulles' brother Alan was head of the CIA. Gray was made head of the Psychological Strategy Board in 1951, and then he was assistant to Eisenhower for national security affairs. Gray sat between Ike and the CIA and all the U.S. military forces. Gray was charged with protecting Eisenhower from any backlash encountered from CIA covert operations. Nixon's connections to Bush went back to '46.'

Schembri sighed and shook his head resignedly.

'Prescott Bush put an ad in a Los Angeles newspaper for the Orange County Republican Party. They wanted a young man to run for Congress. Nixon applied and got the job. He became Vice-President in 1952. In 1960 our friend Nixon was securing funds for his run at the presidency. There beside him was Prescott Bush, Congressman Gerald Ford and Prescott's son, George Bush. When Nixon got in in '68 it was payback time. He made Prescott's son, George, Chairman of the Republican National Committee and ambassador to China.'

Schembri frowned, leaned forward.

'And here we are, a handful of years later, and evidently Mr. Richard Milhous Nixon upset someone badly, because they took him out too. Bullshit Watergate, they have always and forever been in each other's pockets. They record everything, they swap tapes at Christmas for Christ's sake, the Intelligence Community is the Intelligence *Community* . . . National Security, CIA, Division Five of the FBI, the Justice Department, the Attorney General's Office, Office of Naval Intelligence, they're all the same goddamned thing. Nixon pissed someone off, they take him out; Gerald Ford steps in and does whatever Nixon wouldn't, and everything comes back to battery.'

Schembri nodded as if acknowledging himself, and spent a minute or so eating.

I wanted to ask something . . . anything. What did he know about the Ku Klux Klan? What had he heard about me and why I was there? Did he know Nathan? Did he understand what had happened? I had so many questions crowding my mind they seemed to bottleneck. I opened my mouth and nothing came out.

'You remember Kennedy?' he said.

I nodded.

'How old were you then?' Schembri asked.

A moment's mental calculation. 'Seventeen.'

Schembri smiled. 'Hell, you were just a kid.'

I nodded.

'And you remember where you were, what you were doing when you heard?'

I nodded again. I remembered as if it were yesterday. Everyone remembers where they were and what they were doing when they heard.

'Helluva thing,' he said quietly. 'Just a helluva thing.'

He fell silent for a moment.

I clenched my fists. 'What do you know?' I asked. 'What were you going to say about why I'm here?'

He winked. 'Same time . . . same channel,' he whispered, leaning towards me across the table. He started up from his chair. 'See ya tomorrow eh?'

I watched him go, my mouth open, my eyes wide. I felt awkward and ignorant and insubstantial. He disappeared into the throng heading for the doors and I felt nothing.

*

January of '63. The year started with fifty dead as Vietcong guerrillas shot down five helicopters in the Mekong Delta. In February Kennedy warned Cuba off once more as they fired rockets at a U.S. boat. On the upside, the Supreme Court released one hundred and eighty-seven blacks jailed for a protest in South Carolina. Martin Luther King was arrested once more in Alabama. Castro went to see Khrushchev.

These were important times, times of change and upheaval, but however significant these events may have appeared they would be blown away in a heartbeat compared to what was coming our way.

In June Medgar Evers, the civil rights leader, was shot, and with Governor George Wallace of Alabama still arguing with Kennedy, still defying the court order to open the university to negroes, it seemed that these wars would continue endlessly, that just as progress was made another event would turn it backwards upon itself and undo whatever good had been done.

By August of '63 Kennedy was a weary man. He'd lost his second son only thirty-six hours after that son was born. A march of two hundred thousand people came to Washington, and there in the masses were Marlon Brando, Burt Lancaster, Judy Garland and Bob Dylan. The world was watching and listening, waiting to see what would happen, and Kennedy knew it.

In September Governor Wallace ordered his State Troopers to seal off Tuskegee High School, and one hundred and eighty-nine negroes were arrested for protesting.

As the Senate Committee listened to Joseph Valachi deliver the goods on organized crime, as the U.S. officially recognized the South Vietnamese government, discussions about a certain incident that was to occur in Texas occupied the minds of a few men behind closed doors, and the world would change irrevocably.

Nathan Verney and I, however, were consumed with *girls*.

It is difficult now to understand how one single subject could so preoccupy an individual's mind as to exclude almost everything. Yet it did.

I was in 11th grade, and when I should have been working for my high school diploma I was actually working on my strategies to catch the attention of Caroline Lanafeuille or Linny Goldbourne. Perhaps Linny had in some way replaced Sheryl Rose Bogazzi in my dreams. Linny was all light and life and laughter. No-one really knew a great deal about her, 'cept that her father was some heavy political guy. She was always there at the center of things, always the one with the wildest stories and the funniest jokes, and if Caroline represented all the things I would want in a girl, then Linny represented all that I *could* want, but never have. She was dark-haired, hazel-eyed, her mouth full and passionate, and when she laughed a sound came from those lips that could have driven sailors to the rocks. She was as much a part of the world I wanted to belong to as Sheryl Rose had been, but Linny possessed substance, something tangible I suppose, yet something somehow unreachable. Had I known then that both she and Caroline would play such a significant part in my future, perhaps I would have forced myself to look away. But I didn't know. And thus I looked. I was enchanted and entranced and mystified. I was old enough to believe that everything one could ever wish for came with hips and thighs and breasts, and young enough not to push my luck. They existed at the edges of my universe, and though I imagined that perhaps one day I could reach Caroline, I also believed that my fingers would forever stretch towards Linny.

For a brief while I even believed they became friends. Perhaps not friends exactly, more acquaintances, for they were so different. I recall a day at Benny's when I saw them there together. The moment was unnerving beyond belief, for here I was presented with the possibility that they would become close, that they would share everything together, and this terrified me. I sat at a corner table, they were seated at the counter, Linny vivacious, bold, full of herself, and Caroline quiet, perhaps a little pensive. Each of them beautiful and entrancing in their own way, and yet somehow opposites. It would only be years later – when I had more than ample time to turn the significance of these events over in my mind – that I would conjure up that image and see something I found both haunting and somehow ironic. The butterfly and the moth. That's how I would see them – the butterfly and the moth.

Nathan had a different world. Nathan Verney was a handsome guy. Long gone were the jug-handle ears and traffic-light eyes. His face was strong and well-defined, full of character even at that early age it seemed, and the black girls that lived over his side of Greenleaf spent their time working their strategies to interest Nathan in what they might have to offer. Nathan, strangely enough, did not see this. He saw the wrath of his father, the shrieks and hysterics of his mother, for if Nathan had so much as touched a girl it would have been evidence of Lucifer's presence in the bosom of the Verney family.

Perhaps this was the reason he seemed blind to those girls. And they were pretty girls. Beautiful girls. Girls who could possess a heart with a glance and a soul with a kiss.

My scene was not so clear-cut. I was not an ugly kid, more sort of nondescript, neither one thing nor the other. I was neither too tall nor too short, too wide or too narrow, too fat or too skinny. My hair was a medium brown, my eyes blue-gray, and I seemed to excel at nothing in particular that would attract attention. I figured that out early. It was not sex appeal, it wasn't even how good-looking someone might be. It was *attention*. If you could garner attention you became interesting, and if you were interesting then others were interested in you.

Hence the game: seeking attention.

And thus – believing that Linny Goldbourne was somehow destined to be forever beyond my grasp – I was consumed by Caroline Lanafeuille. Caroline seemed quiet upon first impressions, but beneath that gentle exterior was a girl who possessed a strength and self-belief that belied all I imagined her to be. She was pretty: pretty beyond taste or preference. She would have been pretty despite anyone's belief that brunettes or redheads or blondes were best. Her hair was fair, multi-hued between amber and ochre and straw, and her slim figure, her delicate fingers and hands, the way she would tilt her head and sort of half-smile at me, were all indicative of deep currents flowing beneath a still surface.

And yet Caroline was an enigma to me, a distant star, a universe all by herself. She wore short skirts and tight tops, a tiny gold bracelet on her left wrist, and when I sat near her in class I could smell something like that breeze around Lake Marion – pecan pie and vanilla soda all rolled up in a basket of new-mown grass. But there was something else, something that would have been hormones or passion or love. Something that could never be described in a language anyone but me would understand. When Caroline approached me my pulse increased, my strong heart beat stronger, and when she opened her mouth to speak I would hold my breath for fear of my own lungs obscuring the sound that came forth.

Hi Daniel, she would say, and I would smile, and feel something warm around my face, and I would nod and say *Hi* back. And then she might say *How's it going?*, and I might say *Just fine there, Caroline, how's it going with you?*, and she would make some small pleasantry and then be gone. Incidents such as these occurred once, perhaps twice, a month, and the days in between would be spent waiting.

Nothing else.

Just waiting.

Despite her seeming unwillingness to share little more than a *Hi* or a *How's it going?* with me, my teenage heart, big and red and as strong as a stirrup pump, was for some time owned exclusively, and with no right of return, by Caroline Lanafeuille.

And I carried a secret.

And the secret I carried was a picture.

Greenleaf Senior High published a monthly Journal. The Journal of Endeavor. In the Journal were words and pictures demonstrating the attainments of students. In the Journal of August 1962 there was a picture of Caroline standing on the football field in her short-skirted cheerleader outfit, a pom-pom in her outstretched right arm, her legs slightly apart, her head tilted a little to the right, her long neck exposed. I cut out the picture. I covered it with Scotch tape so it wouldn't spoil or crease irretrievably. I carried it well. Like a professional.

The outstretched arm was an invitation into the gates of Heaven. The long graceful neck was a stairway to Paradise and all the gold of Eldorado. The skirt was the work of the Devil.

I yearned for Caroline. I pined for Caroline. I would have walked a thousand miles to Hades with her schoolbooks if I could have held the same hand that held that pom-pom.

For a while she was my life.

Perhaps I would never recover, I thought. Perhaps I would never love like that again. For even now, these many years later, I can remember times I spent with beautiful girls, passionate girls, girls another man might have loved the way I loved Caroline, and yet to me they never quite reached that same Olympic height of perfection that so effortlessly permeated everything she was.

And then November came, Thanksgiving Day, the promise of Christmas, and where my thoughts turned to some vain belief that Caroline Lanafeuille would find it in her heart to look my way with more than just a passing glance, the nation turned its eyes to Dallas and the passage of the King.

I was upstairs lying on my bed beneath the window, which was open just a fraction. Beside me, a small wireless carried sounds from KLMU in Augusta, Georgia, and I was thinking of Caroline. I know I was thinking of her because it was during that time that I thought of little else.

I knew something was wrong, very wrong, when my father appeared in the doorway. It was not how he looked. It was not the drawn expression, the bloodshot eyes, it was that he was there at all. My father had never missed a day's work in his life. Through influenza, a broken wrist, through colds and coughs and an eye infection that blinded his right side for a week, he was ever present, ever correct, to carry the folks of South Carolina on the railroads.

'They've killed him,' he said.

I sat up. For a heartbeat I believed he was speaking of Nathan.

'Who?' I said. 'Killed who?'

'Mister Kennedy,' he replied, and I heard the knot of emotion in his throat unravel.

He reached up and placed his hand against the frame of the door, and then he rested his face against his outstretched upper arm. His body seemed to tighten and then slacken, and not a sound issued from him, and it was all I could do to stand and walk towards him, a long walk, a walk of kings and queens and princes, and I realized only then that I was an inch or more taller than he. He seemed tiny, fragile, mere skin and bones, and as I neared him he turned towards me.

He held me then. I couldn't remember the last time my father had held me, and I started to cry. I felt closer to him then than I ever had, or ever would again.

My mother was there then. She paused at the top of the stairwell as if she wished not to interrupt this moment.

Tears streaked her face, her eyes were round and swollen and dark beneath. She looked like a ghost.

She came towards us, seemed to envelop us both. I could smell her, the hair lacquer, and beneath that the haunt of washing soda and detergent.

We stayed there for an eternity.

No-one said a word.

There was nothing to say.

I think for a day, perhaps two, I didn't think of Caroline once.

Some time later I left the house. People walked the streets aimlessly, broken like straw dolls. I don't think I had ever appreciated the division that existed there in Greenleaf. The path that I had so often taken with Nathan Verney down to the Lake was actually a demarcation between the whites and the coloreds. They had taken one side of Greenleaf, we had taken the other. But on that day it was different.

Kennedy had once said *There are no white or colored signs on the graveyards of battle*.

So it seemed on November 22nd. No white or colored division in our grief.

I saw Mrs. Chantry there. She stood beside Reverend Verney. And when a small boy came running towards them they both held him, comforted him, watched and waited for his mother who came running after him down the sidewalk.

And even now I recall an image from that day; a single, clear image that stands above all else.

Amidst the confusion and grief, the crowds gathered outside the radio store on Hyland, Benny Amundsen kneeling on the sidewalk outside his soda store as if in prayer, there was a moment so bold it stands like a color snapshot amidst a wash of monochrome: my Kodak moment.

A small colored girl, no more than five or six, her hair

tied up in wiry pigtails with bright bows at the ends, as if she wore some strange exotic flowers with sunshine yellow petals and black stems. Along Nine Mile Road she went, tears running down her face, her eyes wide and hopeless. In her arms she clutched a pile of newspapers too heavy for her frame, and as I watched she lost her balance and tripped. She skidded sideways, newspapers spilling out ahead of her, and then she just sat there, her knee grazed and bloody, and she looked up at the sky, as if to God, and those tears came like a river in spring. Too young even to understand the import of what had happened, she was caught in the flood of anguish that tore America apart.

It was Nathan Verney who rescued that child.

I saw him appear from behind the Reverend. He went down there and he lifted her as if she weighed nothing. He gathered the papers that had fallen and handed them to a white man who stood expressionless and dazed at the side of the road. The man took those papers without question.

And then Nathan saw me.

He nodded, walked towards me, and when he was a foot or two from me I held out my arms for the child.

The child reached back, I took her, and her slim arms enwrapped my neck.

She pulled tight, I started walking, and I went to Mrs. Chantry.

I think back now, all of us standing there, the Reverend, the witch who ate her husband, the black kid who floored Marty Hooper in Benny's, and the white misfit, the gangly pale-skinned youth holding this tiny colored girl. I see it now as if it were a photograph, and it makes me think of how it should have been all along. We were the universal family, and there was no difference, and no separate language, and we all breathed the same air and ate the same food and shared the same grief.

It was a day that went on forever, and I still believe now,

in my heart of hearts, that we all carried a little of that day for the rest of our lives.

In December of 1963 my father had a stroke. He would live for another year, a little more, but he would never fully recover his speech. My mother was an anchor, a tower of strength for both him and myself, and without her I believe he would have died much sooner. The Carolina Company gave him an allowance, a generous one for all the years he'd served, and even after he died they continued to pay that allowance to my mother. She went through the motions for another handful of years, but she was never the same. The spirit that was my mother had left with her husband, and even as she spoke, even as she helped me deal with the difficulties I would later experience, I could see so clearly her pain, her loss, her longing to be once again beside him in whatever hereafter may exist. Almost as if she was merely awaiting my permission, some sign of my own independence to surface so she could let go. Let go in the knowledge that I could care for myself.

I think it was in that year that I ceased to be a child and started to become a man. Nathan went with me on that awkward painful journey into adulthood. I seemed to strain at the leashes of the past: those lost summer days where we sat at the edge of Lake Marion with string and bamboo and mischievous thoughts. The County Fair. The football field. The smell of summer mimosa down Nine Mile Road. And Caroline Lanafeuille, heart of my heart, soul of my soul, light of my life and star of my heaven.

I was approaching my eighteenth birthday, talk of the *situation* in Vietnam became ever more prevalent, and Nathan Verney and I sensed trouble on its way.

FIVE

Today is Thursday.

Today we eat creamed beef on toast. Shit on a shingle they call it, and though shit on a shingle is something I cannot recall eating before, creamed beef on toast is a good enough approximation.

While I eat Mr. Timmons speaks to me. He tells me a minister will come down to talk to me today. It is part of the process. Learning how to die I think.

Mr. Timmons tells me his wife has been admitted to South Carolina State Hospital. She has deep vein thrombosis. He tells me she carries too much weight for her height. He is worried. I feel his worry but there is little I can say. I can tell that he loves her dearly, and much as my own mother found it difficult to continue without my father, so Mr. Timmons will find it difficult if his wife dies. I honestly hope she will recover. Mr. Timmons deals with enough death already.

The minister I will meet. I will speak with him. I will listen to what he has to say. Personally I think we keep coming back 'til we get it right. I don't believe in Heaven, and Hell would be so crowded I don't think such a place could exist. The minister will challenge me, tell me that I have to have *faith*, the implication being that I have none.

I do have faith.

I have faith in the truth.

I have faith that the sun will rise and set.

I have faith that the spirit of Nathan Verney lives and breathes and walks the world, and one day I will meet him.

I have faith in the fact that I am going to die.

I recall something then, something that occurred soon after Kennedy's death, and even as Mr. Timmons returns to his duties I see Nathan's face once more.

I close my eyes.

For some reason I feel calm inside.

The world seems silent, patient perhaps, as if time is being afforded me to reminisce, to address my own life, to make some sense of it all before it is complete.

So be it, I think.

Grateful for small mercies.

In March of 1964 Jack Ruby went to Death Row. He'd been found guilty of the first degree murder of Lee Harvey Oswald, the mystical and impressive man who, with no training or experience, had fired three shots into JFK's motorcade and killed the King. Despite the complete impossibility of replicating this feat, even with the highest trained FBI and military marksmen, the Warren Commission, led by the same man who had earlier been sacked by Jack Kennedy, would complete their report, their beautiful whitewash, and announce that it would always and forever be nothing more than a lone gunman.

I never believed it. Hadn't believed it from the first.

In April Sidney Poitier became the first black man to win an Oscar. He won it for a film called *Lilies of the Field*. At first it seemed some progress was being made, but two months later Martin Luther King was back in the Big House for trying to enforce racial integration in a restaurant in Florida.

Later that same month three Civil Rights workers went missing. They would soon be found dead.

In July, Lyndon B. Johnson, the new President of the United States, signed the Civil Rights Act, a sweeping condemnation of segregated restaurants and buses and railroad stations and hotels, an Act that denied the right of any man to choose color as a preference in employment or position.

Nathan and Reverend Verney led a congregation of hundreds that day, but later Nathan told me he didn't think the promised changes would really come within his lifetime.

He didn't know how right he was, though never in the way he intended.

I turned eighteen. I was still a virgin. This caused me a deep-seated sense of concern. As the fall of '64 unfolded I sensed my father's physical condition worsening, and this served to take my attention away from my lack of sexual conquest.

I watched him die then, through the latter part of October and into November and, coincident with the Vietcong launching attacks at Bien Hoa and the declaration of martial law in Saigon, my father the railroad man, the just and lawful railroad man, slipped away silently.

I wanted to bury him in Reverend Verney's churchyard. My mother, understanding, compassionate, said we could not. The Civil Rights Act 1964 hadn't yet reached Greenleaf, South Carolina.

In February of 1965 Malcolm X was shot and killed and the U.S. started bombing North Vietnam. In March LBJ sent the Marines in, and within weeks they were pulling 35,000 recruits a month. Warren Myers, Max's son, was one of those who went, willingly and with duty in his heart; the son of a man I wouldn't meet for close on a decade. There was talk of conscription, the Draft, and Nathan and I would meet and speak of these things – of the war, the promise of the future, and the fact that we were not ready to die.

I don't believe I am a coward. I don't believe I was ever a coward. But the idea of lying dead in some rain-swollen field in the middle of nowhere haunted me.

I remember something from the spring of that year. A man came back, a soldier. He was older than us, perhaps twenty-three or twenty-four, but his face was that of a man in his forties. His left leg was missing below the knee, and he walked with help and a shoulder and a heavy-looking stick. The expression on his face was one of perpetual sadness, as if he was always on the verge of tears. He had been there, out there in Vietnam, and he came to Greenleaf to see his cousin and his cousin brought him to Benny's.

He kept talking of the things they had to carry out there.

Like the things they carried determined who they were.

He spoke of things I didn't understand, this young man with his forty-year-old face.

Things called heat tabs, Kool Aid and C-Rations.

He spoke of a steel helmet with a liner and a camouflage cover; a steel-centered, nylon-covered flak jacket; compress bandages and a plastic poncho. He described an M-16, the cloth bandoliers filled with numerous magazines. He spoke of rods and steel brushes and gun oil, fragmentation and phosphorus grenades, of Claymore anti-personnel mines, and sometimes mosquito netting and canvas tarpaulins. And then he told us there were items of choice, such as razors and chewing gum, paper to write letters home, playing cards and lucky dice. He spoke of a young man from Myrtle Beach – not a dozen miles from where we sat – who carried a rabbit's foot on a string around his neck. Carried it until he died in the arms of a twenty-one-year-old Lieutenant called Shelby White.

We listened, me and Nathan and others I don't recall, and we looked at one another at moments with the same expression.

Then, even then, I knew what was coming, and the fear I'd felt a thousand years before as I stood on a path with a fish in my hands was nothing compared to what I was now feeling.

Nathan Verney felt it too.

We were one and the same, he and I, and I believe now that we knew what was going to happen.

And it did. Not for some time, but it did.

Like a wave breaking for the shore, once started it cannot slow or stop or change its direction.

And it was big, big enough to drown us both.

After my father's death and into the summer of 1965 I spent more time away from home, as if I could see the burden my mother was carrying and did not possess the strength to share it. I hung out at Benny's, I listened to the same scarred and scratched records, and I watched for Caroline.

She would come down there perhaps once or twice a week, and she would sit with her friends drinking soda and talking girl-talk. I would sit alone more often than not, and sense her presence, and feel the distance between us, and remember the Scotch-taped picture I had carried for so long. Where it was by then I didn't know, but I could still feel its smooth surface between my fingers, still recall the sense of longing that possessed me each time I looked at it.

It was at the end of July that she first spoke to me. Spoke to me directly. Her friends had gathered as they ordinarily did, and then one by one they seemed to fade away. I could not have said how they went, or when, but they did, and sure enough I turned and saw Caroline seated alone at her table.

I tensed. I think I prayed a little. I rose from my stool at the counter and walked nonchalantly towards her.

She turned as I came, and she smiled – Lord how she smiled. That same tilt of the head, the way her hair fell sideways from her face, and the flicker of tension around her lips before she let loose with such a radiant smile I could feel sunshine breaking out.

'Daniel Ford,' she said.

I nodded.

'You wanna come sit down?'

I nodded again.

She laughed. 'Cat got your tongue, Mister Ford?'

'No,' I replied, and slid along the seat facing hers.

'Just got the words with more than one syllable, right?'

I laughed. 'I'm sorry,' I said.

'For what?'

I shrugged. I didn't know what I was sorry for. Sorry for being a schmuck perhaps.

'I was gonna get another soda,' she said. 'You want one?'

I nodded.

'Yes, Caroline,' she prompted.

I smiled. 'Yes, Caroline.'

She turned and waved her hand. Benny nodded from behind the counter and went about his business.

'So how ya doing?' she asked.

'I'm okay,' I said. 'My father died you know?' I blushed. I didn't know why I'd said that. It seemed idiotic, like I was trying to win her over with sympathy.

'I know,' she said.

She reached out her hand. I saw it coming in slow-motion. She reached out her fine and delicate hand and she touched my ugly, stumpy, fat-fingered hand.

'I heard,' she said softly. 'I'm sorry.'

'Thank you,' I said, and I really meant it. Someone important to me, someone other than my ma had expressed their sadness about something that in its own way had tortured me silently.

'Your ma's okay?' she asked.

I nodded. 'She's coping.'

Caroline smiled understandingly and withdrew her hand.

Benny brought sodas. We drank silently, and for all the world to see we could have known each other for a thousand years.

It was an important moment, a profound moment, a moment I would remember for years to come. Caroline Lanafeuille was the first, and in some way she would be the last, though the significance of that I would not understand until I believed I was going to die.

'I've seen you here a lot,' she said. 'You always sit on your own.'

I shrugged non-committally.

'Where's Nathan?'

I frowned. I was unaware of the fact that we were so well known together.

'With his folks I s'pose.'

'So when you come down here you should come talk to us,' she said.

I smiled and shook my head. 'Don't see as how I'd fit in with half a dozen girls,' I replied.

She nodded. 'So perhaps you should just come talk to me.'

I felt myself blush. It seemed to please her.

She smiled. 'So that's settled then . . . when you're down here and I'm here too then you come talk to me, okay?'

'Okay,' I said, and in that second I wanted to tell her everything – of the picture, the Journal of Endeavor, of how I had longed and hoped and prayed that she would speak to me just once. And now she was telling me it was okay.

It really was okay.

She stayed a little while – ten, perhaps fifteen minutes – and then she rose slowly, gracefully, from her seat and said she would have to go home.

'I'll walk you,' I said.

'Thank you, Daniel,' she replied, and I did. I walked her home, and though it took the best part of twenty minutes, and though I don't believe more than a dozen words passed between us, it was the most memorable walk of my life.

Arriving at her house she thanked me for being a gentleman, and she reminded me that she would be at Benny's the following Wednesday.

'So you come talk to me, okay?'

'Agreed,' I said.

She held out her hand. We shook.

'Agreed,' she said, and then she passed through the gate at the foot of the path leading to her house.

At the door she paused, and then she turned, and she tilted her head and sort of half-smiled.

I raised my hand. I smiled. She disappeared.

I floated home that night, floated three feet from terra firma with my head in the clouds.

I was nineteen years old, and I did see her again the following week, and two days after that in fact, and the subsequent day as well.

When she stood near me I could smell Bazooka Joe bubble gum and toothpaste. When she held my hand I felt something moving inside me. Something cool and quiet and special.

She spoke with a Southern accent – pronounced and lyrical – and when she talked it sounded like the words of a song.

She was so different from the other girls I knew. She read a lot, things by Hemingway and Robert Frost, and she quoted lines from something called 'Song of Myself' by Walt Whitman.

I had watched her from afar for so long, but never *really* spoken to her. Two weeks became three, and I felt she was the only girl I had ever really shared my thoughts and dreams with, the only girl who ever gave me the feeling she understood something of who I was.

And then there was a day, a day in August, and she came to me that day, came walking towards me as I crossed the Nine Mile Road, and there was something in her expression that told me she'd been looking. The sun was high and hot, and I could see the fine gloss of sweat across her top lip. I wanted to kiss it away. I remember thinking that, and for some reason the thought did not embarrass me. I felt settled somehow, and when she walked beside me it didn't matter that she was there, that she was a girl, that she was pretty or funny or interesting. She was just there.

I remember feeling a sense of accomplishment, but there was no vanity or pride or self-aggrandizement. I felt I could be myself.

And though we had spent so much time together, though we'd shared things that would never transpire between myself and any other, she could never have guessed the depth to which I'd loved her . . . and for so long.

That day in August Caroline Lanafeuille came to find me because *she* wanted to.

That was the most important thing.

'Daniel,' she said, and she reached out and touched my hand.

I smiled. 'Caroline . . . how goes it?'

'It goes,' she said, and her voice was a whisper.

'What you up to?'

'I came to find you,' she said.

'So you found me.'

'I did,' she replied.

And then she touched my hand again, and this time she held it, and we walked for a while saying nothing much of anything at all.

And yet despite this, despite this sense of having arrived, I did not think of touching her. I did not think of her skin, the arch of her neck, the curve and dip of her hip or thigh. I did not think of the smooth, tanned silk of her back, the slender ankle, the short white sock or the cream-colored pump. I did not think of a midnight rendezvous in the back of a Chevrolet Impala, I did not think of breaking a sweat, of fumbling in the semi-darkness with buttons or bows or bra-clips.

Caroline Lanafeuille just walked alongside me down Nine Mile Road, and everything was alright.

Without a thought in my head, I smiled.

We walked for an hour, a little more perhaps, and then she slowed and stopped.

I slowed with her. She faced me, held both my hands, and there was something in her eyes that told me something was making its way towards me. Something that possessed sharp corners and rough edges.

'I have to go now,' she said.

'But . . .'

'I'll come see you later. I'll come see you at your house, okay?'

The way she looked told me not to ask anything. I nodded, smiled as best I could, and watched as she walked away once more.

Seemed like I'd spent almost every hour of every day with her for a month. She'd laughed at my stories, we'd gone skinny-dipping in Lake Marion. She'd even met Nathan and thought him handsome and bright and charming. She'd met my ma, my ma had thought her delightful and witty and one-in-a-million, and when Ma had made baked ham sandwiches she'd made them for two.

That, and that alone, made Caroline Lanafeuille almost family.

And yet despite all these things, these special moments and magic hours, I did not believe she loved me as I loved, and *had* loved, her.

I tried to believe, Lord knows I tried.

Perhaps I did not know what I was trying for.

It was like climbing a mountain, overwhelmingly high, and as I reached each visible peak I found another taller peak beyond it.

It was a good time, that month or so, and it concluded that night . . . suddenly, unexpectedly . . . a sense of beautiful tragedy.

I lost my virginity on August 17th 1965.

I stood on the back porch of my house. The verandah ran

along the side and turned the corner, but the back door possessed its own steps down to the yard. From where I stood I could see the road that ran all the way to the Lake. I was thinking of Nathan. I had not seen him for two or three days, and then I remembered he had gone with his father to Charleston. Reverend Verney was on the fall testimonials, a series of gatherings he held for two or three weeks each year. Folks would come from all over to hear Reverend Verney speak in Charleston. He was a good speaker, he commanded an audience, and when you slipped a dollar or two in that solid silver collection plate it sometimes felt like a fee for a performance. Folks down here appreciated a preacher breaking a sweat in church, and Reverend Verney broke a sweat that would have carried Noah home.

I saw Caroline before she turned off the road and started down the path. I saw her through the trees, her white summer cotton frock, her shoulder-length hair, the breeze flicking it up around her face. She really was a beautiful girl.

When she turned the corner and saw me she waved.

In that moment I seemed to feel something I could never hope to describe.

It was an awareness, a perception, that something would both begin and end today.

I waved back.

She smiled, and though she looked like the same Caroline Lanafeuille there was something in her expression, something in her eyes, that told me something was different.

She reached out and took my hand as I came down the back porch steps. She sort of pulled me towards her and kissed my cheek.

I asked her how she was.

She said she was fine, just fine.

She asked if we could sit on the verandah swing.

I nodded, said I'd fetch some lemonade and bring it out.

She turned and walked towards the side of the house.

I watched her go, why I don't know, but I did, and when she reached the corner of the house she suddenly slowed and glanced back. She had expected to see me disappearing into the house, perhaps just the screen door closing behind me. The fact that I was still standing there surprised her. She smiled, and then she frowned, and then she sort of shooed me into the house like one would shoo a cat or a dog.

The lemonade was cool; chunks of ice floated on the top and clinked against the glasses as I walked back the way I'd come. The sound was like one of those delicate windchimes you would find in bedroom windows.

I went up onto the verandah and sat beside Caroline. She took the glass and sipped. She sipped like a bird. She pursed her lips and kissed the lip of the glass and you would imagine she could drink nothing that way. She did these things, these special little things, and it was for reasons such as these that I loved her.

'I'm leaving Greenleaf,' she said.

She came out with it like that.

Like a stone had dropped from the evening sky right into my lap.

The only thing I could ever remember being so sudden was in Benny's. Nathan had roundhoused Marty Hooper and he flat-fuck fell to the ground. Boom. Down.

And it was like that.

Bang. *I'm leaving Greenleaf.*

'Leaving?' I remember asking.

She nodded, turned away for just a moment, and when she turned back there were tears in her eyes.

'There's been a little trouble,' she said. 'My daddy's gotten himself in a little trouble, Daniel.'

She always called me Daniel. Never Danny or Dan or Danno like the others did. Always Daniel.

She paused as if to catch her breath, and then she reached out and held my hand.

Again I felt that something, something that moved inside of me, something cool and quiet and special.

'So we have to leave,' she said quietly.

I was silent for a time.

'When?' I eventually asked.

She turned away. I could tell she wanted to look at me but could not.

'In the morning,' she whispered, and there was such emotion in her voice I felt like crying myself.

'So soon?' I asked.

'So soon,' she stated matter-of-factly.

She still could not look at me.

I wanted to ask what trouble she meant, what had her father done that was so bad he would have to leave Greenleaf. But I did not ask. For me to have asked would have been unfair. If she'd wished me to know she would have told me.

We stayed like that for a little while longer, Caroline looking out through the trees towards the Lake, every once in a while sipping her lemonade like a bird, and then she turned, eventually she turned, and she said something that I would think of later as I languished in a jail cell in Sumter.

'We should . . . you know, we *should* . . . before I leave . . .'

I felt that *something* inside me again. No longer cool and quiet and special, but alive, a fiery thing, like a catherine wheel or a roman candle in my stomach.

The way she said it – we *should* – required no explanation. I knew what she meant, she knew I knew, and when she turned and smiled I just smiled back.

There was innocence in that moment, innocence and passion, and something that you felt only one time in your life.

There were no trumpets, no rah-rahs, no cheerleader

73

troupe with pom-poms and brass bands playing Sousa marches across the endzone.

There was warmth and silence and promise, and a moment of sweet perfection.

My ma went out that night.

My ma never went out alone.

Night of August 17th 1965 she changed the habit of a lifetime.

I think God had something to do with that.

We lay on the narrow bed beneath the window, the same bed where I had lain when my father came to tell me Mr. Kennedy had died.

She smelled of juniper and toothpaste and a sweet sense of beauty that would linger long after she'd gone. It was cool. There was a breeze beyond the trees, and every once in a while the leaves would rustle like they were whispering delicate secrets one to another.

I had never done this before, neither had she, but somehow we seemed to know where we were going and why.

I remember the moment she stood before me naked. I felt hot and flushed, dizzy almost, and when my hands reached towards her they shook.

'You can touch,' she whispered. 'I won't break.'

She took a single step forward, and my hands reached further, almost grabbed her with a life of their own, and then I could feel her skin, the curves of her thighs, and I could barely hold my eyes open long enough to look.

Her skin was pale and unblemished. Her hair was tied back behind her head with a loose bow. She smiled, she stepped back again, and then she held out her hand and I took it. I rose from where I'd been seated on the edge of my bed.

She pulled me close, Caroline Lanafeuille, and she closed

her arms around me and pulled me tight. Tight like Sunday-best shoelaces.

I stayed there forever it seemed, and then she leaned close to my ear and whispered: 'I think you're s'posed to take your clothes off too, Daniel.'

I smiled, I blushed, I felt simple and naïve.

She released me and I started to remove my shirt, my jeans. For a moment I stood there in my shorts, and then she pushed me back to the bed and sat beside me.

I kissed her hair, her cheek, her neck, her lips. I wanted to kiss every inch of her, wanted to swallow her whole. I felt clumsy and awkward, but somehow my awkwardness seemed to be appropriate. I kissed each closed eye in turn and tasted the salt-sweet tang of tears. And when she lay down I lay there beside her. She moved slightly across me and I felt the weight of her breast upon my shoulder.

'These too,' she said, tugging at my shorts. 'Sex with your shorts on is like taking a bath wearing socks.'

I smiled, inwardly more than visibly, and I tried so hard not to laugh.

Her hand was smooth and delicate, like a ballerina, and when she made small circles across my stomach I felt myself stir and rise.

I believe my heart was beating more slowly than ever.

Time didn't matter.

We had all the time in the world.

Some time later she made a small sound, a sound that was neither pain nor pressure nor anything I knew. The sound she made was one of *completeness*.

I understood that sound, for I felt complete also. Whole and pure and satiated.

Our movement was in unison, a narrow dance, a soft ballet of sounds and emotions and feelings, and all the fears I had possessed about such a moment seemed irrelevant.

And though my eyes were closed I could *see* her, and her

ity was more complete than I could ever have imag-
1.

And it was in that moment that I understood love.

Love more than life itself.

And though there would be times when I would think of
Sheryl Rose and Linny Goldbourne, there would never be a
moment like the one I shared with Caroline Lanafeuille
that night in August when I was nineteen and the world
seemed like heaven.

Later she left.

She left me there half-asleep.

She dressed. She leaned over me. She kissed my forehead,
rested her hand on my cheek, and then she left.

I heard the screen door downstairs, and though I wanted
to lean up towards the window and watch her cross the
yard and start away towards the Lake, I did not.

Could not.

I never wished to remember her leaving.

I wanted my last abiding memory of Caroline Lanafeuille
to be that moment I knew I *truly* loved her.

Nothing else.

I would not see her for many, many years, when we both
had changed irrevocably.

I would never really learn what her father had done that
had taken her away, and I said nothing to Nathan when he
returned from the fall testimonials in Charleston.

I believed that some things, just a handful, were for
yourself and God alone.

SIX

In November of 1965 the Army came to Greenleaf.

Why they chose Greenleaf I don't know, but they came, and with them a tent the size of half a football field.

They sent out buses to bring people from the surrounding towns, and those people came in their hundreds. They saw it perhaps as a family outing, and when they arrived they found the Army had laid on fried chicken and corn and potato salad.

People crowded into that tent, and like an evangelical gathering they sat and waited for *the Army man* to arrive.

Despite the season it was warm, and soon that tent was like an oven, people fanning themselves with the brochures they found on their seats. Children gathered in small crowds along the edge of the tent, chattering and laughing and squabbling.

But when *the Army man* arrived they were hushed and well-behaved.

I sat beside my ma, and to my left was Mrs. Chantry. In the row ahead Reverend and Mrs. Verney sat, with Nathan between then.

The Army man was Sergeant Michael O'Donnelly of the Airborne something-or-other. He told us to call him Sergeant Mike. They'd rigged up a loudspeaker and his voice was clear and measured and precise. He'd done this before, many times I was sure, for it was from places like Greenleaf and Myrtle Beach and Orangeburg that LBJ's 35,000 men a month would come.

They would give fried chicken and corn and potato salad

to America's parents, and in return they would take their sons. Perhaps, to folk in Washington, it seemed a fair exchange.

Sergeant Mike was a spirited speaker, a man of verve and passion. He believed in America. He believed in the Constitution. He believed in freedom of speech and the right to bear arms, and he was doing just fine until Karl Winterson who ran the Radio Store asked him how many of our boys had died out there already.

For a heartbeat there was silence, a palpable tension within the acreage of that tent. Inside that heartbeat it seemed we were all gathered beneath a single blanket.

And then there was a child's voice from the side. A single child's voice that cut through that moment and separated it like a razor. The moment split in half and rolled each way like an orange on a chopping board.

'Serpent Mike . . . is the Vietcong like King Kong?'

A moment's perfect silence, and then laughter broke like a wave.

The tension was shattered.

The question Mr. Winterson asked was never answered.

It was a question Sergeant Mike had not wanted to be asked.

'No, son,' Sergeant Mike eventually said. 'The Vietcong are an awful lot more real than a big monkey.'

Nathan glanced over his shoulder towards me. The expression in his eyes told me that I was not alone in doubting the truthfulness of that statement.

And then the time came, the time to ask, the time to sell us our own freedom, a freedom I believed we already had.

The evangelical minister was asking for money, that's how it felt, and folk were embarrassed because they knew the minister was a drunk and a liar and a philanderer.

But Sergeant Mike had asked before, many times before, and he pounded the crowd with quotes from Lincoln and Robert E. Lee and General Patton.

I realized then that Sergeant Mike was talking to me, talking to me and to Nathan, and to all those others that still hung out at Benny's and believed the world could never reach that far.

And I realized something else. I realized that where we still thought of ourselves as big kids, the world now saw us as men.

Men who should be willing to die in some dark damp jungle on the other side of the world.

Sergeant Mike had violated our innocence and trust, and most of us never even knew.

Marty Hooper stood up first.

He just stood up.

There was nothing, and then he was there, and he stood out like a single flower in the middle of that football field.

Somebody clapped. A single pair of hands that sounded like gunfire.

And because Marty Hooper was on his feet Larry James stood up too.

And then another.

And another.

Someone else started clapping, faster, louder, and before I knew it the tent was filled with riotous applause, and fathers were standing and hugging their sons, and mothers were crying, and the small children were watching this with wide-eyed wonder, asking themselves what was happening, unable to appreciate its significance.

Nathan and I didn't move.

I think if he'd stood up I would have died right where I sat.

I felt my mother's hand gripping mine, and when I looked down I saw her knuckles were white with tension.

I knew she felt me looking at her but she did not turn.

Sergeant Mike was in his element. This was his moment, his own Kodak moment, and even as he was congratulating everyone there were other soldiers, men and women, moving among the crowd to corral the recruits, to guide them to a bank of tables where seated men held forms and pens and documents of release.

I was terrified.

I thought for one awful moment that I might involuntarily stand, that I would be whisked to the side, that I would be clapped on the shoulder, that I would feel strange hands shaking mine, that a man with stern eyes and a sterner voice would want to know my name, my age, my height, my weight.

But I didn't stand.

I sat like a statue.

I barely breathed.

The noise seemed to go on forever. An hour. A day. A week perhaps.

No-one looked at me. There were no accusatory glances. No-one leaned forward to ask me what my problem was, did I not care for my family's freedom, did I not care for the American way of life?

For that small mercy I was eternally grateful.

And when the noise was quelled and the crowds settled I looked up and saw Sergeant Mike had gone.

Serpent Mike, the little boy had said, and of all those who attended that night – the fathers and mothers, the brothers, sisters, cousins and neighbors, those from Myrtle Beach and Orangeburg who thought perhaps there was a circus in town, the little ones who would go home and find their brothers' beds empty – I believed that that little boy had spoken the real and only truth.

I never said a thing.

Like before, there are some things only to be known by yourself and God.

Later, the tent down, the ground scattered with paper plates, chicken bones, brochures trampled into the dirt beneath a thousand feet, Nathan and I stood and watched as soldiers folded the vast canvas and packed it into a truck. The boys who had become men that night had already left in buses.

Forty-six of them in all.

By Christmas all but twelve would be dead.

One of them would return, having left much of the lower half of his body in Da Nang or Ky Lam or some other godforsaken place.

His name was Luke Schaeffer. He was a football player before he went, a good one, a young man who would have walked a scholarship with the speed of that right arm.

He told me stories I cannot bear to recall, even now – older, hardened, a little cynical – there are images of which he spoke that threaten my sanity.

I did not ask why then, I do not ask it now.

There are some things that just are.

They are part of being human.

And that, if nothing else, was never a matter of choice.

SEVEN

The priest who visited me at Sumter possessed an honest enough face. I would later learn that this was a new gig for him, and I believed that perhaps some impropriety or breach of conduct had brought him this position. Counsel to the dead. I couldn't imagine anyone choosing to perform such a task.

His name was Father John Rousseau, he was perhaps in his early forties, and he smoked ceaselessly, one cigarette after the other. The Counselling Room, known as *God's Lounge* to those who still possessed sufficient humor to bother with such things, was a narrow room with a single plain deal table, two chairs, a one-way window through which interviews were video-taped, and a two-shelf book-case. In the center of the upper shelf were two books. A copy of the New Testament & Psalms, and a Gideon's Bible.

John Rousseau brought his own Bible, a beaten-to-shit leather volume which he clutched as one would clutch the hand of a small child in a funfair crowd.

I liked Rousseau's face, and despite our brief weekly meetings being neither a matter of choice nor relevance, I appreciated the fact that I could spend an hour talking to someone who seemed more concerned with my religious and spiritual salvation than my lock-down time.

Our first meeting was in August of 1982. It was a Tuesday, I remember that much, and though I grew to like Father John Rousseau he began our first meeting on the wrong foot.

He greeted me, shook my hand, asked me to sit there at

the plain deal table, and then he told me he cared for neither my innocence nor my guilt.

A man on Death Row thinks of little else but his own innocence or guilt.

He then told me that he knew I was going to die, that he had spoken with Penitentiary Warden Hadfield and there was little hope of any further effective action being taken to either stay my execution or gain a reprieve. He said he understood some of the details of my case and trial, that the issues raised had cast it into the arena of politics, and once it had reached that point there was little anyone would do to reverse the decisions made. It had become a matter of losing face.

I remember feeling the first stirrings of violence within. I was not a violent man – never had been – but the almost complacent nonchalance with which he seemed to pronounce my forthcoming death angered me. I clenched my fists beneath the table, white balls of tense knuckles, and had I believed it would serve any purpose I might have lashed out. If not physically, at least verbally.

I held my hands and my tongue. I was in no position to endanger the sole source of human contact I might have.

And then Father John Rousseau asked me about my faith.

'Faith?' I asked back.

Father John nodded. He gripped that Bible like a lifeline to the shore.

I remember looking towards the one-way window; I smiled for the video camera, and then I shrugged my shoulders.

'I have faith, Father,' I said. 'But I don't know that I have faith in the same things as you.'

Father John smiled. I imagined he'd heard it all.

'And what do you think I have faith in, Daniel?' he said.

I shrugged, half-smiled. I was thinking more about if he would give me a cigarette.

'God,' I said. 'Jesus Christ, the crucifixion, the Virgin

birth, Mary Magdalene, Lazarus and turning water into wine. The loaves and fishes, and the parting of the Red Sea, Moses coming down from the mountain with the Ten Commandments, eternal damnation for me and eternal Paradise for yourself. I imagine those things are what you believe in.'

Father John smiled.

He did exactly what I wanted him to do: he offered me a cigarette.

I took one gratefully. I could not remember the last time I had smoked a whole cigarette to myself.

'I believe in some of those things,' Father John said. 'Though I don't actually believe in eternal damnation for anyone.'

I frowned.

'I think Hell is allegorical,' he went on. 'I think Hell has been marketed as a concept to obtain compliance from the people –'

'Marketed?' I asked.

Father John smiled sardonically. 'The Church has to market a product like anyone else, Daniel.'

I smiled, a little sarcastically perhaps.

'Anyway, I don't think there's such a thing as Hell,' he repeated.

'And Heaven?' I asked.

Father John shook his head. 'I don't think Heaven is a location, I think it's a spiritual state.'

I didn't reply.

'So what do you believe, Daniel?' he eventually asked. He lit another cigarette, his fifth or sixth since he'd sat down.

'Believe?' I asked. 'I believe a lot of things.'

Father John did not say anything; he merely looked at me inquisitively.

'You want to know what I believe?'

Father John nodded affirmatively.

I leaned back and thought for a moment. 'I believe there

are still Cheyenne Dog Soldiers in the Oxbow. I believe that The Rolling Stones killed Brian Jones. I believe that Elvis is alive and well, maybe a hundred and seventy-five or two hundred pounds in weight, and lives somewhere out west on a ranch. I believe that they never really went to the moon, and all the pictures they sent back were manufactured in a studio at NASA. I believe Gus Grissom was gonna blow the whistle and they whacked him . . .'

I looked across at Father John. His expression was intent.

'You want me to go on?' I asked.

He nodded.

'I believe Kennedy was killed by some super-elite political and financial fraternity like the Bilderberg Group because he was too popular, because he was interested in white-black integration, because he was a wild card. I believe Joe Kennedy made a deal with the Mafia, people like Sam Giancana and his crew, to help get his son the presidency and in exchange promised that JFK would go easy on organized crime, but when it got to the real deal JFK reneged and upset everyone in Vegas and L.A. and Florida and New York. I believe Marilyn Monroe was murdered because she slept with JFK. I believe Sirhan Sirhan was part of Operation Artichoke or the CIA's MK Ultra Project, and he was brainwashed into killing Robert Kennedy because it looked like Kennedy might make it to the White House. I think Ted Kennedy was set up for Chappaquiddick so he wouldn't even think of going that way. And I think Martin Luther King and Che Guevara were murdered because they represented too much change and rebellion and running against the grain.'

I reached for another cigarette without asking. Father John made no comment.

'I think Nixon was the golden boy, and then he went crazy, started talking to his dead mother and thinking everyone was following him, and whoever it was that controlled the government knew they couldn't whack the guy in broad daylight like JFK, so they set him up with the whole Watergate fiasco. Bernstein and Woodward were given all the help they needed by someone inside Nixon's administration, and Haldeman and Mitchell and Porter and the others were just the fall guys who happened to be around at the time. And I think that the Cuban missile crisis and the Bay of Pigs and what happened in Dallas were reminders to all Americans that their lives really meant nothing at all. They could go up with an atomic bomb, or they could rise to the greatest position in the country, and it didn't matter a fuck because they could kill you anyway. After the early '60s it all went to hell, and with Vietnam and 35,000 men a month flying into someone else's war, everyone kind of gave up and resigned themselves to a life of TV and Prozac and calorie-counting and aluminum sidings.'

I paused.

'That's what I believe, Father John.'

Father John was quiet for a time, and then he said: 'You didn't go to Vietnam, did you?'

It was a question I had not expected, a question I never liked.

I shook my head.

'What happened?' Father John asked.

'It's a long story,' I said, in a weak attempt at dissuading him from pursuing his line of questioning. My sense of anger had passed, and in its place came a neatly folded package of fatigue and frustration. I did not understand the point of the questions. I could not see what purpose they might serve.

'I've got time,' Father John said.

I smiled. 'But I haven't.'

'You have something better to do?'

I shook my head.

'You have today,' Father John said, 'and one today is better than two tomorrows.'

I looked at him. 'Who said that?'

Father John smiled. 'Benjamin Franklin.'

'One today is better than two tomorrows,' I repeated.

Father John nodded. 'That's right.'

I smiled a little sarcastically. 'Wasn't on Death Row when he said that, was he?'

'I appreciate your bitterness, Daniel.'

I nodded. 'Thank you, Father.'

Father John smiled understandingly. 'And your sarcasm.'

'You think I'm not entitled to a little of both?'

'I think you're entitled to a great deal more than you're getting, but there's little I can do to change that. I'm here to talk to you, to listen, to try and assist you to reconcile yourself to dying.'

'I've been doing that for more than ten years, Father,' I said.

'And to try and foster some sense of hope that there might be something better afterwards.'

He paused then and looked at me. I was unnerved in that moment, for the expression in his face was one I had seen before. The expression of a man with a secret. Was there something happening here he wasn't telling me?

'You believe that?' I asked. 'That there might be something better after this?'

Father John nodded. 'I do.'

I leaned back and closed my eyes. I didn't feel like talking any more. I could see colors behind my eyelids. I felt a little dizzy from the nicotine. There was a bitter coppery taste in my mouth, not unpleasant, just unusual. I could sense Father John was there opposite me, but I felt little requirement to humor him. He was here for me, not the other way round.

'You talk when you feel like talking, Daniel,' Father John said.

I opened one eye fractionally and squinted at him. He seemed as relaxed and settled as I.

'Don't feel much like anything,' I said.

Father John shrugged. 'Okay,' he said.

There was silence for another minute or so.

'Figured you might tell me a little about Nathan,' he eventually said.

I opened my eyes and sat forward. 'Nathan?' I asked.

Father John nodded. 'Nathan.'

'What about Nathan?'

He shrugged again. 'Anything you like.'

'Nathan was like my brother,' I said.

'I know.'

I frowned. 'How do you know?'

'Because when I mentioned his name you looked more like a human being than at any other time.'

'Profound,' I replied. 'What the hell is that s'posed to mean?'

'What it says,' he replied. 'The tone in your voice is less bitter and cynical and frustrated. We could be sat next to one another in a bar just shooting the breeze.'

'Nathan used to say that,' I said.

Father John frowned. 'Used to say what?'

'That expression – *shooting the breeze.*'

He nodded and smiled. 'So you want to tell me a little about him?'

I didn't speak for a moment. I was tired. My head had started to ache. I don't think I had talked so much in the last year.

'You want to?' Father John reiterated.

'I suppose . . . if you want.'

'I want,' the priest said, and his expression was genuine and sincere.

And so I did.

It was like walking backwards and underwater at the same time.

I was surprised at the clarity of my memory, the images I recalled as I spoke. There were things I could remember in crystal detail, things I hadn't thought of for more than fifteen years.

And those things came back, willingly almost, like they wanted to come back, like they'd missed the attention, missed the sound of my voice, because they were part of me just as much as they had been a part of Nathan.

And I let them, not because I felt the need to tell John Rousseau, priest or otherwise, but because it had been so long since I had spoken of Nathan Verney I had started to forget how all of this had happened.

And that I couldn't do, because if I forgot about Nathan I would also forget why South Carolina was going to kill me.

And dying for no reason was something I never wished to do.

EIGHT

1965 ended on a bad note.

Caroline Lanafeuille had been gone four months. No-one spoke of her. No-one spoke of the family. Seemed whatever her daddy had done was sufficient not only to excommunicate them from Greenleaf, but also from our collective memory. That had saddened me. I missed her, and in missing her I confronted the awful truth: that I had done nothing to stop her leaving. I had failed to defend what I had yearned for – yearned for for so long, and with such passion. And in some way I also felt that I had been betrayed, that she had taken what existed of my heart, had filled it with something so strong and seemingly permanent, and then burst it in a single stroke. And when Christmas came and I sensed my mother possessed neither the spirit nor the enthusiasm to celebrate the season I felt truly alone. I did not pity myself, I did not crave sympathy, I merely wished to be *with* people, and I was not.

Reverend Verney took Nathan and the rest of the family to see relatives in Chicago at the beginning of December. Nathan wanted to stay. He was nineteen and fiercely independent but, regardless of his will and desire, the sense of religiously sanctioned discipline so expertly administered by his father was the greater motivation. He went. He had no choice. I remember standing at the edge of the Lake the day before he was due to leave, how he shook my hand, and then hugged me, his broad hands on my shoulders, his grinning face right there before me, and how he told me *hang loose . . . take it easy*. He'd be gone for a month, back in the first week of January, and I should spend the time finding myself a girl.

'So should you,' I said, feeling a small sense of reassurance and self-satisfaction in knowing that Nathan was utterly unaware of what had taken place between Caroline Lanafeuille and myself the August before.

'Let me take care o' my own business,' Nathan said, and there was something in his expression, something in his tone, that made it clear as daylight. He had. He *really had*.

'Who?' I asked, my voice pitching a good three tones above normal.

'Hold it down,' Nathan said, and started laughing.

'So who? Who for Christ's sake?'

He shook his head and smiled. 'No way Mister Motormouth.'

'That girl who does the flowers at the church ... whassername, Melody something-or-other?' I persisted.

Nathan shook his head. 'Not saying. No clues. A promise is a promise.'

'Hey,' I said. 'No deal.'

Nathan shook his head again. 'Hell, man, I tell you, you go tell someone else who tells half the world, and then my father finds out he'll stripe my back for a week.'

'I won't say,' I said, my expression suddenly solemn.

Nathan shook his head. 'No,' he repeated. 'I said I wouldn't say a thing to anyone, so that's the way it's gonna be.'

There it was, that conviction, that stubborn dig-your-heels-in resilience that I had seen before. There would be no moving him. Later, much later, I thought that at any other time I would have pursued him, insisted. I think the real reason I let it go was because I had a secret of my own. A secret called Caroline whom I had loved, and watched ... no, whom I had *let* disappear.

Nathan changed the subject. He told me the reason they were going to Chicago was to see his ma's sister. She had three boys, all around Nathan's age. Two of them had already been killed in Vietnam. They were going out there to help her, to counsel her in her loss. The third son, no more than eighteen, was in a field hospital somewhere. That was all they knew, nothing more nor less. He was just *somewhere*. The Army said they would find him, *promised* they would find him, but they'd been saying that for nigh on a month. Nathan believed he was dead as well.

They wanted to get out to Chicago before his mother found out.

In that light I wanted him to go. I grieved for his cousins, people I neither knew, nor would ever know. I did not know their names, could not recall their faces from some summer picnic we had shared in Myrtle Beach, nor from playing tag with them along the edge of the County Fair grounds, nor from swimming in Lake Marion at the height of a Greenleaf summer when the sun scorched your back and made the rocks too hot to stand on. But I *felt* I knew them. Just like I knew those boys who became men in an Army tent back in November.

I felt I knew them all.

I watched him go when he left. He walked the long way round and took the path that ran out towards the black quarter of Greenleaf.

I watched him grow smaller and smaller, vanishing into the distance like a memory, and when he'd finally disappeared I stood there and looked out over the cool surface of the water.

The Lake was silent. A gray mist hung along the opposite bank and obscured the land. The way the Lake looked it could have been the sea. Swim out there, keep on going, and at some unknown point you'd just fall off the edge of the world.

I remembered the day I met Nathan. The baked ham sandwich. The little kid with jug-handle ears, traffic-light eyes and a mouth that ran from ear to ear with no rest in between.

I did not long for those days to return, but I missed the sense of levity. Seemed to me that growing up was a matter of taking everything more seriously, and I had never found that easy.

I walked home then. I lay on the bed where I had fallen completely in love with Caroline Lanafeuille, and I thought about what I would do when the Army sent for me.

A week after Nathan's departure I went to see Eve Chantry.

Why I went I cannot remember now. Perhaps I fabricated some reason, some purpose to visit, but the true motivation was to remedy my lack of company.

It was the first day of snow. I saw a deer on the way down. It stood in a grove of trees near the bend in Nine Mile Road, and it just watched me. It did not run. It stood stock-still, watched me as I walked, and unnerved me. I even clapped my hands, hollered once or twice, but that deer stood immobile, didn't even blink.

For some reason that brief and unimportant incident made me feel insignificant.

When I arrived at Mrs. Chantry's house there were lightbulbs strung from one side of the verandah to the next. I went up the steps, opened the screen door and knocked.

I waited patiently, I knew she'd walk slowly, and after three or four minutes I knocked again.

I heard a sound above me. I went back through the screen door and started down the steps to the path.

The snow came down like a blanket.

I remember looking up and the sky appeared to be falling towards me.

Suddenly I was on the floor. Snow was in my eyes, my ears, in my mouth even.

And then I heard her laughing.

I finally surfaced and stood up, and there above me, leaning from a window in the front of the house, was Eve Chantry. She had opened a window to see who had come a-calling, and the narrow roof that overhung the porch had let its covering of snow fall.

I had walked backwards down the front steps to meet it. My timing had been immaculate. And then I started laughing too.

It was a strange sight, almost as if I could see myself from a distance, almost as if I stood at the bend in the road that led down to the Chantry house, and there I was, standing no more than three or four feet from the porch steps. Like a ghost.

'You wanna see something?' Mrs. Chantry shouted from the upstairs window.

'Sure,' I shouted back.

She disappeared for a moment, and then suddenly the porch and verandah were ablaze with multi-colored Christmas lights. Red and yellow and blue and violet, every color imaginable.

Mrs. Chantry appeared once again at the window.

'Hell of a thing, Mister Ford,' she shouted.

I held out my arms as if to embrace the moment. 'Hell of a thing, Mrs. Chantry,' I hollered back.

'You spent enough time standing there lookin' like an eejut?'

'Sure have,' I replied.

'I'll come down,' she said, and then her head disappeared once more, the window closed with a thud, sending another small shower of snow down from the sill, and I walked towards the steps again to wait for her.

Whatever she called it – Christmas punch, hot toddy – it was strong.

Beneath the taste of almond and nutmeg, something slightly bitter like new season blueberries, there was the promise of a warm slow death from sourmash or rye. I couldn't decipher it, but I drank it, and when I finished the first glass I asked for more, and it was forthcoming.

She drank too, Eve Chantry, and she didn't even ask why I'd come, merely took my coat and hung it on a stand near the fire to dry, told me to kick off my boots in the front hall and come inside.

Maybe she was short for company too.

'Benny did the lights,' she told me. 'Benny Amundsen from the soda shop.'

I nodded. 'They're cool,' I said.

'Cool,' she said, and smiled.

'So where's your buddy?' she asked me.

'Nathan?'

She nodded.

'Chicago,' I said.

'Seeing relatives?' she asked.

'Yes, his ma's sister.'

Eve Chantry nodded. 'Who died?'

I frowned, looked at her askance. 'What makes you think someone died?'

'Reverend Verney has never left at Christmas. Christmas is serious preaching time. Many souls to save at Christmas. There's a war to fight this time of year, between the birth of the baby Jesus and the shopping mall.'

I smiled. Mrs. Chantry was almost as cynical as I.

'Nathan's ma's sister's kids, two of them, and a third missing somewhere and the Army can't find him.'

'Vietnam,' Eve Chantry stated matter-of-factly.

'Vietnam,' I said.

She shook her head slowly and turned towards the fire burning in the grate.

There was silence for some minutes.

'They sent for you yet?' she asked eventually.

'No.'

She looked at me then. 'They will you know, and for Nathan Verney, and most of the other kids.'

I nodded. 'I know.'

'You willing to go?'

'Willing? No, I'm not willing,' I said. 'Who would be willing to go?'

She smiled knowingly. 'My husband was willing to go,' she said. 'He knew what he was doing, he knew it clear as daybreak. He knew that he'd die as well, but he still went.'

'He knew he'd die?' I asked.

Eve Chantry smiled. There was something beautiful and nostalgic in her face. 'Yes,' she said, her voice soft and measured. 'He knew he was going to die because he should have died in about 1938, and he didn't, and from that point forward he felt he was using up someone else's time.'

I frowned. 'I don't understand.'

Mrs. Chantry settled back in her chair. 'I was born around here,' she said. 'I was born in 1898, a different world back then, a different world entirely. I grew up in Charleston, folks had money, no shortage of money, and I was educated at a real school with real books and a chalkboard and everything. My father wasn't a religious man, but he attended church and he treated people well, treated them with respect, and he never considered I should have anything but the best.'

Eve Chantry reached for the bottle of Christmas punch and refilled her own glass. She handed it to me and I did the same.

'I met the man who would become my husband in 1922. I was twenty-four years old, he was eighteen. He wasn't even a man, he was a grown-up child, but I knew, I really *knew*, that this was the person I wanted to spend the rest of my life with. And he knew it too. His name was Jack Chantry. His father was a fisherman out near Myrtle Beach, and he couldn't read or write or spell his own name. They were poor, poor beyond anything I could imagine, but Jack

Chantry possessed a life and a spirit and a will to live like no-one I'd ever known.'

She paused; she was looking at pictures in her mind, snapshots of Jack and his father, images that conveyed the élan, the vitality of which she spoke, and though I could not see them I could feel the emotion in her voice. She spoke of something powerful, and I was acutely aware that that sense of magic and power was exactly what was missing from my own life. This was something I could perhaps have possessed with Caroline had I been strong enough to hold her.

Perhaps she knew this, perhaps it was her reason for talking.

'We met in secret for more than a year,' she went on. 'We'd meet down by Lake Marion here, and other places, and I took it on myself to teach him to read, to write his name, to learn the alphabet, and never in my life have I ever met anyone who possessed such hunger for under-standing. He learned faster than I thought possible, and soon he was writing letters to me, even poetry.'

Mrs. Chantry smiled. 'It's ironic, but had I not taught him to read and write, perhaps it would never have turned out the way it did.'

I leaned forward. There was something about the way she spoke that made me so much *want* to know more of what happened.

'Jack wrote me a letter telling me he loved me, even suggested we elope together, and it was that letter that my father found. He was a fair man, an honest man, but he was rigid in his belief that there were classes of people, that people should marry within their class. But that was not so much the issue. The real reason he was so mad was because he felt I had betrayed him. That I had been carrying on with this man behind his back, that I had lied for a year or more about where I had been, who I had been with. That was something he felt he could neither understand nor forgive.'

Eve Chantry smiled.

'My father gave me thirty dollars, told me to pack all I wanted in one case, and to leave. If I was so committed to this man, this ignorant fisherman's son, then I could take my lies and my black-hearted deceit and find my own way in the world. I was twenty-five, Jack Chantry was a little more than nineteen, and we went to North Carolina where no-one knew us, and we started our lives together.'

I shook my head. 'Hell,' I said. 'That's tough,' I said.

'It was a different world, Daniel, a world we'll never see again. The main streets were dirt roads, people lived all their lives and died right there in the same town where they were born, and we just rolled into some place and made out we were a newly-married couple. I became Eve Chantry, he became older than me, he started work on a farm and I took in washing, and we found ourselves a little room to rent. It was good, I can't tell you how good it was, and we were happy, Daniel, possibly happier than anyone else in the world.'

She was smiling, a slow-burn glow of color in her cheeks, a light in her eyes that had not been present when she'd started speaking, and I watched with a degree of wonder.

'It was the beginning of the twentieth century, it was a time of change and invention and motor cars and airplanes, and everything was moving so fast and everyone was in such awe of how the world was growing, that they never really had a problem with two young folk moving into town and making themselves useful. People trusted others a whole lot more then. You started out believing someone was telling the truth, and they had to work to convince you otherwise. Now it's the other way round. Now you assume that someone's bullshitting you, and then they have to prove to you they ain't.'

She laughed softly, quietly.

'So we just settled down, settled right in there, and I never wrote to my mother or father, and as far as I know they never made any attempts to find me. Jack's father was different, he didn't give a damn who his son married as long as he was happy, and though he was sorry Jack wouldn't work with him on the boat he also recognized true love.'

Eve smiled, sipped from her glass.

'We'd go down to Myrtle Beach every once in a while and see Jack's folks, and that was fine as far as they were concerned.'

'Did you have children?' I asked.

She nodded. 'I'm getting to that, Daniel Ford. You want some more punch?'

I shook my head.

'You wanna smoke a cigar?'

I frowned.

'I like to smoke a cigar every once in a while,' she said, and got up from her chair. She went over to the mantel, and from a mother-of-pearl inlaid box that sat there by the clock she took two slim dark cigars.

Using a taper from a jar at the other end of the mantel she lit both cigars and handed one to me. They smelled rich, spicy almost, and when I touched that thing to my mouth it was almost as if the haunt of its taste was absorbed through my lips.

I had smoked cigarettes before, many times. Smoking cigarettes was all a part of growing up. A cigar was a new experience, along with Eve Chantry's Christmas punch, and I took it slowly, carefully, and there was a magic in the smell and the taste, even the way the smoke drifted in curlicues and arabesques around our heads, that added to the mysterious ambience of that time.

There was something about the day that was special.

I knew I would remember this day for a long time, perhaps for the rest of my life. My one disappointment was that Nathan was not there. Nathan *should* have been there, but he was out in Chicago dealing with the brutality of war and the dissolution of a family.

Mrs. Chantry sat down again.

'Our daughter was born in 1926. I was all of twenty-eight years old, Jack was twenty-two, but for reasons of social acceptance we always gave our ages the other way round. We weren't even married, never did get married, but everyone knew us as Mr. and Mrs. Chantry, and never had reason to suspect otherwise. And our daughter was an angel, bright and beautiful and the happiest child I've ever known. Her name was Jennifer, and Jack Chantry, fisherman's son, turned out to be the best father any child might ever wish for.'

Eve Chantry paused a little while and smoked her cigar. The smoke obscured her face, and for a moment she seemed to disappear completely. I glanced to my left, and there through the window I could see the multi-colored ghosts of lights from the verandah, reflected up against the glass from the snow beneath.

'We stayed there near Wilmington, just over the state line, for ten years, and then when my father died we decided to return to Charleston. My mother was of a similar mind to Jack's father, a lot of time had passed, and she understood that sometimes when you love someone it doesn't matter what people think or say. You know what you know, you know what's in your heart, and sometimes you just have to follow it.'

Eve paused again, her eyes softened with memories, and I watched her intently.

'Summer of 1938 we came down here. I got to know my mother all over again. Jack bought a small boat and he took it out across Lake Marion and he taught Jennifer to fish. She loved to be with her father, her world revolved around him, and if there was something he could do then she wanted to do it too. We stayed up here the whole summer in a house we rented, and every day they'd go out across the Lake and work on her fishing. Two weeks and she never caught a thing. Jack was patience itself, but Jennifer was frustrated. It didn't matter whether she could fish or not, she knew that really, but it was something that made her father happy so she wanted to master it. So she went out on her own, took that little boat out across the water one morning before either myself or Jack was awake . . .'

Eve Chantry looked at me, and in her eyes I could see what was coming.

'She caught something alright, found her rod floating in among the weeds, and on the end of that line was a fish. But she was gone, drowned . . .'

Eve's eyes were filling up, and from the small table beside her she took a silk handkerchief and held it to her face.

'Jack went running down there when he found her bed empty. He knew. He knew what had happened. He was shouting and crying before he even reached the edge of the Lake.'

Eve paused again. Her cigar had gone out. She lit it once more, needful of a brief hiatus in the telling of this tragedy.

'I remember looking from the window of the house . . .' She raised her hand and sort of indicated a direction out towards the Lake.

'I saw him standing there. And then he went down. He was holding her limp body, her long hair wet and trailing on the ground. He was on his knees, his head was thrown back, and never in my life have I heard anything like the sound that came from him. It sounded like his soul had been wrenched from his body . . .'

Eve raised the handkerchief again and wiped her eyes.

'She was twelve years old . . . 1938 it was, and for the few years between her death and his own he was a ghost of himself. He went to the war in '44, and apparently he saved some boys, nothing more than boys they were. Three boys from Boise, Idaho, who wouldn't have known him from

Adam. He gave his own life saving them. But he wasn't saving them, he was saving Jennifer . . .'

I leaned back in my chair.

I was overwhelmed, exhausted, and yet my head was clear despite the quantity of punch I'd drunk, the cigar I'd smoked, despite the warmth of the fire.

I looked at Eve Chantry and she seemed ageless and perfect, an island of calm amidst some raging torrential sea.

My heart, for what it was worth, went out to her, and losing Caroline Lanafeuille, even seeing Nathan disappear at the end of the road, even losing my father, meant nothing in that moment.

Jack Chantry had lost his world in Lake Marion, lived for a few years on borrowed time, and then committed himself to die because he couldn't bear the burden any more.

Eve Chantry had lost her daughter, then her husband, and since that time had lived alone here in Greenleaf.

'Too much,' I remember saying, my voice sounding thin and weak. I couldn't imagine saying anything that would have been fitting or relevant to the situation.

'Or not enough,' Mrs. Chantry said, 'depending on which way you look at it.'

During that month while Nathan was in Chicago I spent a great deal of time with Eve Chantry. I invited her down to Christmas at our house, but she didn't come. I remember standing there on the porch watching the road, my mother calling for me to close the door against the wind, and I did close it, but I stayed outside for nigh on an hour. Folks came and went, but none of them was Mrs. Chantry.

Later, after dinner, I walked down to the edge of Lake Marion and looked over the water.

I imagined Jack Chantry stumbling up towards me, the limp body of his twelve-year-old daughter in his arms, a sound like a wrenched soul rushing from his lungs. I felt a tight fist of emotion in my chest, my throat, felt that fist turn back on itself and grip my heart. I could feel veins and arteries swelling between its relentless fingers.

I started to cry. I cried for someone I neither knew nor had ever seen, but in that release was perhaps the loss of Caroline, of Nathan, of my father.

Later I walked back and stood at the end of the road near Eve Chantry's house. The lights were still on, their multi-colored reflections against the snow.

I didn't walk up there. I figured if she hadn't come out it was because she wanted to be alone.

Perhaps she wished to share Christmas with the memory of her daughter and her husband.

Perhaps she wished to share memories that were simply between herself and God.

Some things are like that.

I understand that now.

Understand that the best of all.

NINE

Two hours after Father John Rousseau's departure that day in August, Max Myers came up to see me. From his overalls he produced four packs of Lucky Strikes and pushed them through the bars. They were from John Rousseau.

I gave one pack to Max and asked him to give another pack to Lyman Greeve. Lyman Greeve didn't smoke, but he was saving trade-ins for a harmonica. He wanted to learn to play 'My Darling Clementine' before he died. He'd seen some guy do it in some old cowboy movie with Audie Murphy or Randolph Scott. It had become his life's purpose.

The other two packs I kept myself, and though I wanted to smoke them all I took four cigarettes, wrapped them in some paper, and pushed them into a gap between the wall and the edge of my sink. They would be safe there.

When I knew it was all over, when I had a time and a date that I knew wouldn't change, I would take them out and smoke them.

Two for me and two for Nathan, because we had always shared everything.

It had begun with a baked ham sandwich, the best in South Carolina, and it would end with a Lucky Strike and an inevitable promise of death.

Seemed to make sense to me.

Simple, like most things should be but, ironically, like most things never are.

My time was coming, crawling backwards towards me relentlessly. And Mr. West knew my time was coming too, and as it approached I seemed to see him more frequently. I watched him just as he would watch me. I tried to place myself behind his eyes and see the world from his viewpoint.

I believed Mr. West saw faces, more faces than those who inhabited D-Block.

And when he dreamt, he dreamt in monochrome, and the faces were there too.

Most often they were silent, but sometimes, only *sometimes*, they spoke, and when they spoke they said terrible things.

He listened, but he did not reply. If you talked back to your own memories you'd go crazy.

And Mr. West wasn't crazy.

He was just *necessary*.

He believed all men possessed a purpose. Some to father children. Some to build scrapers that towered over the earth. Some to plant trees and corn and pomegranates.

Some men were born to die, and then there were those born to kill them.

Such was his belief, and neither desire nor pleasure nor emotion entered into it. What he did was functional and precise.

Most of all it was *necessary*.

And so it was that he watched me, and other times he watched Max Myers as he wheeled his trolley away from my cell, and understood that for now he was here merely to see that all of us met our just end. It was neither his duty nor interest to question why, to ascertain innocence or guilt, for all men were guilty – if not of the thing with which they were charged, then of other sins.

Sins Mr. West knew all about.

For these last thirty years he had served other men, men with political and judicial ends, men without names and faces, and he had taken care to execute his duties with professionalism and pride.

Now, in these latter years, he had walked these corridors and gantries, listening to the guilty as they cried and prayed in the dark of night, and he had fulfilled his function: to take them down along those same corridors to their rightful and punctual deaths.

To Mr. West I was such a man, and though I did not cry or pray, he believed I would.

Time would come that I would.

I had walked where I shouldn't have, and though I seemed no more capable than a Girl Scout of America of killing a man, I had nevertheless crossed the line.

The law was the law, written or otherwise, and the Bible said what the Bible said, and people like Richard Gold-bourne – a man Mr. West had never met, but knew a little of – would not have tolerated such a violation of his own sense of morals, however twisted those morals might have been.

And so the nightmare had to unfold – as slow as Sunday chess, as tragic as a child suicide.

The details of these events, I was certain, were unknown to Mr. West. He had not been involved, had not wished to be involved, but he knew of people who knew people who would have taken care of such a detail.

I would pay the price for my omission.

My sentence was served, and would be carried out, and come the day I twitched and jumped and smouldered, come the day my blood boiled beneath my skin, a natural imbalance would be rectified.

Such was life and death and justice in the motherland, the good ol' U.S. of A.

One time I watched Mr. West smile as Max Myers disappeared around the corner at the far end of the corridor.

He turned himself, turned quietly, for he believed that half the punishment served here was the stealth and swiftness with which he appeared and disappeared, the readiness to twist the nerve when it was bared, to turn the light of truth upon these sad victims and help them see the raw and bloody ugliness of their own dark and twisted hearts.

He smiled again.

My time would come, and Mr. West – in his whiter-than-angels shirt and his black glass shoes – would be there to see me home.

In some small way I wished to speak with him, to tell him of how these things had occurred. He would not have listened. I knew that. But nevertheless some part of me wished to be understood, by anyone I think. I wanted to let him know that within these walls resided a human being, a *real person*, not just a name, a face, a number. I wanted him to know that behind these eyes were memories, each of them a thread, and in pulling that thread an entire world would unravel behind it. I wanted him to know of Jack and Eve Chantry, of the events of that Christmas, of things I had said and done that would perhaps redress the balance of my humanity in his eyes. But the difficulty was never my humanity, it was his. He possessed none, and would not have understood anyway.

I watched him come and go, his quiet movements, his darker thoughts, and saw the cloud of hatred that ever settled over him like a mantle. I would turn my eyes away, close them perhaps, and in closing them begin the process of opening yet another verse, another chapter of my thoughts.

These were all that remained, and as such they were the most precious thoughts of all.

I thought of Nathan, and how he did not return from Chicago until the second week of the New Year.

It was 1966, I would be twenty soon, and adulthood, its threat and promise, was arriving with greater vigor and tenacity as each new day unfolded.

The third cousin was dead. They had heard on January 2nd, and the Verneys had stayed the extra week to see the boy's body flown home and buried.

Nathan had changed. That was obvious from the first moment I saw him standing there at the end of my drive, his hands in his pockets, his head down, his manner subdued.

As children we would have shouted and screamed and run towards each other. We would have chattered back and forth, each interrupting the other until we were exhausted from laughing.

That day in January the mood was that of a funeral. And no black Methodist gospel affair, but a silent white suburban melodrama, tempered with Excedrin and single malt.

We spent a little time at the Lake but it was cold, and much of the time we did not speak. I remember asking him if he had thought about the war, about receiving his Draft Notice, and he just shrugged. He didn't say anything. He'd had enough of the war already.

When we left, Nathan walked with me to the top of my drive, and before he turned he hugged me like the brother that I was, and when he let me go he looked right at me and said: 'We'll see this thing through together, Danny.'

The same words I had uttered after our escape from Benny's when Nathan had floored Marty Hooper.

Marty Hooper was dead, as was Larry James and the other boys from Myrtle Beach. Their bodies were probably still out there, buried beneath mud or scorched foliage, or scattered in a hundred parts across a waterlogged field beneath tall trees and clear cerulean skies.

And we were here – Nathan Verney and I – and the threat of that other world was growing closer with each heartbeat.

I thought then of Jack Chantry, his belief that after the death of his daughter he was living on borrowed time. He had believed he should have died instead of her.

Was it the same for us?

Should we have stood up in front of Sergeant Mike and pledged our allegiance to the flag, the Constitution, the American way of life?

Should we have walked out there carrying things called heat tabs, Kool Aid and C-Rations, carrying steel helmets with liners and camouflage covers, carrying compress bandages, steel brushes, gun oil and fragmentation grenades, carrying our own chewing gum and lucky dice? Should we have walked out there carrying the weight of our broken hearts and our fear?

Should we have done those things?

And should we now be dead in Da Nang or Ky Lam or Saigon?

The war, though a million miles away, seemed right there across the state line. But it was the borders within that counted, and with each revolution of the earth I felt the invasion coming.

For the first time in my life I felt *real* fear.

And that, along with everything else since that day at Lake Marion, Nathan Verney shared with me too.

In March of '66 I took a part-time job at Karl Winterson's Radio Store. It wasn't so much that we needed the money – the Carolina Railroad Company pension was still coming in month after month – but more because I wanted something to do with my time. It didn't seem to matter what it was, anything would have done, and I had a chance to listen to all the music I would have missed at home.

Nathan would come down when Mr. Winterson was out, and together we'd find small back-porch radio stations out of Memphis and New Orleans. The reception was awful but still we heard things like Howlin' Wolf and Sonny Boy Williamson. There was a world of great music out there, and just because we lived in some small town in South Carolina didn't mean we had to miss it.

Those hours we spent together were some of the closest

we ever shared, for hours would go by when not a soul would come down there to disturb the atmosphere within the store. Made me wonder sometimes how Mr. Winterson made a living. With the windows wide and the front door open, the sun beating on the sidewalk like a tyrannical stepfather, Nathan and I would simply sit back and share the silences between the songs. Sometimes we'd talk – of where we were going, a few dreams, some other things – but mostly we just talked of nothing consequential at all. Nathan would make up stories, and his imagination would grow out beyond the confines of the walls, and I would marvel at the sheer quantity of ideas that could be carried inside a single head.

'Most people are actually aliens,' he told me one time. 'Most of the people we know are actually aliens.'

He paused and looked at me, his expression certain, indignant almost, utterly believable.

'Your mother is an alien,' he said. 'She's from Arcturus 7, a small satellite star that orbits Jupiter . . . and she has two skins. Her outward skin she takes off at night, and inside she's nothing but gloop and boogers. And one day soon, when you least expect it, she's gonna creep into your room when you're sleeping and bite off your Johnson.'

'Shut the fuck up, Nathan.'

His expression didn't change.

'Sure as shit I'm tellin' the truth . . . and Eve Chantry is the same you know?'

'Outta your freakin' tree,' I said. 'You've lost whatever you got when you came into this world and a handful more besides.'

Nathan nodded. He peered at me like a condescending professor. 'So tell me this,' he said. 'How come, if your mother isn't an alien, your right eye can go one way and your left can go the other at the same time?'

I frowned. 'They can't.'

'Yeh right,' Nathan said sarcastically. 'You wanna know what people call you when you ain't around?'

I raised my eyebrows.

'Bughead.'

'What the fuck are you talking about?'

'Bughead . . . that's what people call you when you ain't there.'

'Horseshit.'

'So go get a mirror . . . go get a mirror and look see what happens when you stare at something. Your right eye goes one way and your left eye goes the other.'

'That's just so much crap.'

Nathan shrugged. 'Please yourself . . . bughead.'

So, sure as hell, I went and got the mirror, and fool me if I didn't stare at the thing for a good five minutes. Only stopped when I caught Nathan's reflection behind me, his face fit to burst, even holding his crotch like he was going to piss himself right there and then on Karl Winterson's chequerboard linoleum floor.

After he stopped laughing he told me I was dumb as milk. Told me that I actually believed that my mother was an alien.

'The fuck I did,' I said defensively.

'Then what the hell did you go get the mirror for?'

I stood looking at him.

'Asshole,' I said.

'Bughead,' he replied, and started laughing once more.

Such conversations, too many of them to remember. Stupid things, meaningless things, but things that would seem so important later. That was what we were like – Nathan Verney and I – before the real world came a-calling.

It was one of those days in June when we heard about James Meredith. It came down as a newsflash from KLMU in Augusta, the same station I had been listening to when my father told me JFK had been killed. James Meredith was the first black student to enroll at Mississippi University in

1962, and all we knew was that he'd been shot in his back and his legs on a march someplace.

Nathan was stunned speechless. He'd believed the white-negro situation was resolving, and things had in fact been quieter for some time. Evidently things were all aflame as much as they'd ever been; we just hadn't been paying a mind to it.

He didn't speak of it as I expected him to. He left for home, went to see his father, and I didn't see him for two or three days.

Seemed to me as the summer passed through Greenleaf we were spending less and less time together, and though I never felt we were losing touch I believed that those subjects where we shared the same viewpoint and under-standing were diminishing in number.

I felt in limbo, waiting for notification that my presence was required at a boot camp somewhere in the South while praying that the war would end before it came. It was as if waiting was my station for the time being, and those of us who had not volunteered in that tent with the fried chicken and potato salad felt that we would all just have to keep quiet and sit it out. There was no point making any plans. None at all. What would plans mean until we knew? Once upon a time I had thought of college, learning a trade, somesuch thing as that, but the war had changed everything. My ma knew this, and she didn't push either way. She was happy I was doing something with my time rather than sitting in my bedroom reading comic books and trying to hide the fact that I was smoking Lucky Strikes.

At the end of June we started bombing Hanoi. I referred to the U.S. as *we* even though I felt that the bombing of Hanoi was nothing personal. I did not wish to bomb anyone. I was still naïve, trusting that the powers that be must have at least believed with all they had that such an action was required. We knew nothing of the atrocities that were being perpetrated out there, and would not know for some time yet.

I worked on through the summer at the Radio Store, and though I saw Nathan less than I would have liked, we stayed on the same wavelength. We never spoke of the Draft directly; to do so would have been to grant it energy and spirit, but we referred to *the thing*, how we would react if *the thing* came, if we walked downstairs one sleepy-eyed morning, and there it was.

And so it went that way, all through '66, and it was in that year that I had more time and yet achieved less than in any previous year. Or so it seemed to me. Perhaps it was merely that I no longer felt a child, something I had believed would occur at sixteen or seventeen. It hadn't. The fragment of child within me stayed alive and well and living in Greenleaf until gone Christmas and the start of 1967. I believe I hung onto that child, the wide-eyed innocence, the sense of trust in humanity, the conviction that all folks were fundamentally well-intentioned, and that when it came down to it they would always decide in favor of good and right and equity.

I learned this was not the case in February.

It was obvious from her manner and speech that Eve Chantry was unwell. She appeared outside her house less and less frequently, and sometimes I felt like I was her last lifeline to the known world. I would visit two, perhaps three, times a week, and more often than not I would find her still in bed in the mid-afternoon. I had taken to entering unannounced, and one Wednesday afternoon in the middle of that month I went as usual. I took fresh milk, some eggs, some pancakes my mother had made. I found Eve asleep, a tray of food from the previous night still untouched on the bed. I knew enough to understand that as long as she continued to eat regularly then she would be fine. Alarm bells were installed and operational from that moment.

She woke easily, but even as she slurred into consciousness I could tell that there was something wrong. Her face seemed different, her speech a little awkward, and I recognized the indications of a stroke that had been so present in my father's manner.

I insisted she see a doctor, and after much disagreement she conceded defeat. She was a proud woman, a single-minded and ferociously independent fighter, and the possibility that she would be unable to fend for herself was perhaps more damaging than any other single threat.

Dr. Backermann came unhesitatingly. He examined, he questioned, he tested, he scribbled copious notes in a grubby little book, and then he took me aside and peered at me slightly suspiciously over gold-rimmed half-moon spectacles.

'You are not a relative, Daniel Ford,' he stated with authority. He delivered this message as if it was an unfortunate and brutal revelation.

'No Sir,' I replied.

'I do not therefore understand your involvement.'

I remember smiling, as if humoring a child.

'Eve . . . Mrs. Chantry and I are friends,' I said.

'Friends?' Dr. Backermann asked.

'Sure,' I said. 'I visit a couple of times a week, bring some food over, keep her company.'

'Mmm,' Backermann grunted, a further hint of suspicion in his tone.

He again peered at me inquisitively over his spectacles.

'You understand that I am not at liberty to discuss her medical condition with you,' Backermann said drily.

I nodded. 'She's gonna be okay, though?'

I heard myself ask the question, and already there was that strained sense of hope present. It sounded like a plea.

'Okay?' Backermann asked, almost to himself. 'She has had a stroke, much the same as your father . . .'

Backermann looked at me to see if I would react. The last thing he wanted was some over-emotional youth on his hands.

'So it is with a stroke,' he went on. 'You have a body that is worn out, that's the basis of it, and when the body starts to wear out there is little that you can do. Sometimes things improve significantly by themselves, and sometimes they don't.'

'What about hospital?' I asked.

'Hospital?' Backermann echoed. 'There are places you can send folks in this condition, places where specialists in such fields work to improve conditions for them, but we're talking a great deal of money, and unfortunately Eve Chantry never got it into her mind to take care of such things as medical insurance.'

I was confused.

'So you're not going to do anything?' I asked.

'Not going to do anything?' Backermann asked back. 'And what would you have me do?'

I frowned, shrugged my shoulders. 'I don't know, you're the doctor.'

Backermann smiled deprecatingly. 'It is a money-driven world, Mister Ford,' he said, his tone condescending. 'If you care to find something in the region of ten or twenty thousand dollars then I would be more than happy to refer Eve Chantry to Charleston State Hospital and instruct they start work tomorrow.'

I stood immobile and silent.

Backermann seemed to be waiting for me to say something.

My head was empty.

Backermann sighed a little impatiently, and then walked to the head of the stairwell.

'I'll check on her, Mister Ford,' he said. 'When I'm down

this way I'll check on her. If something happens you can call me or my assistant. Aside from that she should rest, take plenty of fluids, eat some proteins . . .'

He was already starting down the stairs.

There was no money here; his work was done; everything else was platitudes.

I stood there for some time. I perceived then the utter emptiness of the house. Its size dwarfed me, made me feel grandly insignificant, and when I crossed the landing and entered Eve's room, I was aware also of how tiny she seemed beneath the covers.

'I will die you know,' was her greeting.

I sat there on the edge of the bed and took her hand.

She smiled. The tension down the right side of her face seemed to have eased a little, but it was still obvious that the stroke had done its work.

'You cannot expect me to be anything but the candle-moth,' she added.

I frowned.

'The what?'

'The candlemoth,' she repeated.

I had heard her correctly.

I shook my head.

Eve Chantry used my hand to pull herself up into a sitting position.

'There is the biological view of life, and then there is everything else,' she started. 'The butterfly is proud to be so colored and graceful, to spread its wings in the sun. The moth however, its closest relative, is a night creature. The moth possesses beauty equal to a butterfly, but it does not see it . . . more importantly, people don't see it because it is primarily nocturnal. And moths are attracted to light because they wish to be seen, to have their own magical beauty recognized.'

Eve Chantry squeezed my hand and smiled.

'Leave a candle on the porch at night and watch them

come. A biologist will tell you that the reason the moth circles the flame is because it naturally flies towards a source of light, that the wing nearest the source will take shorter strokes thus creating the ever-decreasing circle.'

She shook her head.

'That's not true. They see the beauty of their own wing in the light, and wishing to emphasize it, wishing everyone around to see it, they draw ever closer in order to illuminate it further. The heat is a worthwhile price to pay for being a butterfly. They gather momentum, the circle decreases, and suddenly, unexpectedly, in that last split second, in that last beat of the fragile wing, they catch fire . . . and whoosh! The body aflame, bright yellow and red and blue . . . the moth becomes a butterfly at last.'

Eve nodded.

'That's a candlemoth.'

I smiled, squeezed her hand. I did not understand the significance.

'And the reason I tell you this, Daniel Ford,' she said, interrupting my half-formed questions, 'is that I am an old woman, and soon I will die, and there is nothing that you or I can do to change the fact that I am an old woman about to die.'

She looked away towards the window for a moment.

'People change, of course they do,' she went on. 'People change a little every day, and sometimes you can meet someone down the road and they are utterly different from the person you thought they were . . . but then sometimes it's you who has changed, and they stayed exactly the same, and now you merely see them from a different point of view . . .'

Eve paused as if to catch her breath a little.

'Truth is truth, you are who you are, and though your viewpoint might change, and though you might possess a different perspective about something, your heart and what you believe and who you are inside is only ever you . . . and you have to follow that heart, you have to believe what you're doing is right, and no matter what anyone might say or think or do you have to trust yourself to make the right decision.'

She fell silent for a minute or two.

The window was slightly open. The cooling breeze lifted the netting and flicked it into the room like a sail.

Three sheets to the breeze, I thought. She sails towards her own death with three sheets to the breeze. I said nothing however. I sat silent, immobile.

I could feel my own heart beating.

'So when it comes,' she whispered, 'remember that it's your choice, and your faith, and your heart you follow. If you don't want to go to war, then don't go . . . but only you, *only you* can decide that. You hear me?'

I nodded; I heard her.

Even here, even after suffering a stroke, she was still the most perceptive and direct person I had ever known.

She knew what was in my mind. She saw inside my thoughts, my heart, my soul, and she knew also that at least half of any decision I might make would depend on Nathan Verney.

She was telling me to decide alone.

I asked myself if I had ever really decided anything alone.

'And so at some point I will turn towards the candle, and I will fly ever closer, and in one last brilliant burst I will be gone,' she whispered. 'And you, Daniel Ford . . . you must let me go.'

I looked back at the window. I didn't wish to see her eyes.

'There,' she said.

She pointed at a chest of drawers against the wall.

'The lower drawer to the right,' she said. 'Open it.'

I rose, crossed the room, opened the drawer. Among neatly folded sheets and pillowcases was a square wooden box.

'Take it out,' Eve said.

I lifted the box, and turning it over I realized it was not a box at all, but a small wooden picture frame.

Behind the glass was a perfectly preserved moth, its wingspan no more than two or three inches, but within those wings every hue of gold and brown and russet and sienna captured.

'Jack made it for our daughter,' Eve Chantry said. 'And you shall take it with you today.'

I looked at her.

She raised her hand, a single finger extended.

'Not a word,' she whispered. 'Not a word, Daniel Ford.'

I nodded.

There would be no arguing today.

Or any other day.

Eve Chantry was dead within a week.

She left no will, no family could be traced, and then a gray man with deep shadows beneath his eyes appeared. He said he was a representative of Carolina & North Eastern United Trust And Savings, that Mrs. Chantry had owed more than a thousand dollars on the house, that the house would now be repossessed by the bank, sold at auction, they would recoup their losses and the remainder would be turned over to something called the Community Fund.

The gray man with deep shadows seemed to be completely unconcerned with any funeral arrangements or expenses. He was there to collect his dues, and collect his dues he would.

So Eve Chantry was buried after a simple ceremony in Reverend Verney's church. She was not, however, buried in Reverend Verney's cemetery, but in a white plot, unmarked and obscure, beside a wall that separated the cemetery from the far end of Nine Mile Road.

With the money I had earned that summer I paid for a headstone.

It was plain white marble, and on it was the simple inscription:

Eve Chantry.

Mother.

Wife.

Friend.

Rest In Peace

My mother attended the service and the burial. She understood enough to know why I had spent my money this way and she neither questioned nor protested. This was my way of giving something back, and she respected that.

In losing Eve Chantry I had lost a lifeline, an anchor to a reality more real than that within which I lived, and I felt a greater wrenching of the soul than ever I had for my father.

I would remember 1967, for this was the watershed.

The circle grew smaller, bringing me ever nearer that flame.

On a small nail I hung the candlemoth above my bed. It was the last thing I saw before I slept, the first as I woke.

It was a reminder to be true to myself, to believe what I believed, and never to compromise.

That would prove, of all else, the hardest lesson of all.

TEN

It was a harsh winter. Folks who had been alive two and three times my lifespan spoke of it as the worst that ever was. Snow drifted eight and nine feet high, cars were buried, and in February a cow was found frozen upright against a fence. Ben Tyler and Quinn Stowell tied a rope around its neck to drag it away with a GMC Jimmy, but the cow's head snapped right off like a branch. It was that cold. Really that cold.

I stayed indoors much of the time, either at home or at the Radio Store. The post sometimes got through, but more often than not it would be delayed for up to a week. I was not certain if this was better or worse, for the thought of my Draft Notice lying in a sack somewhere near Myrtle Beach – something like that with my name on it and I just didn't know – gnawed at me relentlessly. I spoke with Nathan, and each conversation seemed abrupt, as if every word was strained and unnatural. We understood the significance of what would happen when those notices came, that we would be caught then, caught between a rock and a hard place, and though the thought of leaving haunted my thoughts, an ever-present shadow, I could not bring myself to voice it. Nathan possessed that thought too. I could read it in his eyes, and the aura of fear it precipitated was not even close to what we had experienced a thousand years before in Benny's. This was nothing to do with race or color or religion, this was life and death. Sometimes I pretended this thing would never come, but pretense it was.

Eve Chantry's house stayed empty, much of the back half

buried beneath the snow drifts, and it wouldn't be until spring that the gray people with dark shadowed eyes would come to lay up signage and put fliers out for the auction.

If I'd had enough money I would have bought that house. Just for the way the light came in through the upper floor windows. Just for the smell. Just because it was hers.

But winter, despite itself, despite the tenacity with which it held the world in its icy grip, eventually released us into the quiet concession of a new season. The spring run-offs flooded the fields, and small children – black and white – skidded in the mud, fraying both their clothes and their folks' tempers, until the color they'd arrived in had transformed to a uniform gray-brown. Only from the length of their hair could you tell who was white and who was not. From where I watched from the Radio Store window I could see life emerging once more. It seemed like a new beginning, but somehow I knew that our time was coming, and our time was not a new beginning, but an end.

In May the boxer Muhammad Ali was indicted for refusing the Draft. That was a premonition. He was black. He was famous. They could still kick his ass.

Nathan Verney came to see me that day, and it was that day I told him of Eve Chantry. I showed him the candlemoth, and as if in validation of my decision to hold him in his confidence, the original decision to have Nathan Verney as my blood brother, he was both enchanted and impassioned.

'She was right, you know,' he said later.

I looked across at him.

'That you can only make the decision yourself.'

I nodded.

'My decision is made,' he said quietly.

I didn't look up. I didn't want him to tell me. I wanted it to be mine and mine alone, and to hear what he had decided could only sway my thoughts.

'I won't go,' he said. 'I have decided that no matter what happens I won't go to Vietnam.'

His voice possessed such clarity and authority there was no mistaking his intent.

'It isn't cowardice,' he went on – a phrase I would hear as the opening of every explanation from every Draft dodger I would ever meet – 'it's the principle of the thing. It is not my war. I do not wish to kill people. I don't even know any Vietnamese people . . . I don't even know any communists come to that . . . so why should I go out and kill them? What did they ever do to me?'

'Killed your cousins,' I said.

Nathan was quiet for a moment, then, 'Sure, they got killed, but they wouldn't have been killed if they hadn't gone, would they?'

'And if everyone said they weren't going then no-one would be dead, and there would never have been a war in the first place . . . and then there would be communists everywhere.'

Nathan shook his head. 'You really believe that?'

I smiled. 'No, I don't believe that.'

'Then why do you think there's a war?' he asked.

'I heard that someone bet LBJ a dollar that we would win.'

Nathan laughed.

'I don't know, Nathan, I really don't know. I also don't need to know why you have decided not to go, but I wish you hadn't told me.'

Nathan frowned. 'How come?'

'Because I have to make my own decision and I don't want to be influenced by anyone else.'

Nathan smiled. 'Then you've missed the whole point of what Eve Chantry told you.'

I looked questioningly at him.

'The point, Danno, is that you have to stick to what you

think regardless of what anyone says whether you know what they're gonna say or not.'

I shook my head. 'But –'

Nathan raised his hand. 'But nothing, Danny. You think what you think and everyone else thinks what they think, and you go ahead and do whatever you're gonna do regardless.'

I didn't reply.

He was right.

More often than not Nathan was right. His daddy was a minister and sometimes I believed he had God on his side.

We didn't speak of it again that day, nor the week following, or the week beyond that. In fact, I can't remember speaking to him about it again until much, much later, and by then words were as meaningful as the nineteen-year-old lives that went out to Vietnam.

Nathan had his wireless radio with him. He found KLMU on the dial and we listened to Johnny Burnette and Willie Nelson.

The mood between us changed, the challenge was gone, and I for one was grateful. This was a subject so close to home I did not believe I could be challenged and survive with my sanity intact.

Dark times were coming, I knew that much, and still the decision evaded me. Perhaps I believed in some small way that the war would skid right by me, miss me in its hurry to collect the youth of America and slaughter them wholesale. Someone was reaping children, less than children, and beneath the great sweep of its scythe I would duck and become nothing for just a heartbeat.

It would take just that long to be missed perhaps.

About the same amount of time it took to die.

In October the largest anti-war demonstration in history moved on the Pentagon. There were two hundred and fifty arrests, including that of Norman Mailer. The government's response was to step up the bombing of North Vietnam.

I remember watching the demo on TV at the Radio Store. I don't believe I'd ever seen so many people gathered with one united voice in all my life. With the death of Jack Kennedy we wept as a people, but on this day we raised our hearts, our voices, our fists in anger. It was a release, an impassioned and desperate plea for someone out there to listen, to understand, to hear us. That cry fell on deaf ears. Another 35,000 filed quietly up gangways and into aircraft, strapped themselves into helicopters, checked their weapons for operational status, chewed their gum, closed their eyes and remembered their sweethearts' faces, said a brief prayer to a God they doubted could really exist, and looked down at American soil for the last time.

In most cases they were dead within hours; the rest got a week or two.

The year ended as it had started. America felt like a clenched fist, a seized heart, a twisted muscle. So much power, so little use.

And it hurt.

The strain was beginning to show.

1968 began with the indictment of Benjamin Spock for anti-Draft activities. He was a hero, and though his voice was loud it was like the creaking of a door in a hurricane. Only if you hid behind it could you hear it, and the protection it would afford you was of no value.

In February Richard Milhous Nixon said he would run for president. That face, the expressive gesture, everything that would become more recognized than perhaps any president before him, was not the image that we remembered from that time.

There was a photograph. It leapt at us from the TV, from the newspapers, from the human interest magazines: South Vietnamese Army General Loan holding a revolver against the head of a suspect in a Saigon public square. The suspect's head was tilted to the viewer's right, his face twisted in a grimace of horrified anticipation.

General Loan was quoted.

He said: *Buddha will understand.*

Some people asked who Buddha was; was he responsible for the war?

Some people asked why General Loan thought Buddha would want anything to do with such a thing.

Some people just turned away, sickened, repulsed, disbelieving.

The picture haunted me for days.

Perhaps it was that picture that gave me closure.

In March LBJ said he would not run for office again. To temper the sense of loss many would feel at such an announcement he sent another 35,000 to Vietnam.

Robert Kennedy said he would run. That gave people a lift somehow. He was so like his fallen brother.

They came crashing to earth once more in April.

Like Marty Hooper. Boom. Down.

Martin Luther King was killed in Memphis.

Reverend Verney, a sequoia of a man, wept openly in the street. He hugged his wife and his son to him and they wept with him.

The negro quarter of Greenleaf was deserted. In times such as these we had learned there were no such things as divisions and quarters. United only in war and grief it seemed.

I did not understand the reality of what had happened.

I knew enough of King to appreciate that all the progress made had been carried forward on his shoulders. There was no-one to take his place, no-one who *could* take his place. I felt that the ignorant whites were responsible. The same ignorant whites who'd started the war.

When they named James Earl Ray I wondered why they

always used all three names. Lee Harvey Oswald. James Earl Ray. John Wilkes Booth. Why did they do that?

And when Nathan told me they were going to Atlanta for the funeral I knew I would go with them.

I considered it was not necessary to understand all the details to get the message.

My blood brother was a black man. We were different. Of course we were different, we would always be different. But we were not so different as to justify different streets and different bars and different jobs or houses or salaries. Martin Luther King believed in what he was doing. I believed in him. I felt I owed him enough to go to Atlanta.

There were, in fact, about 150,000 people who felt the same, Jacqueline Kennedy and Hubert Humphrey among us, and when I arrived in Atlanta in the back of Reverend Verney's station wagon – tired and nauseous from the endless jolting – I sensed a collective consciousness had arrived.

I had never witnessed nor experienced anything like it in my life.

The streets were impassable. I gripped Nathan's hand for dear life, and Nathan held onto his daddy like our only connection to the shore. People wept and screamed, people sang, people hugged one another and kneeled and prayed, and some folks lay prostrate right there on the sidewalk and cared not that they were trampled underfoot.

The noise and heat and commotion tested both my patience and my lungs, but beneath this there was a tangible sense of brotherhood and unity. I did not feel threatened, either by the crowds or the police, and where I had assumed I would be the only white man there, I was overwhelmed by the sheer number of people, color immaterial. We were just people, grief-stricken, outraged people.

That was the only important thing.

Until I saw Linda Goldbourne.

We had stopped to get a drink at a diner somewhere in

downtown Atlanta. I was weak, dehydrated and exhausted, and sweat ran off me in rivers. Sweat like a fall testimonial.

Linny Goldbourne stood at the counter. Her hair was long and dark, and around her forehead she'd tied a beaded headband. She wore rings in her ears, a necklace made of a leather lace with a stone tied to the end, and when she turned towards me she knew who I was.

Images of all those I had loved from afar in my own quiet way came flooding back, and when she smiled – genuinely thrilled to see me – my heart leapt.

'Danny!' she shouted across the room, and elbowed her way through the crowd towards me, her arms wide.

When we met she threw those same arms around me and pulled me tight.

'Wow!' she said. 'Wow! Danny Ford! Christ, man, what are you doing here?'

I turned and glanced at Nathan and Reverend Verney.

She shook her head, realizing she'd asked the most obvious of questions.

'Of course,' she said, tempering her enthusiasm for a moment.

I had not spoken with Linda Goldbourne since 11th grade. I had seen her, of course, the girl I believed would have been reserved for a far better man than I, but we had never connected. Now, in that moment, there it was: a connection.

'So you're travelling back?' she said.

I nodded. 'Yes, I'm going back tonight with Nathan.'

I looked at her face, her eyes, her lips. She was more beautiful than ever.

'Me too,' she said. 'I haven't been home for about six months.'

'Where've you been?' I asked.

'California,' she said. 'San Francisco, Haight-Ashbury, L.A. for a couple of weeks, travelling around you know?'

I did not know. I was not a traveller. I had been in Greenleaf all my life.

'So we should connect up when we get home,' she said.

She used the word, not me. We should *connect* up.

I nodded. 'I would really like that, Linny. I would really like to do that.'

She smiled. She hugged me again. She held me a little too long for this just to be the excitement of a chance meeting.

Then she withdrew, and as she withdrew she held her cheek against mine for just a split second, but in that second I felt all the warmth of the world encapsulated within a touch.

My heart was racing.

I could feel my pulse in my temples.

In that second I believed every loss I'd ever felt was healed. My father, Eve Chantry, even Caroline Lanafeuille – all seemed insignificant as I held Linny Goldbourne against me. I could smell her skin, feel the power of her presence, and around me the hubbub of the crowd within which we stood was silenced.

And then suddenly, all too suddenly, she was gone, breezing past me with her grace, her beauty, the scent of something autumnal from her hair.

I watched her go.

She did not look back.

I did not want her to.

My cheeks burned with something close to a fever, closer perhaps to passion.

I would think back later, and despite the reason I was in Atlanta, despite this being the first time I had left the State of South Carolina, I did not think of Martin Luther King again that day.

I thought of Linny Goldbourne and how her body might feel against mine in the coolness of the night.

ELEVEN

Had I known that years later I would meet Father John Rousseau in Sumter, that he would have asked so many questions of that time, I perhaps would have kept a journal. My memory of those months after the shooting of Martin Luther King were somewhat vague. So many things happened, so many incidents of moment, that it became hard to maintain any frame of reference within which to hold them.

Two days after King's burial in Atlanta, New York Mayor Lindsay was stoned by a black crowd in Harlem. In Detroit two police officers were shot, and down south in Tallahassee a white youth was burned to death. The same day LBJ signed the Civil Rights Bill making it illegal for landlords to refuse housing on grounds of race. The second day of May one thousand people went on the Poor People's March from Memphis to Washington. Five days later Robert Kennedy won the first primary in Indiana, and a week later the second in Nebraska. Simultaneously, talks began in Paris between the U.S. and the North Vietnamese, talks instigated by Johnson with his promise to stop bombing North Vietnam above the 20th parallel.

These were historical things, events people would write about for years to come, but these events melted into one another effortlessly when compared to Linda Goldbourne.

She came and found me two days after my return from Atlanta.

She found me at Karl Winterson's Radio Store. I was

alone. Karl was out in Charleston and Nathan was fetching groceries for his ma.

Linda Goldbourne was a special girl, had always been. Her beauty and wit, her culture and intelligence were not the only things that kept her far beyond reach.

She was ex-Congressman Richard L. Goldbourne's daughter. A staunch Southerner, a towering monolith of a man, he really was a force to be reckoned with. Much of the land east of Greenleaf's central suburbs belonged to the Goldbournes. They had owned that land since before the War of Secession, and with that land had come crops and slaves and leverage and money. Goldbourne, even now, seventy years old or more, could swing an opinion with a nod of his head or a glance one way or the other. He had been consulted by every Congressman, senator and state representative ever to take office in South Carolina, his brother-in-law owned two of the largest newspaper chains in the State, and Goldbourne Automotive was the most profitable retail chain for agricultural and domestic vehicles from Charleston, South Carolina to Montgomery, Alabama.

This was Linda Goldbourne's family, her history, her birthright, and on May 11th 1968 she walked into Karl Winterson's Radio Store and asked me if I wanted to go out and party.

Linda, or Linny as she was known, had more life in her than a thousand of her contemporaries. She was neither naïve nor irresponsible, neither over-enthusiastic nor brashly false; she possessed no airs or graces, affected nothing but her own individuality, and unashamedly and without inhibition opened her mouth and said what she thought. She did not offend or upset people, for what she said contained an element of truth that was as reassuring as it was direct. She did not make enemies. Who could make an enemy of life? Children sought her as an oasis of sanity and like-mindedness. Those her own age found her child-like spirit revitalizing and passionate. The older members of

131

Greenleaf's community, my mother included, described her as *a breath of fresh air* and *a ray of sunshine*.

This was Linny Goldbourne, and for a little of the summer of '68 she decided I was hers and hers alone. Perhaps she was short of company, but I did not complain; I did not question her decision; I reserved the right to maintain equanimity in all discussions as to her motives or agenda. She loved being alive, and for this brief part of her life she had concluded that I should share it with her. Which was fine, just fine by me.

That night of May 11th 1968 was the first night we went out together. We went to a bar on Doyle Street. She ordered tequila with lemon and salt and taught me how to drink it, and while I retched and vomited in the gutter along the sidewalk she kneeled beside me and rubbed my back with a smooth, strong circular motion that seemed both a reprimand and a comfort at the same time. And then she walked me home. My ma was asleep. She helped me to my bed, undressed me, and rolled me beneath the covers. I remember she leaned across me, kissed my forehead, and then she left.

I slept like a dead man.

And it was she who woke me some seven or eight hours later, her eyes bright and luminous, her energy unfettered, and suggested I haul my useless carcass out of bed, get some breakfast, and she would drive us to the coast.

She prepared eggs and ham and pancakes, and sat across from me as I struggled to eat.

'What happened with you and Caroline?' was the first question she asked me.

I almost choked, had to thump my chest to catch my breath.

'Caroline?' I asked back.

Linny nodded. 'Caroline,' she repeated. 'You and she went out for a while, didn't you?'

I nodded in the affirmative. 'For a while, yes.'

'And then she left,' Linny said matter-of-factly.

'Yes, she left.'

'Because you got her pregnant?'

I stopped and looked across at Linny, my eyes wide, scarcely believing my ears.

'I heard you got her pregnant and her father had to give her an abortion, and that's why she left so suddenly.'

I shook my head. I didn't know what to say.

'So you didn't get her pregnant?' Linny asked.

'I didn't get her pregnant,' I said.

'Okay,' Linny replied, and then the subject was dropped. It went as suddenly and unexpectedly as it had come. Rather like Caroline herself.

'And you always had a thing for me, didn't you, Daniel Ford?'

That was the next question she asked. It was something that I would learn all too quickly about Linny. She never hedged or hesitated; she never sounded uncertain or vague. She had a thought, always a big thought, and when she opened her mouth that thought fell from her mouth. She didn't say it, it just fell out. After a while, a very short while, it became one of her most valuable and endearing qualities. With Linny Goldbourne you always knew exactly where you were and why. If you had any degree of uncertainty she would sure as hell tell you in no uncertain terms.

I smiled at her question. It didn't embarrass me, didn't make me feel awkward. Linny's honesty engendered honesty in others, and I myself was caught in that wave without thinking.

'Yes,' I said. 'I always had a thing for you.'

'That's good,' she said.

'Good?'

'Sure,' she went on. 'I wouldn't want to get involved with someone who didn't have a thing for me, right? I mean, would you like to be really in love with someone and have

133

the feeling at the back of your mind that they didn't really love you the same way?'

I thought of Caroline, that that was exactly how it had felt.

'No, I wouldn't,' I said, and believed that that was the most honest answer I could ever have given.

'Which is not to say we're in love,' Linny said, again matter-of-factly. 'But then I have time, and you do too, and hell, we're young and intelligent and stuffed with hormones, right?'

I started to laugh, and when I looked up from the breakfast she had prepared for me I saw her beaming, contagious smile, her hair tumbling around her face, her bright eyes, her winning charm.

I wanted to kiss her.

'You can kiss me now,' she said.

'I can?' I asked, unnecessarily.

'Sure,' she said. 'Free of charge an' everything.'

I leaned across the table and kissed her, a brief and insignificant connection, yet so meaningful. Imperfect, yet perfect. Like Linny herself.

Ahead of our house, parked against the curb, was Linny Goldbourne's Buick Skylark, deep blue, cream leather interior, a hundred miles of bright chrome, wire wheels and style.

Within an hour of my surfacing from some dark hell of tequila-fueled unconsciousness we were on our way, Linny talking endlessly of San Francisco, of *The Scene*, of someone called Roky Erickson, The Thirteenth Floor Elevators, Doug Sahm, The Grateful Dead, John Cippolina and The Quicksilver Messenger Service. The roof of the car was down, the sun was high and warm, and the wind took her long hair and sent it dancing out behind her in a bold wave of color and life and beauty.

I said little. I watched her. I absorbed her energy until I

felt replete, and still it came – boundless, infinite, rich and heady.

We drove east towards the mouth of the Santee River, and then south-west to Port Royal Sound, right there on the Georgia border where the Savannah River hurried out to meet the Atlantic as if late for their appointment.

I felt no ill effects from the night before by the time we arrived, and had I done I believe Linny would not have allowed them a moment of consideration. She was out of the car and down the street towards the beach before I had a second to question her plans.

I followed on that wave of enthusiasm and energy, and I saw her run ahead of me to the sand just as I had seen her in school.

But this time was different.

This time I was here because *she* wanted me to be here.

Later, seated there in the sand beside her, she rolled some grass in a neat twist of paper and lit it. She inhaled and held her breath, and slowly her eyes widened, her cheeks colored, and then she released that breath in a sudden rush.

She held that thing out towards me, and gingerly, cautiously, I took it.

I felt afraid, but I could not say no.

I felt that here was my first moment of trial, my first test of mettle against the attitude and viewpoint of another.

I felt Eve Chantry watching me.

She was saying: *Don't do it, Danny, don't do it until you have decided first. It has to be your decision, and your decision alone. Nathan was right. Nathan's daddy is a minister and sometimes he does have God on his side. It is a moment such as this that counts the most. Right now, right here.*

But I did not decide.

The moment decided for me.

I pressed the thing to my lips and inhaled.

At first it tasted bitter, and then beneath that something sweet, and though I had imagined myself choking and coughing and spluttering over Linny I did not. I did as she had done. I inhaled and held my breath. I waited a while and nothing happened. I inhaled again, and yet again a moment later. And then I felt something coming, not at first, but a few moments later, or minutes perhaps, I cannot remember. But it came, it most definitely came, and when it came it was like the small weathered blanket you carried as a child, your best toy, the feeling of warm security that closes around you when your ma holds you after a bad dream . . . the sound of your father's voice as he lifts you from the sidewalk, your knee grazed, your confidence bruised . . . the rush of excitement as daylight fades and the lights of the funfair can be seen all across town . . . the rushing whirl of music as the carousel starts up . . . and the smell of popcorn, fresh donuts, red and white spiral sugarcanes . . .

'Here,' Linny said, and passed me another joint – fatter, coned like a trumpet, and when it burned it crackled and hissed, and the smoke filled my eyes, my mouth, my nostrils. I smoked it for a while, and when I passed it to her she shook her head.

'Have my own,' she said, and held it up to show me.

How much I smoked I can't remember, two, perhaps three, maybe more. I wasn't counting, and neither was Linny, and after a while she got up and walked away. She returned a moment later, a bottle of tequila in her hand, and with it two small glasses she had brought from the car.

'Prepared for every eventuality,' she whispered as she leaned close to me, and she filled both glasses, urged me to swallow in one, and then she poured yet another and another.

She kissed me then, and then her tongue was behind my ear, inside it, beneath it, and all I could remember doing was laughing.

I felt I would burst with laughter.

I felt whatever seams had been sewn into my body would

unravel in one great rush and whatever was inside me would scatter across the sand and be washed out into the Atlantic.

And then I felt I *was* the Atlantic, and inside me was the Savannah River, and over in my right hand a thousand miles away was Greenleaf and my ma and Karl Winterson's Radio Store . . . and the war was someone else's problem, and they weren't looking for me . . . no, they weren't looking for me . . . perhaps for Nathan Verney, but not me.

Later, much later, I opened my eyes. The sun was setting along the horizon.

We were both naked.

Beneath us was a blanket from Linny's car, and over us were draped her dress, my shirt, and to the left, just there in the corner of my vision, I could see my right shoe on its side.

Linny stirred but did not open her eyes. I could feel the weight of her breast against my arm. Like Caroline Lanafeuille, but not. Different. Not better, just different.

And different was good.

I closed my eyes again. I did not want this time to end.

I felt nothing. No guilt, no pain, no loss, no sense of heartache for anything at all. I had not felt *nothing* for a long time it seemed, and in its absence, in its deep and echoing hollowness, it felt good.

Linny felt good. Too good perhaps.

I slept then I think, for when I opened my eyes again it was dark and cool and the sound of the sea closing up against the shore for the night was all I could hear.

Apart from Linny's breathing.

And those sounds, those reverberations of the soul, would be something I would remember for the rest of my life.

Seemed to me the most beautiful sounds in the world.

And they were mine.

That we had smoked grass and drunk tequila and slept on the beach seemed crazy. At least to me. I wanted to tell Linny Goldbourne that this had been something magical, that such a thing as this was so new to me it was scary, but there was something about her that warned me to say nothing. It was not that I felt unable to share my thoughts and feelings with her, it was that I imagined such a confidence would really have no great significance for her. She appeared so worldly, she drove her own car, she smoked grass. Christ, she brought grass *with* her. I would not even have known how to go about getting some had I wanted to.

So I said nothing, and that was okay.

When I opened my eyes the second time I could hear the radio from the car.

Linny was not beside me, she was out there in the sea and, acutely aware of my nakedness, I hurriedly donned my pants and walked down to meet her.

Linny Goldbourne possessed no such inhibitions. She was naked, and the water barely reached the tops of her thighs. She came up out of the water, and for a moment – even as she walked towards me – I felt invisible. For one horrible moment I felt I could have been anyone to her. And then she called my name, and the feeling passed, and I shrugged away my misgivings and uncertainty.

I was here because she wanted me. After all, had she not returned from Atlanta and found me out?

'You wanna go home, or somewhere else?' she asked.

I tried hard to keep my eyes on her face as she came closer.

I shrugged my shoulders. 'Whatever,' I replied, intending to sound relaxed and nonchalant, but it came out weak and indecisive.

She smiled. 'You hungry?'

I nodded. I had not paid much mind to eating, but now

she mentioned it I was aware of the ravenous craving in the pit of my stomach.

'We'll go get lobster or something,' she said as we reached the car. She leaned over the door to gather her dress from the back seat. I saw the sheer elegance of her form, the way her breasts barely moved as she stretched, the way she raised her arms to lift the dress over her head, and in the moment her face was obscured I looked down to her stomach and, below that, the dark triangle of color at once so magical and perfect.

I looked away, out towards the sea, the Atlantic Ocean, and when I turned back she was watching me.

She stepped towards me, she raised her hands, and placing them on my shoulders she pulled me close.

Then her arms were around my waist, I felt the side of her face against my neck, and then she was leaning up towards me, kissing me, her tongue between my lips, in my mouth.

I felt as if I was being swallowed. Emotionally swallowed. It was powerful and intoxicating. A drug. There was little I could do but be devoured. Quietly, gratefully, thankfully devoured.

This was Linny Goldbourne. She did not touch, she grasped. She did not caress, she enclosed. She did not hesitate, she acted, and acted with certainty.

And yet, for all these things, she was never anything but a woman. Nathan, who in time to come would also learn to love her, said being with Linda was like being mugged by a beauty queen.

'You're okay,' she said, as we sat beside one another in the car.

It was not a question, more a statement of fact. My perception in that moment was that she had sensed some slight misgiving on my part, something in my demeanor that told her I was not here on the same terms as she was.

'I'm okay,' I said.

'I know you loved Caroline,' she said, almost in a

whisper. 'I saw you together a couple of times, and you can always tell.'

I looked sideways at Linny, and there was something in her eyes, something in her expression that told me she perhaps understood more of what I was feeling than I did myself.

'You can lose someone, Danny, lose someone without ever really losing them. You have to recognize that there was a time and a place back there which you will never find again . . .'

Linny's hand closed over mine.

Her skin was warm and soft, like a summer peach.

'You just keep the emotion somewhere quiet where it cannot be disturbed, and when you're alone you can reflect on it, enjoy it once more as if it had never gone . . . but when you're *not* alone you have to realize that there is no place for that emotion. You have to be wherever you are, have to be *with* whoever you are with when you're with them . . . and if you can't do that, then wherever you might find yourself, and whoever might be there, then you're always going to be alone . . .'

She squeezed my hand gently.

'You understand what I'm saying?'

I smiled. I nodded. I leaned towards her.

She closed her hand around my neck and pressed her cheek to mine.

We stayed that way for a long time, and she was the one who drew back slightly, and then she kissed me, and she kissed me forever too, and then she released me.

'Lobster,' she said, and turned the key in the ignition.

And we did eat lobster. Fresh, caught right there off the Sound. We sat on wooden chairs on a pier with the sound of the sea beneath us, and we drank wine, red and strong, and we stayed there talking, smoking cigarettes, watching the world go about its business but with no wish to become involved.

Boats went by, fishers and shrimpers, and the rough faces of seafaring men observed us with a wry and curious detachment: kids from the city come down to see how real life can get. I had always felt that people like that would live more life in a day, an hour, than I would in three score and ten.

But my viewpoint was changing. I was going on twenty-two, I had lost my father, I had heard of Kennedy's death the day it happened, I had fallen in love with Caroline Lanafeuille, at first from a distance and then up close, and now I was losing my mind and my heart to someone called Linny Goldbourne whose father was perhaps the third or fourth most important man in the State. I had been to Atlanta to mourn for Martin Luther King. I had grown up with boys who were now dead in some vast wilderness of jungle on the other side of the world. I had smoked grass, made love in the sand near Port Royal Sound, had drunk tequila with salt and lemon until I believed I would lose my stomach to the gutter. I had shared time with a woman called Eve Chantry, and she had shared with me the candlemoth.

And soon ... soon enough, someone would write and tell me to go to Vietnam.

It came then – that thought, the name, the place, the things I imagined would happen there. A shadow passed across me, and within its passing I felt myself shudder. The war was out there, it was calling my name, and though I pressed my hands against my ears and hummed a tune to myself, I could hear it echoing through everything.

I closed my eyes.

Was this not a life?

Surely, yes.

I felt the breeze coming up off the sea that day, could almost taste the salt in the air, and as that day closed I lay in the back seat of a Buick Skylark with a girl I could so easily have loved for the rest of my life, and she whispered secrets that meant everything, and yet nothing at all.

I felt things had somehow simplified.

That was the only way I could describe it.

As if things now had some meaning, and thus everything else could be aligned and given its rightful importance.

For now, Linny Goldbourne was the most important thing in my life.

TWELVE

Throughout May of 1968 I cannot recall a day I did not see Linny.

Looking back at it now I can so clearly see how I pushed Nathan aside. Hindsight, our cruellest and most astute adviser, so easily illuminates our errors of judgement, and yet in the middle of life one seizes upon things that seem to mean so much. Looking back, they could never have meant as much as those things that came before or after. If they had, well, if they had they would still be present.

Had I known that my involvement with Linny Goldbourne would last less than a month, and had I known how and why it would so abruptly end, I would have kept my distance, but – as ever, the moth to a flame – I found her whirlwind of passion and enthusiasm so addictive I could not withdraw.

Throughout that month I drank tequila and Crown Royal, red wine and beer; I smoked Colombian hashish and opiated marijuana; I read books by William Burroughs and Jack Kerouac, I listened to 'Subterranean Homesick Blues' a thousand times and believed that all the answers of life were somewhere contained within the spaces between the words . . . and all for Linny Goldbourne, ex-Congressman's daughter, my Svengali, my savior, my nemesis.

I did love her, I know I did, and in return she loved me. Linny enclosed everything within her own self-created world, and for that time I was the center of her focus, the fulcrum. I saw this in the way she smiled when she saw me, the way she reached and held my hand as we walked, and there was something so strong in the way she felt that my memory of Caroline faded. Faded gently, but faded nonetheless. I had loved Caroline, yes, but as a teenager with a teenager's heart and mind and soul. When I loved Linny I had become a man. Or so I thought then. Different, not necessarily better, but different. My feelings for Caroline were now tinged with a sense of betrayal, as if she had somehow cast me aside for something that should not have meant so much. She was my first. That meant something special, and yet I had recalled her leaving with a sense of bitterness and pain. Those emotions – my passion alongside my loss – had felt like a bruise that would always ache and never heal. Linny somehow healed it, at least from within, so although the bruise still colored my skin it did not gnaw at me as it had once done.

Linny swept me up inside everything that she was, and she became a part of me that I would, and could, never lose.

Had I never lost Caroline, perhaps what now happened would not have affected me so. But I *had* lost her, and that earlier sense of betrayal grew all the more relevant and pressing and real. That was how it felt, and time would not change that . . . for in the years to come I would begin to see them both in the same light, as if each – though necessarily and remarkably different – had been born to punish me in the same way. It would only be later, much later, that I understood the import of what might have taken place within Linny's family, and thus gained some sense of closure on why she did what she did, but in that moment she had become everything, and then suddenly nothing.

The last time I saw Linny Goldbourne was the day Bobby Kennedy was killed in Los Angeles.

Kennedy had just won the California primary and was speaking at the Ambassador Hotel.

Someone called Sirhan Sirhan, who later said he couldn't

even remember shooting the presidential candidate, walked towards him in the crowd and killed him.

Shot him five times.

How do you shoot someone five times and not remember?

They did him, just like *they* did his brother.

And who were *they*? Same folks who bet a dollar we could win in Vietnam.

I was with Linny when we heard. I had just closed the Radio Store for the afternoon, and we were planning to drive down to Orangeburg and see one of her girlfriends.

Linny started the car, the radio was already on, and we heard.

She stopped the car. She looked at me with an expression I had never seen before, would never see again.

She looked at me and there was nothing.

She was hollow.

She shook her head, looked down, and when she looked up her eyes were filled with tears.

'I have to go home,' she said quietly. 'I have to go home now, Danny. You understand, don't you?'

I looked back at her with nothing to say.

She leaned across me and lifted the door lever.

The door swung open.

'I love you, Danny,' she said, but she did not look at me as she said it. 'I love you . . . but I have to go now.'

She started the car. She sat there looking right ahead. She was waiting for me to get out.

I wanted to say something, anything, but when I opened my mouth I felt hollow also.

Never so hollow.

I edged sideways. My foot was on the sidewalk. I levered myself up and stood there for a moment, the car door open, Linny sitting stock-still, looking right ahead through the windscreen at the road, and then I closed the door.

She revved the engine, eased the handbrake, depressed the accelerator, and she was gone.

She drove more slowly than was usual, and even as I watched her go I knew she would turn back, raise her hand perhaps, anything to indicate that she had changed her mind, her plans, *our* plans. Even though Bobby Kennedy was dead, it still meant something that I was left there on the sidewalk watching Linny disappear.

But she did not look back.

She did not raise her hand.

I felt the same as I had at that moment when she'd walked out of the sea towards me at Port Royal Sound.

Invisible.

I stayed there for some minutes.

I saw Caroline's face for one fleeting moment, the way her head tilted, the way her hair tumbled across her face. I felt nineteen again. I felt ashamed and confused and naïve.

My heart was beating slowly, I remember that, but what else may have occurred in my mind is no longer there.

And then I turned and walked towards Lake Marion to find Nathan Verney.

Somehow, for some unknown reason, something had changed.

I did not suspect for one moment that I would not see her again.

The *connection*, for now, was gone.

We never got drunk again. We did not smoke weed or listen to Dylan or read sections from Albert Camus or *Tortilla Flats*. We did not drive out to Myrtle Beach in the Buick Skylark and watch the sunset naked.

And had there been more time I perhaps would have stayed to learn what had happened. Had events not spiralled so quickly out of control, beyond anything I could have imagined, I perhaps would have allowed myself time to grieve, to ask myself why, to beg some understanding of Linny's motives.

But time had run out – so quick, so sudden, and yet in some way so *expected*. To live, to love, to lose: these things are just human, and perhaps say something of the way the world is. To do them twice says something about you.

June 8th 1968 was a Saturday.

Had it been a weekday I would have been at Karl Winterson's Radio Store when Nathan Verney came down.

But I was asleep, and when Nathan came he carried a burden the like of which would crush a man.

The burden weighed three grams. It was a pale manila color, and within it a single sheet of white paper with an official seal at the top and a printed signature at the bottom. It weighed more than heat tabs and Kool Aid and C-Rations and steel helmets and liners and camouflage covers, more than compress bandages and steel brushes and gun oil and fragmentation grenades, more than the weight of all our mothers' broken hearts, our fathers' vanished hopes . . .

It came in the disguise of a letter, and upon the letter was printed Nathan Verney's name.

It called upon his duty and his honor. It called upon his national allegiance. It called upon his sense of rightness and equity. It called upon his belief in the Constitution and the American way of life.

It called upon *him*.

More than anything, the burden called upon his fear.

And Nathan came prepared. He carried a shoulder-sack and a holdall. He carried a polythene bag within which he'd stowed clean socks and a bar of soap, a toothbrush, a shaving razor and a kitchen knife. In his coat pockets he carried a packet of Kools, a Zippo lighter, a comb, loose change and a small roll of one and five-dollar bills which couldn't have amounted to more than thirty or forty bucks all told. In his heart he carried guilt and fear and an indescribable sense of loss and disassociation.

And in his hand he carried the burden.

My ma was out fetching provisions.

The sound of his feet on the path below woke me, and I leaned from the window to see who was there.

As I looked out he looked up, and with that one glance, that one image of his upturned face, I read everything that could be said.

My body became cold, and yet I twitched as if with a fever.

My palms sweated so much I couldn't tighten my belt, and as I went downstairs I almost tripped and fell.

As I reached the front door Nathan was walking up the front steps towards the screen. He paused there, and in that second he glanced back over his shoulder towards the road, towards Lake Marion beyond, and in that glance I recognized his deep sense of longing, his heartache.

In that glance was perhaps the belief that he would never see this place again.

'You okay?' I asked. A stupid and thoughtless question.

Nathan didn't reply, couldn't reply. What was there that anyone could have said?

He passed by me and walked down the hall to the kitchen. He hesitated in the doorway, and then he crossed the room and sat down. He sat where he always sat, back to the window, his hands in his lap, his eyes downcast to the floor.

We were six years old when we met, sixteen years before, and Nathan had perhaps sat right there two or three times a week in every week since, but never, never in all those thousands of times, had he looked like this.

He placed the burden on the table.

I believed the table would buckle with the weight.

'My folks don't know,' he started. 'My folks believe I am going north to find work. I have been talking about it for six months. I knew the time would come and I wanted to be ready.'

I sat down opposite Nathan. Even then I could picture my ma turning from the stove with fresh corn and potatoes, Nathan's round cherubic face grinning up at her as she spooned more food onto his plate than he could possibly eat.

I saw us sitting there playing cards, the sun going down through the window behind him and, as it touched the horizon, the last brief burst of orange that would throw a halo of gold through his short wiry hair.

I saw Nathan sitting there nursing a bleeding elbow, tears in his eyes, the temptation to touch it growing ever stronger as he looked.

I saw myself laughing as we tried to chase a bird out through the back door and into the yard.

I saw all these things.

And then I looked at Nathan once more.

'And you?' he asked.

I turned away. I could not face him. My heart thundered in my chest. My fists were clenching and releasing. My pulse raced like a derailed freight train.

I opened my mouth to speak, not knowing what to say.

'Your decision,' Nathan said quietly.

I closed my mouth.

I thought of my mother, the memory of my father. I thought of Eve Chantry, of Dr. Backermann. I thought of Marty Hooper and Larry James lying dead and stiff and cold in the middle of nowhere. I thought of Caroline Lanafeuille, of Linny Goldbourne, of Sheryl Rose Bogazzi whom I had never touched, never kissed, but still somehow managed to love from afar despite her ultimate betrayal.

I thought least of all of myself.

'I –'

Nathan raised his hand.

'Your decision,' he repeated quietly.

I looked at him, and for a moment I did not recognize the man who sat facing me. He seemed a stranger.

'I cannot let you go alone,' I said.

'That isn't a decision, Danny,' Nathan replied.

I felt like crying.

'I haven't received my notice,' I said.

My voice sounded unfamiliar.

Nathan didn't reply, merely looked back at me with that same detached expression.

'My ma . . .'

Nathan started to rise from the chair.

'Wait,' I said. 'Sit down, Nathan. Talk to me . . .'

Nathan shook his head. 'I don't want to talk any more, Danny. We've done all the talking we need to. I've made a decision, and the decision stands whether you come or not.'

'I'm coming,' I blurted out, and even as the words left my lips I realized that once again there had been no self-determined decision.

My response was involuntary.

I was running on automatic.

'You're coming?' Nathan asked.

I started to nod my head. I felt as if someone was moving my neck from behind.

'I'm coming,' I said. 'I'm definitely coming.'

Nathan nodded. He did not smile. He didn't hug me or shake my hand, he didn't clap me on the shoulder or anything else.

He just nodded.

I felt my insides turn cold and loose.

'So get ready,' Nathan said matter-of-factly.

'Yes . . . get ready,' I mumbled.

I made for the door, my legs like lead, my feet like large wooden blocks tenuously attached. I could see my father's face, that expression of admonishment he wore when the Daniel he'd raised was not being the Daniel he wished for.

I saw my mother, her expression of quiet patience as my

father scolded me, and then her comfort afterwards, the way she would make me believe it was all for my own good.

And I had believed her, believed her so well I could never doubt her.

I started upstairs towards my room. I felt the weight of the entire universe slowing me down, and with each footfall on each riser the sound of my narrow heart came in unison.

I felt Nathan waiting downstairs.

I felt pulled in all directions, and how much of that I could stand I had no idea.

I believed – perhaps for the first time in my life – that the real world had arrived.

And with it came all these things, and they weighed so much, and they bore down upon me like a mountain and an ocean and a thousand fallen trees.

But the greatest weight was the lie.

That it had been my decision.

It had not, and I knew it, and I believed Nathan did too.

I closed the bedroom door behind me and started to pack.

THIRTEEN

Clarence Timmons came down to speak with me today. I asked after his wife. He seemed pleased that I remembered. He said she was doing a little better, that some physiotherapy had been recommended and he would help her with that.

And then he said: 'But I didn't come down to talk to you about my wife.'

He said it as though I would have been surprised.

'They're coming down to weigh you,' he said.

Clarence Timmons nodded in an almost avuncular fashion.

'They're going to weigh you every week from now on . . . they're also going to do a medical check every month to make sure you're . . .'

'Healthy enough to die,' I said, which was unfair, because Clarence Timmons was a good man and he had difficulty dealing with this.

I had learned that there were those who chose to work on D-Block and there were those who were posted without choice. Such a man was Mr. Timmons. Perhaps he had believed he could help, make some reforms, assist some convicts to recover a sense of self-esteem and personal worth. Perhaps he even believed he could return to the world some men who had been truly rehabilitated. Instead, he had been charged with looking after them until they were killed by the State.

'I'm sorry, Mister Timmons,' I said.

Mr. Timmons waved his hand, brushed the comment aside.

'So they will come down and weigh you today,' he repeated.

I nodded, thanked him for telling me, and when he left I leaned back and closed my eyes.

Perhaps my weight determined the voltage.

That's all I could think of.

Back while I was in Charleston – the first year or so after Nathan's death, the trial, all those things – America wrestled with its collective conscience.

At the tail-end of 1960 they had given Jack Kennedy their vote over Richard Nixon. In November 1968, only after Johnson said he wouldn't run again, only after the death of Robert Kennedy, did they give Nixon his chance.

By the time Nixon was inaugurated Nathan Verney and I were long gone, and in the months following our departure from Greenleaf events took place that we only caught on the hop. Nixon won the Republican nomination for President with Spiro Agnew beside him, the August riots broke out in Watts, and then in October Johnson said he had ordered a halt to the bombing of North Vietnam.

But the most important thing was Nixon's victory.

Nixon had promised that he would end the war, but Nixon was a crazy man. Nathan knew that. I knew that. But at the same time we believed that his craziness might make things different, that perhaps the law would change, that perhaps he wouldn't be so harsh on those who'd refused to fulfill their apparent national obligation to die in South-East Asia.

It wasn't long before we realized that this was not to be the case.

In September Nixon ordered the B52s to keep on bombing those gook motherfuckers for as long as it took. Not in those words exactly, but the sentiment was there.

In November, Lieutenant William Calley, U.S. Armed Forces, would be tried by court martial for the massacre at My Lai. An Army photographer called Ron Haeberle, a witness to the killing of one hundred and nine people, the youngest of whom was only two years old, said *the bones were flying in the air, chip by chip*.

America heard these words, asked itself what was happening in Vietnam, asked itself what had become of its sons.

But America did not act.

Father John Rousseau would speak of these things, I would tell him what I remembered, but what remains in my memory of those times is neither politics nor protest, nor the growing awareness of just how many millions really believed that the Vietnam War was a complete fiasco, but Nathan Verney standing at the end of Nine Mile Road looking back towards Greenleaf.

To describe how I felt at that time seems impossible now. Greenleaf had been my home for my entire life. Everything I had ever been had been born in that town. Everything I knew, every*one* I knew, was a part of that place just as much as I.

I did not know where we were going, and in my hurry to gather some things together and leave the house I had almost forgotten why, but every article of clothing, each postcard and picture and letter I sorted through . . . all bore some memory of who I had become in this place. My childhood years, each of them encapsulated within a thought, and within each thought an image, and within each image an emotion that unfolded itself silently around me and reminded me who I was. This place was who I was. And I was leaving. Forever? I did not know.

I wanted to speak, I wanted to ask Nathan if there was any other way this could be done, but I knew such questions were pointless. Nathan would look at me – not with the eyes of the child he was, but with the eyes of the man he had become, and in becoming that man he had worked through all of his own fears and doubts and reservations about where he was going and why.

I had not. I felt empty and insubstantial. I felt . . . nothing.

Coming down the stairs, my bag in my hand, I could feel the weight and pressure of everything I was leaving behind. Here was my family, my mother and father, and here also were Eve and Caroline and all that they had shared with me. I was leaving this behind, and in doing so would leave behind a part of myself. Always and forever beyond this point I would be missing something. It was wrenched out of me and cast aside. I would look back and see the boy I was standing at the side of the road, and in his eyes were loss and pain and a strange sense of failure. *You are not who I wanted you to be*, that small child would say, and I would know he told the truth.

I wrote a note for my mother. I left it on the kitchen table, and looking back at it from the doorway I saw it for what it was: a lie.

We left together, Nathan and I, silently, hopelessly it seemed, and looking back from the road my own house seemed so small and frail. We walked on in silence, and though I tried to catch Nathan's eyes, tried to glean some sense of compassion and empathy for what I was feeling, he looked straight ahead, never flinching, neither erring nor wavering in his intent. We reached Nine Mile Road, the scene of so many significant moments, and it seemed a thousand years since I'd stood in almost the exact same place and watched that small negro girl bear the grief of Kennedy's death until she fell beneath its weight.

I remembered the universal family – myself and Nathan and Reverend Verney and Eve Chantry – and I asked myself how I could ever have believed that things could stay the same.

Nathan had walked ahead of me with a determined and

forthright stride, and I had caught his coat-tails – or that's how it felt. Swept along once again in the fury and passion of the moment.

I thought of the note I'd left my ma, the lack of anything specific I had said, only that I had gone with Nathan, we were going to find work, that I would call her soon.

That was all.

I had left $100 behind, and in my pocket I carried a little more than $300, all the money I'd earned at Karl Winterson's Radio Store.

I knew people would talk of us. I kind of knew that there would be no coming back to Greenleaf, at least until the war was over, and I also believed that the general opinion of me would be that it was Nathan Verney's influence.

Why?

Simple: because he was black.

Nice white Anglo-Saxon Protestant boys didn't do things like this.

And so I watched Nathan walk on ahead, and had he walked to the edge of the world I would have followed him.

I believed in his belief.

That was all.

For now, at least for now, that had to be enough.

Sometimes I get a little confused. I lose the sequence of things, dates become muddled.

It is only when Father John comes down and asks me about all these things that the patchwork seems to mend. Things come back, things I haven't thought of for years, and as they return there is a growing sense of realization about what is going to happen to me.

America, the same America I turned my back on and betrayed, was now returning that favor in kind.

Father John told me that a final date of execution would be confirmed within the week.

I thought of the cigarettes wrapped in paper and wedged down the side of the sink.

Soon, Nathan, I thought.

Soon.

They did come down and weigh me. One hundred and fifty-two pounds. I had lost weight and never noticed.

I made a joke, something like *Seems to me you'd only have to plug me into the wall to finish me off with a body weight like that*, but the guy in the white tunic didn't smile, didn't even look at me. He was either deaf, or just numb to such things, going through the routine without ever connecting with whoever was there ahead of him. Maybe he thought like Mr. West. *Dead meat*.

I watched him leave. He didn't look at me. He walked with his head down, like he was ashamed.

There were times when I believed I wished for nothing less than to talk with Father John. Other times I looked forward to his visits as if they were the only reason for staying alive. His job was to draw me out of myself, to have me speak, to remember, to recount the other details, the things that were never said in the myriad court appearances I made back then. Here was my opportunity to understand myself, to gain awareness of why I was here.

Father John told me that we created our own destinies. He did not believe in the ever-present hand of God. He told me he didn't believe our lives and fates were bound by some ethereal and omniscient force. He said he wanted me to look, to soul-search, to try and understand why I was here. He basically said that if we were in the shit, then we got ourselves there.

That was something I didn't want to believe. For so long I had carried the certainty that it was all because of someone else, that it was political, that there were people who really believed that what happened was what *should* have happened, and there was nothing I could have done about it. I believed I could have been anyone, that purposes would have been served any which way. I believed in bad luck. I *wanted* to believe in bad luck. If I could believe in that then I did not have to take any responsibility at all.

Father John Rousseau knew how I felt, and he started to take it all away. For a while I hated him for that, despised him for challenging all that I had held so close. This was my belief system. He had his. I had mine. What right did he have to challenge that?

But he did. Challenged it with ferocity. And as I watched that Jericho crumble beneath the onslaught of questions and memories and recognition, I began to remember more; details that had slipped away soundlessly, things that I never believed it would be possible to remember. It seemed that everything was there, every second, every heartbeat, every thought, and as I spoke of those things, as Father John listened, I imagined that Nathan was there beside me, perhaps seated at a third plain deal chair in *God's Lounge*, sharing Luckys and shooting the breeze, smiling like he once had in Ma's kitchen, looking like he had when he came with *the burden*, looking like the kid with jug-handle ears, traffic-light eyes, and a mouth that ran from ear to ear with no rest in between.

Perhaps that was the only reason I went on talking, for as long as I talked I was still alive, and as long as I was alive I could still remember Nathan Verney.

And as long as I remembered Nathan then perhaps I could believe there was some sense to it all.

There wasn't, I knew that, but like Father John kept on telling me: *You have to keep on believing . . . you just have to keep on believing.*

'South?' I had asked Nathan. 'Are you fucking crazy?'

Nathan was seated. He didn't flinch, didn't move a muscle, almost as if he'd predicted my exact reaction.

'You understand what's going on down there?' I asked,

my voice incredulous. 'Hey! Wake up, man! Smell the coffee for Christ's sake.'

Nathan glanced at me, his expression cold. Nothing justified blasphemy.

'You're a black man,' I said, 'a negro, an African-American . . . you don't go *south*.'

'Which is exactly why we go south,' Nathan said quietly.

'We go south we get killed,' I said matter-of-factly.

Nathan nodded. 'We go south because that's the last place anyone will think we're gonna go for exactly the reason you're saying. We go south because any kinda nigger with half a brain would *never* go south, and that's exactly why they'll look for us north.'

'But hell, Nathan, you gotta understand that with what's going on right now there is no reason in the world you ain't gonna get yourself killed and dumped in some swamp.'

Nathan looked up at me and smiled.

'A swamp here is better than a swamp in some country I never even heard of until a few months ago.'

I sat down.

There was method in his madness.

'Look,' he said. 'You gotta take everything into consideration. We go north then there's a greater chance we'll be identified. I don't know what kinda arrangement they have for dealing with this kinda thing, people who just disappear when their Draft Notice comes, but sure as hell they're gonna have something. They'll think we're going north because it would be crazier than shit to go south, and so we go south, make sense?'

I shrugged. It was too much. Too overwhelming for me to take everything on board.

'Let me make the decisions, okay?' he said calmly.

Have already, I thought. *Hell, Nathan, you have already*.

I gave Nathan Verney control of my life at that time. I let him lead the way, I let him direct us both, almost as if there was one spirit and two bodies. I had cheated him, I knew that. Cheated him into thinking that going with him had really been my decision too. I felt guilty for that, for lying, for all my slight deceptions, and yet now I was here there was little I could do. I could not turn back, that would have been worse, and so I followed ... quietly, obediently, I followed.

We took a bus out of Greenleaf and headed first for Augusta and Macon, and then down through Cordele and Albany towards the Florida state line.

I remember that journey, the hours we spent with our knees up against the backs of the seats in front, the endless road ahead, the fields and trees, the sky like a roof on the world. It rained at one point, rained for maybe ten, fifteen minutes, and through the rain-spattered window the world was distorted enough for it to be a new place. *If only*, I had thought, *if only the world had changed its face that day and become something else entirely.*

At first Nathan said little, he was subdued and internal, and I wished so hard I could have read what he was thinking. Every once in a while he'd turn and smile, almost as if reassuring me that everything would be alright. I didn't believe that for a minute. And then he seemed to ease somewhat, to relax a little, and for a while he talked of things that had happened when we were kids.

'The fish,' he said. 'You remember the fish?'

I smiled; I remembered it like it was yesterday.

Nathan shook his head. 'I remember when we were running down the street away from Benny Amundsen's place, those kids chasing us ... Christ, you looked like you were gonna shit yourself.'

'Me? You shoulda seen *your*self. And then when Eve Chantry appeared you nearly fainted right there in the street.'

Nathan laughed. 'You were the one who thought she was

a witch. You were the one who told me she'd eaten her freakin' husband.'

'Everyone thought she was a witch, not just me.'

Nathan shook his head. 'No, man, you were the chicken-shit one, Danny, as chickenshit as they came.'

'Go fuck yourself,' I retorted.

Nathan pulled a face, a face like a scared weepy kid. 'Oooh, the witch is coming, Nathan,' he whined. 'Watch out for the witch who ate her husband.'

I turned to look out of the window, feigning indignance.

Nathan nudged me in the shoulder.

'Eat shit, Nathan,' I said.

'Eat shit, Nathan,' he mimicked in a simpering voice.

I turned suddenly and thumped him hard on the upper arm.

Nathan started laughing and rubbing his arm simultaneously. 'Fuck, Danny, that hurt!'

'Ooh, ooh, Danny, that hurt,' I replied.

And then he was laughing so much the woman ahead of us turned and looked at him like a reprimanding schoolma'am.

She turned back and Nathan pulled a face, pouting like a spoiled child. He pointed at the woman and mouthed *witch*.

And so that journey went – laughing like we possessed not a care in the world. Perhaps a pretense, a brave face for the world, but it didn't matter. Whatever that world was, it felt like we were driving away from it, and that was fine by me. We stayed in Georgia the first night, in a motel outside of Waycross, but I did not sleep, can neither remember closing my eyes nor ever really forgetting for a second why I was there. I sat up at one point, looked out through the window towards the fields beyond the highway, and somewhere within those fields I saw shadows moving, shadows like people, and I imagined they were out there looking for me, looking for us, already aware of our betrayal and plotting our capture and return.

I asked myself if I should go back. I asked myself if I would have ever actually received *the burden* myself. That was a question that would never be answered until I did go back. *If* I went back.

I remember walking back from the window and sitting on the edge of Nathan's bed. He slept soundly. I watched him for a while, and I realized that he slept so well because this was his decision. He had been committed and realistic, he had determined his course of action, and would have carried it through regardless of my agreement or presence. He had been true to whatever ideal he possessed. That's why he slept. And that was why I could not.

For a time, seated on the edge of that bed, I felt like nothing, with no more substance than one of the shadows out there in the fields beyond the highway. Perhaps those shadows didn't see Nathan because he was real. And perhaps Nathan would not have seen them either.

They were my ghosts, destined perhaps to follow me until I finally made a decision of my own.

My own private ghosts, neither taunting nor threatening, neither questioning nor scolding, they were just there.

I remembered the candlemoth, the small wooden frame that still hung over my bed back there in Greenleaf. It was a fitting gift from Eve Chantry, something that was trying so hard to be something else, and failing to recognize its own worth it kept on trying to be something else until it died.

As if in echo of that thought I remember looking to my left, and there, right there against the window, there was a flutter of wings. A single moth. It was beating its wings against the glass to come inside. It wanted the light. Wanted to reach the light. Wanted the light so much it would die to get it.

I did not open the window. I merely pressed my face

against the glass to watch that thing tirelessly attempt the impossible.

And it watched me back, I was sure of that, and perhaps was puzzled why one who was so near the light would want to leave it.

And then I lay down again, a strange bed, a strange room, and with the sound of Nathan's breathing I tried to pace myself, to measure my own thoughts, and lose the sounds of rushing thunder that so relentlessly filled my head.

I knew I would not find peace. It was ironic, for this lack of internal peace had only come about because I was trying to avoid a war.

Someone else's war. I had to believe that, had to keep telling myself that it had nothing to do with me.

When dawn broke, daylight growing from the horizon, I dressed and went out and stood on the edge of the highway until the last of my ghosts had left the fields.

I must have been there an hour, perhaps more, and when I returned Nathan Verney was still sleeping.

Slept like a dead man.

I remember thinking that: *Nathan Verney sleeps like a dead man*.

I stood over him for a minute or two, and then I reached out and put my hand on his shoulder. He stirred, turned, breathed deeply, and then opened his eyes. He had been elsewhere, for when he rolled back and looked up at me there was a moment of puzzlement, and then realization dawned as to where he was and why.

'The war's over, right?' he said, and I smiled half-heartedly.

For a while, the few hours he had slept, he had been elsewhere. For a few hours he had been granted the blessing of forgiveness. He had taken it, taken it willingly, and in taking it was now learning how it felt to have it withdrawn.

He was quiet for a little while, and then he rose, he

washed, he dressed and, saying nothing to me, he went to the door and opened it.

I stood up, put my bag over my shoulder, and the pair of us walked down to meet the world once more.

The world was out there, it was the same as before, and it was as ready as it had ever been to take us on.

FOURTEEN

Even after reaching Sumter, even after watching the first and second appeals fall on deaf ears, I still believed that someone somewhere would realize the terrible mistake that had been made. I believed there was still a war to be waged, and – more importantly than that – I believed I possessed the spirit to fight it. I don't think it really ever came home to me, and I don't believe I lost that spirit, until Father John Rousseau sat across from me in *God's Lounge* and gave me the date.

November 11th 1982.

He told me on October 5th. Told me on October 5th that someone somewhere had decided I had thirty-six days left.

Coincidentally, one day for each year I'd been alive.

Father John said he would increase my visits, that he would now come for two hours every other day, that we would talk more, that we would have time to talk of everything before . . .

'Before what?' I remember asking him, which was unfair.

Before you die, Daniel, he'd said, and I'd turned to him and there was such a look of hard reality in his eyes I couldn't bear it for more than a second.

He'd reached out, reached out across the table there in *God's Lounge*, and he'd gripped my hand and squeezed it tight.

I realized that in that moment I had felt the first human contact for many weeks. Perhaps months.

Message delivered, Father John had left.

Clarence Timmons came soon after to return me to my

cell. He didn't say a word. He knew the date had come. I was relieved he said nothing because I would not have known what to say in return.

Mr. West, however, knew exactly what to say. I was sleeping when he came, and he took a wooden chair from the corridor, just a plain deal straight-backed chair, and he dragged it all of ten yards towards my cell. Dragged it slowly, as noisily as he could, knowing full well it would stir me into consciousness.

When I opened my eyes I could see his half-lit face right there above me through the bars.

'Jesus Christ!' I started.

Mr. West raised his hand and pressed his finger to his lips.

'Ssshhh,' he whispered. 'Quiet now . . . don't want to be wasting what little breath you have left there, Daniel.'

I closed my eyes and tried to shut him out.

I could smell him, the boot polish, the detergent, and beneath that something bitter and acrid and rotten . . . like some long-dead thing preserved in formaldehyde.

'Got your date eh?' West went on.

His voice was sibilant, insistent, penetrative.

'You know I'll be coming for you then, don'tcha?' he asked, a rhetorical question that required no answer at all.

'I'll be coming for you . . . and you'll piss yourself and cry and plead like all the others.'

I could hear in his voice that he was smiling.

'But there won't be a goddam thing you can do, Daniel, 'cause no-one gives a rat's ass what happens to you . . . hell, I doubt if anyone even remembers you're here. These lawyers and judges and pro bono social conscience para-legals, hell they get on their high horse about some bullshit, some weak-minded pathetic sense of guilt about how we shouldn't be frying your ass . . . but they get bored awful quick don't they? Get bored and go off to chase some crap about the ozone layer and chemical pollutants near playgrounds and Christ only knows what.'

West sighed, as if tolerating such people was a necessary part of his work.

'These people don't know what they're dealing with ... they know nothing of life and death, eh Daniel?'

I opened my eyes.

Mr. West had leaned even closer.

I could see he was smiling.

'Life and death is a little simpler, a little more straightforward than they could ever imagine. And that's something that we both know a great deal about, isn't it?'

I opened my mouth to say something, but West stared at me, again pressing his finger to his lips.

'I'm gonna share something with you, Daniel, and hell you better listen 'cause I'm not the sharing kind see?'

I breathed out silently. I couldn't imagine being anywhere more terrifying in that moment.

'Eight years old I was, just eight years old, and the little town I came from was just a nothing place. Kids down there didn't get much of an education, but there was a schoolhouse, plain room wooden schoolhouse, and we went down there each morning and did what was asked of us –'

A sudden stabbing pain in my shoulder.

I jumped.

A nervous exhalation escaped my lips.

'Wake the fuck up, Ford,' Mr. West hissed. 'Don't you go fallin' asleep on me.'

I shook my head.

'Should think the fuck not.'

I opened my eyes wide.

'So we'd go down there, and on the way was this house, and on the porch of this house was some big old ugly mean sonofabitch dog, all teeth and noise, slavering jaws, snappin' and snarlin' and scarin' the living shit outta these little kids. Guy who owned the dog, fat ugly motherfucker, he'd just watch through the window and laugh as the kids scattered past. He fuckin' loved it, man, fuckin' loved every minute of it . . . but I saw him, I saw what he was doing, and hell if I was gonna let him carry on frightening those little kids the way he was. Let it go for a month, and then I took a big piece of steak, ground up some sleeping tablets my ma used to take when she got the fever, and I covered that meat in enough of that shit to floor a horse. Rode down there on my bike one night and hurled that meat up and onto the porch. Motherfuckin' dog didn't even wait to smell the thing, just wolfed it down in one mouthful.'

West laughed to himself, a cold and disquieting sound.

'And then I waited, waited for no more than ten minutes, and that dog was snoring like a rattlesnake in a tin can. I climbed over the fence, had a canvas sack, some rope and a tire iron. Went up those steps like I was on eggshells and then I tugged that bag under that dog until he was all trussed up inside like a Thanksgiving turkey. And then I took my tire iron and I smashed the living fuck out of its head, kept on smacking into that bloody pulp of brain and skull until I could see how soaked with blood the canvas was. I dragged that sack across the porch, down the steps and all the way over the yard to the street. I tied a rope to the sack, the other end to my bike, and then I cycled away, dragged that poor motherfuckin' mess of shit all the way to the end of the highway.'

Mr. West laughed again.

I felt sick to my stomach, the vision of a demented eight-year-old kid with a tire iron and a canvas sack with a dead dog inside.

'And then I set that fucking thing on fire, stood there while it burned . . . and hell if roasting a dog don't smell like a Sunday afternoon barbecue.'

Mr. West was silent for a few seconds, and those seconds

stretched into some dark forever where humanity and empathy and compassion could never exist.

'And you know what, Daniel? Smells just like yo' gon' smell come your fuckin' birthday.'

West started to laugh – softly at first, like a distant train rumbling somewhere across the state line – and then he appeared to be caught in the contagion of the moment and his laugh became louder, more raucous, ugly and threatening.

'My daddy knew about people like you,' he said. 'Sympathisin' with the niggers and the Jews and all the other dregs of humanity. Worked his guts out trying to keep our home clean of scum. And hell, if they didn't kill him for it . . .'

West paused, and in his eyes was a sense of something as close to emotion as I had ever seen, was ever likely to see.

'People like you will never understand the war we're fighting . . . the war we will go on fighting until we take our country back. And my daddy knew that, and his daddy 'fore him, and as far as we're concerned you did us a service by killin' one of them niggers so we didn't have to do it ourselves.'

West sneered, his face twisted and contemptuous.

'You know what it feels like to see your daddy get killed, boy? See him dragged along the road by his own father, blood spilling from his head where those niggers beat him with sticks . . . niggers that weren't good enough to be shinin' his shoes . . .'

He stood up, dragged the chair back to the wall.

He paused for a moment, catching his breath perhaps, and then he crossed the corridor again and looked down at me.

'Sleep well you piece of shit,' he whispered.

I lay there, my eyes closed, and I listened until his footsteps had faded into nothing.

And then I started to cry.

*

Max Myers came down later, reached his hand through the bars and touched my hair. I had been drifting away, losing all sense of reality, and then I heard Max's voice saying *I heard you got your date, Danny boy. We all gon' miss you, kid. Let me know if you need anything, okay? Let me know if you need anything at all.*

And I reached up and touched Max's hand, and he gripped it, and I gripped back, and then his fingers slipped from mine and I heard him walking down the block, his soft-soled shoes on the linoleum, the squeaking wheels of his magazine trolley.

They would all come in turn, one by one, and say what they had to say, and express whatever emotion they were capable of expressing at such a time, and I would nod and smile as best I could, and hear them, and reply with whatever words I could, and believe that never would it be possible for anyone to understand how such a thing felt.

Except Nathan.

Perhaps Nathan.

Nathan knew exactly what it was like to know you were going to die.

But that's another story.

I'll tell Father John, tell him everything, and I've got thirty-six days to do it.

We'd left Greenleaf at the beginning of the second week of June. We'd left on a Saturday. By the following Monday we were in Jacksonville, Florida, we had spent nigh on $100 and we needed work. We stayed one night in a motel off of Highway 36, and then we went down to the coast.

I remember leaving the motel that morning, the cool clear sky the brightest blue, and for a moment I felt free. There was no other way to describe it, just *free*. That feeling lasted no more than a fleeting second or two, because as we turned right at the end of the pathway towards the street I saw a squad car idling against the sidewalk, motor running, one officer inside eating a sandwich, the other standing on the curb, radio in his hand, talking to someone. I didn't hear what he said, couldn't have done from where we were, but I knew, I just *knew* my name was in among those sounds somewhere.

I glanced at Nathan, he was looking straight ahead, oblivious it seemed. The thought struck me that he couldn't have seen the car, but we were fifteen yards away, only a glance to the left and they were there, and even as we levelled with them I knew the officer inside was watching us intently. He had stopped eating, his attention so fixed upon me he hadn't cared to wipe the smear of mayonnaise from his chin . . . and I knew we were done for.

I knew it in my heart of darkened hearts.

My knees were weak, my insides churning, and I anticipated the sound of his voice, the *Hey you!* that would come any second.

I walked on.

One foot after the other.

One footstep for every three heartbeats it seemed, and I knew they would hear my heart, hear it clamoring inside my chest like a frightened crazy man beating at the door of a burning house.

Any moment now the door would give and my heart would burst from my chest and land on the sidewalk like a handful of raw red guilt.

I turned suddenly at the sound of someone laughing. A child. Then another. A single-file crocodile of children suddenly turning towards us at the junction.

A man was at their head, tall and stern-looking, and as he passed he looked at us with an air of disdain.

I glanced back at the squad car, and the officer who had been seated inside was even then rising to his feet, stepping out of the car, taking one, two, three steps in our direction.

I thought to run.

Hey!

My heart froze.

I didn't want to look back.

Couldn't help myself.

My eyes took on a life of their own, and even as I felt my head angle awkwardly to my left I could see the man at the head of the crocodile of children greeting the police officer warmly, shaking his hand, smiling. The line of kids came to a staggered halt as they realized it was now time to stop.

I looked at Nathan. He looked back at me and smiled.

He *was* oblivious.

Once more it came home to me that we were running on Nathan's decision, not mine, and as it was his own uninfluenced decision he had shouldered the responsibility of any consequences that might unfold. Shouldered that responsibility along with his rucksack and meagre possessions.

I, however, had not.

I was alone in this despite Nathan's company.

Thirty, forty yards from the motel, the squad car, the line of kids now out of view, I glanced back the way we'd come.

I wasn't looking for the police; I was looking towards my home.

It was summer and already brutally hot, and down along the piers and wharfs there were fishing boats coming in from the Atlantic. Unloading catches was not a trade that required any qualifications except the willingness to sweat, to smell of fish all day and night, and a backbreaking persistence.

We earned barely enough to cover a room and food, but we were out there, we were unknown, and no-one asked questions. That, of all things, was predominant in our thoughts.

It stayed that way through June and the best part of July, stayed that way until one night in the last week of the month when we decided we would go out and get drunk.

We couldn't afford it, but we felt we deserved it. Six or seven weeks we had worked without a break, twelve, sometimes fourteen-hour shifts, and we had gotten into a groove, a tolerable groove, and we had forgotten why we were there, what we were escaping from.

So we went into Jacksonville, found a small bar on Oak Street near the bus station, and there we sat and drank Budweiser and Crown Royal, listened to Willie Nelson and Chet Atkins on the juke, minding our own business and making small talk between ourselves.

Which is the way it should have stayed, but I got it in mind that we should shoot a game or two of pool, and though Nathan was not interested I convinced him it was a good game to play.

He had not played before, and though he gave it his best he was bad. The extent of his inability was commented on by some guy at the bar, an overweight dungaree'd redneck who smelled like he was rotting right where he stood and used the word *fuck* as many times as possible in each sentence. Like *Fuck me, what the fuck is that fuckin' guy doin' on a fuckin' pool table for fuck's sake.*

Nathan took offence. Nathan was a preacher's boy, and when the bad-smelling guy said something about how blacks shouldn't be allowed to play pool, that pool was a white man's game, that a pool cue wasn't a spear and maybe he should just stick to running fast and screwing his sisters, Nathan got mad.

It was ugly from the start.

The bad-smelling guy wasn't alone. As if by magic three others appeared, equally stupid and bad-smelling, and when they rounded on Nathan he looked at me and realized a little of what he'd gotten himself into.

He hit the first one and broke the cue.

The guy didn't move. It was like hitting a tree. A bad-smelling tree.

I took a cue ball from the table, and when I raised my

hand to launch it someone grabbed me from behind and knocked me down with one punch. A kidney punch hurts, hurts like hell, and while I was trying to get up, clutching my side and feeling like I would puke most of my internal organs, Nathan was being kicked left and right and down the bar to the door.

The man who'd hit me figured there was more fun to be had beating on a nigger and he went with them.

I came up roaring, the man turned, and in some kind of instinctive moment, no thought, no regard for consequences, I grabbed the glass of Crown Royal and threw the contents in his face.

The man screamed in agony as the spirit met his eyes. He clutched his face, couldn't see a thing, and I let go with the most almighty kick to his balls.

The moment of connection brought the most amazing reaction.

The man fell silent, dead silent, and then he went down like the proverbial plank.

Like Marty Hooper in Benny's.

As I ran past him I kicked him in the small of the back. Not a sound.

I reached the back of the bar just as Nathan was being hurled headlong into the alleyway behind the building.

I went limping down there, my side feeling like it had been opened up for surgery and then forgotten about.

I could see them down there, three of them, Nathan kneeling and locking his arms over his head as they rained punches down on him.

He wasn't screaming, and that was perhaps the most unnerving thing of all. He didn't make a sound.

The men grunted with the exertion, they didn't hear me, didn't see me, and from the floor I grabbed the lid of a trash can. With all the strength I possessed I hurled it sideways like a frisbee. The sound of that thing connecting with the back of a man's head reminded me of church days in Greenleaf. Like a bell. A goddam bell!

The sound reverberated down that alleyway.

The middle man went down, his hands clutching the back of his damaged skull.

The other two turned, shock evident on their red drunken faces, and then they came for me, hulking and menacing like cartoon villains.

I thought this was it. This is the moment I die. This is when it goes really ugly and they kick the living crap out of me, and *Oh Lord Jesus Christ Almighty, Mary Mother of God* . . .

Nathan came up behind them like a shadow.

He seemed overpowering, towering like a redwood, and I saw the bar in his hand, heavy like steel or iron, three, perhaps four feet in length, and when it came sweeping sideways towards the two men that approached me I knew that this was going to be something more than a knock-down drag-out fight in some alleyway somewhere. This was getting to be life and death.

I knew the blow was crippling even as I heard it. The force drove the man on my left into the second man with such velocity that they both careened into the wall. The second man's head connected with the lower rungs of a suspended fire escape, and again that sound, the sound of a bell ringing, echoed clearly out into the darkness.

They went down like collapsing buildings, one over the other, and even as they lay there, even as silence suddenly filled the alleyway, we knew we were in the deepest shit imaginable.

I wondered if the man on the left was dead.

We moved then. Moved like lightning.

Nathan went back the way he'd come to the end of the alleyway. With one leap he seemed to leave the ground and gain the top of the wall. He perched there like Spiderman, beckoned for me to get a move on, and then I could feel myself being dragged upwards and over the top. We dropped like thieves into the lee of the wall, and pausing there for no more than a few seconds I could only sense the pressure, the sweat that covered my body, my heart running away with itself. Though I would find a bruise the color of raw steak covering much of the lower half of my back when I woke the next day, in that moment I felt nothing. The panic had gone, the terror was a vague and distant memory, and all I felt was a sense of *aliveness* that was new.

I looked at Nathan. His eyes were wide, his expression one of tense concentration, and then he was moving, me beside him, the pair of us hurrying back across Oak Street towards the room we shared.

My naïveté surprised Nathan.

'Leave?' I'd asked him once we were inside.

'Hell, Danny, you understand what happened here? That guy could be dead. Least of all he's gonna have half his head stitched up in the Emergency Room. You think they're gonna let such a thing lie?'

I shook my head. I hesitated. 'I don't know –' I started.

Nathan looked amazed, dumbstruck.

'You don't know? You don't know *what*, Danny? You understand that we're in violation of a government Draft Notice. That's a felony at least, a goddam felony.'

I realized then it was serious. Nathan never, *never* used God's name in vain.

'We're committing an illegal act, and on top of that we've more than likely got aggravated assault, wounding, Lord only knows what . . . get wise, Danny, this isn't an adventure, this is real life, this is the most serious shit you ever got yourself into.'

'So we're leaving?' I asked.

Nathan threw up his hands in despair.

'No, Danny, we're going back down Oak Street and see those good ol' boys and see if we can't share a drink and shake hands and let bygones be bygones. Of course we're leaving. Get your shit together. We're outta here in five minutes.'

More panic . . .

I was ready in four.

We left together.

I didn't ask any more questions.

We followed the coast down through St. Augustine and Daytona Beach, and there we stayed for a day or two while we healed up. I was sure at least two of Nathan's ribs were snapped, but he said he wouldn't go to the hospital. If he went to the hospital they would require a name, some I.D., an explanation of how he'd gotten banged up so bad. We'd learned a lesson, that was all he said about it; we had learned a lesson.

Though the bruise across my back looked close to fatal I was not in a great deal of pain. I'd held up, I had done something effective to deal with the situation that night, and I felt good. I had not backed down. I had not run. I was not a coward.

'Well shit, Danny, you owed me for flooring Marty Hooper that time,' Nathan said.

We laughed a little, not too much because Nathan's chest hurt bad and laughing made it worse.

Daytona Beach was quiet, we took a room in a motel on the edge of town and no-one asked questions. We decided to stay there until Nathan was up to travelling again, and then we would go east towards Ocala and Gainesville.

We kept ourselves to ourselves, we spoke only to those we had to, and when we needed tickets or provisions only one of us went. Even on the streets we walked a few feet apart. This was something we neither discussed nor planned. It just happened, a tacit understanding that this was the way it needed to be. There were certain places where the black-white division was evident, startlingly so, and we paid it no mind. We couldn't afford either the time or the attention to concern ourselves with this. We had more important things going on.

The police seemed to be everywhere, as if special programs had been implemented in every town and suburb we entered to enlist all surrounding units in the search. Never once did I consider the sheer number of teenagers and young men across the nation who were doing just as we had done. Never once did I consider the possibility that my imagination was working overtime, that I was merely *looking* for the police, for the State Troopers, and therefore seeing them more and more. As has been so often said *It isn't paranoia if they really are out to get you.* It seemed that on every street corner and junction, in every store and parking lot, every 7–11 I entered, they were there, waiting, watching, saying nothing, just *absorbing* my presence. I felt like John Dillinger, like Babyface Nelson, and that after weeks of pursuit this would end with me seventy foot up, screaming *Top of the world, Ma!* from some gas tower along the freeway.

We left Daytona Beach on September 14th. We'd been gone a little more than two months. I had not called my ma, I couldn't face hearing her voice and lying to her. I lied in a letter, said I'd headed up towards Winston-Salem, had considered carrying on up into Virginia, but we'd see what happened. I told her Nathan was with me, that we were doing just fine, and though I was sorry to have left in such a hurry I'd felt there was opportunity and means to do something bigger with my life. I'd told her I couldn't go on working in Karl Winterson's Radio Store for the rest of my years. I knew she'd understand that. Her husband, my father, had been a railroad man all his life, and everyone knew how he should have done something with his passion for making things, his skill with wood, his natural eye. He never did, never even mentioned it, but if you got close enough you could see it in his face.

It was only later that I realized the letter would have a mark on it showing its point of origin.

I didn't mention that to Nathan, didn't tell him that my letter, my inability to face my mother, had thus erased all possibility of people believing either of us had gone north.

No, I figured telling Nathan that would do more harm than good.

Another little thing for just me and God.

I tried to speak to him of my concerns, my fears, the ever-present sense of foreboding that haunted me like my own shadow. Sometimes, when I thought those feelings were not there, I would turn and see them lingering beside me. It was not escaping the Draft that gave me these emotions, it was the sense of betrayal. I had never believed myself to be anything other than honest, straight as a die, implacable almost in my attention to those things that were right and just and equitable. Justifications and explanations aside, I believed that there was a *sense* to what was being done in Vietnam, but a sense in the principle, not the action. Perhaps it was nothing more than the result of some long-ingrained propaganda, but I believed in freedom, freedom of speech and action and belief, and the communist overthrow of territory and humanity struck me with such a sense of inequity. I did not believe for a moment that the communists would take the world, had not believed that even as the Bay of Pigs unfolded so many years before. But I did believe in a human being's right to be himself, to believe what he believed, to express his thoughts and emotions and words in whichever way he wished. It was the betrayal of this belief that hurt the most. And though I imagined that had I ever gone I would never have survived, I still felt that even those that went unwillingly, terror in their hearts, the blessings of their loved ones carried with them; even as they'd lain in some filthy ditch, their lives bleeding out from holes filled to bursting with fire and pain and hell; even as they'd grasped at some final breath . . .

even then, they'd known that they did what they were asked to do, what they had been called upon to do, and there was some sense of justice and rightness in that and that alone.

I believed then, and believe now, that there is some universal balance present in all things.

Perhaps I had cheated death, extended my life beyond its allotted time.

I recalled a story my father had once told me. A Persian merchant, visiting a soothsayer, had been told that Death would find him that day. The merchant, terrified, asked where Death would find him, and the soothsayer said that such information could not be revealed. The merchant, a man of great method and predictability, knew that today was the day he always visited the market. He rushed home, and speaking with his servant, told him he would not be going to the market as was ordinarily the case, but he would head to Baghdad. He took his fastest horse and fled towards the city, hoping he would find some place to hide in the great capital. The servant, confused, distressed by his master's behavior, himself went to the market as usual. There he saw Death, and Death approached him. The servant, horrified and perplexed, asked Death why he was approaching him. Surely it was not his day to die? Death smiled coldly, and said that he was merely surprised to see the servant here without his master, the merchant. The servant asked why, and Death – leaning close, his cool breath against the servant's face – whispered that he had an appointment that very afternoon with the merchant in Baghdad.

Death was out there looking, and he came with the faces of policemen and State Troopers, in the faces of old women watching us cross the street and pause there at the junction, in the faces of innocent children who seemed curious that a white man and a black man would walk so close together down here . . .

He came looking with all these things, and no matter how fast I could run I believed he would find me.

There appear to be brief moments during our lives when, despite all circumstance, the humanity of others shines through. It is as if the indomitability of the human spirit – at once oppressed and assaulted – nevertheless rises, a phoenix from the ashes, and we are reminded that people do care. They *really* do care.

There was one such time with Nathan. In itself it was perhaps of little significance, but it highlighted for me the fundamental difference between us. Later, many years later, I would weigh the burden of guilt I carried, and a moment such as this tipped the scales of justice so effortlessly towards Nathan Verney.

In all things I had considered myself first. In leaving Greenleaf I had so easily thought of what *I* wanted, what would become of *me*. Nathan would have left Greenleaf alone. I would not. I would not have left alone for fear of loneliness itself, but for fear of my own survival had someone else not been there to assist and protect me. This was how we differed.

I considered how events would affect me.

Nathan Verney considered the effects on others.

Where we were I cannot recall even now. There were so many places, so much traveling, and after a while the towns and suburbs blurred seamlessly, one into the other.

I remember a street however, nondescript, eminently forgettable. I recall the frontage of a grain store, that unmistakable rusty smell that emanates from the bales and bins within.

I remember standing talking to Nathan of something inconsequential.

'You wanna eat now or later?' he asked.

'Later's fine,' I replied.

He nodded, and then turned suddenly to the left as his

attention was drawn to some commotion at the end of the street.

A child on a bicycle came into view, a young girl no more than eight or nine, and she was pedalling like fury, like the devil was on her heels. Behind her, snapping at the wheels of the bicycle, was a large and ugly dog, jaws slavering, teeth snapping. A man ran behind the dog, calling its name, hollering at it to *Stay! Stay!*

The girl was terrified, her face white and drawn, her every ounce of strength pummeling at the pedals as if her very life depended on it.

Nathan flew from the bench where we had been seated, flew like the wind, and before I knew it he had raced between the girl and the dog and was standing there, his fists raised, his shoulders hunched forward.

I was reminded vividly of the moment when Nathan had faced Larry James and Marty Hooper in Benny's Soda Shop a million years before.

With the dog no more than ten feet from him Nathan released an almighty roar and started pounding his chest.

The dog almost fell over its own front legs as it came to a dead stop.

It hunkered there in the street, at first confused, and then suddenly it was down on its haunches, teeth bared once more, a guttural growl emanating from the base of its wide and muscular throat.

'Come on you motherfucker,' I heard Nathan hiss. 'Come on you ugly motherfucker . . . come get me, come get a piece of me.'

Nathan lunged forward then, suddenly, unexpectedly, and the dog, shocked beyond belief, gave out some kind of desperate whimper. It backed up one step, whimpered again, and then it turned and hightailed it down the street.

In that instant I had a vision of Larry James and Marty Hooper turning and running from Eve Chantry so many years before.

I was speechless.

And it was only in the silence that followed that I realized the girl had fallen from her bike no more than fifteen feet from where I still sat, stone-still.

I came to my feet, started towards her, but Nathan was there before me, kneeling beside her, comforting her, brushing small chips of gravel from the graze on her knee.

I watched him without a word.

Words had escaped some minutes before, and however hard I looked I could not find them.

I opened my mouth and sheer silence floated out like organdy.

Nathan had acted before I'd had a chance to think of acting.

Again, just for a moment, I felt invisible beside him.

FIFTEEN

By mid-September we were on the west coast of Florida near Apalachee Bay. We figured we'd work on the boats again, the season would run for a little while longer and then we'd decide where to go next. For the first week we slept on the beach. It was still warm, people hung out down there, folks with guitars, folks smoking weed and drinking, folks living life the way they wanted to live it. Little did we know but those years, the late 1960s, would be years people would speak of in terms of revolution, a revolution of mind and spirit, a revolution of sexual freedom and peace on earth. The people we met down there seemed worldly, the same way Linny Goldbourne had seemed to me, and we listened to the stories they told of San Francisco, Haight-Ashbury, of acid and Jimi Hendrix and Janis Joplin.

Nathan was caught up in it, perhaps even more than I, for here he seemed to find release from the strictness and discipline of his father's world. His upbringing had not been harsh, he had never gone without, but the world from which he'd come was black and white, clean, reverential and temperate.

Nathan smoked weed with these people. I did too, but I didn't smoke like Nathan. We'd work all day, break our backs in the sun, our hands shovelling fish from nets into boxes packed with ice, loading those heavy boxes onto trucks and watching them drive out to Tallahassee and Orlando. There was an endless convoy of vehicles, and the drivers would get restless waiting for their maximum load to be stowed, and we worked like crazy people. Come the end of the day we would walk down to the beach, strip our clothes off and wash in the sea, and then we would sleep for a while, sleep until the evening grew cold, and then we would light fires and wait for the others to arrive. They drove down in pickups and Volkswagen vans, guys and girls, kids even, their long flowing hair, bright clothes, bottles of sourmash and wraps of weed and this old music player that hooked right into a generator in the trunk of someone's car. We gathered in circles, and the circles became wider, the fires became brighter and somewhere beyond the point where the light reached there were couples making out. You could hear them. They sounded like free people.

Nathan was enchanted and empowered by this stuff. He learned guitar down there, half a dozen chords that's all, but with his gospel-church trained voice he could sing above the sound of the sea. His voice carried, an unearthly sound, and he proved something I had figured many years ago at high school. It was neither your color nor your looks that counted, and not a great deal to do with your personality at first: it was all to do with attention. He got their attention, he really got their attention, and there was barely a night that Nathan wouldn't be one half of a couple out there where the light didn't reach.

For a time I felt I was losing him, but he always came back, always searched me out to see how I was doing, and it was he who brought the Devereau sisters, the Devereau *twins*, back to where I sat by the fire one night towards the end of the month.

Rosalind and Emily Devereau were from somewhere in Louisiana. I never knew exactly where; but you could tell from their looks, that wild-eyed, dark-haired, bold and confident spirit that there was something about these girls that wasn't anything close to what I'd experienced before. They were not identical, but they were close, and they possessed an uncanny ability to sense what the other was feeling. They completed each other's sentences, would stop mid-flight and suddenly leave to find one another. Later, in conference, Nathan and I would discover that though we had been three hundred yards apart down the beach the two of them had gotten up simultaneously and walked in each other's direction. They did things like this, and had it not been unnerving it would have been funny.

They seemed to gravitate towards us, and though I spent more time with Emily and Nathan spent more time with Rosalind, it was almost as if it wouldn't have mattered the other way around. They were so alike in everything, almost as if you could start a conversation with one, finish it with the other, and never notice the break in between.

We took an apartment, Nathan and I, right there overlooking the beach, and though it was small, though we shared a single room with two mattresses on the floor, we really felt that there was something special to be experienced in this place. Rosalind and Emily Devereau, for the months between October 1968 and the early part of 1969, became part of our family. That's the way it felt: that we were family.

I remember a night we spent in that apartment. Rosalind and Emily had come down to the beach as they always did, and after a little while Rosalind suggested we go home, take some Thunderbird wine and hang out for a while.

We went, all too eagerly we went, and by the time we arrived Nathan had drunk half of that bottle and was laughing as Rosalind tried to waltz him down the sidewalk.

Once inside they collapsed together on the mattresses, and I watched them, happy to see Nathan free of every vestige of South Carolina and his father's world.

'You guys want some of this?' Rosalind asked. She held the bottle out towards her sister.

Emily took it, asked me to get some cups from the kitchen, and when I returned the three of them were seated back to back in an outward-facing triangle on the floor. I joined them – seated there cross-legged, Rosalind behind me, Nathan to my right, Emily to my left. I felt at ease. I felt strong-willed. I felt like I was exactly where I wanted to be, sharing my time with people whom I had chosen.

'So how long you planning on staying here?' Emily asked.

'As long as it takes,' Nathan said.

'As long as *what* takes?'

'The war.'

For a moment there was silence.

'You jumped the Draft,' Rosalind said matter-of-factly.

'We jumped the Draft,' I said, and even as I said it I imagined it was possibly the hardest thing I had ever uttered.

No-one spoke, not a word, until Nathan sort of leaned forward to reach his cup, and then he said something that surprised me more than anything I might have guessed.

'Danny made it happen,' he said.

I frowned, turned to look at him, and he smiled at me.

'There was a time many years ago,' Nathan went on. 'We were in South Carolina, our home town. The whole black-white thing was really getting itself up to speed, and we were in this soda place where the kids hung out. Some kid grabbed this girl's ass or something, some girl that Danny was sweet on . . .'

There was a smile in Nathan's voice, an underlying element of humor that was hard to miss.

'Anyhows, this kid grabbed this girl's ass . . . what was her name, Danno?'

'Sheryl Rose Bogazzi,' I said.

'Right, Sheryl Rose Bogazzi –'

'Oh come on,' Emily interjected. 'No-one's called Sheryl Rose Bogazzi.'

'Go tell Sheryl Rose that,' I said.

Rosalind laughed. 'That's like Betty Sue Windmill or Mary Joe Plankboard.'

'One of those Southern places where you grow up only to find out that your mother's really your sister, and when you reach thirteen you have to marry your grandfather,' Emily added.

'Enough already,' Nathan said. 'Anyway, you pair of crazy witches can talk . . . you came straight up out of a swamp. Mad freakin' Appalachian mountain people with snakes in the house and learnin' the Bible by heart.'

'The story,' I said, wanting more than anyone present to know what Nathan was going to say.

'Right, the story . . . so this girl gets her ass grabbed by a guy called Marty Hooper, and he had this sidekick, Larry James –'

'You sure it wasn't Cletus Knackerback and Billy Bob Dickweed?' Rosalind asked.

'I'm sure it wasn't,' Nathan said. 'Now will you pair shut the fuck up and let me finish?'

'Sorry, Nathan,' Emily said.

'Me sorry too,' Rosalind echoed.

'So Danny fronts up to these guys, all ready to get the shit kicked out of him, and I yank him back and floor the asshole.'

Nathan started laughing.

'This kid goes down like a house of cards, Danny's standing there not knowing whether to be pissed off I hit the guy or relieved he didn't get his teeth knocked out through his ass, and then someone calls me a nigger . . . just like that. Nigger he says, and silence fills up the place to bursting.'

Nathan pauses, and there is a quiet tension in the room. Four of us seated together and there isn't a sound. Not even a breath.

'And then someone else says it,' Nathan goes on. 'And someone else . . . and we hightail it out of there like someone lit our fuses.'

'So what does that have to do with dodging the Draft?' Emily asked.

Nathan smiled as he looked at me. 'You have any idea what kind of guts it took to side with a black guy like that?'

Neither Emily nor Rosalind said a word.

'Twenty, thirty kids, crazy kids, all fired up, angry . . . and Danno takes off with the only black kid there. We ran out of there and they chased us, threw stones, ready to catch us and fucking lynch us . . . and Danno runs with me all the way.'

'And what happened?' Rosalind asked.

'We were saved by the witch,' I said. 'The witch who ate her husband.'

'You what?' Emily asked.

'The witch,' Nathan said.

'There was a witch?'

Nathan laughed. 'There was indeed a witch . . . but that is a totally different story. The point is that Danno did something that no-one else did. He stuck by me when everything told him he shouldn't have . . . and that taught me something. Taught me that you do what you think is right no matter what anyone thinks.'

Nathan turned and looked at me. He didn't smile; he just looked at me. I felt he could see right through me, right through to the lie that sat inside me like a tumor. Maybe that time I had done what I'd believed was right, perhaps out of fear, out of self-preservation, or just out of sheer terror. That time. But this time was different. This time I had come because I didn't have the courage to say no.

I would think back in years to come, think back on all that was said and done in Florida, and I would see that there I found my feet, my balance, my *self*.

The Devereau sisters were a special breed of person, they were wise and deep and at once passionate and irresponsible. Never in my life would I meet people so spontaneous and impulsive. They wrote poetry together, poetry for us, and then they would have Nathan play guitar while they sang love songs to us. Love songs to me and Nathan Verney. And sex. There was so much sex. We stayed with the same partners, always the same, but there were moments when the four of us would lie down on those mattresses, mattresses that had been pushed closer together by either Emily or Rosalind, and somewhere in the midst of our passion I would catch a glimpse of Nathan, and he would look upwards, and they were there, these sisters, and though we were there in body they were looking at one another. Like they were on the same spiritual wavelength, feeding off one another's arousal and intimacy, and we just happened to be there to appreciate the closeness these girls felt.

It was not perverse, it wasn't ugly or degraded. It was none of these things. It transcended the physical, it entered the realm of nirvana and the mountains of the moon. And though sometimes I would lie close to Emily and in some small way wish it had been Caroline, or Linny, I did my best not to think of such things. I did my best to live for that moment, and that moment alone. In my mind the past was like a collage of sounds and faces and colors, of the love I'd felt for Caroline and Linny, of betrayal and loss.

This, now, was a time I would never forget.

A time of learning, of self-discovery, and more than everything, of promise.

The Devereau sisters left in the latter part of January 1969. There were no tears, no regrets, no recriminations, no sense of loss even. They had come, they had visited, they were leaving. They intended to return to Louisiana, their family, their previous lives perhaps, and Nathan and I felt nothing as we watched them go.

I remember turning towards him as the bus took a bend in the road and disappeared, and his face was blank, expressionless, neither happy nor sad nor anything else identifiable.

'Gone,' he said quietly.

'Gone,' I replied.

We turned together and walked back the way we'd come.

We didn't speak of them again.

Like it had all been a dream.

And later that same day Nathan turned to me and asked, 'You ever fall in love, Danny?'

I smiled. 'Helluva question, Nate.'

'So?' he prompted, and I leaned back and looked at him, feeling strangely awkward.

Nathan was my closest friend, had always been, ever since that day beside Lake Marion and the baked ham sandwich, but in all that time I could not recall him ever having asked me such a close-to-the-heart question.

Nathan Verney was a rock, an anchor, an island. He appeared distant, uncommunicative perhaps, and yet behind that wall beat a heart so large it could have swallowed the world.

'I've been in love, yes,' I replied.

'Tell me.'

I shrugged my shoulders. 'What's there to tell?'

'How it is, what it feels like, how you know . . .'

'You're not serious?'

'As I'll ever be,' he said.

And there was something in his eyes, something in his entire being that told me just how serious, that he really wanted an answer to his question.

'I don't understand –' I began.

'I'm here,' he said. 'I've left my home, my folks, everything I've known throughout my life. I'm here because I don't want to die right now . . . and seeing as how things have been going recently I don't know that I stand a much better chance down here than I would in some godforsaken jungle in the middle of nowhere. I've been thinking about what makes a life matter, about important things, things like family and friends and having something to believe in. I've thought about faith and God, all the things my father told me as I was growing up . . . and I can't say that any of them are as important as loving someone, being loved by someone, and knowing that whatever might happen you'll always be there for one another . . .'

Nathan Verney turned and looked at me.

I believed, just for a second, that there were tears in his eyes.

'When I die, Daniel . . . when I die I want to be able to say that I loved someone . . .'

I was quiet for a time, and then I started to speak, and words came from my mouth that I never knew I possessed.

'There was Caroline,' I said. 'You remember Caroline Lanafeuille?'

Nathan smiled and nodded.

'I loved her as much as I imagined anyone could love anyone. She was my first, the very first one, and there was something truly amazing about how she made me feel.'

Nathan shifted his weight from one leg to the other and watched me intently.

'She made me feel strong . . . strong and passionate. She'd laugh at things I said, not because they were stupid, you know? But because they actually just made her laugh. She stood close to me, just stood close sometimes and said nothing, and the way she did that made me feel like the most important person in the world.'

I paused for a moment, and saw that Nathan had never felt such a thing.

'And then there was Linny Goldbourne . . . and Linny was like a firework, a mad firework going off inside your head.'

I smiled. I laughed.

'She would rush at you with everything she had and

there was something about her that made you feel as though nothing else in the world mattered while she was around. She made me feel loved, a different way than Caroline . . . not better, just different. I loved Caroline, but I don't believe she loved me the same. But with Linny that love came back threefold, almost overwhelming in some way, and it was addictive . . . like a drug.'

I hesitated, and in hesitating I realized I was talking of things I no longer felt. For a moment a strange sense of panic overtook me, of loneliness, a fear that having felt that way twice in my life would be all I would ever receive. I believed – just for a second – that I would never have the chance to love like that again.

In my throat a fist had swollen and strangled any other words I might have found.

'I want –' Nathan said quietly.

I looked up.

'One day . . . I want to feel something like that, Danny.'

In that moment I believed that Nathan Verney was more important than anything in the world, more important than anyone . . . and I couldn't find a single, solitary word to give him.

If I had known how that moment would haunt me later I would have told him anything. But I wasn't to know, and so it did haunt me, followed me like a ghost.

Followed both of us, resolutely, irrevocably, each to our own deaths.

Later he seemed quiet, distant and withdrawn.

'You okay?' I asked him.

He turned, smiled as if in philosophical resignation, and asked me a question.

'What is it that you want, Danny?'

I was a little taken aback. 'Want? How d'you mean?'

'Out of life. What do you want out of your life?'

I shook my head. 'Can't say I've thought a great deal about it.'

Nathan smiled. 'Everyone thinks about it, Danny ... about being happy, about what might make them happy.'

'Happiness,' I asked. 'What the hell is that when it's at home?'

Nathan shrugged. 'My father says it's faith ... faith is happiness.'

'But he's a minister ... of course he's gonna say that.'

Nathan shook his head. 'Didn't mean it like that. Not faith in God or anything, just faith.'

I was puzzled.

'Faith in something,' Nathan went on, as if talking to himself. 'Faith in yourself even. Having such a strong belief in something that it really is the most important thing in your life.'

'I don't know that I have ever really believed in something that strongly,' I said.

Nathan looked at me. 'You believed enough in what we were doing to leave home,' he said.

Believed enough in you, I thought to myself, but didn't say it. Instead I said, 'Yes, I believed enough in that.'

'And what *was* that?' he asked. 'What was it that we believed in?'

'Life?' I asked, rhetorically almost.

'Maybe,' Nathan replied.

He was quiet for a moment.

'But only our own,' he added after a while. 'Believed only in our own lives, not the lives of others.'

'I don't get you.'

'What about my folks, what about your ma ... what do they think about this?'

'They think we've gone to find work.'

Nathan shook his head. 'You're kidding yourself, Danny. They know why we left. They know exactly why we left.'

'You figure?'

'I figure.'

'Well, if they know that we haven't gone north then I don't know what they think.'

Nathan turned, closed his eyes for a second. 'They think that we have betrayed them, betrayed our country . . . and they have lost their faith in *us*.'

I didn't know what to say.

'And therefore we have taken away their happiness.'

'But they would be more unhappy if we'd gone out there and been killed,' I said.

'Would they?'

'Of course they would,' I retorted.

'You're sure?'

I didn't reply. Nathan was unnerving me. Guilt was invading my thoughts.

'People get over losing their friends, their family,' he said. 'Somehow they always recover. And it's never the things that people have done that they regret, it's only the things they haven't done. I know my father will think of all the things he never said to me, all the times he could have asked me what I felt about the war, about being an American, about serving my country, and he will tear himself to pieces over it. If I'd gone, if I'd gone out there and been killed, then at least he would have had time to grieve for me, to convince himself that I had done the right thing. Now he has no such chance. All he knows is that his son didn't face up to his responsibilities. That is something he will never forgive himself for.'

'You really believe that?'

Nathan nodded. 'I do.'

I looked away. I felt such pain inside. I thought of my mother, of how my father might have felt had he been alive.

'So we took away their faith,' Nathan said. 'And that, of all things, is possibly the worst of all.'

I closed my eyes. I wanted to cry. Not for me, not for

Nathan or Caroline Lanafeuille or Linny Goldbourne, not for my mother.

I wanted to cry for myself.

Because I had no faith.

I recognized later how much Nathan had changed. Where he'd once been almost too considerate he became single-minded and stubborn. Where he'd once possessed the patience of Job he had learned the value of acting quickly, decisively, and taken it to the extreme. Where he'd once allowed that perhaps I had some choice in the direction we'd take, he now treated anything I might have to say merely as a test of his will to execute what he wanted.

And so it was in March of '69 that we were moving again, further east, out towards Panama City and Pensacola.

I did not argue, I had learned already the pointlessness of such a venture, and I allowed Nathan to lead the way. We had some money now, money we had worked for during our months near Apalachee Bay and, at least on a physical level, I was not concerned for our survival and well-being.

Emotionally, spiritually, I was not so sure.

I thought often of my mother. We had been gone seven months, and in all that time the only communication she had received from me was a single letter containing a multiple of lies. This was not how I had treated her before, certainly not how I'd have wished to be treated myself, and though I spoke often with Nathan of contacting her, he remained resolute. We had left. We were not going back. This was final.

I conceded defeat following the third or fourth attempt to resolve this, and it was soon after my concession that he told me we should move on, that we were becoming settled, becoming familiar.

'Too many people know our names,' he said. 'Someone comes down this way looking for us and there are a hundred or more people who know us by name and face.

You forget too quickly, Danny. You forget we're still on the run.'

And though I could have questioned and challenged him I did not.

He *had* changed, there was something inside of him, something our recent experiences had released, and that something held shadows and dark aspects that I did not wish to test.

Had I known then what would occur I would have left him alone, let him go wherever he wanted to go. I could have stayed, could have remained right where I was, and perhaps enjoyed my freedom right through until the war was over. But Nathan was stronger than me, his personality had always held sway over our relationship, and I was afraid of being alone. Nathan Verney was the one man who knew where I had come from, why I was running, and why I didn't wish to be found. With such a secret it was easier to be with someone who knew – even though that someone might be a little crazy – rather than alone. I believed that then, perhaps still do. But now my belief is tempered with hindsight, and I see all the things I could have done and said that might have changed the outcome. Who knows? I don't, and now I don't care to know. It was what it was, I saw what I saw, and what I believed then is not what I believe now. I have changed more than I could have imagined possible, and part of that change was the result of knowing Nathan Verney, following his lead, trusting him to take care of what we had and to ensure we came to no harm. I trusted him to do that much. If nothing else, I trusted him with that.

So we went. We closed out our apartment, packed what we could carry into shoulder bags, and we moved on. We did not return to say goodbye to anyone. Again that was Nathan's choice. He said people would ask questions, and unless we worked out what we were going to say it would become awkward and complex, and he really couldn't be

197

doing with the hassle. So we would just go. Disappear. For my part, I felt our sudden disappearance would raise suspicion, that someone might think we had drowned, that a report might be filed, and then there would be questions. But I said nothing. Again I said nothing, and I could see from Nathan's expression, could hear in the tone of his voice, that he had made his decision and I either went along with it or left.

And so I went, like a child, like a lamb, and Nathan Verney – a good man, a preacher's son – led us all the way to Hell.

SIXTEEN

When I think of the events that appear to have carried me here, I think again of Robert Schembri and the days he spoke to me in August of 1972. I think of a man who wove his threads of conspiracy into the most fantastic and brightly-colored quilt.

I believe I was the sleeper, the fall guy, in some minor conspiracy of my own.

I was no Lee Harvey Oswald, no James Earl Ray, but in the smaller scheme of things I had a part to play and I played it well. I walked into it like a deaf, dumb and blind kid.

Nathan and I used to talk politics, and though we never really either agreed or disagreed on anything specific we did concur that Nixon was dangerous. January 20th 1969 had seen him inaugurated as President of the United States. Finally he had achieved the position he'd been working towards since the early 1940s. We believed that a committed and criminal fraternity of judges and lawyers and international financiers had supported Nixon throughout his political career, but it was Robert Schembri, the man who'd sat and talked to me about Kennedy, who gave me a far greater understanding.

Schembri had spoken to me over three meal periods, always with that same distant look in his eyes, that feeling that I could have been anyone at all, but simultaneously the sense that here I was listening to something valuable enough never to miss a word. Like Schembri himself said: *a channel from the gods.*

I seem to recall it was a Tuesday, the second day I

searched him out in the mess hall at Sumter. Craning my neck across the hundreds of seated men, I saw him at his usual corner table. I took my food and made a beeline for him, sat down, and waited patiently while he arranged his food in neat concentric circles. First the rice, then peas, and finally a neat pile of chicken pieces in the center. When he was done he looked right at me, just for a moment, as if simply to acknowledge I was there, and then he looked down and started talking. Momentarily his speech would slow, his voice become quieter, and not wishing to interrupt his flow I found myself leaning ever closer to hear every word that came from his lips.

'In 1960, the evening before the New Hampshire primary,' Robert Schembri began, 'Frank Sinatra introduced a girl called Judith Exner to John Kennedy. A few weeks after that Mister Sinatra introduced the same girl to Sam Giancana, the Chicago Mafia boss. This girl continued an affair simultaneously with the most powerful mobster in America and the most powerful political leader in the world. Giancana had been hired by a former FBI and CIA operative called Robert Maheu to form up assassination teams to go after Castro. Maheu told Giancana that wealthy Cuban exiles were behind this thing, that that's where the money would come from, but the money came directly from the CIA. Giancana put his L.A. lieutenant, Johnny Roselli, in charge of the hit squads.

'In 1978, when the House Select Committee questioned him, Roselli said that those teams were trained up for the Kennedy assassination as well. Shortly after his testimony his body was found floating in an oil drum off the Florida coast. Giancana never got a chance to testify. He was shot in Chicago. One point that Roselli made was that the Warren Commission never questioned the possibility that there were more than three shots fired at Kennedy. They listened to the eyewitnesses, the eyewitnesses heard only three shots, and they took that as gospel . . .'

Schembri looked up at me. 'You payin' attention, kid?'

I nodded a yes.

'Sure as shit hope so . . . you only get this stuff once, you understand . . . and we don't get into any kind of question and answer period later, eh?'

I shook my head. Okay.

Schembri nodded, spooned another mound of rice and peas into his mouth and seemed to swallow without chewing.

'Roselli intimated that there were up to three different assassination teams in Dallas that day, and that many more shots were fired, the majority of them with silenced weapons. Reports indicated from inspection of the road around the vehicle, from the bodywork of the vehicle itself, that a great many more than three bullets were aimed at JFK.'

Schembri smiled knowingly, held up his spoon and moved it to emphasize each word he was saying.

'And now there's Nixon. Nixon's presidency was planned meticulously. Military fanatics and industrialists were upset with Kennedy, upset that he didn't go to war with the Soviet Union. The publisher of the *Dallas News*, a known militant paper, told Kennedy that America needed a man on horseback to lead the nation, that too many people in Texas and the Southwest saw him as riding Caroline's tricycle.'

He smiled sardonically.

'Kennedy said he wanted to splinter the CIA into a thousand pieces and scatter it to the wind. Soon after he said that he was killed. After his death the South-East Asian situation escalated with no visible provocation. John Foster Dulles, ex-Secretary of State, still held phenomenal power in this Warfare State they had created, and his brother Alan was head of OSS. With his brother protecting him from any unpleasant consequences, Alan Dulles went ahead to satisfy the military-industrial demands of the Far Right. Alan

Dulles was the same guy who'd run Operation Paperclip towards the end of the Second World War. He'd been posted in Switzerland, his function to round up and assist German specialists in all the fields of armaments and military production. Between 1945 and 1952 they brought six hundred and forty-two German and foreign specialists – scientists and the like – and their families into the U.S. and placed them in senior positions within aerospace programs, war industries, armaments manufacture and defense systems. In 1945 ex-General Reinhard Gehlen joined forces with the OSS. Gehlen was placed in charge of wartime intelligence for Foreign Armies East. Gehlen met with the main players at the Pentagon itself – Hoover, Dulles, some others. That affiliation, Gehlen's intelligence network and the OSS, became what is now known as the CIA.'

Schembri lowered his spoon and leaned towards me. 'You didn't know this shit did you?' he whispered.

I shook my head.

'Tomorrow I'll tell you about the fucking Ku Klux Klan, same folks you collided with down in Carolina, eh?'

I leaned closer. 'Tell me . . . tell me now.'

But my informant leaned back slightly, and again smiled, that wry knowing smile that made you feel he knew everything there was to know in the world, and all of it was true.

'And so there you had it . . . the Nazi experts in clandestine assassinations and reversal of judicial proceedings became the tutors for Dulles and Richard Helms. These were the people who invented the American-Soviet conflict and the Cold War.'

I felt frustration for a moment, a sense of agitation. 'What about the Ku Klux Klan?' I asked. 'Tell me what you know about that.'

Schembri again spooned in a mouthful of food and swallowed it without chewing. He looked at me without seeing me.

'And our friend Nixon . . . he applied to the FBI after graduating from law school. They never replied to him. With the outbreak of World War Two he requested sea duty and was assigned to the South Pacific Combat Air Transport Command. He was out there fifteen months and then he was posted to Alameda, California with Fleet Air Wing 8 under special orders from the Navy Bureau of Aeronautics. His job was to wind up active contracts with aircraft firms such as Bell and Glenn Martin. Those same six hundred and forty-two scientists were coming in at this time, and with a healthy donation from the Guggenheim Foundation they secured a hundred and sixty acres and the medieval castle built by the financier Jay Gould at Sands Point on Long Island.

'Those German and foreign scientists were stationed there under the auspices of the Navy's Office of Research & Inventions. And the American states that were most likely to benefit from this influx of German scientific brilliance were those in the South and Southwest. The segregated, racist states were fuelled by propaganda machines funded by those same departments, and it was in those states that the majority of the military-industrial production facilities were based.

'Nixon himself was in New York, wondering where he would go career-wise. He decided to move to Maryland, and coincidental with his move an advertisement appeared in twenty-six different newspapers. The ad asked for a Congressman candidate, no previous political experience, no political strings or obligations, but with a few ideas for betterment of the country. Herman Perry, Vice-President of the Bank of America, called Richard Nixon and asked if he was a Republican, and if he was available.'

Schembri nodded as if to grant Papal indulgence to his statement.

'Nixon was a creation of some very interested people, a creation that was born as an idea by the Committee of One

Hundred Men in California in August of 1945, and wound up here, the early 1970s, with the realization that Nixon is a fucking loon and he needs to disappear quietly.'

Schembri smiled and again emphasized his words with his spoon.

'And I'll tell you something else, kid . . . if they hadn't shot Kennedy back then in '63, if they'd gotten him out through the legal process or perhaps exposed his sexual history and predilection, they would have shot Nixon instead of cooking up this bullshit longwinded Watergate fiasco. They can't shoot Nixon, they wish they could, but even they figure they might have a hard time pulling it off twice. Anyway, Nixon's crazy enough to do himself in if someone doesn't get there first.'

Suddenly there was a commotion behind us. I turned to see the majority of General Populace making its way towards the exits. The end of meal bell had sounded and I hadn't noticed. My own food sat untouched in front of me. I snatched a piece of bread, folded it, stuffed as much chicken as I could between the two halves and buried it in my pocket.

'They're all a bunch of crazies, kid . . . and you ran foul of a very small corner of that world . . . you and your man Goldbourne, and all that shit that went down with Jack Kennedy's brother. Tomorrow,' Schembri said, 'I'll tell you all about that tomorrow.'

He winked knowingly, put one last spoonful of rice into his mouth, and then he stood and waited for the guard to come down and take him to his cell.

That move in March of '69, the journey we took out to Panama City and Pensacola, was really the beginning of the end.

If I try to collapse this thing into one statement, like trying to synthesize the extent and scope of my life into one paragraph, it is really about nothing more than a friendship. My friendship with Nathan Verney was really the beginning and end of everything. It was with Nathan Verney that I discovered the world, and I cannot think of any significant event that occurred prior to his death that we didn't share. It was always the two of us. From six to twenty-four years old we ran parallel lives, and though one or other would veer momentarily to the left or right, perhaps pause or slow or miss a step, there would always be that moment a little way up the line where we would coincide once more.

Truth be known, it would have been difficult to create a life after Nathan's death. With him gone it was perhaps simpler to just vanish into the American judicial and criminal system, to become a non-person, to disappear from the eyes and minds of the world. That's what I had done, and sometimes I would wonder if I hadn't *wanted* it that way.

There have been times when I have tried to imagine what it would have been like to grow old, to sit on some porch stoop or verandah, to recount tales of Eve Chantry, of Sheryl Rose Bogazzi, of Caroline Lanafeuille and Linny Goldbourne, of Marty Hooper and Larry James; to talk of the day the Army came to Greenleaf, of Reverend Verney and the day Kennedy died; to reminisce about the baked ham sandwich by Lake Marion where the smell was like the flowers and the fish and the trees, and summer mimosa down near Nine Mile Road, and something like pecan pie and vanilla soda all wrapped up in a basket of new-mown grass.

I have *tried* to imagine.

But I cannot imagine any of it without Nathan beside me.

Truth be told, I don't *want* to imagine without Nathan.

We were never brothers, we were more than that, for in the same way that I believed so hard that he'd died for me, I try now to convince myself that my death will serve some other purpose, redress some universal imbalance perhaps.

It was never meant to be this way, I know that much, but at the time it all seemed so innocent and simple and magical.

Smoke and mirrors, Nathan would say whenever he felt there was something he didn't understand, something we weren't being told, something that didn't make sense.

Well, the smoke and mirrors were there, and we, in our passion, our naïveté and our desire to really live, walked in between them.

One of us lived to speak of it.

And one of us . . . well, one of us just disappeared.

SEVENTEEN

I knew from the moment we arrived that Panama City was a mistake.

Father John would ask me what I meant when I told him that later, and I would be vague and uncertain. Sometimes you just *know*, I would tell him, an intuition, a sixth sense, call it what you will, sometimes you just *know*.

Until Panama City we had stayed in smaller places, towns or suburbs, but here we were colliding with the real world once more. Seemed to me that as soon as we arrived we were treated with suspicion and curiosity. Nathan said I'd smoked too much weed and gotten paranoid, but I didn't believe that to be the case. I felt people were looking, watching us, wondering what the black guy was doing with the white guy and vice versa. Nathan had grown his hair, he wore a headband, his clothes were a mixture of things we had traded and bought from the beach people in Apalachee, and in Panama City he stood out like Hendrix at a Methodist Chapter. I warned him, told him to dress down, to be a little less conspicuous, but Nathan used words like *square* and *off-track*. He didn't listen, he was of a mind to be what he wanted to be, and when he was in such a mood there was no purpose in arguing.

'The problem with you,' he said, 'is that you're always anticipating trouble. You go looking for trouble and it'll find you.'

'But I don't go inviting it,' I replied. 'There's a difference between being aware and just being fucking obvious.'

He smiled like he knew best.

He'd started doing that, the *leave it to me* routine, and it pissed me off.

'Look, Danny, you gotta understand something about people. People don't naturally want to upset their own lives. They want everything plain and simple and straight-forward. The ones who start trouble only start it because they figured you were starting first . . .'

'That is so fucking naïve, Nathan.'

Nathan laughed. 'Naïve? You're calling me naïve?'

It was worded as a question, but I understood the intention.

'You seem all set to create a problem when there isn't one,' he went on. 'There are times when I really don't get where you're comin' from.'

'Same place as you,' I replied.

'Yeah, right,' he stated, his tone sharp and sarcastic.

I wanted to tell him that I had only come along because of him, that had he left me to my own devices I would still be in Greenleaf, still be right there at Karl Winterson's Radio Store earning some money and minding my own business. I didn't say it, it was weak and feeble-minded, and if there was one thing I believed this escape had taught me it was that there was no place for weakness. Indecision was what had started the war in Vietnam; indecision was back of all the dead bodies that lay burned and black and without identity in some place that was once a country; indecision was what had brought me out here with Nathan. Had I been there again, back home when he came down the path with the letter, I would have told him *No, you make your own way now. I have a life here, perhaps not a great deal as far as lives go, but I have time.* And indecision was the cause of losing both Caroline and Linny.

I felt my fists clenching and unclenching as he spoke.

'You ever figure out how to have an original thought you let me know,' Nathan said, an unnecessary and vicious comment.

I wanted to slug him upside the head; I bit my tongue and said nothing.

There was silence for some time, stilted and awkward, but eventually he turned and smiled at me.

'Figure that's enough arguing for this week,' he said.

I nodded. 'Enough,' I replied.

'Don't want to fight with you, Danny, but hell, man, you gotta relax a little, okay?'

I nodded in agreement, but back of the agreement there was no feeling. I let it slide, but even as I watched that ghost depart I believed that a time would come when Nathan Verney would have to stand down against me. I vowed there would be.

'Truce,' he added.

'Truce,' I said.

I found work easily, warehouse labor, simple, basic-wage stuff. Nathan tried to get work at the same place and they didn't want to know. He said it was his color, I said it was his attitude. He said *You go be a lowly Uncle Tom nigger boy and see how it feels*.

I left him alone for some time and he came back to battery. He had me cut his hair, he bought some straight pants, white tee-shirts, a denim jacket. Next day he got a job unloading dead chickens at a factory on the outskirts. There was a little community, ten or fifteen black guys, and come the end of the day I'd walk over there and watch them playing craps. They didn't seem bothered by me, a single white guy. They thought I was retarded or somesuch and left me alone. No white boy in their right mind would go down there and hang out.

Nathan eased up a little, he made some friends, he didn't smoke weed or drink too much, and within two weeks we had a small place on Rosemont Street, a couple of rooms over a laundromat. Rent was low, it was close enough to where we worked for both of us to walk, and we figured maybe we could hang out there until the war was done.

I thought once again of calling my ma, writing at least, but still the thought of how it might affect her worried me. I knew she would want me to go back, just for a little while perhaps, just to visit. I knew I couldn't do that. They'd be onto us within hours. Someone in Greenleaf would see me, that someone would say something, and before I knew it someone else would have made a call and it would all be over. I think I believed the war couldn't go on for much longer. I think I fooled myself every which way I could.

So I didn't call. I kept my mouth shut, kept my head down, and we worked until we could afford a car. It was some beat-up piece of shit but it went, and for the first time since we'd left Greenleaf we felt as if we had arrived somewhere. We were no longer the vagrants, the hobos – we had an apartment on Rosemont, a car, some money in our pockets. And it was that attitude, that sense of confidence, that started the trouble.

It was the end of June. America was all aflame about the Space Program, that we would be the first to land a man on the moon. It had been three months since we'd left Apalachee, almost six months since the Devereau sisters had graced our lives with their bizarre Louisiana magic.

Our thoughts turned to girls.

Like moths to a flame.

It was a Saturday night, between us we carried more than a hundred dollars, and we drove out towards the south side of the city. Here were the bars, the nightclubs, the gambling joints, the brothels. We made a deal: if we hadn't both connected with someone by midnight then we'd take half of whatever money we might have left over and go pay to get laid.

It seemed a good plan, a simple plan, and a plan that rolled out just fine and dandy until we hit Ramone's Retreat on Wintergreen and Macey.

I sensed no alarm when we entered. It was perhaps the fourth or fifth joint we'd drunk in that night, and though there were no blacks inside that wasn't something I even noticed until afterwards.

We played pool. Nathan's game had much improved and his playing wasn't the thing that prompted a reaction; his color was.

Leaning against the bar was a group of three men. Later I would recognize that something in their faces was similar to that of Mr. West at Sumter. They possessed dark aspects, shadows where shadows should not have been, and it was these three who said the thing that started the trouble.

As Nathan passed ahead of them to gain the far side of the table and line his shot, the center man made a sound like a pig. It was a brief snort. Like someone clearing their throat. Nothing more than that.

Nathan merely glanced towards him. Just for a second. Less than a second. Half a second.

But that was enough to prompt a question.

Why was Nathan looking at him?

What did he want?

Was there something he wanted to say?

Nathan merely smiled and nodded.

Was Nathan now laughing at them?

Was there something funny Nathan had on his mind?

And they called him *Boy*, like *Hey boy, you got something funny to say?*

We had been here before – both of us – and this particular place was not somewhere we wished to visit again.

Nathan looked towards me. He glanced quickly to the left indicating the door, and then he gently laid down his cue and started to walk. He didn't pick up his jacket, left his glass there on the edge of the pool table, and though he was quiet and slow and nonchalant it was still very obvious that he had every intention of leaving the bar without another word passing between him and the group that had challenged him.

And they knew it.

Knew it instantly.

The center one picked up the cue.

He said something which was indistinguishable among the grunts from the other two.

'Go!' Nathan hissed, and without any further prompting I ran for the door.

Nathan was beside me, heel-to-toe, and we burst out through that door and started down the street. I caught an image of him as he flew past me – not the young, strong man he now was, but a small kid with jug-handle ears. We were running from the baying mob at Benny's, we were running towards the witch.

My heart thundering like an interstate hauler, my insides cool and loose, I barreled down the sidewalk, the sound of raised angry voices behind us.

'Faster!' Nathan was shouting. 'Go faster, Danny,' and it was only then that I realized the trouble we had collided with was not staying put.

The sound of feet, a door slamming shut, and then an engine . . . a car engine.

'Motherfuckers,' Nathan hissed, and before the word had barely left his lips the lights of the car illuminated us against the night.

'Oooh shee-it!' I remembered screaming, and even as I tried to turn the corner at the end of the street I collided with the wall. I felt the skin had been torn from my shoulder beneath my jacket.

The sound of the engine was louder, roaring in my ears, and then I could hear the sound of their voices beneath that.

Fucking nigger-lover! The voice screamed. *Fucking niggeeer-looover!*

I knew we were done for when I turned the next corner.

A dead-end. We'd run right into a dead-end. The car came upon us, the headlights brilliant, and I turned to see Nathan backed up against the wall, his eyes wide, his mouth open in an expression of frozen terror.

I started to scream. I don't know what, but hell I started to scream.

The car came forward, backing us even further into the cul-de-sac, and even as it slowed the first man came out of the passenger side brandishing a pool cue.

'Fucking nigger and his nigger-loving buddy,' he said, and faster than either of us could react he lurched forward and brought the cue down over his head onto Nathan's back.

Nathan didn't go down but he arched forward and howled in agony.

I made a run down the side of the car, but the driver jerked open the door and floored me. He floored me with a single roundhouse to the side of the head.

I'd felt that before, back there in Benny's. Then it had been for the honor of Sheryl Rose Bogazzi. Now it was for my life.

I tasted blood in my mouth. I could hear nothing but a rushing tide in my head, beneath that an insistent squealing that neither fluctuated in tone or pitch.

I tried to get up. A foot came from somewhere, a foot encased in a heavy work boot, and that boot seemed to drive a hole the size of California through my stomach and chest.

I believed, I *really* believed, that I was going to die.

I remember wondering then if there had been anything that day that had been an omen, a portent of what would happen, and then my attention was snatched from wherever I had put it by the sound of Nathan screaming.

There were two of them beating on him, the man who'd come first from the car, and the third man from the rear. The passenger still held the pool cue, and with the heavier end he was just whipping Nathan across the back and shoulders. Nathan was curled up like an embryo, howling excruciatingly with every collision of that cue, and as I tried to stand I felt every color and sound imaginable rush through my head like a tidal wave of broken glass.

And then Nathan fell silent.

All I could hear was the labored breathing of the two men standing over him. The one who had floored me had stepped over me and joined his buddies at the end of the passageway.

You think he's dead?

Fuck knows.

Let's get 'em the fuck outta here.

Where d'ya wanna take 'em?

Fuck knows . . . any place, far as you can get.

You go get your car.

Fuck it, you go get yours . . . I ain't havin' no nigger bleed all over my upholstery.

I think I went then.

Lost it completely.

There was a sound like a freight train grinding to a halt on a broken rail line somewhere behind my ears. I remember staggering to my feet, gasping for breath, and even as I stood, even as I raised my arm to hurl it I felt blackness rushing towards me.

And then there was nothing.

For a long time there was absolutely nothing at all.

And then I could smell something. Something bad. Smelled like someone had eaten a dead raccoon and thrown it up over my clothes. I could feel something cool and moist on my hands. And that smell. Never smelled anything so bad in my life.

When I moved I heard sounds like rustling paper, something skidding beneath my foot, something solid and unforgiving, and as I raised my arm and stretched it I felt a cool metal surface.

It was dark, but there was also the sound of cars somewhere.

I tried to sit up. I felt like a bridge had fallen on me. I closed my eyes and strained to move. There was no traction, nothing to grab onto, and in my fumbling and groping there in the darkness I felt my hand brush across something.

It was Nathan's hair.

I struggled again, somehow managing to maneuver myself into a semi-seated position. I raised my hand, and again found a cool metal surface, something that didn't resist me as I pushed upwards. With every ounce of strength I possessed I heaved upwards, the surface seemed to rush away from me, and suddenly my eyes were almost blown out the back of my head by the daylight.

We were inside something.

It took a minute or two for my eyes to become accustomed to the light, and then I looked downwards.

Garbage, rotten, stinking, infested with mould and shit and Christ only knew what. We'd been thrown into a garbage dumpster.

I remember cursing and swearing, retching even, and then I tried to rouse Nathan.

There was blood all over his eyes and nose and the upper part of his head. I grabbed his arm, pulled it, shook him, shouted his name – *Nathan! Nathan! Nathan!* – but there was nothing.

For a little while I thought he was dead.

I grabbed his wrist, and pressing there against the artery I could feel a weak pulse.

I knew then, knew with greater certainty than anything I'd known before, that if I didn't get him to a hospital he would die.

Nothing else was important then. Not our identities,

where we'd come from, how we'd ended up in a garbage dumpster in Panama City . . . none of these things were relevant or significant. If I didn't find medical help Nathan would be dead. I came up out of that dumpster like a crazy man, and within minutes I had found a phone, called Emergency, and there was a medic unit on its way.

I sat there on the side of the road, stinking and bleeding, crap in my hair, in my shoes, and I watched the waves of red and black fighting with my consciousness until I heard voices around me. I looked up and saw a man inside the dumpster trying to help Nathan out and onto a stretcher, and everything was washed out and vague, and the sound of the cars sounded like the coastline up around Apalachee when you'd smoked too much weed and Emily Devereau was trying to get your shirt off and laughing so much you thought you'd spontaneously combust right there on the sand . . .

And then there was nothing once more.

The most appreciated and welcome nothing I'd ever known.

They wanted names, home towns, dates of birth, all manner of things. They wanted to know where we'd come from, why we'd been beaten up. They wanted to know if we'd beaten each other up and gotten into the dumpster to sleep it off. They wanted to know my address, my Social Security number, my mother's and father's names, they wanted to know who to call and when they would be there and if we'd be willing to make a statement to the police and look at some mugshots.

Every question they asked me, I told a lie. I lied good. Like a professional.

And finally they told me that Nathan had a couple of broken ribs, but they'd not been broken the previous night, they'd been broken some time before. He had a gash across the top of his head, needed fourteen sutures, and the thumb on his right hand was dislocated.

That was it. Apart from the bruising and some abrasions that was it.

My certainty that he would die had been wrong.

Later I would see that as a premonition, a misplaced premonition, and with that premonition came that oh so familiar sense of guilt. I was carrying it like a sleeping child, carrying it close and tight for fear of losing my grip. I believed perhaps that my duty to carry this guilt served as some reason to go on.

The nurse who dealt with me said we'd be there just as long as it took to check all our details, sort out some way of paying for this, and then the police would want to question us about the incident. I agreed with everything, agreed and kept on asking if I could see Nathan. After an hour or more the nurse said okay.

They took me to where Nathan lay in another curtained area. They'd given him painkillers, he was drowsy but coherent, and when I explained what they wanted to know, that they wanted us to talk to the police, he told me I had to figure us some way out of there.

I left him there, returned within a minute or two with a wheelchair.

Nathan levered himself off of the gurney and dropped into the chair like a dead weight. He grunted painfully.

'You okay?'

He nodded. 'Figured I'd race you to the street corner and do some press-ups.'

I smiled.

'Whup your ass any time white boy.'

'Can it, Nathan . . . just can it.'

We seemed to glide then, glide mysteriously from the hospital emergency room, and there must have been a guardian angel because there were no voices calling after us, and even as we approached the Reception desk the girl there turned and looked away as we passed, and I knew there was something else going on.

I would tell Father John Rousseau of this many years later, and he would smile, and nod, and then he would say the last thing in the world I would have expected him to say.

'Nothing to do with God,' he'd say. 'Nothing to do with the Archangel Gabriel or secret guardians of the Nether-world ... all comes down to decision. People make powerful enough decisions and they can do some incredible things. You ever hear of a woman lifting a car off of her child's legs? Skinny little woman, nothing to her, little more than a hundred pounds, and she lifts a car off of her child. That isn't God, Danny ... that's people.'

Whatever the reason, we made it out of there, and then we were on the street, the wheelchair abandoned in the lobby, Nathan Verney limping along, me holding him up so he didn't fall flat on the sidewalk, and me with my face all swelled up on one side like I was trying to chew a baseball.

We made it out of there and we were three blocks away before we realized that things like this were not supposed to happen. Despite the pain, despite the previous night's events, we were laughing. Laughing together. If I think back now that moment was the closest moment we would share before the end.

Seems odd to me that the most terrible circumstances seem to bind people together. But they do, and that's what happened to me and Nathan Verney in Panama City, Florida in the summer of '69.

We didn't leave, we stayed right where we were. We avoided Ramone's Retreat, we stayed on the north side of the city where things seemed a little more liberal and understanding. We kept our jobs, our car, and every once in a while we'd go out and find some company. It was simple, uncomplicated, and it stayed that way until Christmas. For the best part of six months there was no Vietnam, there were no questions, no-one looking for us, and Nathan and me got along just fine, possibly better than we'd ever done.

Nathan had forgotten *the burden*, either that or he was remarkably good at pretending there was nothing on his mind.

I had not. I thought of it often. And more often than that I thought of my ma.

And it was she who closed up the chapter of Florida in December. It had been a comfortable chapter, the sort of chapter you go back to and read once more, perhaps again and again, because there seems to be some kind of emotion encapsulated there that you connect with. I connected, at least I thought I did, but like all things it came to a final paragraph, a final line, a final word.

The word was *family*.

Helluva thing.

Christmas was coming and we – Nathan Verney and I – figured it might be okay to call home, just one call each, just to check everything was fine, that there was nothing too serious going down.

We'd been gone eighteen months, and whoever might have been sent down to find us had given up by now.

Surely.

There was only one way to tell.

We called on December 17th, eight days before Christmas, and it was that date, that date and no other, when the real nightmare began.

EIGHTEEN

'She's dead.'

It was Dr. Backermann, his voice like the dry scratching of insects trapped in a cardboard box.

He'd been there when Eve had died, and now he was here, here on the end of a telephone line telling me something I couldn't even begin to comprehend.

'Daniel? Daniel, you there?'

'Yes,' I mumbled.

'Back in August, the first week of August. She passed away in her sleep, Daniel, no pain . . . but she did die, Daniel. The house has been closed up since then waiting for you to come back . . . where did you say you were?'

I was numbed into silence.

'Daniel?'

Backermann's voice sounded distant, as if he was whispering at me from the bottom of a Pepsi can.

'Daniel . . . you still there?'

'Yes,' I said, or at least I *thought* I said it.

'I think you need to come back, Daniel, come back and sort everything out. You can't spend your whole life running away from things.'

I was surprised by his words, angered even.

'What d'you mean, running away from things?'

I could hear Dr. Backermann smiling. How that happens I don't know, but you can hear the slightest change in timbre and pitch and know that someone is smiling, somewhat condescendingly, even though you can't see them.

'We understand what happened, Daniel, we understand that you were influenced by the negro boy.'

'The *what*?'

'You know, the Verney boy, the negro you used to spend so much time hanging around –'

I exploded. 'Asshole, you're a fucking asshole. You're a Jew, Backermann, and the last fucking person in the world I'd expect that kind of bigoted redneck bullshit from is you –'

'Now steady on there, Daniel –'

'*You* steady on, you dumb fucked-up piece of shit, you steady on . . . you go fuck yourself, you go goddam fuck yourself!'

I hung up.

I was seething.

My heart was thundering, my mouth was dry, a taste like I'd been chewing copper filings.

I turned and saw Nathan standing no more than three or four feet away.

We were in a diner near our apartment.

People were looking at me.

I felt as if the world could suddenly close up around me, suffocate me. Never felt anything like it before, never ever felt anything like it any time in my life.

The expression on Nathan's face was one of complete shock and bewilderment. I shook my head. I didn't want to speak. I walked towards the door. Nathan came after me.

'Danny? Hey, what's happenin', man?'

I said nothing, didn't turn, merely shoved the door and walked out into the street. I could feel the eyes of people in the diner following me. I didn't care. They could go fuck themselves too.

'Danny! Hey, Danny, hold up there!'

I didn't stop, I didn't slow down, and when Nathan's hand touched my shoulder I turned suddenly.

My expression must have surprised him because he stepped back suddenly and raised his hands.

'Whoa, man, what's the fucking problem here?'

I shook my head. I looked down at my shoes. Somewhere inside of me, somewhere buried beneath a ton of memories, emotion was beginning to stir.

'She's dead,' I said, and my voice was cold and flat and strange.

'Dead? Who's dead?' he was asking.

His voice sounded like Backermann's, somewhere out there, somewhere in the distance, echoing all the way from Greenleaf perhaps . . . a whisper carried back from the glassy, still surface of Lake Marion . . .

'My ma . . . she's dead, Nathan, she's gone an' died, man . . .'

'Oh shit,' I heard him say.

I felt the emotion even stronger, reaching up towards me from somewhere I didn't even want to look, and it came, it all came on home, and I could see myself sitting there on the sidewalk, my head in my hands, my hands resting on my knees, and sobbing I think, sobbing or crying or something. It was a new thing. A new emotion. A release perhaps.

Even now I don't really know what happened.

Seemed like the world closed up some place and opened up somewhere else.

After that moment I would never see anything the same.

I had to go back. I knew that. I thought little of consequences, repercussions, of what people might say or do when I got there. My mother had died and the house was empty, and she was buried somewhere and I hadn't even said goodbye. In eighteen months she'd heard from me once. A single letter, full of lies. That was how she'd have remembered me. Her son, the liar. She died with that thought, with the wish to see me, to find out what had happened, and I hadn't been there. I believe now, perhaps, that that was the point I decided my own fate. Didn't have anything to do with God, just me and my own conscience.

And despite everything that happened, despite *everything* that happened, my conscience was the worst judge of all.

NINETEEN

After the trial, after the move from Charleston to Sumter, I had time to think. Time was my greatest asset, the one thing I had no shortage of, and yet the weeks blurred into months and even the years seemed to lose their seams and divisions. I would find it hard to recall exactly when everything had happened.

During that time I seemed to lose myself in the events that transpired across America. It was a monumental handful of years, of events that would change the course of history, that would sour the minds and hearts of a nation irretrievably, and those events seemed to open up like gangrenous wounds one after the other.

In Charleston we had newspapers, a day late yes, but still we had newspapers. At Sumter we were not permitted them, they could be rolled tightly and jammed into someone's throat, you could smash their windpipe, even break their neck if you carried enough force behind it. But we did have a transistor radio, a small one that hung from a piece of string at the end of the walkway. Mr. Timmons would hang it there and put it on when Mr. West was off the Block. That happened frequently enough for us to follow everything that happened through the news flashes and daily bulletins.

We listened to a local station, CKKL, a small station with two reporters, a guy called Frank Wallace and a girl called Cindy Giddings.

Frank Wallace had the voice of someone who believed himself to be very important. He rolled his words out like carpets, unnecessarily lengthy and overly precise, but Cindy? Cindy was a different breed altogether. Cindy Giddings should not have been a reporter on CKKL, she should have been an NBC anchorwoman. I created her look, her age, her height, weight and hair color, personal interests and hobbies, the name of her cat, the kind of house she lived in, and after two years of listening to her almost daily I felt a closeness, a sensitivity and depth to our imagined relationship that was perhaps more meaningful than anything I could remember. When she transferred to some station in Georgia in 1973 I felt as if I had experienced a protracted and ugly divorce, a divorce based on nothing more substantial than a difference in location. I even asked Mr. Timmons if we could find the new station on the transistor, but Clarence Timmons – understanding as he was – could not get that little transistor to hear that far.

It was Cindy Giddings who kept me alive during those first years: the sound of her voice, her measured and rhythmic tone, the undercurrent of sensuality I perceived when she said *Well thank you, Frank, and thank you to all our listeners today. It certainly has been a day of revelation, hasn't it?*

One time I thought of writing to her.

I didn't know, wouldn't have known, what to say, but I did know from experience that at times like that it was better to say nothing at all.

Richard Milhous Nixon was the mainstay of my interest. Curiously, I felt a certain camaraderie with this bizarre character. There was no doubt in my mind that he was crazy as a loon. By that time I was cynical enough to believe that the only people who were ever installed at the White House had to be at least half gone.

Richard Nixon was an enigma, a walking contradiction. Why I felt some sense of empathy with the man I didn't know. I believed he was caught, just as I had been, and though there were crimes and felonies perpetrated, though

I did not doubt he had in fact known everything that was going on, there were those behind him who wanted him to vanish any which way he could.

Like me.

We were different, so very different, but in some small way, some fraction of reality, we were just the same.

On one hand Nixon would spend much of his time working on political and economic relations with the Chinese and the Soviets, on the other he was bugging the Oval Office and listening to himself and his aides. He was trapped in the Vietnam fiasco, and while attempting to divert attention from the war by publicizing his overseas trips, the war was pulling America's attention ever back to the atrocities that had been perpetrated there.

In February of 1970 five U.S. Marines were arrested for murdering eleven women and children. April saw the anti-war protest at Kent State and the shooting of seven students. Racial violence erupted once more in Georgia and six blacks were killed. Through September and into Christmas there was the Kent State student body burning their Draft cards, Lieutenant William Calley began his court martial for the My Lai massacre, and members of his own unit came forward to testify that Calley had knowingly and wilfully shot civilians.

The quote that everyone remembered came from Henry Kissinger. Justifying the U.S. invasion of Cambodia he said *We are all the President's men.*

In the early part of 1971, William Calley, guilty of murder, pronounced *I will be extremely proud if My Lai shows the world what war is.*

This was a sentiment the Americans did not want to hear, least of all Nixon, and two days later Nixon ordered Calley's release while his conviction was reviewed.

In May, 30,000 anti-war protesters demonstrated on the banks of the Potomac in Washington. The presidency had the Supreme Court clear Muhammad Ali of draft-dodging.

Captain Ernest Medina, also present at My Lai, was cleared of all charges, and Nixon promised that 45,000 troops would be out of Vietnam by the early part of '72. He gave five and a half billion dollars to space shuttle research and announced he would stand for re-election, simultaneously intensifying the U.S. bombing campaign. A seven hundred-plane B-52 Strato-Fortress fleet pounded Hanoi and Haiphong. Nixon went to China, then to the Soviet Union. He hoped, he prayed, and his words fell on deaf ears.

In June of 1972 five men were arrested at the Democratic National Committee Offices in the Watergate Complex. Former CIA operative James McCord, Security Co-ordinator for the Republican Committee to Re-Elect the President, and two others, both CIA, both with histories of serving anti-Castro groups in Florida, were among them.

Richard Milhous Nixon's nightmare had begun.

John Mitchell resigned as Presidential Campaign Manager just as the last U.S. Ground Combat Unit, the 3rd Battalion 21st Infantry, left Da Nang. Newspapers told America and the world that the Vietnam War had cost a hundred billion dollars.

The air war continued however, with those same B-52 Strato-Fortresses bombing the communist supply routes that fed the invasion of the south.

Gordon Liddy and Howard Hunt were indicted for Watergate. A spokesman for the White House stated categorically that there was 'absolutely no evidence that anyone else was involved'.

Henry Kissinger, Nixon's National Security Adviser, said peace with Vietnam was at hand, and in November of 1972 Nixon won a landslide re-election victory. He ordered the suspension of the Hanoi bombing after twelve days of the heaviest raids the war had seen. Three days after Nixon was sworn in, a ceasefire was declared in Vietnam. The U.S. Army Court upheld the death sentence for William Calley, prisoner exchanges between the Americans and the Vietnamese began, and eleven reporters from three major newspapers were subpoenaed to testify on Watergate. Liddy refused to answer questions and was jailed for eighteen months. Bob Haldeman, Nixon's Chief of Staff, his Chief Domestic Affairs Adviser, John Ehrlichman, Attorney General of the United States Richard Kleindienst and John Dean, Nixon's Legal Counsel, all resigned. Presidential aides John Mitchell and Maurice Stans were indicted for perjury.

Nixon admitted that there had been a White House cover-up of the Watergate scandal, and the Senate began its hearings. In July 1973, Nixon refused to hand over the Watergate tapes to Senate investigators, and John Dean was heard again. He said that Nixon knew of the Watergate burglary and was actively involved in the cover-up. Dean also said that from Nixon's own lips had come a promise: *We could find in the region of a million dollars in hush money.*

The President was served with Court orders to hand over the tapes of White House conversations. He refused. The Appeal Court stepped in and reiterated the order. Nixon refused once more.

Four days later he consented. He ordered Attorney General Elliot Richardson to dismiss Archibald Cox, the Watergate Special Prosecutor. Richardson refused and resigned. Richardson's deputy, William Ruckelshaus, got the same order. He refused. Cox was finally dismissed by the Solicitor General Robert Bork, and with this action came the first mention of impeachment.

The New Year of 1974, the first year in fifteen that America was not reporting weekly deaths in Vietnam, saw Nixon rejecting the Court order to hand over more than five hundred tapes. He finally conceded defeat. The Court received them, but there were five gaps.

Special Prosecutor Leon Jaworski spoke with Nixon. Nixon said he would not hand over the key Watergate tapes, and found himself named as an unindicted co-conspirator. The Congressional Committee warned Nixon he would be impeached. The Supreme Court ordered him once again. Again, the President refused on the grounds of executive privilege. The House Judiciary voted 27–11 in favor of impeachment.

On August 8th 1974 Richard Milhous Nixon resigned the Office of the President of the United States. Spiro Agnew, his Vice-President, had already gone after pleading guilty to tax evasion, and the former Republican Minority Leader of the House of Representatives, Gerald Ford, the newly assigned Vice-President, became Nixon's successor.

There was an interesting turn. Nelson Rockefeller, a man whose grandfather owned Standard Oil, a man with a major involvement in the Chase Manhattan Bank and the Federal Reserve, became Vice-President. He was sworn in on December 19th, a full five months after his selection, and – coincident with the official assumption of his new duties – John Dean, John Ehrlichman, Bob Haldeman, John Mitchell, and Robert Mardian, Assistant Attorney General, were jailed.

The Nixon empire had fallen.

The Vietnam War was over.

A new era had begun.

Such was America during the first years of my imprisonment. I listened to these events transpire from a small wireless, and beneath those thoughts was the memory of what had happened that Christmas of 1969, the few weeks, the few days even, when all we had believed to be a freedom had become its dark and complex opposite.

In some small way my own life had begun to mirror the life of the nation. As I believed nothing could get worse, so it worsened. As I believed there could be no darker shadows, so a deeper darkness was revealed.

And it was into that darkness I fell: boom, down like a stone.

TWENTY

'How did you feel when you realized that you'd never been drafted?'

I looked across the narrow table at Father John Rousseau.

'How did I feel? I felt cheated . . . I don't know, confused perhaps. I don't suppose I took time to think how I felt. My mother was dead. Backermann was there. Nathan came back with me but no-one knew. I moved into my mother's house and Nathan stayed inside, didn't go out. If anyone visited he hid down in the basement.'

Rousseau smiled. 'He hid in the basement?'

I nodded. 'Right, he hid in the basement. He had been drafted, he'd jumped the State. If anyone had known he was there the authorities would have been told and he'd have been arrested.'

'Why did he come back with you?'

I shrugged my shoulders. 'I asked him to. I didn't want to go back alone.'

'And he was willing to go back despite the fact that he might be discovered and arrested?'

'We were friends, had been friends nearly our whole lives. Despite anything that had happened we were still as close as brothers.'

'You think he came back with you because you had left with him in the first place?'

'Like he owed me?' I asked.

Rousseau nodded. 'Perhaps.'

I shook my head. 'I didn't ask him why he came. I asked

him to go back to Greenleaf with me and he said yes, it was as simple as that.'

Rousseau didn't ask anything else.

He lit a cigarette, handed it to me, lit one for himself.

We sat silently for some time. There seemed to be little restriction on the number of times Rousseau could come, the amount of time I could spend in *God's Lounge* when he was there, and I took advantage of it.

I had thirty-one days left. Thirty-one days and I'd be dead. It was a disquieting, sobering, unreal thought.

'So tell me about going back,' Rousseau said. 'Tell me everything that happened.'

I leaned back slightly in the chair. I wanted to stand, to walk around, but such movement was not possible in the narrow confines of the room.

I was restless and agitated. I wanted it to finish now, be done with. It was a simple request, but it would be dragged out, all the way to November 11th.

I was getting medical checks, they were ensuring I ate properly, maintained my personal hygiene. They were not willing to be cheated of their moment of retribution. My watch had increased, my exercise time was constantly supervised, and whereas I would ordinarily walk in the yard with one or two other inmates, there was now simply myself and a warder. Ordinarily Mr. Timmons would come, sometimes one of the others.

It was on my walk two days before that I'd found a small piece of wood. Almost flat, perhaps three inches wide and two inches long, somewhere around quarter of an inch thick. It was like a slice of wood from a tree trunk, something like that, and across it was the most striking grain, three or four shades of brown. Mr. Timmons was with me, I asked if I could keep it, and he said yes. He said I could because he trusted me. He said that if I was asked I was to say I'd found it somewhere else, that he would deny ever speaking with me of such a thing. I agreed.

Later that evening, I took a spoon and rubbed the end of the handle against the wall until it possessed somewhat of an edge. With the sharpened end I carefully drew the shape I wanted, and then fraction by fraction, millimeter by millimeter, I started the endlessly laborious process of chipping away tiny fragments of wood. After more than two hours I had the shape I wanted, vaguely symmetrical, a little square perhaps but nevertheless identifiable. A moth. Its body and wings, the grain of wood across it following the outer curve of the wings on each side. I held it up towards the light, and its silhouette was unmistakable.

I remembered the last time I saw such a shape, hanging right there over the bed I'd slept in, the bedroom I'd grown up in a million lifetimes ago.

Backermann stood behind me.

His greeting had been almost avuncular. I think he was pleased to see me standing there on the front steps of my mother's house, standing there alone, standing there without the *negro boy*.

We had entered the house together, and as I walked through the rooms one after the other, dampness and emptiness hovering around us like ghosts, Backermann was there, a step behind me all the way. I walked upstairs, he came with me, and as I slowly opened the door to what had been my bedroom, still was my bedroom, he seemed finely tuned to everything that was happening, waiting for the emotion to come, waiting for whatever words of comfort he may have been able to afford.

But there was nothing. I really felt nothing. Until I saw that little wooden frame hanging back of my headboard: the candlemoth.

It all came back to me. Eve Chantry, her husband Jack, their daughter Jennifer.

A man staggering from the banks of Lake Marion bearing

his only child, her hair hanging wet and limp, her body like a rag doll, the man's face a tortured mask of utter devastation.

I felt myself exhale.

I thought it would never stop, that I would empty out into that room, fold up like origami and be carried away by some errant breeze.

Dr. Backermann's hand closed over my shoulder. I could smell him. His cologne. The vague taint of pipe tobacco. Something beneath that. Perhaps red wine. Perhaps sherry.

He sort of pulled me closer. I didn't resist. He stood there, solid like a tree, and I just sort of leaned into him, appreciated the sense of stability and support.

I remember starting to apologize for what I'd said on the phone.

Dr. Backermann cut me short, told me it was nothing, that he was sorry too, that he'd been out of line, that we'd both been upset, stressed by recent events . . .

His words faded into nothing.

I just stood there. I couldn't think of anything to say, anything to feel. I was sort of numb. Displaced.

Later – an hour, a day, a week, I don't know really – I recall sitting talking with Backermann. He told me the house was mine, that it would take some time to pass through the legalities, but it was my inheritance, and that he was happy to see me home. He told me he knew why I'd gone, that he'd been interested to see if I ever did receive a Draft Notice. I hadn't. He was sure of that. He'd checked with my ma every week until she'd died. They'd sent for Nathan, but not for me. An irony.

During those moments, I didn't take time to wonder what would have happened had I stayed. I didn't punish myself with thoughts about how my mother might still have been alive had I stayed. I didn't allow myself to consider anything about anything had I stayed.

It was safer that way.

I was home. My mother was dead, but I was home.

After eighteen months of running it was just that simple.

Dr. Backermann left after some time. He left feeling that I'd be okay. I walked out to a callbox and called Nathan. He was at the bus station. He asked me if I was okay, I told him I was, and I suggested he wait until nightfall and then walk into town. I said he should come the back way, cut across Nine Mile Road near the I-88 intersection, and come down through the bank of trees that separated the Interstate from the main freeway.

He did come that way. He was certain no-one had seen him.

It felt good to have him there, have him in my house again, and for a little while I imagined we were back ten years, that we were kids again, that any moment now my ma would call us in for potatoes and greens and homemade corned beef, and she would sit Nathan down and present him with a plate loaded with more food than he could ever possibly eat . . .

But she didn't. She was dead.

We ate in the same kitchen. We ate from the same plates. *What* we ate didn't taste the same. Never would. We had changed along with the world, and back here in Greenleaf it was so much more evident than when we were away. We really had grown up. We were men, no longer boys, and I think some part of me wished we could go backwards and change it all. I wondered for a moment what would have happened had a different decision been made, what would have occurred had we not run. Nathan Verney would have gone to Vietnam, I would have stayed here, perhaps my mother and I would be sitting here, right where Nathan and I were sitting, and we would have been talking about Nathan, what a friend he was, how much a part of both our lives that little black kid with jug-handle ears, traffic-light eyes and a mouth that ran from ear to ear with no rest in between had been . . .

That first day back he asked me a question.

'You think we did the right thing?' he said.

I was surprised. I had never doubted his commitment and resolve.

'Yes,' I said – as much for myself as for Nathan. 'We did the right thing.'

He nodded, he smiled, he looked away towards the window.

I looked out there too, towards the rear of the house. I half-expected to hear our own voices from the yard. Kids' voices. Laughter. Someone shouting at us as we ran from some trouble we'd caused. Something such as that. I imagined we could even go out walking and see ourselves playing, ghosts of who we once were, still haunting the back yards, the open grass fields near Nine Mile Road, Benny's Soda Shop, Karl Winterson's Radio Store . . .

But we were gone. The children we once were had disappeared forever. I think perhaps I grieved for that more than anything else.

We decided then that we would stay for a little while, that this was my home, that no-one was going to come looking for me. Nathan would stay too, I would go see his parents, let them know he was fine, that he'd stayed up north and would be back before the spring. In reality he would stay right in the house, he wouldn't leave, and if people came visiting, as they were bound to do, he would hide down in the basement. Meanwhile he could help me sort the place out, fix it up from all the months of neglect, and we even spoke of selling up, taking the money and going somewhere else entirely, perhaps L.A., New York, even overseas.

They were dreams, nothing-dreams really, but we shared them, and it made us laugh, and after all this time it felt good to be somewhere where we didn't need to be afraid of who might come looking.

That's what we believed.

There was no reason to believe otherwise.

TWENTY-ONE

Rousseau came again the following day. I asked him if he had no place better to go. He smiled, and though he smiled there was something in his expression that spoke of his own sadness. He would spend this handful of weeks with me, and once I was dead there would be another, and yet another. How long could someone stay doing this without losing their mind completely?

That's why I asked him the question, and though I knew it was unfair, though I knew I had no right to put him in such a position, I was aware of my own lack of concern. Hell, I was going to die. I could afford to upset some people before I went.

'The death penalty?' he said, repeating what I'd asked him.

He sat down, and as was his routine he produced two packs of Lucky Strikes from his jacket pocket.

We'd get through a pack each in every sitting. I figured he got a nicotine expense account.

'It depends entirely on whether or not someone is guilty,' he said.

I was surprised at his answer, and then I figured it as the *eye for an eye* philosophy that many of the Southern-state Christians possessed.

'If a man kills someone, and he did kill them, and he says he killed them and there is no doubt that he did, then I think perhaps those who were closest to the victim should decide whether he dies or not.'

'Hell, that would be a good deal for me,' I said, thinking of Reverend and Mrs. Verney.

'Wouldn't be applicable to you,' Rousseau said.

I looked up, frowned.

'You say you didn't kill Nathan, and as far as I can tell there really isn't anything but circumstantial evidence to support that you did.'

I smiled. 'How would you know?'

'From the trial records.'

I was puzzled. 'You read the trial records?'

Rousseau nodded. 'Yes.'

'All of them?'

He nodded again. 'All of them.'

'And your opinion?' I asked, genuinely curious.

'That there was someone who should have been there to give evidence and they weren't ... perhaps the most significant person in the whole case.'

'I know that,' I said. 'That's old history. What I meant was whether or not you thought I was guilty.'

Rousseau shook his head. 'I don't think you were guilty of murder, but I do think you were guilty of something else.'

I looked at him.

He smiled, tried to look sympathetic, understanding perhaps, but it came out like he was hiding something, that there was something he really didn't want to say.

'I think you were guilty of compromising, of cowardice, but most of all of being untruthful with yourself.'

I laughed, a hollow and slightly irritated sound. 'What gives you the right to say that?'

Rousseau shook his head. 'You asked me.'

'And that's what you think?'

'The only thing I can think is what I can gather from the trial records. I wasn't there, Danny, not when they found you, not when they arrested you or interrogated you. I wasn't there in your house listening to what was going on before or after. The only opinion I have is based on hearsay, second and third-hand reports, and the answers you gave to so many leading questions during the trial. That's the sum total of what I know.'

'But that's not all that happened, and certainly not the way it happened.'

'So tell me.'

I sighed. 'Christ, so many times I've been through this . . . seems I've spent the last ten years doing nothing but explaining myself over and over again.'

Rousseau smiled. 'I know, Danny, but I think I need to know. I have some explaining to do as well, you know?'

I frowned. 'Explaining? Who do you have to explain to?'

Rousseau smiled, looked up towards the ceiling.

'God?' I asked. 'You have to explain yourself to God?'

Rousseau shook his head. 'No, Danny, I have to explain *you* to God.'

I laughed. 'Me? What the fuck has that got to do with anything? I don't know that I even believe in God.'

'Because you're here . . . because of what's happened to you?'

'No,' I said. 'Not because of what happened to me.'

'Then why?'

I looked away towards the vague, gray reflection of my face in the one-way window.

'Because, if there is a God, he let Nathan die, Father John . . . because he let Nathan die.'

The room was quiet for some time.

I could hear the sound of my own breathing.

All these years you take your own life for granted, and it is symbolized by something so simple as the sound of breathing. You pay no mind to it, it's always there, never even give it a second thought.

I wondered, in that moment of quiet, what it would be like to hear nothing, to hear absolutely nothing at all.

I think – for the first moment in all the time I'd been waiting – I felt afraid.

Truly afraid.

People did come over. Benny came the day after I'd arrived back in Greenleaf. He seemed so much older than I remembered him, and the day we'd run from the soda shop, the other kids chasing us, seemed a thousand years ago. He spoke of that moment, and there was something in the way he spoke that sounded like he wished to be forgiven for failing to defend us. I felt no resentment towards him, I was happy to see him, but all the while my attention was on the fact that Nathan was down in the basement.

Benny stayed for nigh on two hours, and when he'd left I went down to get Nathan and found he'd pissed in a bucket in the corner.

'Christ, Nathan, you pissed in the bucket.'

'Hell, you didn't get rid of him. What the hell did you expect me to do?'

'I couldn't just send him away.'

'Sure, but you didn't have to keep him here two hours.'

I stood looking at him, his unshaven face, his hair twisted upside his head, and he reminded me of the Nathan I'd wheeled from a hospital in a stolen chair. His clothes were dirty, dishevelled and sweat-stained, and when he moved he moved like a beaten man. He took a step forward and slumped in a chair.

'Two fucking hours, Danny . . . you know what it's like to sit down there in the fucking dark for two hours wondering what the hell is going on up there?'

He thumped the arm of the chair with his clenched fist and cursed again. He was on edge. He wanted to see his folks. He felt he couldn't, not yet, not until the Draft situation had been resolved completely. Either that or the war ended.

I believed I understood what he felt; I'd felt the same way until I'd arrived back and found there'd been no call for me.

This reality created a tension between us, but the moments of tension were brief and inconsequential in the grand scheme of things.

The abiding feeling was one of relief. We were no longer running, no longer living hand-to-mouth or wondering who might ask questions about who we were and why we were there. That sense of ever-present anxiety had disappeared. I had not realized how great an effect that had had on me.

Nathan, though, was a different story. He became increasingly agitated, understandably so, and though he spent much of his time listening to the radio and reading, he appeared always restless. We had no TV, my ma had never wished for one, and though Karl Winterson's Radio Store now stocked such things I never considered buying one. For some reason I believed my stay in the house would be short, perhaps through Christmas, the early part of the New Year, but no longer. Why I felt that I didn't know, but the feeling was there and establishing roots was the last thing on my mind.

As Christmas approached Nathan's invisibility became more and more difficult to maintain. People came to visit, people called and asked me to go visit them, and try as I could to maintain some distance it became ever more real to me that to avoid everyone, to ignore every invitation, was merely to feed any sense of suspicion that might already exist. The human mind – concerned, afraid perhaps – always errs towards thinking the worst when there is no real reason to think such things. Nevertheless, I felt that way, careful, tentative, alert to what I said, always conscious of never allowing myself to refer inadvertently to Nathan Verney. So I would go out, and was out most evenings during the last week before Christmas, and though I would return as quickly as I could I found that Nathan would be drunk more often than not. Drinking had become his solution to the interminable boredom. We had spent eighteen months working, travelling, doing something different almost every day, and now he was housebound. I could appreciate how he felt to some degree, but we started arguing, and one evening I returned and found he'd broken plates and cups across the kitchen floor.

I was incensed. These had been my mother's possessions. He had no right.

'Right?' he shouted. 'Don't talk to me about rights. I have rights. I'm stuck in this fucking place because someone who doesn't even know me thinks I have the right to die for something I don't even believe in. That's my fucking right, Danny, a right that was never granted you –'

'Sit the fuck down, Nathan, and stop shouting.'

Nathan paced back and forth across the room for a while. His fists were clenched, he seemed all wound up inside, tightened like a clock spring. He'd worn the same jeans and tee-shirt for days, and for the life of me I could not remember when he'd last bathed.

I opened my mouth to say something.

The sound of someone knocking on the front door stopped me dead.

'Oh hell,' I remember saying.

I looked at Nathan.

He looked at me.

I looked towards the basement door there behind me in the hallway.

Nathan shook his head.

'Nathan –'

'Fuck it,' he said. 'Fuck it, I'm here . . . I can't bear to stay locked up in this fucking house any more. Let whatever comes come, I'm ready.'

'Nathan,' I said again.

Nathan shook his head again.

'Fuck it, Danny . . . might as well face the music as go crazy in here.'

I sighed inwardly. There was nothing audible. It was like some internal collapse. The walls of the soul were giving way.

I turned and walked to the door.

I raised my hand.

I could see a silhouette through the frosted glass.

The latch snapped back.

I could sense Nathan behind me, right there in direct line of sight.

I slowly opened the door, and I recall trying to fill the ever-widening gap with my body, knowing at once that such an action was futile. If Nathan had given up hiding then he would be seen whether I tried to hide him or not.

I gave up my resistance.

I pulled the door wide.

'Danny!'

TWENTY-TWO

'You were surprised to see Linny Goldbourne?'

I looked across at Father John. 'Surprised? I was stunned. Christ, I never thought I'd see the girl again.'

'What made her come, d'you think?'

I shrugged my shoulders. 'I don't know. There was something about her, something distant, like you could never really nail down exactly what she was feeling or thinking. Apparently she was like that with everyone, had been all her life, and that was part of the reason people found it so easy to accept that she'd gone crazy. They were comfortable with the idea of Linny Goldbourne being crazy because it explained their own difficulty in relating to her.'

'You thought she was crazy?' Father John asked.

I smiled, shook my head. 'No, I never thought she was crazy, no more crazy than me or Nathan or anyone else.'

I leaned forward and looked at Father John. 'The truth? The truth was that I loved the girl . . . loved her as much as I'd loved anyone, and the way she left, everything that happened at that time –'

I stopped mid-flight. I didn't know what I was saying.

'Go on,' Father John prompted.

'She was different, that was all, and I think that was her method of dealing with her family situation.'

Father John frowned. 'Her family situation?'

I waved my hand nonchalantly. 'People said her father was Klan, this kind of thing. He was an influential man, big money, big opinions, and rumor had it that he was Klan. A guy I knew in Sumter, a guy called Schembri . . . even he told me something of the guy's reputation. Even heard her father was in some way involved with Robert Kennedy's death.'

Father John raised his eyebrows. 'You think he was?'

'I try not to think about it now.'

'How come?' Father John leaned towards me.

I looked at him. I looked to his left at the one-way window. Everything I said here would be taped. I shook my head. 'Whatever he was into was whatever he was into, I have no opinion about it. There were rumors, hearsay . . . nothing else. Linny Goldbourne sat in a car with me, we heard on the radio that Robert Kennedy had been killed, and that was the moment she left.'

'When she heard Kennedy had been killed?'

'Right.'

'And you think her father was involved?' Father John asked.

I shrugged. 'All I know was that we heard he'd died, and she changed . . . everything changed at that point. She left and I didn't see her until after we came back to Greenleaf.'

'And you think she suspected her father had some involvement in the assassination?'

I shook my head. 'There were people at the time, later, weeks later . . . people who said that Goldbourne had business interests, millions, billions even, tied up in industry throughout the South. There was an opinion that the industrialists and money men were as afraid of Robert getting to the White House as they had been of his brother before him. There was even some guy, an investigator, Stroud I think his name was, and he was mouthing off about how Goldbourne was implicated in all manner of things that might lead back to the Kennedy administration.'

I sighed. I felt agitated. 'Linny left . . . she went home, and that was the end of the era.'

'But you suspected she might have known something, and when she heard Robert had been killed she got scared?'

'I don't have an opinion about that.'

'Have none or don't want to have one?'

I sighed. 'You want me to tell you what happened?'

Father John relaxed slightly. He leaned back in his chair, lit another cigarette. 'That's why I'm here,' he said.

I smiled. 'I thought you were here to save my soul.'

Father John nodded. 'That too.'

I noticed he was not carrying his Bible today. I thought to mention it but decided not. Right now Father John Rousseau was the only man I could speak to and I didn't wish to unsettle this relationship.

'It was the week before Christmas 1969, the end of the '60s, the end of an era in a lot of ways . . .'

Linny Goldbourne had heard from Marty Hooper's elder sister, who in turn had heard from Karl Winterson, who in turn had heard from Benny Amundsen. She didn't tell me that right away, she told me a little later, and the mere fact that so many people were talking about my return to Greenleaf gave me slight cause for concern. Greenleaf was a small place, but not that small. This was no seven hundred population miss-it-with-a-blink watering hole, it was bigger, much bigger than that. I presumed that people were interested because Ma had died. I put it down to that.

Linny hadn't changed. She was still as beautiful as ever, stunningly so, and the verve and enthusiasm with which she breezed into the house was almost overwhelming. She once again encapsulated me within everything she was, and I was swallowed. Jonah and the whale.

I remember standing there, standing breathless and still and silent as she embraced me, embraced me as if nothing had happened.

And then she saw Nathan.

'Oh my God . . . oh my God . . . oh my God! Nathan!

Nathan Verney! Come here, Nathan Verney . . . oh my God, you're alive!'

Nathan stood rooted to the spot at the other end of the hall.

His expression was a complete mystery.

Linny rushed towards him, her arms out, almost running, and when she reached him she seemed to enclose him completely.

Nathan was caught off-balance and almost fell backwards.

I thought nothing of her reaction to seeing him at the time, for Linny was always so enthused about everything.

'My God, Nathan,' she shouted. 'When did you get back?'

'His parents had told everyone that he went to Vietnam,' I said.

Father John nodded.

'They were ashamed of what he'd done, at least that's what Nathan felt, and so they told everyone that he'd gone to Vietnam and died.'

'They didn't expect to see him again?' Father John asked.

'Nathan said they must have *hoped* they wouldn't see him again.'

'Why?'

'So they wouldn't have to explain how come he wasn't dead.'

'But he never spoke to them?' Father John asked.

I shook my head.

'And you never went to see them to tell them he was alive?'

'No, I never went to see them . . . didn't see them again until after.'

'After what?'

'After he was dead,' I said.

'Yeah, right, sorry,' Father John said.

I raised my hand. 'I actually feel really tired,' I said.

'Okay, just tell me what happened with Nathan and you after Linny came back.'

'Tomorrow,' I said. 'Let's talk about it tomorrow.'

'Tell me now, Danny.'

'Why the hurry?'

Father John looked momentarily awkward. 'The tape,' he suddenly replied. 'Use up the video tape.'

I glanced at the one-way window, remembered the camera behind, the fact that every word, every sound, every expression was being recorded.

I was puzzled.

'You wanna talk about this today because you don't want to waste a video tape? That's the problem? What is it, you payin' for them or something?'

Father John smiled. He looked a little embarrassed. He shook his head. 'No, I'm not paying for them, Danny. It's just that –'

'Just that we don't have that much time do we, Father? Four weeks, give or take, right?'

Father John smiled, something reassuring in his expression. 'Right,' he said.

I was quiet for a moment.

'So how come all of this is so important to know?' I asked.

He shrugged his shoulders, an effort at nonchalance. 'Important? I just feel I want to know exactly what happened, Danny. I've read the trial records, read the statements, listened to the taped interviews –'

I smiled. 'You've listened to the tape where I confessed?'

'Yes,' Father John said. 'I've listened to your confession.'

'So you've heard everything.'

'I've heard everything that I'm meant to hear, read everything that I'm supposed to read, but there's so much missing.'

I looked up. I wanted a cigarette. 'Missing?' I asked.

Father John shook his head slowly. 'You take in every-thing, you study all of that stuff, and you come away . . . at least *I* came away with a definite feeling that here was a man who didn't fight back.'

I smiled. 'Didn't fight back? Fight back against what? Against the might of the South Carolina District Attorney's Office, the Federal Court, the Fifth Circuit, the State Appellate, the Supreme Court, the Governor? Or was there someone else involved that maybe I should have argued with?'

Father John leaned back. 'I'm sorry,' he said. 'I do understand what happened.'

I nodded. 'And what happened was what was meant to happen, and for all I know had been arranged long before Linny Goldbourne came back.'

'And how did it make you feel, the fact that she'd left so suddenly after Robert Kennedy's death the year before, and now had returned so unexpectedly?'

I smiled. 'It made me feel great, Father John, it made me feel . . . Hell, I don't know. I don't think I'd ever stopped loving her.'

'Tell me.'

I took another cigarette. I was smoking so much now. Had I possessed any reason to concern myself with the subjects of health and physical well-being I would have slowed down.

But I had no reason to think of these things.

A month and I'd be dead.

I looked at him, this priest, this man of God, and in his face I saw all the weatherworn signs, the moments when his own faith must have been tested to its limit. It was hard in a world such as this to consider that things were arranged in any other fashion than to bring a man down.

'Danny?'

'Uh huh?'

'Tell me,' Father John repeated.

*

'Get back?' Nathan asked, as soon as Linny had climbed down off of him. 'Get back from where?'

He was laughing, shocked by her reaction, and when she told him that she thought he'd gone to Vietnam and died, a dark cloud seemed to descend on the room.

I was still standing by the front door, a little amazed at the speed and enthusiasm with which she'd hurtled down the hall and enveloped Nathan. As far as I knew they could never really have had anything to do with each other. Linny Goldbourne had been distant from anyone but her peers, and with her father's apparent racial persuasion she would have been forbidden to even speak to blacks, let alone make lifelong friends.

I knew Nathan had figured it out even as I closed the front door and joined them in the kitchen.

Reverend and Mrs. Verney, reading his note, not believing for a moment that he'd gone north for work, had told all and sundry he'd gone to Vietnam and died. That had been their solution. A solution to shame, to reputation, to the Reverend's credibility and position.

They had killed their son to save face.

In that moment I was glad I'd never gone over and seen them, never told them that Nathan was back in Greenleaf.

We sat around the kitchen table, the same table where Nathan and I had sat as kids, and we talked.

'You gotta understand that you cannot tell anyone I'm here,' he told her.

Linny smiled. 'Take it easy, Nathan . . . not a word.'

'I'm serious,' he said. 'You say something and word'll get around, and before I know it there'll be State Troopers or the fuckin' National Guard down here.'

Linny raised her hand in a placatory fashion. 'Nathan, look,' she said. 'I have no reason to say anything. I wouldn't even consider saying anything. Besides, if I said something and they slung you in jail I wouldn't get to come down here and see you guys.'

She turned to me and I looked at her – the dark hair, the hazel eyes, the full and passionate mouth. She reached out and closed her hand against the side of my face.

'I missed you,' she said softly. 'I missed you so much, Daniel Ford.'

'And me you,' I said, and raised my hand to cover hers.

She leaned across the table and kissed me, her lips against mine for what seemed an age and everything that I'd felt – the loss and betrayal, the heartache I had worn on my sleeve since the day she'd left – seemed to evaporate.

I looked at Linny Goldbourne.

Linny Goldbourne looked at me.

There was something smooth and electric passing between us.

I sensed it, could almost reach out and touch it. There was a wavelength that flowed in slow-motion: psychic molasses.

She smiled once more, withdrew her hand, and turned to look at Nathan.

'But Christ, you can't stay inside the whole time . . . the war might go on for years,' she said.

Nathan shrugged his shoulders.

There was silence for a moment.

'Look,' she said. 'I understand what you're getting at, but hell, Nathan, a prison is a prison whatever the hell it looks like. You stay here you'll go out of your mind.'

And then she turned to look at me again. To look and to smile. And I perceived it: that thing that was so much Linny, so much whoever she was. Her *magic*.

'I'm not going to argue with you,' she said, and both her expression and her voice had warmed. 'I'm here, and I can make things a little more interesting for you guys.'

She looked at me. 'Okay?'

I nodded. 'Okay.'

'Let's have a drink,' she said. 'Fuck it, let's have seven and get completely shitfaced and puke in the garden, huh?'

Nathan looked at me and smiled, a genuine smile, and then he started to laugh, a sound I hadn't heard for as long as I could recall. The tension was broken, and I thanked her for that, thanked her silently from the bottom of my heart.

'Sure, let's drink,' Nathan said. 'Let's drink the place dry.'

I fetched a bottle of Crown Royal, opened it, took glasses from the side.

'So maybe we could go out some,' Linny suggested.

Nathan shook his head. 'Going no place,' he replied.

'I don't mean now, right now, Nathan. I mean sometime soon, maybe when things have settled down.'

Nathan shook his head. 'Believe me, things won't settle down 'til this goddam war is over.'

Goddam. He said *Goddam.* So unlike Nathan.

'They'll settle,' she said. 'And I think you'd be surprised how little people really care about who went to the war and who didn't. The mood has changed . . . people are beginning to resent the fact that it ever started, and the ones that jumped the Draft are being talked about as the ones who really had guts.'

I watched Linny. I knew what she was doing, knew she always moved towards opportunities. Here was a girl who could have anything she wanted, had always had anything she wanted, and to be denied something that piqued her interest was a violation of her fundamental rights as a human being. I felt like saying something, even opened my mouth, but nothing came out. She would convince Nathan that going out was the only real solution to anything he was feeling.

I poured another drink. I didn't want to talk of the war. I didn't even want to talk of whether we would ever leave the house. Now Linny was here I would have been content to be under house arrest for the duration.

She laughed suddenly, loudly, a little drunkenly perhaps. 'It's so great to be here with people that have lived some kind of life . . . I mean, for Christ's sake, everyone here is so narrow-minded and predictable, don'tcha think? Get up, go to work, mow the lawn, read the paper . . . Jesus, could you imagine having a life like that?'

She reached out once again and touched my hand. 'So rare to collide with someone on the same wavelength, eh?'

Some*one*.

That's what she said.

And again she looked at me, and for the first time since leaving Greenleaf I felt that something right was happening. Just for a moment I felt that the past had all disappeared behind me and meant nothing at all.

A little later we smoked some weed that Linny had brought, and despite everything she seemed to lift the mood and atmosphere for a while. Nathan and I had become introverted, spending too much time thinking about what had happened, what was happening, what might happen if this or that occurred.

Linny Goldbourne had arrived, and with her arrival the seriousness of our situation was eased briefly. I think both of us – regardless of those things that were never really voiced – were grateful for that.

When she left she held me close, pulled me tight towards her and kissed me again. 'I would stay,' she said, 'but I can't. It's good to see you.'

'And you,' I said, and buried my face in her hair, smelled the rich and heady scent of her perfume, the whisky, everything that she was.

She promised to return the following day, to bring some provisions, to make some dinner for us.

Nathan had again asked for her discretion, to say nothing, to come and go quietly.

She had smiled, reached up her hand and held it there against his cheek. She said she would be quiet, like a ghost, and she hugged him.

I watched her go from the door, and when I closed it I felt the light had gone out.

I was drunk, but I did not sleep.

She had held me the same way she'd held me in a diner in Atlanta on the day Martin Luther King was buried. Held me slowly and closely – a little too long to be simply the pleasure of a chance meeting, a reunion, an acquaintance missed and reconnected.

I hadn't asked her why she had suddenly disappeared back then, that afternoon in June of the previous year. So sudden. So unexpected and unexplained.

And Linny Goldbourne hadn't offered up any explanation herself.

If I'd realized then that she was the messenger, the carrier of our destiny, I would have locked the doors, bolted the windows, and convinced Nathan we should both hide in the basement until she lost interest.

But I did not. I was still enchanted by her.

Nathan Verney – a man possessed of his own loneliness and longing – was, I think, enchanted too.

How much, I didn't know, and how far this thing would eventually travel I had no idea. And so I watched her leave, even walked to the front window and saw her make her way down to the sidewalk and turn away. She glanced back, and I was glad of that, for it told me that this was not the same departure as before.

Perhaps I'd felt I'd lost too much already: my folks, Caroline Lanafeuille, Eve Chantry. Like life had been a chain of losses with some vague and forgettable interruptions in between.

Hell of a way to think of your life, but I felt that Linny Goldbourne's return had served to begin a redress of wrongs, a correction of the universal balance that had so precariously tipped away from me.

And Nathan was excited too, he spoke of her endlessly after her departure. He asked me for every detail of the time she and I had spent together that summer.

Seemed Linny Goldbourne was the last important thing

that had occurred prior to our departure, and the first on our return. *How* important we would soon know.

For now, I was content to lose myself in some vague and drunken bliss of remembering, and Nathan was content to listen.

She would come the following day, she would come every day, and the more she came the more I seemed to lose myself. We slept together, we laughed and got drunk, we smoked weed, and then we fucked again. Nathan seemed oblivious to any degree of exclusion, and I suppose I saw myself as the one who deserved this association. I had been the follower, the one who had compromised what I wanted, what I believed, and now it was my turn to have something exclusively for myself.

Or so I believed.

'You believed?' Father John asked. 'What d'you mean?'

'I sensed that she started to lose interest in me.'

Father John raised his eyebrows.

'Little things. At first I didn't notice . . . but they were there.'

'Like what?'

'The way she said his name. The way she would look at him a little too long . . . things like that.'

'And it wasn't your imagination?'

I smiled and shook my head. 'No, it wasn't my imagination.'

'You felt you were losing her?'

'Yes, I felt I was losing her . . . she'd been with us a week, perhaps ten days, and already she was fading.'

'What did Nathan say to you about her . . . about her father?'

'Nathan said he didn't care who her father was or what he might do. I let him think whatever he wanted. It was his life, not mine, and he didn't owe me anything.'

'And you felt that he was taking her away from you?'

I shook my head. 'Not at first. I felt like she was taking him away from me . . . and then I felt that she'd used me, and then that she was using both of us. I got confused. All I knew was that she'd come down almost every day, and when she came it was to see me and me alone . . . and then she started spending time with Nathan, telling me she felt bad because he was on his own downstairs.'

'Was it jealousy?'

I looked at Father John. Sometimes I was surprised at the directness and detail of his questions.

Sometimes I felt he was interrogating me.

'Jealousy? Hell yes, it was jealousy. I think it had more to do with the fact that she did not grant any substance to what we had shared before Nathan and I had left, before she drove away that afternoon. And then she'd come back and I had been the center of her attention for a week or so, and then that attention faded . . . it just grew narrower and narrower until there seemed to be nothing left at all.'

I paused; I had not considered these events in such detail for a very long time.

I cleared my throat.

'If she'd said something . . . like she knew she'd left suddenly, that she'd not given any reason for leaving, that she was sorry even, I might have felt different. Maybe if she'd been completely straight with me, told me that what we had the summer before was really nothing at all, a bit of fun, a distraction, and now we were back she was happy to see me, to spend some time with me . . .'

I leaned back and sighed. 'I loved her, loved her once, loved her twice, but the way it happened made me feel like . . . like . . .'

'Like you'd been betrayed by her again?'

I nodded. 'Yes, like I'd been betrayed again.'

'What did you want her to say?'

I shook my head. 'I don't know . . . perhaps that what I'd thought was love was merely an infatuation, a crush or something. Maybe that she felt good with me, but it was just a sex thing, a physical thing . . . and now she'd had enough of that and she really wanted to spend some time with Nathan. Maybe if she'd said that I would have felt differently.'

'Or maybe not,' Father John said.

'Or maybe not,' I replied. 'Hard to know how you'd feel about something that *could* have been different.'

'So tell me how you *did* feel when you realized what had happened between them.'

'Angry, confused, hurt . . . all those things. Betrayed by her, and by Nathan too.'

'In detail . . . tell me exactly how it came about.'

I shook my head. 'Hell, this is some pile of tapes they're gonna have when we're through.'

Father John Rousseau smiled but said nothing.

'You wanna know in detail everything that happened then?'

'Seems to be the most important point, Danny, don't you think?'

'Maybe,' I said. 'You're gonna have to be the judge of that.'

'So let me judge,' Father John said.

'Overstepping the bounds of your jurisdiction?' I asked, and I glanced upwards as he had done, up towards the ceiling, to Father John's boss.

Father John smiled. 'The secret of maintaining authority is the ability to delegate down.'

'Okay,' I said. 'You be the judge.'

TWENTY-THREE

I remember waking one day with a headache the size of Mount Rushmore. I had not smoked weed or drunk so much since Florida. And just as that first night after Atlanta when Linny took me out and taught me the evils of tequila, and then arrived the following morning to drive me to the coast, she appeared in my room that morning with the same enthusiasm and boundless energy that seemed to be her trademark.

She told me to *drag my useless carcass out of bed*, and then she laughed and went back downstairs.

As I surfaced I could hear Linny and Nathan talking downstairs. They were making breakfast, the radio was playing, and between the other sounds I could hear laughter, the sort of laughter that people share when they have *connected*.

I went down quietly and stood there in the hallway listening to those voices.

You want eggs, Naaa-than?

Sure.

Anything else you want?

What you offering?

Anything you see, baby.

Nathan laughing.

What I see is a whole heap of trouble.

Kinda trouble you like though, ain't it?

You're a bad girl, Linny Goldbourne.

When I'm good I'm good . . . when I'm bad I'm better . . .

Silence for a moment.

Danny awake yet?

Don't you worry about Danny.

He knows, you know?

He'd be blind not to know, Naaa-than.

Don't seem altogether right.

Ah, to hell with what's right and what's not. You want something, you take it baby.

And what do you want, Linny?

I think you know what I want, Mister Verney.

I closed my eyes and breathed deeply. I should not have been standing there listening, but I couldn't help myself. There was something magnetic about the way she bound everyone into her spirited passion for life. She cast spells, and we of weak minds and weaker hearts didn't stand a chance.

Had I not loved her, had I not given her everything of me, I don't believe I would have felt anything more than a fleeting interest in what was occurring between them, but it was in that moment that I felt I'd lost her. There was *something* about her that defied description, something that made me feel transparent in her presence. Her attention was transitory and impermanent; she held your gaze unflinchingly for a moment, you really felt you were getting through, and then it was gone. Like a breeze that lifts the leaves of a tree, just for a moment, and then they are again still.

Nathan knew little of how she was, he was caught up in the whirlwind of life and light and laughter, and when I paused there at the bottom of the stairwell and watched them in the kitchen I could see how easily she enchanted him. She would smile a little too long. She would laugh and touch his arm, his shoulder, his hand. I even believed she waited until he reached for something and then she'd reach in the same moment so their hands connected, and these things would prompt further eye contact, further smiles and laughter.

I believe I had the right to be envious. Though there had been no spoken agreement, no contract, no tacit consent, I still felt that the depth of emotion I had felt for Linny had been reciprocated. She had known that, *must* have known that, but in that second it appeared that she possessed no memory at all of such things.

I crept back up the stairs, walking on eggshells, and then I turned at the top and came thundering down like a freight train. I announced my arrival in order to give them a moment to collect themselves.

I walked into the kitchen as if nothing had happened, and there they were, at either end of the counter-top, she cracking eggs into a bowl, he frying mushrooms in a pan at the stove. They had so obviously been standing next to one another, and in hearing me had moved apart.

They knew, all too well they knew how such a connection might hurt me.

'Hey,' Linny greeted me.

I smiled and nodded.

'Smells good,' I said.

'You want eggs, Danny?' she asked.

I glanced at Nathan. 'Sure thing.'

Anything else you're offering? I thought.

Linny busied herself.

'Sleep good?' Nathan asked.

'Good enough,' I replied, and took a seat at the table. I did not offer to help. They were in collusion against me. They could at least make the fucking breakfast.

'And you?' I asked.

Did he glance at Linny then? Did she glance back at him? Did a slight knowing smile flicker across her cherry-red, pouting, selfish-bitch lips?

I closed down my thoughts. Such thoughts would get me nowhere.

'I slept fine,' Nathan said.

Linny carried plates to the table and set them down.

She leaned closer to me. I could smell her perfume, the natural scent of her body. Smelled like that day on the beach, and with that thought I could see her stretching her arms above her head, the way her form so elegantly defined each curve and swell and dip. I wanted to reach up and touch her face, to run my fingers through her hair, to kiss her, to taste the salt-sweet tang of her lips . . .

'Coffee?' she asked.

I could feel myself blushing.

'Ye-yes,' I said.

And then she touched me, and her fingers on my cheek were like small stabs of soft electricity, and I could feel that electricity pulsating through my skin, and I wanted so much to reach back. But I couldn't. Dared not to.

'You're okay, right?' she asked.

I feigned a moment of perplexity. 'Okay? Sure I'm okay. Why'd you ask?'

She smiled, withdrew her hand. 'Just checkin',' she said, and turned once more towards the counter-top.

Checking if you've hurt me? I thought. *Checking if I'm going to be okay with the fact that you have cast me aside for someone else? Checking to see if there's something I might want to say about how effortlessly you seem to flit from one person to the next?*

I closed my eyes for a moment. I breathed deeply once more. I let it go. I *had* to let it go.

They finished preparing breakfast and we ate together, almost in silence.

They sat beside one another facing me.

I wanted to move, wanted to do something, *anything*. But I said nothing, as always the one who was led, not the leader. For despite the things that Nathan had said to the Devereau sisters in Florida, his belief that we had left because of me, I believed otherwise. I felt that recent events had strengthened me – the death of my mother, my return to Greenleaf – and emotions I once would have suppressed were now simmering beneath the surface. I felt like fighting back, like marking my territory. This was *my* home, these people were *my* guests, they were here by the grace of me. They were owed no right of possession, no law of jurisdiction over my feelings and thoughts, and yet here they were, playing with things of far greater substance and significance than they were granting. Resentment, unexpressed or otherwise, set in. It came slowly at first, and then those flickering uncertainties about my own importance in these matters gathered speed, rolling up together like a thunderhead across the horizon. Lightning would strike I believed, not now, not yet, but it would, and I wondered what I would do to redress the balance.

For the time being I was quiet. I watched, I waited, I listened and made mental notes. Later I would refer to them in trying to reconstruct this chapter of my past.

And thus it was not my idea that we go out, but Linny's. That we wait until dark, leave in her car, with Nathan lying across the back seat covered with a blanket, and go somewhere, somewhere across the state line, Savannah perhaps, or Augusta.

'Fucking crazy,' I remember telling them.

Nathan was excited – by Linny, by the prospect of leaving the house for the first time since his arrival, even excited by the risk. Linny possessed sufficient enthusiasm to make even armed robbery sound like a swell idea.

'It'll be okay, Danny, it really will be okay. We'll just go out, just for a few hours.'

Again it was that same persistence of Nathan's that wore me down.

I agreed, but there was a condition.

'No playing pool, right Danny, no playing pool . . . whatever you say.'

Linny asked about it, Nathan told her: that the two times we'd played pool were the two times we'd had ten shades of shit kicked out of us.

Linny found this hysterical, either that or the weed she was smoking.

'Hurled the lid of a trash can into the back of some guy's head,' Nathan told her. 'Danny came up out of the alleyway like a freakin' tornado. Had he not been there, had he not done that, I think those motherfuckers would have kicked me to death.'

Linny looked at me. There was no smile, no expression of surprise, just this cool and measured sense of being impressed. I felt for a second I had turned her thoughts back, that now I was the one who would hold her interest, and then she looked back at Nathan. And there it was again, that flow of emotional and physical energy that passed between them. Almost tangible. She was thanking me, I later felt. Thanking me perhaps for saving Nathan's life. Thanking me for ensuring that he came home safely to Greenleaf so she could own him for a while. Maybe my imagination. Jealousy is a powerfully narcotic drug. I was addicted, for in each such moment I read everything there was to read, and when there was nothing to read I made it up as I went along.

Later, so much later, when they took her, when they finally closed down her life, I would ask myself if she hadn't deserved it. Deserved everything she got. Perhaps it was who she was, perhaps she couldn't help but be that way. I watched her then, I thought of her later, and I asked myself if I could forgive her for being that way. I could not. Perhaps *would* not. Wanted to believe that she had engineered everything in some subtle Machiavellian fashion to gain everything she wanted, whatever the cost. She paid for her sins, as I did, and forgiveness was not something I felt was a natural right for anyone. I had not been forgiven, and thus everyone else involved was as guilty as I.

Nathan told his stories, and every other word he mentioned my name, what *Danny* had done, what *Danny* had said, almost as if he was forcing her to think of me. Like he knew how I felt and was making an effort to balance things backwards. He had taken her, he must have known that, but by speaking of me, by telling her how resolute and courageous I had been, he was paying his dues. Perhaps. Perhaps not.

And later we did go. We went down to Savannah on the Georgia state line. It was two days before Christmas. People were drunk wherever we went. No-one was paying much of a mind to anything except what they themselves were involved in. That was fine by me. I felt I passed through those bars like a ghost.

I drank like a ghost too – a short here, a beer there – but Linny and Nathan drank like they'd seen the sign *Drink Canada Dry*, and taken it as an instruction. They'd start in Georgia and work their way north until they reached the St. Lawrence Seaway and Montreal.

They were loud, they sang together, and when we left some place called The Watering Hole a little before 1 a.m. they appeared incapable of standing without one another's assistance.

I steered them like new-born heifers to the car, their legs giving way beneath them, all elastic knees and rubber feet.

They lay across one another on the back seat of Linny's car, side by side, their faces touching, and in the cool light cast by the streetlamps they appeared to be one entity, two-headed and multi-limbed.

I drove us back. My head was clear. I smoked a couple of cigarettes, I watched the world unfold through each window – the Christmas lights, the trees, the fields that seemed to gather along the edges of the highway to guard my return. Like they'd been waiting. Like they wanted to make sure I got home safely before they slept.

I felt insubstantial against all of this. I felt I could have been anyone, anyone at all. Tonight I was the chauffeur, the help, nothing more than that, and when we arrived back at my house I was almost tempted to leave them out there in the car.

There was a color to my thoughts that had not been present for many years. Perhaps the last time I had really felt this way was a Summer Dance when Caroline Lanafeuille reputedly lost her virginity to Larry James. It should have been me. That was my thought then. *It should have been me.* Then it was Larry James, Marty Hooper's sidekick, and now it was Nathan, Nathan Verney, my brother, my blood, the man I had left Greenleaf for eighteen months earlier.

But I was strong, and I cast such thoughts aside. I hadn't left Greenleaf for no reason. I had left because I believed my own *burden* would arrive imminently, but most of all because of the friendship between me and Nathan – I would have expected him to come with me had I gone first, and thus felt I should afford him the same. I convinced myself that I felt nothing for Linny Goldbourne, and that night – sitting in her car smoking a cigarette and turning recent events over in my mind for a few minutes before I hauled them out the back and helped them to their beds – I forced myself to believe that I couldn't care less what happened between them.

'But you did care?'

I nodded. I reached forward and ground the end of my cigarette into the ash tray.

'How much?' Father John asked.

'How much did I care?'

Father John nodded.

'More than I realized. I wanted to be part of everything that was going on. I didn't want to feel on the outside, even on the edge. I wanted to be right in the middle of everything.'

'And what happened between Nathan and Linny was an exclusion?'

I smiled. 'I don't know how they could have made me feel *more* excluded than that.'

'When did it happen?'

'The day after.'

'The day after you drove back from Savannah?'

'Right,' I said. 'The day after I drove back from Savannah.'

'Tell me what happened.'

I arched my back. The muscles in my shoulders and neck were tense. There was that unmistakable taste in my mouth from too many cigarettes.

'You think there's any way to get a drink, a cup of coffee or something?'

'Sure,' Father John said.

He reached behind him and pushed the buzzer set just beneath the one-way window.

It was less than a minute before the door was unlocked and a guard stepped in.

'Any hope of some coffee?' Father John asked.

'You can use the machine down the corridor by Incoming Administration,' the guard said.

'Would you wait here while I go down and get some?'

'Sure, Mister Rousseau,' the guard said.

Father John smiled, stood up. He took a step towards the guard and pointed at his own collar. 'Father Rousseau,' he said. 'Father Rousseau.'

The guard looked awkward for a second. 'I'm sorry, Father ... I'm so used to Mister this and Mister that –'

Father John slapped him on the shoulder as he stepped out through the door. 'Should attend your church a little more often perhaps,' he said. 'Now keep an eye on him, son ... I'll be back in five.'

And he was, less than five even, and with him came two styrofoam cups of coffee, and after the guard had left he produced a packet of Orio Cookies from his jacket.

The coffee was good, machine or otherwise, and out of four cookies Father John ate only one. I ate three, barely tasted them, but hell they were good, as good as anything I'd tasted in months.

'So tell me what happened after you came back from Savannah,' Father John said.

I smiled. These memories had so long been folded neatly in some drawer at the back of my mind. Now, as I unfolded them, held them up, aired them to the breeze of my words, I was so aware of their tone and smell, their colors and sounds and feelings. It was amazing to me that I could close my eyes, close my eyes and almost reach out and touch these things. They were *that* real.

I wondered what would happen to these memories when I was dead.

'After Savannah,' I said, and for a moment my voice sounded like someone else's. 'After Savannah things went strange . . .'

TWENTY-FOUR

'The Invisible Empire,' Robert Schembri whispered across a plastic tray of boiled chicken pieces and dry mashed potato. It was our third meeting in August of 1972, and I was filled to bursting with questions.

'That's what they considered they possessed ... an Invisible Empire.'

I glanced over my shoulder. Someone was arguing on the other side of the mess hall. Apparently someone-or-other was *gonna get themselves bitch-slapped if they didn't mind their fucking mouth*.

Schembri was oblivious to all distractions.

'After the Civil War six Confederate officers got together in Pulaski, Tennessee, December 24th 1865 it was, and they formed this society. The name was based on the Greek word *kuklos* which meant circle. They were opposed to the Republican representatives of the Reconstruction governments that came into power in 1867. They regarded the Reconstruction governments as hostile and oppressive, and they believed in the innate inferiority of the blacks. They saw their own former slaves rising to positions of civil equality and political influence and this galled them. They committed themselves to destroying the Reconstruction from the Carolinas to Arkansas. They all dressed in white cloaks and hoods, terrorized people, doing everything they could to prevent undesirables from voting and holding office. They burned crosses near the homes of those they wanted to scare up. They started flogging people, mutilating them, killing them sometimes; anything that would produce the desired degree of fear to prevent a continuation of the black-white integration and equalization that was building momentum.

'In Nashville in 1867 they adopted a declaration which upheld their belief in the Constitution, and their determination to "protect the weak, the innocent and defenseless, to relieve the injured and oppressed, and to succor the suffering". They called themselves the Invisible Empire and elected a senior official called the Grand Wizard of the Empire. He carried almost autocratic power and back of him were ten lieutenants called the Genii. They also elected the Grand Dragon of the Realm who was assisted by eight Hydras, the Grand Titan of the Dominion who had six Furies, and the Grand Cyclops of the Den who had two Nighthawks.'

Schembri smiled. 'Fuckin' nuts, eh?'

I smiled and nodded, but once again felt that I could have been anyone, could have been anywhere. Schembri was going to talk any which way as long as he considered someone was listening.

'Anyways, from 1868 to 1870, as the Federal occupation troops were being withdrawn from the Southern states and Democratic administrations were being established, the Klan was infiltrated by elements which the Klan themselves considered distasteful and dangerous. The local organizations, the klaverns, became so out of control that the Grand Wizard, Confederate General Nathan Forrest, officially disbanded the Klan in 1869. The klaverns operated independently then, and in 1871 Congress passed the Force Bill to implement the Fourteenth Amendment to the U.S. Constitution which guaranteed rights to all citizens. President Grant made a request to all illegal organizations to disarm and disband, and hundreds of Klansmen were arrested.

'In 1915 a new organization appeared in Georgia. A

preacher and soldier, Colonel William Simmons, established the Invisible Empire, Knights of the Ku Klux Klan. Membership requirements were simple. The new Klan was open to native-born, white Protestant males, sixteen years old and above. Roman Catholics and Jews were excluded, and these people joined the ranks of the blacks and themselves became targets of defamation and attack. They sort of existed somewhere in the background until about 1920, and after World War One, the whole financial and economic slide that occurred in the '20s, the Klan expanded rapidly and appeared strong in Oregon, Kansas, Texas, and down through the South, across Georgia, into Illinois, Indiana, Ohio, Pennsylvania ... all over the country. They opposed the Roman Catholic Church heavily, said that the Catholics actively threatened the American way of life. They attacked liberals, trade unions, any non-nationals; even striking workers were labeled subversives and targeted for terrorism and hate campaigns.'

Schembri sighed resignedly and leaned back in his chair.

'It was a time of huge political dissent and social unrest, people wanted someone to target, and the Klan effectively did what the National Socialists did in Germany in the 1930s. They gave people a reason, a target, somewhere to direct their frustration and hatred. Combined with the natural sense of xenophobia that people felt, they couldn't help but hit home. They had money, they bribed officials, they held marches, they burned crosses, they dragged people from their houses and flogged them in public. They got away with it for a short while, and then the papers got hold of what was going on and a Congressional inquiry was instigated in 1921. The Klan changed their tactics, and as a result of the publicity they received from that inquiry the membership exploded. By 1924 the Klan claimed a membership in excess of three million. The National Convention of the Democratic Party denounced the Klan, and attempted to outlaw them once again. That attempt was defeated.'

Schembri smiled knowingly and leaned forward. 'The government, whatever they might have said in public, didn't want the Klan disbanded. The Klan kept folks in line, they terrorized the trade unions, and the government was all in favor of that kind of activity. They didn't want the blacks to be equal, whatever the result of the Civil War might have indicated. That was clear when they whacked Martin Luther King.'

Schembri spooned a mess of chicken and potato into his mouth. His eyes were alight, on fire almost. He was in his element.

'The Depression of the '30s reduced the membership greatly, apparently, and the Klan was rife with internal corruption, immoral leadership, all manner of travails. They didn't fold however, and they continued to attack their primary targets – trade union organizers and blacks trying to vote. In 1940 they affiliated themselves with the German-American Bund, a group financed by the German National Socialist Party. They held a huge rally at Camp Nordland in New Jersey, and it was believed at that point that the Klan had never been so organized or well-funded as it was then. The U.S. government knew exactly what was going on, they knew exactly where the money was coming from, and with that kind of network being strengthened they could so easily have investigated and prosecuted the ringleaders. But they didn't. The Klan were like the hydra, cut one head off and another one would grow, and it was estimated that in excess of thirty percent of Congressional and Federal officials were either part of, or in favor of, the Klan's actions.'

Schembri raised his spoon and emphasized each word with a downward motion.

'Shit like this doesn't happen because it happens. Shit

like this happens because people want it to happen, you know?'

I nodded. I knew.

'The Federal government kicked up a fuss about unpaid taxes after World War Two and Georgia revoked the Klan Charter in 1947. The Klan's current leader, Samuel Green, died and the structure of the Klan weakened for a short while. However, with the Supreme Court ruling in May of 1954 that racial segregation in schools was illegal and unconstitutional, the Klan got all stirred up again, re-established itself, and went on a heightened recruitment drive. They started bombing places, stepped up the reprisal killings and terrorist activities, and after the Civil Rights Act of 1964 they experienced a huge resurgence in member-ship. It was estimated that the Klan was as strong in the mid-'60s as it had been in the '20s, though folks obviously didn't publicize their membership so it was hard to determine exactly how big they had become. By the 1970s they were big enough to put known and acknowledged Klan leaders up for Federal and local elections, and these people amassed huge voting constituencies. They now possessed a unity of voice, and whether it was the Knights of the Ku Klux Klan or the National Klan or the United Klans of America, it was still the same thing. And now you have the Union of the Snake, the Valkyrie Charter, the Grand Order of White Supremacy, all these white Anglo-Saxon Protestant neo-Nazi groups right across the country, and they have money, and they have allies and members in the Senate, in Congress, everywhere you look.'

Schembri smiled knowingly and cynically.

'And that, my friend, was what you ran into in South Carolina.'

I looked up. Before speaking to him I had no idea Schembri even knew who I was, let alone the fact that I'd come from South Carolina.

'You think you were targeted because you were there,

well you're right. Only thing they might have regretted was that you weren't a nigger. But hell, you were a hippy, as good as damn it, and hippies were communists or Jews or homosexuals whichever way they looked at it. You got involved with someone you shouldn'a gotten involved with, that's the truth my friend. You stuck your little candy cane in a beehive and they done stung your pecker, eh?'

Schembri laughed coarsely and shovelled some food into his mouth.

'And I understand they're planning to kill you, right?'

I nodded. I talked about it with no real connection to what it meant. The death penalty had been presented as the only acceptable penalty by the prosecuting attorney. I knew someone, somewhere had already made the decision. Characteristically, I would be the last to know. At that time it all seemed so unreal and distant and beyond belief that I could have been talking about someone else. It would not be for the best part of a year that the actual truth of what would happen to me would become real.

'You gon' go to your Maker with a clean heart, right?'

I nodded.

'Shee-it, boy, I heard you didn't even put up a fight,' Schembri said.

I opened my mouth to say something, but he cut me short.

'Seems to me anyone who knows anything about you knows you were railroaded, boy . . . but the fact that they know ain't gonna help you none. People you pissed off are an awful lot more powerful than a few convicts and a couple of Penitentiary wardens.'

He spoke the truth.

'So don't go gettin' yourself involved with any politicians' daughters again, eh? Let that be your lesson this time around.'

Schembri spooned the last mound of chicken into his mouth and stood up.

I opened my mouth to speak, to ask any one of the ten thousand questions I had planned to ask him.

'I gotta go take a piss now, boy . . . been nice talkin'. I'll see y'around.'

He stepped out from behind the table and started walking.

And then he stopped, suddenly, as if someone had tugged him with a rope, and he turned, slowly, silently, and looked at me with such a strange and disconcerting expression.

He started back towards me, his expression focused, intent, and when he reached the table he leaned towards me.

His voice was a whisper, barely that much.

'One more thing,' he said. 'When you go up there –' he nodded towards D-Block on the other side of the building '– you're likely to meet someone. His name is West, Mister West, and he runs that place all by hisself. He's the bossman up there, don't let anyone tell you different. He's a bad, bad man, the very worst . . . and some long time back he was working for the government on things the government don't like to tell you about. He was employed to take care of certain – shall we say – embarrassments, for folks like Cavanaugh, Young and Goldbourne.'

I was stunned into open-mouthed silence.

Schembri continued.

'Not a word, my boy, not a word of this. You got yourself involved with those people, people who I believe may as well have pulled the trigger on the Kennedys themselves. And look what happened to you and your buddy, eh? West is born out of the same egg, and you let him know what I just told you and they'll find you hanged in your cell just like they found Frank Rayburn. There ain't nothin' you can do about it so I wouldn't even try. You keep that secret, take it to your grave if you have to, 'cause you ain't never gonna prove nothin' an' the only one who'll hurt for it is you.'

Schembri stood up straight.

He nodded his head.

'Not a word,' he repeated, and walked away.

He didn't look back. His stride was purposeful and determined.

As I watched him go, I was none the wiser, all the more frustrated for realizing I really knew nothing significant at all about what had taken place. I wanted to speak with him again, I *needed* to speak with him, but I never found him again.

A little more than a month later he went up against the Warden of Sumter Penitentiary with an armful of legal books and some quotes from the Constitution. Apparently he intended to sue South Carolina State for violation of his basic human rights.

Two days after that particular conversation he collapsed in his cell with a massive coronary seizure. The bruising he suffered to his chest and back was apparently the result of falling against the sink when he went down. How someone can fall both backwards and forwards simultaneously I don't know, but Robert Schembri did it, and did it with style.

He was buried in a Penitentiary plot. No-one came. Apparently he had no living relatives. He was one of a kind.

Some months after his death I was moved to D-Block, the place of my execution, and I would look back and recall the people I knew and realize that, aside from Schembri, I never really connected with anyone. I had spoken to the man no more than three or four times, and more often than not there was that feeling that he didn't even know I was there. But what he said influenced my thinking, broadened my perspective of the world from which I'd come, the world from which I would depart. And above all this he had placed a belief in my mind. That perhaps this Mr. West knew something of Nathan Verney, that he might have been involved in the very reason I was there. But I could not let myself believe that, could not dare to imagine that such a thing could run in so concentric a circle. But the thought was there, and as someone once said *a mind stretched by an idea never again regains its former proportions*.

My mind was stretched. It would never again be the same.

The world was crazy. We knew that in Florida. We knew that when we heard of the tens of thousands of dead in some far-away war that possessed neither motive nor meaning.

It was becoming harder and harder to gain anchorage.

I took some sense of comfort in the belief that there was a reason for everything.

Shame that no-one told me what it was.

TWENTY-FIVE

Christmas Eve 1969.

I remember standing on the porch of my house watching a dog run back and forth across the road. Crazy fucking dog. Chasing something I couldn't see. Eventually it paused right there in the middle of the road and started barking. It vanished as soon as a car appeared around the corner.

I turned and walked back into the house.

Nathan was upstairs, sleeping off whatever had happened the night before. Linny had gone early, a little after six, said she'd be back before the middle of the day, would bring food, make us a meal.

I couldn't have cared less whether I saw her again. Her enthusiasm had begun to grate on me.

I sat in the kitchen for a little while. The house was silent. I smoked, drank some coffee, closed my eyes and remembered times I had sat there before. Times when things had been simpler, less complicated, times when things had seemed to make some kind of sense.

Reality challenged me. I felt an injustice had been perpetrated, and though I cared for Nathan Verney perhaps more than for any other person alive, I was concerned that he hadn't considered the effect his burgeoning relationship with Linny Goldbourne might have had upon me.

I wanted to feel nothing about it. I wanted it to be of no consequence at all. I wanted to be strong and independent and uninfluenced by anything anyone said or did. But I was not. I knew that. Perhaps that was the real source of my irritation.

Nathan came down a little later. I said nothing. If Linny Goldbourne felt the same way about Nathan that she had evidently once felt about me, then she would be gone in a month, perhaps less.

I hoped that would be the case.

He asked me if I was bothered by her.

'Bothered?' I asked, feigning surprise at his question.

'Yeah,' he said. 'You know, bothered that she's obviously into me.'

I smiled and shook my head.

'You're welcome to her, Nathan,' I replied, and in my tone was the intended intimation that I knew something about her that he didn't. Something that he perhaps wouldn't like. The purpose of what I said went over his head completely. He merely grunted in acknowledgement and poured himself some coffee. He possessed thicker skin than I, and cared little for what people thought.

'She's coming back,' I commented a little later. 'Gonna make us some Christmas dinner.'

'Shit, hell yes, it's Christmas Eve,' he replied. 'I'd completely forgotten.'

'So you didn't get me a gift?'

He smiled. 'Sure, I spent about the same amount of money on you as you did on me, you asshole.'

We laughed, just for a minute we laughed, and for that minute it seemed that we were ten years younger, ten years more naïve, and whatever had transpired through that decade was now gone and forgotten.

And then the moment itself passed, and I realized that the things we had shared were now just memories and could not be recreated. What was gone was gone, and despite whatever I might have wished Nathan had no desire to see them return.

We were no longer kids. I think I missed that more than anything else.

Linny came in a whirlwind of noise and laughter. She stumbled through the front door carrying two or three grocery bags, and across the hall rolled fruit, cans of beer, bread and cheese and vegetables.

We went out to help her, and as she called for Nathan from the front drive I realized that she was advertising his presence.

Nathan went without thinking, an automatic response, and even as they returned, even as I warned them to be less public, the only reaction I got was a casual lack of concern.

'Hell, Danny, take it easy,' Linny told me.

She reached out and touched my face, and for a second she looked at me: looked at me just as she had when we'd gone down to Port Royal Sound, when we'd sat out on some pier eating lobster and watching boats on the Savannah River.

And then nothing. Holding her attention was like trying to hold a ring of smoke.

She breezed past me, again calling for Nathan, and I stood in the hallway and watched as they unloaded bags and started preparing food.

I was not hungry. I went upstairs and lay on my bed. I could hear the indistinct murmur of their voices downstairs. I imagined what they were saying.

Want you.

Want you too.

Fuck me here, right now, right here on the kitchen floor.

But Danny –

To hell with Danny –

Christ, Linny, he's my friend.

And I'm not?

Sure you are.

So fuck me, Nathan, fuck me . . . fuck me . . . fuck me . . .

I turned over and closed my eyes.

I thought of Caroline Lanafeuille, and for the first time in

. . . well, more than four years, I really missed her.

Really.

They called me down when food was ready and I went.

I ate with them, I drank red wine, I sat and listened and smoked cigarettes, and for all the hours we spent together I couldn't have said more than a dozen words.

I didn't want to be there. It was my house and I didn't want to be there.

'Where did you want to be?' Father John asked.

I smiled, shrugged my shoulders. 'Somewhere else . . . anywhere else, I s'pose. Two's company, three's a crowd.'

'Did you resent her being there?'

'No, I didn't resent her. She had every right to choose where she wanted to be. I just felt it would have been better for the both of them to be elsewhere.'

'Did you wish Nathan gone?'

'Wish him gone? No, I didn't wish him gone. I wished he would come back.'

Father John frowned. 'What d'you mean?'

'So much had changed in those eighteen months. I don't know why I thought it wouldn't, but it had. I think I expected everything to be back the way it was before we left. The thing with Linny wasn't the only thing. We had changed, both of us, changed in ways that I didn't even realize then. What I wanted was for everything to be how it was before, that's what I meant.'

Father John nodded. 'And what happened then, after the dinner?'

'I went out, took a walk.'

'And that's when you met them?'

I nodded. 'That's when I met them.'

'Two of them?'

I nodded again. 'Two of them.'

'And they didn't say who they were?'

I shook my head. 'They didn't need to.'

'You knew who they were?' Father John asked.

'I didn't know who they were, but I knew where they'd come from.'

'Linny's father.'

'Right. Linny's father.'

'They said that?'

'No, they didn't say that, but they were the kind of people that Linny's father would use.'

'Would use?' Father John asked.

'For any kind of action like that.'

Father John paused, and then he leaned forward across the table towards me. 'You know that he's dead now.'

I looked up. 'Who?'

'Linny's father, Richard Goldbourne.'

I shook my head. 'No, I didn't know he was dead.'

Father John nodded. 'Yes, died about six months ago.'

'And Linny?'

'She's okay, okay as can be expected as far as I know.'

'You know her?'

Father John shook his head and looked away. 'I don't know her, no.'

He looked back at me.

I opened my mouth to ask him how he knew of her at all but he interrupted me with his next question.

'So what happened when they approached you?'

'They warned me . . . well, they warned me on behalf of Nathan.'

'And you told this to the police?'

I frowned. 'I thought you'd read the trial records.'

'I did.'

'So you know the answer to these questions.'

Father John smiled. 'Humor me, Danny . . . tell me again.'

'Why?' I asked.

Father John shook his head. 'I don't know, I just feel I need to understand everything that happened.'

'And this serves some purpose?'

'Gives us both something to do,' he said, which surprised me.

'You really want me go through all of this again?'

He nodded. 'Yes,' he replied. 'All of it again.'

TWENTY-SIX

Today is October 11th. A month from now and I will be in the Death Watch cell. A month from now and it will be three or four hours until I die. I thought of this when I woke, and I cried. I cried for the first time in almost twelve years.

Before now I don't think I was capable of crying, but all this talk of Nathan, all this talk of the things that brought me here have served to bring me to the surface. That's the only way I can describe it. I have *surfaced*.

Sometimes I hate Father John Rousseau. Hate his questions. Hate his weatherworn Bible. Hate the sound of his voice as he asks me to go over these things time and again. Hate the plain walls of *God's Lounge* where I seem to have spent more waking hours than anywhere else. He says he means well, but until now I had somehow managed to keep reality at bay. Who's to say it would not have happened whether he had come or not? Who's to say that this *surfacing* would not have begun regardless of anyone asking me anything? All I know is that with his arrival came the first real thoughts, the first real emotions about everything that had taken place.

The years I have lived here at Sumter seem to have merged one into the other. I cannot even recall the names of the people I have spoken to through the bars of my cell, in the Visiting Room, in the Interview Section when civil rights lawyers and youthful law graduates have questioned me again and again. Seemed to me at one point everyone had something to gain from my death. It would prove to the blacks that there was no prejudice in the Court systems. It would prove to the whites that no matter your color you couldn't kill a man and expect any kind of leniency. It would prove the relentless and committed attention to the letter of the law of the District Attorney's Office. What it would prove to me I didn't know.

Perhaps I would find out in a month.

They came to take some blood after lunch.

Took half a pint through a needle the size of a pencil lead which they put into the vein at the top of my leg. Hurt like fuck. Didn't say a thing. Didn't even move.

Fuck 'em, I thought. *Fuck 'em all.*

Clarence Timmons came down to talk with me. He told me about the Death Watch cell. Told me I'd be moved there on November 4th, a week before the date. Told me there was twenty-four-hour surveillance. They didn't want you offing yourself before the party started.

He told me there'd be an open line to the Governor and the District Attorney's Office from the moment I moved to Death Watch until 12.01 p.m. on November 11th. He told me they'd ask me what I wanted to eat for my last meal.

'Baked ham sandwich,' I told him.

'You've thought about it?' he asked, and seemed surprised.

I shook my head. 'Don't have to think about it . . . know what I want, that's all.'

He said *Fine, just fine*, but if I should change my mind I should tell him or the Duty Officer because I could pretty much have anything I wanted.

I told him I wouldn't change my mind.

He let it go.

Then he told me about the Procedure Room. That's what he called it: *The Procedure Room.*

'When they take you to the Procedure Room they'll ask you if you want a sedative,' Mr. Timmons said, and his voice was hushed, like he was telling a bedtime story to a little kid.

'They move you into the Procedure Room an hour before the Procedure is due to begin, and they'll put you on a glucose drip and put in a line in case you need to use the restroom. You see, once you're in the Procedure Room you can't come out again –'

'Unless the Governor or the D.A. decides to call,' I said.

Clarence Timmons smiled understandingly. 'Unless the Governor or the D.A. calls,' he repeated, and in his voice was the certainty that such a thing would never occur.

'And once you're cooked you can come out, right?' I asked.

Clarence looked embarrassed.

'Otherwise it would get too crowded for the next guy . . . and the smell –'

Clarence Timmons raised his hand.

I had made him feel bad.

Fuck him, I thought. *Fuck them all*.

'I'll be going now,' Clarence Timmons said. 'You let the Duty Officer know if there's anything you need, okay?'

I nodded, didn't say anything. Didn't have anything to say.

I lay down when he'd gone, lay down and put my pillow over my head. I closed my eyes and thought of Eve Chantry's place, how it had looked that late Christmas Eve afternoon, the russet leaves, the wind gathering them in handfuls and scattering them along the path . . .

And the broken window.

I stood there on the path. Even as I looked I could imagine myself in the lower half of the house. I thought my way through it, up the stairs, and then looked out through the broken window. The broken window was in Eve's bedroom, the bedroom where she'd lain and told me of the candle-moth.

I could almost smell the place, that fresh scent of lavender and cinnamon, and the way the sun cut through those upper floor windows and created such space within.

The reasons I would have bought that house if I'd had the money. But I hadn't. Seemed no-one else had either. Or no-one else wanted it.

The place was falling apart, damp had set in along the edge of the porch and around the verandah. The mesh in the screen door was torn like someone had hurled a stone through it. The paint was peeling from the outer walls, like leaves, like the tongues of cheeky kids pulling faces at the strange guy standing on the path staring at them. The strange guy who used to come down here and see the crazy old witch a hundred years ago.

Place had been empty since she'd died back in the beginning of '67. Nearly three years.

I felt something I could not have described. Loss? Anger? A sense of worthlessness?

I walked towards the front door, went up those same steps where I'd stood and been showered in snow. I remembered the Christmas lights Benny Amundsen had hung along the front, the way Eve Chantry had leaned from the window and hollered at me.

Hell of a thing, Mister Ford.

Hell of a thing, Mrs. Chantry.

I remembered everything. And it hurt.

I reached for the handle, felt the damp mouldy surface of swollen wood, and when I turned it, the rusty latch creaked against the striker plate. I shoved the door and it gave, and pushing it back against the raised carpet I stepped inside.

This was no longer Eve Chantry's house.

Everything had been taken away, the furniture, her personal effects. The atmosphere.

That was the main thing. Eve Chantry's house had been

the way it was because of her. With her gone it was just a house. Nothing more.

Perhaps the rumors she herself had created had been sufficient to convince people the place was haunted.

I had a fleeting thought: that I should sell my mother's house and buy this one, restore it, recreate the atmosphere that was present when Eve was alive.

Do that for her. For myself. I smiled. It was a crazy thought.

I surveyed the hallway, saw through the door into the kitchen where she had baked those cookies, the ones that tasted of nutmeg and sweet cherry and something else indescribable that made you want two or three more.

I stepped forward and looked into the room where we had drunk Christmas punch and smoked cigars, where we had remembered Jack and Jennifer and a terrible day in the summer of '38.

All these things.

I turned and looked up towards the landing. Taking each riser slowly, testing my weight with care, listening to the creak of the damp wood beneath my feet, I went up.

I stood in the upper hallway, and when I moved I could almost see her there, see her lying on her bed, the tray of food untouched by her feet, that smell of lavender, the sense of losing . . .

I stood right where I had when I'd come to see her.

I remembered Dr. Backermann, his words, his platitudes, and how I'd wished I'd had all the money in the world to send her to Charleston State and have people who knew what they were doing give Eve Chantry back to me.

I remembered the candlemoth.

I turned at the sound of a car engine. Reaching that same broken window I had seen from the path below I lifted the net curtain aside and saw a dark sedan pull along the path and approach the house.

I frowned.

I released the curtain and went back to the upper landing. I started down the stairs, quietly, slowly, and without asking myself why I was going with such care. If I had stopped to think I perhaps would have been puzzled by the coincidental appearance of someone else. The house had been empty for years. Perhaps this was a buyer. A real estate agent. But it was Christmas Eve.

Back in the lower hall, I approached the front door and, as I reached for the door handle, I saw a silhouette through the frosted glass of someone out there on the porch steps.

Something tight and cold clutched at the pit of my stomach.

I stepped back as I realized whoever was out there was coming in. I was at the kitchen doorway by the time they had turned the handle and opened the door.

A man stood there. Tall, dark hair, long overcoat. He was not alone. I glimpsed a movement to his right.

'Mister Ford,' he said, and smiled.

I felt like someone had slapped my face.

'They knew your name?' Father John asked.

I nodded.

'But you'd never seen them before?'

I shook my head. 'Not that I could remember.'

'And the second man came in alongside the first?'

'Yes, but he sort of hung back, like he didn't really want to be seen as much, like he was trying to avoid showing his face.'

'But you did see them both clearly?'

'I saw them both clearly.'

'And you remember what they looked like?'

I frowned, puzzled. 'Why d'you ask?'

Father John leaned forward and rested his forearms on the table. He looked like a schoolteacher explaining something once more to a slightly backward child.

'I'm just fascinated,' he said. 'It's like gangster stuff. You go down to this house and these two guys turn up, long overcoats, menacing, all this kind of stuff. And also the thing that this guy Schembri told you about Mister West being in the employ of Senator Goldbourne.'

'Robert Schembri was a lot of things,' I said. 'And just plain crazy may well have been one of them.'

'You don't want to believe that Mister West knew something about what happened with Nathan?'

'What I want, what I believe, none of these things count for much right now. It doesn't matter whether Mister West knew anything about it or not . . .'

'Doesn't matter?'

'Say he did. What the hell am I gonna do about it now? I'm here, right here on Death Row, and he's doing whatever he does and there's nothing that's gonna change our places, right? It was what it was . . . I said all along that that's what happened. I went down there, they said what they came to say, they left.'

'And they threatened you?'

'Not directly . . . they didn't say they were gonna kill me or anything, but their purpose for coming down was clear.'

'And what was that?'

'Your friend,' the first man said. 'Your negro friend, Mister Ford.'

He took a step towards me. There was something in his face that I would recognize years later in that of Mr. West.

These people possessed dark aspects. They carried shadows and ghosts. Ghosts of what they had done, what they were about to do. Ghosts of what they would *like* to do if there was some way they could.

'Who the fuck are you?' I asked. I could hear the tension and fear in my voice. I sounded like a frightened ten-year-old.

'Let's say we are associates of an interested party,' the first man said. 'Anyways, who we are and who you are isn't the issue at hand, Mister Ford. The issue at hand is a certain Mister Verney who happens to be spending a little too much time and showing a little too much interest in a particular young lady.'

He smiled, and again there were dark aspects, shadows beneath his eyes that seemed to flicker out from someplace and return just as swiftly.

'So who the fuck are you?' I asked again. 'You're like paid fucking thugs or something?'

The second man appeared to emanate from behind the left shoulder of the first. He was slightly taller, he wore a wide-brimmed hat, and the light from the frosted pane in the front door cast a shadow that obscured all but his chin. It was a strong chin. Clean-shaven. I could see the muscles along his jawline tensing and relaxing back and forth as if something was alive and breathing inside his mouth.

I felt nauseous.

'We're no-one,' the first man said. 'We're messengers, nothing more than that. There's no threat to you, Mister Ford, none at all. We merely bring you a message that we would appreciate you passing on to your negro friend.'

'Message?' I said. 'What message?'

The first man smiled. 'I think you have the message loud and clear, Mister Ford . . . loud and clear.'

He turned as if to leave.

'Hey wait!' I said. 'What are you saying? That if Nathan keeps on seeing this girl there'll be some kind of problem for him?'

It was a stupid question, and even as I said it I felt awkward and naïve. They had delivered a message, I *had* received that message loud and clear, and these people were very simply the kind of people that stayed over their side of the field and you didn't proffer invitations.

The first man turned back.

He smiled, but there was something so sinister in that

expression, that slight flicker of tension around the lips and eyes.

'We're not here any more, Mister Ford . . . we're gone . . . we were never here in the first place . . .'

The second man had already backed out through the front door and was standing on the porch.

The first man went then, slowly, deliberately, his eyes never leaving me, and even as he reached the door the second man was walking away towards the sedan.

People didn't operate like this without a great deal of practice.

I was gripped by an indescribable sense of terror that seemed to pervade every nerve, every sinew, every muscle, everything inside of me.

The first man nodded, smiled again, and then he turned and closed the front door behind him.

I watched his silhouette as he went down the front steps and started along the path.

I walked to the stairs and sat down on the third riser.

I heard the sound of the car pull away towards the road.

I listened until the sound vanished into nothing, and then I buried my face in my hands and started to shake.

'And you didn't see them again?' Father John asked.

'Not that day, no.'

'Later?'

I nodded.

'And you were sure it was the same men?'

'Sure then, sure now . . . always will be sure it was the same men.'

'No question about it?'

I shook my head.

'The second man . . . you never saw his face clearly?'

'I saw his face clearly enough as he was leaving. He walked backwards towards the front door, and there was a

291

moment when the light from the side window in the hallway illuminated his face.'

'So you saw them both clearly?'

'Jesus,' I replied. 'This really is the third degree.'

Father John laughed. 'I'm sorry, Danny. The whole thing intrigues me. The fact that Goldbourne would send two heavies down to threaten you because his daughter was seeing someone . . .'

'Not just someone,' I interjected. 'Seeing a nigger.'

Father John looked at me. 'Right, right, of course . . . that really was the issue at hand, wasn't it?'

I shrugged. 'I don't know whether that was the only issue, maybe there was something else going on, but sure as hell if the rumors about who he was were true it would be an awful slur on his reputation for his daughter to be seen with a black guy.'

'The rumors?' Father John asked.

'That he was Klan . . . that he was Grand Wizard of the Empire or Grand Dickhead of the Realm . . . whatever these fuckers call themselves –'

Father John was laughing.

'What?'

'I like that,' he said.

'What?'

'Grand Dickhead of the Realm.'

I smiled. 'You know about these characters?' I asked.

'Some.'

'They're fuckin' nuts, man, fuckin' nuts. Grand-this and Grand-that, and the Invisible Empire, and the Union of the Snake. Robert Schembri told me all about the shit they used to do . . .'

'*Still* do,' Father John said.

'Right, still do,' I said.

Father John paused for a moment and looked away towards the window.

'So they left,' he said.

I nodded.

'And you went home?'

'Right,' I said.

'And that's when you saw them . . . Nathan and Linny.'

I nodded again. 'That's when I saw them.'

'Tell me . . .'

I was tired. Once more I had smoked too much, and now we could get coffee I was drinking too much of that as well. My guts hurt, that kind of acidic burning when you eat crap and chuck your system full of caffeine.

Carry on like this and it would kill me.

Irony, bitter-sweet and poisonous, filled my thoughts.

'Danny?'

I looked up.

'Tell me,' Father John prompted once more.

I nodded, resigning myself to talk until the end.

I could do that. I could talk.

Father John seemed willing to listen, and hell, talking to someone was better than talking to myself.

My memories were clearer than they'd ever been, and whether this was good or bad I didn't know.

Again, for some reason, I wondered where those memories would go after November 11th.

Father John would keep them, I thought. Father John would keep them for a while, and then perhaps he would pass them on to someone else. Perhaps we all carried around five-thousand-year-old memories that had travelled from generation to generation all down the line. Maybe a hundred years from now someone would be talking about me, this guy from South Carolina who fucked it all up so badly he got himself electrocuted in Sumter.

Or maybe not.

Maybe it wasn't that important.

I had wanted so much for my life to mean something. Something of worth, something of value, something to be proud of. Not for my parents, not for anyone but me. *I* wanted to feel like I'd done something. And how would I be remembered? A white guy who killed his best friend in a fit of jealousy and rage.

That's not how it was. Not how it was at all. And there had been a time I believed everyone involved knew that it could never have been that way.

But now, more than ten years later, I no longer believed anyone cared.

'Danny?'

I looked up. 'Father John,' I said, a little sarcastically. 'You're still here?'

'You're tired,' he said. 'We'll talk some more tomorrow.'

'Tomorrow?' I said. 'I thought we missed a day.'

'I'll come tomorrow,' he said. 'We don't have much time. A fortnight will disappear before you know it.'

I frowned. 'A fortnight? I have a month.'

'Right, Danny,' Father John said. 'But I only get to see you for the next two weeks, and then once more on the tenth.'

I frowned. 'How come?'

Father John shrugged. 'It's the rules.'

'They don't tell you why?'

He shook his head. 'No, they don't tell me why.'

'Strange shit goes on here,' I said.

'So, tomorrow,' Father John said as he rose from his chair.

'Tomorrow,' I replied.

He lifted a half empty pack of Luckies. 'You want these?'

I nodded. 'Sure, thanks.'

'Welcome,' he said, and reached for the buzzer to call the Duty Officer.

I would remember that day for a little while – not because of what I'd said, not because of the clear reminder that Rousseau had given me about my forthcoming rendezvous with *The Procedure Room* – but because of something I saw as I left *God's Lounge* and waited for the Duty Second to come and get me.

Rousseau walked away, down the corridor, a long and seemingly endless corridor that would take him out of this place. Thirty yards from where I stood he suddenly paused, looked to his right down an intersecting walkway, and then he was joined by Warden Hadfield.

They spoke for a few seconds, and then Rousseau turned, turned and looked directly at me, and seeing me standing there he seemed to emanate a sense of surprise. It was not something I saw, more something I felt. He seemed awkward for a second, standing there beside Hadfield, and then he took Hadfield's arm and directed him down the walkway and out of my line of sight.

I wondered what they were saying, whether they were speaking of me or something else entirely unrelated. That moment left me with a disquieting sense of unease, and I considered all the discussions, all the conversations that were taking place, that *had* taken place, about me. About what would happen. About who I was. About my death.

I turned as I heard Duty Second approaching. I looked down at my shoes. They seemed a million miles away, but the sense of foreboding, of fear, was as close as anything had ever been.

That sense of fear was within, it was now part of me, and – no matter what happened – it would walk with me all the way.

TWENTY-SEVEN

That night, a couple of hours after John Rousseau left, Clarence Timmons came down to see me.

He told me that he'd been assigned Duty Officer on my Death Watch. From November 4th until the end he would spend twelve hours a day with me in two six-hour shifts. He explained how I would be shackled to wall stanchions, a wide leather belt circumventing my waist and my hands cuffed to the belt at my sides. He said he had tried it once, that it wasn't uncomfortable, just exceptionally difficult to do anything but sit or lie down.

I listened to him silently. I barely breathed. And when he had gone I waited until the lights went down and then I sat on my bed in the darkness and imagined I was elsewhere.

Port Royal Sound.

Panama City.

Anywhere but here.

Eventually I lay down and slept, slept like Nathan used to sleep.

No dreams.

No nightmares.

Nothing but the sound of my own breathing whispering back at me from the dark.

But for that I could have been dead.

The following morning I woke before the bell. I knew it wasn't yet six, but I had no way of telling the time. From where my cell was situated I could not see the clock.

Mr. West was on the Block, you could tell that right away,

for as soon as the bell went everyone was up and making noise, getting busy. Mr. West did not, would not, tolerate late sleepers.

Plenty of time to sleep when you're dead, he'd say.

The Duty Second came down and told me I was on exercise time at nine, a half-hour round the yard and back. He said if I had cigarettes I could smoke out there.

I shaved, washed and dressed. We went up for breakfast, three at a time, an evolution that took more than an hour and a half for twenty-one people. D-Block could hold forty in all, but it seemed they were slightly more willing to consider life terms these days. Why, I didn't know. Didn't make any difference to me.

Breakfast was cereal, skimmed milk made with powder, two pieces of dry toast, no butter, a couple of spoonfuls of overcooked eggs and a cup of coffee that tasted like tepid raccoon piss.

It didn't take long to eat such a meal. It went down due to necessity alone.

Nine o'clock came and went. The Duty Second came down maybe fifteen, twenty minutes later and told me exercise time had been cancelled. Mr. West had decided on a cell search instead.

Duty Second should never have told me. Duty Second would have gotten his ass kicked if Mr. West knew. To tell me was to give me warning, and though I didn't carry drugs or a knife or anything else, I did carry a small wooden moth. Not exactly dangerous contraband, but Mr. West was a man who would have taken his time breaking it to pieces and kicking it out into the corridor. He would have done such a thing for the revs, no other reason, and he would have gone home later and jerked off about how excited he'd been.

Though I had seen him many times, though he had spoken to me on many occasions, I found it impossible to find the least understanding of Mr. West's passionate desire for cruelty. He was a precise and systematic thug, a vicious and uncompromising sadist, and I wondered what could have driven a child to become such a man. From what he'd said, his father had been killed, murdered by blacks someplace, but I knew West well enough to be convinced that West was merely a reflection of his father. I had no doubt that his father had been killed by people defending themselves, and perhaps he thought that all men were responsible for how his own life had been. Thus his life had become a means by which he could exact revenge, and what better place to do that than the Federal Detention system? What better place to find victims who were incapable of fighting back, men who had long since given up all hope of reprieve, who were already beaten and broken and cowed? He was singular in his predilection for ridicule and abuse, exacting in his demands for subservience, and with every word that passed his lips he would find a target. This was his life, this was who he was, and he took the greatest pleasure in practising until perfection was achieved.

I didn't see Mr. West until after my cell had been searched. I was given clearance without any question. The moth I'd held in my hand the whole time. They didn't look at my hands. They felt along the cuffs of my pants, around my waistband, they checked inside my shoes, the collar of my shirt, but they didn't check my hands. Figured perhaps that anyone stupid enough to actually hold something during a cell search was ballsy enough to get away with it.

And I did.

After they'd gone I lay on my bed and slept for an hour or so.

Father Rousseau would come later, mid-afternoon, and between now and lunch there wasn't anything to interest me.

Lunch came and went, another revolving evolution of

three men in, three men out, and by the time the meal was over it was close to 2.30 p.m.

Rousseau would be here within the hour. I wanted him to come. I *needed* him to come. He'd told me he'd read the trial records, that he'd come away with the feeling that I'd never fought back. He was right. I went down, and I went down easy. They weighted evidence against me. I even gave them a confession, a bullshit confession granted, but good enough to get me here.

But Rousseau was right about my not fighting back. And now? Now, for the first time in more than ten years I was angered by what had happened. Talking about these events had made me resentful and bitter, and though getting angry about facing execution less than a month before the due date was kind of pointless, it nevertheless felt right to be so.

I was going to die. Least I could do was tell people how pissed off I was about it.

Why had I not fought back? Why had I let the law graduates and pro bono paralegals come and go? People had read of my case. People had gotten all righteous about the injustice, the extent of circumstantial evidence, and they had come down here determined to get me out. I had answered their questions, perhaps not to the degree that I had responded to Father John Rousseau, but answering at all had been a formality. As if I hadn't wanted the distraction. As if I was so tired of all the bullshit I just wanted to wait it out. Wait until the lights went down for good.

Maybe I would have felt like this whether Father John had appeared or not. Maybe it was the fact that I had a date. Now it was real. Now it was going to happen for sure. I didn't know. Would never know. Couldn't go backwards . . .

'Ford?'

I opened my eyes, turned onto my side.

Duty Second stood in the corridor.

'Father John's here, time to go confess.'

I sat up, rose to my feet.

The Duty Second hollered down the corridor. The buzzer went, the door slid back and clanged against its frame.

Duty Second came in and put the belt around my waist, cuffed my hands to the belt, shackled my ankles together. He walked me out, hollered again for the door to be closed, and together we went down the corridor to *God's Lounge*.

Rousseau looked tired, dog-tired.

He was already smoking, already had a cup of coffee in front of him on the table when I entered the room.

Duty Second un-cuffed my wrists, removed the belt, unhooked my ankles and took the hardware away.

I sat down.

Best part of twenty-four hours had passed since I'd last sat here. Seemed like five minutes. I wondered if the next twenty-something days would go this fast.

'How you doing?' Father John asked.

'As good as.'

'You sleep okay?'

I smiled. 'Better than you it seems.'

He smiled back. 'Lot of work to do.'

'Lot of souls to save, right?'

'Right.'

'You got a new tape in?'

Father John frowned.

'In the video through there,' I said, indicating the one-way window.

'Sure, yes, a new tape.'

'Where do the tapes go?'

Father John shrugged his shoulders. 'Christ only knows.'

I leaned back, slightly surprised. 'Christ only knows? That's a little blasphemous isn't it?'

'Well he probably does know . . . I sure as shit don't.'

'Maybe you should go sleep a couple of hours and come back later,' I suggested.

Father John shook his head. 'I'm okay. I'm fine. Let's just pick up where we left off yesterday, okay?'

I nodded. 'Okay.'

I walked back from Eve Chantry's house. I took the path where I'd seen the deer watching me before. I remembered the moment vividly. The emotion I'd felt back then was the emotion I felt now: insignificance.

I didn't know what to say to Nathan. Or to Linny.

Hell, you know what, guys? A couple of heavies came down and saw me at Eve Chantry's place. Said as how Linny's daddy didn't like his little girl hangin' round with no niggers. They said as how I should pass that message onto you guys loud and clear, so you get the point an' all. Whaddaya figure huh? Ain't some folk prejudiced or what?

I thought not.

I decided I would speak to Nathan alone. Speak to him after Linny had gone. He would perhaps understand the situation better than she. After all, he'd been there in Florida, in Panama City. He'd been there when someone had taken such offense at his pool-playing they'd kicked the crap out of the pair of us.

I reached home within ten, maybe fifteen minutes. I stood at the end of the path and looked up at the house. The house of my childhood.

Even as I entered I knew there was a situation. I sensed it, couldn't tell how, but I *sensed* it.

I heard them before I reached the end of the hallway.

The door to the front room was slightly open, and peering through the gap between the edge of the door and the frame I could see movement on the floor behind the chair.

She came up then, Linny Goldbourne, and from where I stood I saw the upper half of her naked torso, her head thrown back, her eyes closed, a sound escaping from her open lips like an animal.

Stepping forward a foot or so I could see over the chair.

Nathan was on his back on the floor, she was straddling his waist, and as I looked his hands came up and enclosed her breasts.

Such big hands. Hands big enough to floor Marty Hooper, sensitive enough to fold an origami bird in Benny's Soda Shop.

Now they were hanging onto Linny Goldbourne like she'd levitate if he let go.

Her back arched, she continued to moan, and then she was moving back and forth, her hips rotating like a carousel at the County Fair.

All aboard!

I stepped back.

I felt the color rise in my face, my cheeks burning with embarrassment, with rage, most of all with jealousy. I felt hatred – real hatred – rising inside me like a wave, a gagging, spinning tortuous wave of something I could barely contain. I stepped back, almost lost my footing, and when I regained my balance I felt the stinging anguish of tears flood my eyes. My throat was tight, constricted, my breathing short and sharp, and when I stepped closer to the door once more my mind was filled with something dark that could have killed them both.

I pressed my face against the cool surface of the woodwork.

I could hear them – every word, every sound, every labored panting breath – and I wanted to burst in there, wanted them to know, to *really* know, to *really* understand, what their complicity and betrayal had done to me.

I wanted them to hurt like I was hurting.

I *really* wanted them to hurt.

I leaned forward one more time as Nathan came upwards and closed his mouth around one of her nipples.

She screamed and started laughing.

'Don't bite!' she hollered. 'Ow, ow, ow, you fucking animal!'

Nathan was laughing too then, and suddenly she lifted herself free of him, pushed his shoulders back and her head disappeared towards his stomach, lower to his groin.

Nathan moaned.

I stepped back. I imagined my fist driving through his face like a jackhammer. I pictured my knuckles whitening as my hands stretched around her throat and choked every last cheating breath from her lungs.

I wanted to scream, to burst open with rage and take both of them with me.

I knew, I knew then, that if I didn't leave I could not contain myself; that if I didn't run from the house, I would do something that I could only ever regret.

I grabbed the handle and slammed the door shut.

And then I ran.

'They must have heard you.'

'Sure they must have heard me. I *wanted* them to hear me.'

Father John nodded. 'You wanted them to know you were there.'

'Yes, I wanted them to know that I was there, that I was angry, that it was all well and good they were gonna fuck each other, but for Christ's sake, in my front room, on my carpet ... Jesus!'

I looked at Father John. 'Sorry,' I said.

He waved his hand. 'No problem.'

He paused to light a cigarette.

'And that's why you never said anything to Nathan about the men who came to Eve Chantry's house?'

'Yes.'

'Because you were pissed off with him and Linny?'

'Yes.'

'How d'you feel about that now?'

I paused, looked away for a moment. 'I think that whether I'd told them or not it wouldn't have changed a great deal in the end.'

'But they were unable to make a choice for themselves,' Father John said.

'That's right, but you'd have to understand a little of Nathan and something of Linny Goldbourne to understand that they more than likely would have ignored the whole thing.'

'Or thought you'd made it up?'

I frowned. 'Why would I have made it up?'

'Jealousy,' Father John said. 'They could perhaps have read it as jealousy, that you wanted to see them split up because you wanted her for yourself.'

'Could have,' I said. 'That wasn't the case . . . I was pissed off with them, more with Nathan than Linny, and once she'd left it seemed less important . . .'

'So where d'you go then?'

'Walked around,' I said. 'Walked back the way I'd come, turned around and went to the other side of town. Went to Benny's, had a soda, settled down. I was sure as hell angry for a while, just a while . . . and then I calmed down and went back.'

'And when you got back?'

'When I got back she'd gone.'

And Nathan was standing in the kitchen drinking a cup of coffee. He nodded as I walked into the room. He could tell I'd left in anger. I waited for him to say something, got the feeling he didn't know what to say, and so I said something first.

'It's okay,' I said. 'I was mad, and now I'm not.'

He seemed relieved. 'Hell, Danny, if I'd known you were coming back . . . well, if I'd known you were coming back we wouldn't –'

'It's okay,' I said. 'It's gone.'

And what I wanted to say was *well, friend, I got her for a month, and now you're gonna get her for a month if past experience is anything to go by*. But I didn't.

I shut my bad mouth, kept my thoughts to myself.

'You want some coffee?' Nathan asked me.

'Sure,' I said, and I sat down.

'And you didn't speak of it again?' Father John asked.

'No, we didn't speak of it again. Hell, it was Christmas Eve. We relaxed, we had a drink and a smoke. I think we even played cards or something.'

'And when did you see her again?'

'Not until after Christmas, a couple of days after Christmas.'

'And that was the last day you would see her?'

I nodded. 'Right, the last day.'

Father John leaned back in his chair and sighed resignedly. 'Hell of a thing, Danny,' he said.

I smiled. 'Hell of a thing, Father John.'

TWENTY-EIGHT

Christmas Day came and went.

Linny, presumably with her parents that day, didn't come down. We didn't see her until the 27th, and by then I had spent enough time with Nathan for our friendship to have resurfaced.

Christmas Day itself we ate hot dogs, relish and sweetcorn. We drank red wine, three bottles between us. We talked of things we hadn't spoken of for years, things like Kennedy, Martin Luther King, and though we discussed these monumental events the war was never mentioned. It never even crossed my mind, and though I cannot speak for Nathan, I believe I knew him well enough to have known if he carried some unspoken thought. There was no such perception.

We were relaxed, at one with the world it seemed, and when I fell asleep across the chair with the radio playing Tony Bennett out of someplace in Virginia, Nathan left me there. He knew I would have wanted to be left.

The day after Christmas I visited my mother's grave. I knelt there for some time, in my hand some flowers, and though I tried with everything I could to feel some deep sense of loss, I didn't. The guilt I had experienced when I'd heard of her death had gone. I had faced the fact that I had not been there, and wish though I might, I couldn't turn time backwards. She was gone, much the same as my father, as Linny – if not in person then surely in spirit – and then there was Caroline. For some reason my attention turned increasingly to her, and the more I remembered what we had shared the more important it became.

I had never discovered why Caroline Lanafeuille had left Greenleaf, what her father had done that had precipitated such a reaction. The truth was, she was the first. And despite the girls in Florida, the beach-dwellers, despite the Devereau sisters and all they brought with them, there really was only one girl who had ever touched me with something more than the physical. If I would cry for losing anyone, it would be for Caroline.

I did not stay long at the grave, I did not see the purpose. I visited, I paid my respects, I did not say a prayer for I didn't believe anyone was listening. I said a few words *to* my mother: how grateful I was that she had cared for me, that I hoped she'd found peace, hoped she'd found my father. Then I walked from the cemetery at the end of Nine Mile Road and went home.

The remainder of the day passed uneventfully. Every once in a while Nathan would walk to the front window and look out towards the road. I knew he was looking for Linny. Again, just as before, she had engineered that sense of uncertainty: was she with you, was she not? How she did that . . . well, I don't believe even she knew how. She was beside you, possessed you, swallowed you up completely, and then she was a million miles away and growing more distant with each heartbeat. She could make you feel as if you were the center of the universe, and then as nothing. I thought she was perhaps a little crazy.

But Nathan was a man, his own life was right there in front of him, and he would learn too.

Learn the hard way perhaps, but hell, was there any other way?

Later, evening closing up around the house, I lay in a chair in the front room and listened to the radio without really hearing much of anything at all. I was tired, as if the past eighteen months of running had finally caught up with me. Nathan was somewhere – the kitchen, upstairs, back in the kitchen again – and I sensed his restlessness. He wanted something to happen, and I reckoned the best thing for everyone concerned would have been for him to leave then, to go see his folks, to get things straightened out.

But he stayed. Stayed with no intention of seeing anyone but Linny Goldbourne, for she, in her own inimitable style, had captured him and wouldn't let go until she decided she wished for something else.

'You think she did such things on purpose?' Father John asked.

I shook my head. 'I don't think so. I think she came from the kind of background where she could have pretty much anything she wanted without a great deal of effort. Live like that for a while and I think things begin to lose their value. Relationships too. Figure if you've got money there's always a line of people waiting in the background to be your best friend.'

Father John smiled. 'To have and have not.'

I shook my head.

'It's the name of a book,' he said. 'Deals with similar sorts of things.'

'Right, okay.'

'So you don't think there was any malice intent on her part?'

'Malice intent, no. I don't think she was even aware of what she was doing. If I hadn't seen Nathan pacing about like a caged animal that day I might have thought it was just me, but I could see he was feeling the same things as I once had. It was the *not knowing* that did it. Was she with you? Was she not? Was she off with someone else? Was she using you for some brief amusement, and then you were forgotten? It was the way she looked at you sometimes, like she was looking right through you . . . it was odd.'

'Did you know much about her father?'

'No,' I said. 'I didn't really know anything about him at all. Some rumors perhaps.'

'Rumors?'

'The stuff I told you, that he was something significant in the Klan, that he controlled a great deal of land, possessed endless millions of dollars, could buy anything he wanted including people, votes . . . that kind of stuff.'

'You know he's dead.'

'You told me that already.'

'Right,' Father John said, and for a moment he looked distracted.

'His position was what got her where she ended up, you know?' I said.

Father John nodded. 'I'd thought of that as well.'

'If he hadn't been who he was I don't think that would have happened to her . . . she wasn't that bad.'

There was quiet for a moment, Father John looking down at his hands, his expression distant.

Then he looked up and smiled. 'So, the next day, the day she came back?'

'Right,' I said. 'The next day –'

I felt good when I woke. I had stayed off the weed and the wine the day before and felt better for it.

Nathan slept through until close to lunchtime and I appreciated the couple of hours alone. I walked through the house, spent a little time in each room, moved some things around, found some photos I hadn't seen for years, photos of myself as a child, my parents in their twenties and thirties. I recognized how much I looked like my father, and somehow that pleased me.

I walked out into the back. The yard was overgrown. Under an eave that projected from the rear of the building, a small shelter where my mother had stored wood and tools, I took an axe and split some logs. The axe was heavy, rusted around the join between the blade and the haft, but it did the job. It felt good to be doing something physical, felt good to get some clean South Carolina air in my lungs. It felt good to be alive without the fear of someone finding me.

I made breakfast, waffles and bacon, and I sat alone in the kitchen and ate. It felt right to be back there. That house had always been an anchor, a safe harbor, and though I was no longer running from anything, it still gave me a feeling of security. Here I could stay, regardless of what the world might think, and I felt lucky to have it.

When Nathan came down he had a headache. He didn't want to eat, but he drank two or three cups of coffee.

'Figure we should clean the place up,' I said. 'Thought I might stay here for a while.'

Nathan nodded. 'Sure thing,' he said.

'You can stay here as long as you want, but I reckon you should give some thought to what you're gonna do 'bout your folks.'

'My folks?'

I sat down facing him. 'Sure, your folks. You can't leave them trying to convince everybody that you're dead, Nathan.'

'Why not?'

I gave a forced, unnatural laugh. This was a response I had not expected. 'It ain't right. They're your parents for God's sake. You want them to keep pretending you're dead for the rest of their lives?'

Nathan shrugged. 'Figure they'll get over it,' he said. 'Hell, perhaps they already have.'

'You don't think they'd be happy to see you?'

'Shock would more 'n likely kill my pa,' Nathan said, and there was something in his tone that made me suspect he could actually believe such a thing.

I shook my head in disagreement. 'You are their son. Whatever the hell has happened, you are still their son.'

'The prodigal returns,' he said.

'Jesus, Nathan, sometimes I just don't get your viewpoint.'

Nathan stopped with his coffee cup halfway to his mouth. 'I don't know that you need to get my viewpoint, Danny. I am who I am. I think what I want to think. I say what I want to say. It's as simple as that.'

'Shit, you've changed, man –'

'Changed?' he said, his tone one of surprise. 'We've *all* changed. The world has changed. The world has become some crazy fucked-up place with people killin' each other like there's no tomorrow. What the hell d'you think this has all been about, Danny? Do you ever wonder about why we're here? D'you ever stop to think about what's going on around you? Hell, sometimes you are so blind.'

'Meaning?' I asked defensively.

'Meaning nothing.'

'If you meant nothing you wouldn't have said it,' I snapped.

'Oh shit,' he replied. 'What is this now? Kids in the sandbox? I won't come if I can't win bullshit?'

And then I thought of them. Thought of the men at Eve Chantry's house.

I was on the edge of saying something. But I didn't. Didn't say a thing. I didn't ask myself why I said nothing. I didn't even question my motives, or lack of them. I just decided then and there to say nothing. It seemed ridiculous that anyone would really do anything just because their daughter was seeing some black guy. Maybe I believed that. Maybe I deluded myself. Whatever. But I didn't mention it.

And then the moment was gone.

'Forget it,' I said.

'Already have,' Nathan replied.

I walked over to the sink. I started to wash some plates. I wanted to turn and hurl one right at Nathan Verney and crack his head in half.

But I didn't do a thing. Like so many times before.

There was silence between us, and I let that silence grow and fill my house as if it could suffocate Nathan, could suffocate how I felt, could bury us both in emptiness and dissolve everything.

And perhaps that atmosphere would have stayed, stayed and mushroomed like some dark fungus, but Linny arrived within the hour, and with her arrival everything shifted to a different level altogether.

'A different level, how d'you mean?' Father John asked.

I smiled. 'She was so enthusiastic about everything. She would always bring something – something great, something stupid – it didn't matter. That day she brought Christmas party hats and balloons, all kinds of things from her own house. She brought bottles of champagne and some cigars she'd stolen from her father, these foot-long Havanas. That was what she did, she assumed control, she made everything revolve around herself.'

'And she stayed the rest of the day?'

I nodded. 'Yes, the whole day.'

'And when did these men come back?'

'The exact time I could never be sure of, midnight, sometime after midnight I think. I'd drunk a lot of champagne, smoked some weed too, and I slept heavily . . . and if it hadn't been for the sheer volume and intensity of screaming I don't think I would have woken at all.'

'But you did wake up?'

I nodded, lit another cigarette.

'And what happened when you woke up?'

'First of all I was conscious of something in the house that didn't belong there . . . you know . . . when you just *know* that something isn't right?'

'Yes,' Father John replied.

'That feeling, that awareness, whatever you wanna call it . . . I just knew there was something in the house that shouldn't have been.'

'And what else?'

The darkness.

The darkness was intense.

I didn't know how to describe it. Darkness is darkness, right?

I knew something was happening.

For a long time there seemed to be silence, but I knew there'd been some sound that hadn't belonged here.

That's what had woken me.

At least I *felt* that that's what had woken me.

I believed I had heard someone screaming.

I sat up in my bed and listened.

There was movement, I could hear movement, and I believed it was coming from the room facing mine, the room where Nathan and Linny were sleeping.

I moved to sit on the edge of my bed and then I stood up. I felt a little uneasy with the sudden awakening, the champagne I'd drunk the night before, the sense of confusion and disorientation I was experiencing. All these things contributed to a feeling that my anchors to reality had slipped, the ropes were spooling out and I was floating into some errant tide that would lose me.

I gathered my thoughts.

I moved towards the door.

Thud!

A definite sound, something heavy falling to the floor, heavier than a footstep.

I was puzzled.

I figured perhaps Nathan and Linny were fooling around, but by the time I reached the door the feeling that something was wrong had gathered substance.

Intuition was not my strongest point, but there was something about the atmosphere, something about the way the hair crawled across the back of my neck, something about the tension I felt in my lower gut, that told me I was walking towards something fearful.

And then she screamed.

'You knew it was her?' Father John asked.

'It could only have been her. And besides, I knew her voice well enough to know it was her. Like you can tell someone by their laugh –'

'But you'd heard her laugh many times. How many times had you heard her scream?'

'She was a screamer.'

Father John looked at me questioningly.

'She screamed when she got excited, she screamed when she was making out sometimes, she screamed when Nathan bit her that time . . . she was a screamer, okay?'

'But this would have been a different kind of screaming . . . this would have been terrified screaming or something –'

'It was her,' I said emphatically. 'And besides, when I opened the door it was Linny standing there – screaming.'

'So you did actually see her screaming?'

'Yes, but you didn't let me get that far. I heard someone screaming, I thought it was Linny Goldbourne, and then when I opened the door I *saw* that it was Linny Goldbourne screaming . . . are we clear on that now?'

'We're clear on that now,' Father John said. 'I'm sorry . . . go on.'

'You gonna interrupt me again?'

Father John shook his head. 'Not unless there's something I don't understand.'

'Okay,' I said. 'So I'm standing there in my room and I hear someone screaming who I think is Linny Goldbourne –'

And even as I reached for the door handle I could feel this

sensation in my lower gut. Felt like a snake was unravelling itself in my intestines.

That sense of tension increased right through me. I started to open the door.

She screamed again.

The door was three, four inches ajar, and that sound came at me like a freight train.

I started, took a step backwards, and for one awful, horrifying second I believed Nathan was killing Linny Goldbourne.

It seemed such a ridiculous thought that I found myself smiling, but it was the smile of someone afraid.

Something was happening in my house.

Something was happening ten yards from where I stood in the shadow within my room, and I had no idea of what was going on.

Except that it was bad.

I looked around the room for something to defend myself, something with which I could protect Linny, but there was nothing.

I stepped towards the door again, opened it a little further, and then the screaming became a continuous rage of sound, a torrent, a rush of madness exploding from the door facing mine.

I went out like a crazed man, fear cowering behind me, some inner force impelled me, drove me, took over my body and propelled me across the hall towards the opposite doorway.

Linny was standing beside the bed, her eyes wide, her hands reaching out towards the center of the room. Her whole body was spattered and coursed with bright red blood, covered in it.

Nathan lay on the bed, his form barely visible among the scarlet sheets.

I opened my mouth.

The man I'd seen at Eve Chantry's house, the man who'd

spoken, appeared out of left field like a shadow and I felt a pain the like of which I'd never experienced.

My head felt as if it had been smashed with a baseball bat.

Like Babe Ruth had hit a home run through my forehead.

As I went down I could see the second man wrestling with Linny.

Linny was screaming still, sounded like her body was being wrenched in two; I staggered to my feet, felt myself skidding awkwardly. I looked down, and my feet, my own bare feet, were sliding back and forth in runnels of blood that seemed to be moving beneath me as if they possessed a will of their own. I lost my balance, grabbed the side of the bed and went crashing down to the ground once more.

I began screaming too, and then I felt a tremendous pain collide with the side of my body.

Everything was turning black.

Black and gray with red waves inside it . . .

And I could smell something, something like dirt, and later I would think that perhaps it was the smell of so much blood . . . and I could see the blood as I fell . . . like someone had gutted a pig and swung it round the room . . . and then there was blackness coming like ink through water, like indigo to midnight to lampblack to ebony to jet . . .

I tried to stand again, reached for the sheet that hung from the side of the mattress, and used it to haul myself up. As I came to my knees, a second collision impacted against my body.

I howled in agony. I rolled sideways bringing the sheet down across me, a wet, heavy sheet, so red and so warm . . .

I tried to slide underneath the bed, tried to gain some purchase against the wet floor, but it was useless, and I was losing consciousness . . .

Kill the motherfucker, someone said.

And I thought I heard my mother's voice.

No, not my mother . . . it was Eve Chantry.

And then it sounded like Caroline Lanafeuille.

She was saying something, quoting something like she used to, something from Frost or Whitman . . .

My surface is myself . . . under which to witness . . . youth is buried . . . Roots? . . . Everybody has roots . . .

I opened my mouth to scream again and felt a hand around my throat, a hand that was squeezing every ounce of breath from my lungs.

I flailed my arms wildly, I connected with something, something hard . . .

Asshole motherfucker!

A fist collided with the side of my face. I felt as if all my teeth had moved from one side to the other, and then I was gasping as my head was forced down against the floor, and I could smell the blood, taste it in my mouth. My own? I didn't know. Christ, there was so much blood . . . so much blood . . .

I was dragged across the room.

I heard Linny screaming again.

I tried to shout her name.

There was a sound like when Nathan hit Marty Hooper in Benny's and then there was silence but for my own breathing . . . my own desperate struggle for breath as the two men started raining punches down on me.

I moved sideways, sideways again, and somehow I managed to roll onto my side and get to my knees. Pushing my back against the wall I started to rise, and then heaved myself forward, propelling myself towards the bed as if there I could find some sanctuary.

And he was there.

Nathan was there.

Nathan's eyes staring back at me from his head.

Nathan's head lying on its side amidst a still wave of blood that had erupted from his body and covered much of the room.

His body lay still, his arms outstretched like Christ crucified.

His head on the side of the mattress.

Disconnected. Detached.

I opened my mouth to scream again, and a shoe collided with my lower jaw and sent me hurtling back against the wall.

I saw nothing but blackness . . . blackness and the image of Nathan's decapitated head staring back at me from the torrent of red . . .

I heard Caroline's voice as I slid into the darkness.

She was smiling.

We should . . . you know, we should . . . before I leave . . .

And then there was nothing.

TWENTY-NINE

'Were the police there when you came round?' Father John asked.

'Yes, they were there.'

'And you were already cuffed?'

'Yes. I was on my stomach on the upper landing floor, face against the banister, hands cuffed behind my back. I could taste blood in my mouth, and this excruciating pain was pounding through the side of my head. There was so much noise, so many voices.'

'And you saw them take Nathan out?'

'Yes.'

'How could you see that?'

'I was able to see through the banister posts and down the stairs. They carried him down on a stretcher but he wasn't covered up then.'

'And his head?'

I closed my eyes.

I could see it vividly – too vividly – even now.

'His head was carried by someone else. In a see-through polythene bag.'

'And what happened then?'

'They took him out, presumably to the coroner's car or an ambulance or something, and then they came back to get me.'

'And Lieutenant Garrett was there?'

'Yes, he was there.'

'And he was the one who told you that you were going to be charged with Nathan's killing.'

I nodded. 'Yes.'

'And Linny wasn't there, and no-one mentioned her name?'

'No, she was gone. It wasn't until much later that day that she was found.'

'In a field about a mile away.'

I nodded.

'Naked, covered in Nathan's blood.'

'Apparently so. I was told she was hysterical, delusional, in shock, all manner of things. It was intimated I had tried to kill her too, killed Nathan in a jealous rage and then tried to kill her.'

'But you were never charged with attempted murder?'

'It was not that I was never charged with attempted murder, it was that charges were never brought by Linny or the police for attempted murder.'

'And she went straight to Charleston.'

'To the State Psychiatric Hospital, yes,' I said.

'And for the duration of the trial she was classified mentally unfit to testify?'

'You're asking me questions you know the answers to.'

Father John smiled. 'I'm sorry. It's just that even now I find it so hard to believe that the entire thing was constructed around circumstantial evidence, that the only witness was classified as mentally unfit to testify and kept in Charleston State Psychiatric Hospital, and the State Defender never challenged any one of the aspects of evidence put forward by the prosecution.'

I shrugged. 'I think he was paid not to challenge them.'

Father John looked up. 'By whom?'

'Linny's father.'

'Because it was his people that killed Nathan, the two men that stopped you at Eve Chantry's house.'

'Right.'

Father John sighed resignedly. 'And then there was the axe,' he said quietly.

I nodded. 'The axe from the woodshed, the axe I'd used that very same day to cut logs outside.'

'And that was what they used to decapitate Nathan Verney.'

I nodded in the affirmative.

'And there were no other fingerprints?'

'That's what I was told.'

'By Garrett?'

'Yes,' I said. 'And then all the details over again in the trial. Forensics said there were no indications of anyone but Nathan, myself and Linny having been in the room, that the axe had only my fingerprints on it, that the footprints left in the blood on the floor and the landing were concurrent with my entry and exit to the room, with Linny's running away . . . you know the routine.'

'Okay,' Father John said. 'Enough for today.'

'You have somewhere better to be?' I asked.

'Somewhere to be, though not necessarily somewhere better,' he answered.

He started to rise from his chair.

'Father John?'

He looked at me.

'I wondered if you could do something for me.'

'Sure,' he said. 'What?'

'Do you think you could find someone?'

He shrugged. 'Who do you want me to find?'

'There was a girl I knew in Greenleaf, a girl I went out with for a short while. Her name was Caroline Lanafeuille, spelled L-A-N-A-F-E-U-I-L-L-E. She left Greenleaf suddenly in August of '65, and I never knew where she went.'

'And you want me to find out where she is now, seventeen years later?'

I nodded. 'If you can.'

Father John sat down again. 'Why, Danny?'

I smiled and shrugged. 'Curiosity. She was the first girl I

loved . . . hell, the way I see things now, she was the *only* girl I ever loved.'

'And what do you want to know?'

'If she's okay, if she's married, does she have kids, anything at all really . . . if it's possible.'

'Anything's possible, Danny,' Father John said.

He reached out and closed his hand over mine.

'And if you find out these things or – a worse scenario – you find out she's not okay, or even that she's dead . . . what then?'

'Then nothing,' I said. 'I just want to know, that's all. Whatever the situation, I just want to know. You think you can do that for me?'

Father John nodded. 'I can try, Danny, best I can do is try.'

'Then try, okay?'

Father John smiled, squeezed my hand reassuringly, and once again rose to his feet.

'I'm gonna be gone a couple of days now, Danny, maybe three.'

I looked up. 'I will miss my interrogations,' I said.

'As will I,' he replied. 'You take care, okay?'

'I'll take care.'

Father John reached for the buzzer.

I stood up and waited for the Duty Officer to come take me home.

Later, much later, I lay on the thin mattress in my cell, my eyes closed, and replayed the events of that terrible night. I was tired, my eyes scattered with sand, but I could not sleep. I turned everything over and over time and again, and I could never get away from the feeling that I had created my own fate by my omissions. Hindsight – our cruellest and most astute adviser – flickered in the rearview mirror of my mind. It haunted me, taunted me with names and accusations, and I watched it close up against me and then retreat, and then close up against me once more as if to remind me that whatever I might think, however I might seek to justify my actions, it would always be there. Every once in a while it carried Nathan's face, and then the face of my mother, and at one point it looked like Caroline as she walked away from my house that morning.

My thoughts were disturbed by a sound to my right. I turned and, my eyes accustomed to the dark, I saw a figure standing against the far wall a good fifteen feet from where I lay.

The figure moved, moved again, and then with half a dozen swift steps whoever it was had reached the bars of my cell and stopped.

'Can't sleep, little man?'

Mr. West.

My breath stopped in my lungs. My throat swelled and tightened with tension. I tried to close my eyes, to block him out, but there was something far more powerful forcing me to watch him.

He shifted sideways and gripped the bars ahead of him. He brought his face up close, and even through the darkness I could see the shadows beneath his eyes, and above those shadows the direct and unflinching gaze that held me cornered, barely able to move.

'Have been thinking of you, Ford,' he whispered.

The idea of Mr. West thinking of me disturbed me greatly. Like a killer selecting you as his next victim, tailing you, stalking you, learning your routines and habits, and all the while you know nothing.

'Have been thinking about the hollowness you must feel right now, the pointlessness of everything that you are, everything you have ever done . . . except when you killed the nigger.'

West laughed, a gentle creeping sound that echoed back at me from the walls and ceiling.

'That, my friend, was perhaps the only worthwhile thing you ever did.'

West moved again, squatted down on his haunches so his eyeline was level with mine. He was a good ten feet away, but in that moment it was almost as if I could feel his breath against my skin as he spoke.

'And the priest . . . what the fuck he comes down here for I don't know. Wasting what little time you have left justifying your pitiful existence. Haven't you figured out that there is no God yet? If there was a God would he have let you rot here? Would he have seen you walk all the way to the chair and never once raised his hand to help you? I think not.'

I closed my eyes for a second or two. There was blackness behind my eyelids, black and deep enough to swallow me. In that moment I wished it would.

West stood up. He pushed himself away from the bars.

'Count the days, Ford . . . count the days. Sleep if you can, but remember that for every hour you sleep you lose another hour of the few you have remaining. It goes so fast. Look at the last year . . . seems to have vanished into yesterday, right?'

I shuddered. He was right. The last *twelve* years had folded neatly into a heartbeat that I hadn't even noticed.

'Watch it disappear, Ford . . . watch it all disappear . . .'

And then he was gone. In the moment that it took to close and open my eyes he was gone.

I could hear the sound of my own heart beating. Conscious then more than ever of that sound, I imagined it was slowing down. My heart knew the end was coming. It was preparing itself. Preparing itself to stop.

And I would stop with it.

That simple.

THIRTY

It was the 17th by the time Father John Rousseau came back.

The previous four days had disappeared quietly, soundlessly, into nothing. Time had become intangible, immeasurable, and though I knew when the days began and ended because the lights came on and went out, it was still unsettling to realize that only twenty-four remained. A little more than five hundred hours.

Clarence Timmons came down to tell me Father John had arrived.

'How you doing there, Danny?' Mister Timmons had asked.

I looked up. I felt the heaviness of my face, the nothingness in my eyes.

'Don't want to die, Mr. Timmons,' I said.

'I know, son, I know.' His tone was that of a father comforting a child. 'You go see Father Rousseau now, you talk to him, okay?'

I nodded, rose from my bed, and waited for Mr. Timmons to pass the belt through.

'I found her,' Father John said as I walked into the room.

I frowned.

'Your girlfriend, the Lanafeuille woman.'

The Lanafeuille *woman*. She would be as old as me. I had not thought of this. When I thought of her I saw a teenager.

'You found her?'

I didn't know what I felt. Something powerful. Something indescribable.

Father John sat down. 'And you won't believe what she's doing.'

'What?'

Father John smiled. 'She's a lawyer.'

I started to laugh. I laughed at the irony, perhaps at the fact that she even existed.

'You spoke to her?' I asked.

'No, Danny, of course I didn't speak to her.'

'How did you find her?'

'I called Greenleaf High School, got the details of the school she transferred to in 1965, and then I just followed the trail. It was easy to find her, a lot easier than I thought.'

'Where does she live?'

'In Charleston.'

'She's still here, in South Carolina?'

Father John nodded. 'Yes, she's still here.'

'And she's a lawyer.'

'A conservation lawyer,' Father John said.

'A what?'

'A conservation lawyer. She handles cases to do with land rights and violations of public ordinances regarding waste dumping, that kind of thing.'

I was quiet for a moment. I could see her face. I could smell her as she leaned over and kissed me as she left. I could remember not wanting to look out the window. Not wanting to remember her leaving.

'Danny?'

I looked up.

'You okay?'

'Sure,' I said. 'Sure.'

'Does this upset you?' Father John asked.

I shrugged my shoulders. 'I don't know what I feel ... upset, happy to hear she's okay ... I don't know.'

'Why did you want me to find out?'

I shook my head. There was a tightness in my chest, a feeling that tears would well into my eyes if I didn't grit my teeth, clench my fists, hold it all in . . .

But I couldn't.

Someone, something, was gently, irrevocably pushing me towards somewhere I didn't want to go. I started to cry. I could feel the rush of pain through my chest, my head, my whole body. I began to shake, to sob, and I sat there rocking back and forth as Father John came round the table and placed his hands on my shoulders.

'Let it go, Danny . . . let it go,' I could hear him saying.

And I did.

And it kept on coming.

Like twelve years' worth.

It must have been an hour or so later that Father John asked me about the events that immediately followed my arrest.

I was tired of talking, a bone-deep exhaustion pervaded my thoughts, my actions. But I talked anyway, talked because talking was an exorcism, a catharsis, and because Father John Rousseau wanted me to.

'Garrett was the first interviewer?' Father John asked.

'Yes, Lieutenant Garrett . . . hard bastard, unforgiving.'

'And the first interview you had was without any legal representation present?'

I nodded. 'It wasn't classed as an interview, that's why the information from it wasn't thrown out in court. They read my rights back at the house, apparently told me I could wait until legal representation arrived before I spoke, but Garrett said that I'd started talking, that he was there at the time . . . like it was just a coincidence that he heard what I had to say.'

'And what did you say?'

I shook my head. It was hard to recall the exact sequence of events.

'I remember talking about the men that came to the

house, that I'd seen them at Eve Chantry's house, things like that.'

'And Garrett didn't question any of it?'

'No, he didn't say anything really. He sat there with this patient expression on his face, like he was waiting for a bus or something. He prompted me every once in a while, but he never really asked me a direct question.'

'And you were in shock?'

I smiled. 'I was on a different planet. I was sat in Greenleaf First Precinct in an interview room, my clothes covered in blood, my hands and feet cuffed . . . and I was dying to take a piss, I remember that, like I was gonna burst.'

'And a lawyer came down?'

'Yes, a lawyer came down, someone from the D.A.'s Office or someplace, but he seemed like he really didn't want to be there. I remember how he first appeared to me, like we'd woken him up, or dragged him out of a dinner party, something like that. He seemed in an awful hurry to get out.'

'And while he was there Garrett asked questions?'

'Yes,' I said. 'He asked a lot of questions. He asked me how I knew Nathan. He seemed to know about the fact that we'd been gone from Greenleaf for eighteen months. He knew about Nathan's Draft Notice. He knew who Nathan's parents were.'

'And all of this within a couple of hours of your arrest?' Father John asked.

'Less, maybe an hour . . . it wasn't long between when I got to the Precinct and the lawyer coming down.'

'And what else did he ask you?'

I shrugged. 'What we'd done when we left Greenleaf, where we'd been. He asked me about my parents, about where I'd gone to school . . . all kind of things.'

'And during this interview neither he nor the lawyer mentioned Linny Goldbourne.'

'Right,' I said. 'Her name didn't come up 'til the second or third interview –'

'And there was no lawyer present at that interview?'

I shook my head. Details were becoming clearer, almost as if the more I looked the more I remembered.

'So what was the scene with the confession?'

I shook my head and sighed. 'It was not a confession.'

Father John leaned forward expectantly, a sudden look of heightened interest in his expression.

He nodded, prompting me to go on.

'I was talking, rambling a little . . . I remember I was tired, really tired. Garrett was asking me about my relationship with Nathan, asking me about things we'd done together, how my ma had felt about me befriending a negro in the '60s, how many times I'd been to Nathan's house, how I got on with Nathan's folks . . . that kind of thing. He asked me about these men at Eve Chantry's house –'

'I told you already.'

Garrett smiled, a practised smile. He was a hard-faced, brutal-looking man, a man who looked like he had little time for emotions other than suspicion and anger. From the moment I met him he frightened me.

'Tell me again,' he said, trying his damnedest to sound interested, to sound understanding and compassionate, though no such qualities were in his emotional vocabulary.

'Dark complexions, the first one shorter, heavier-set, the second one tall, thinner altogether,' I said. 'Suits and ties, dressed like Feds or something.'

Garrett smiled again, a little sarcasm in his expression. 'Like Feds?'

I nodded. 'You know, dark suits, white shirts, dark ties, and the car they drove was this sort of nondescript sedan.'

'Nothing specific, nothing about them that could help us make some kind of identification?'

I thought for a while. I thought of nothing. I shook my head.

Garrett nodded, and for a split second there was a smirk of satisfaction around his mouth, as though he was pleased I could give him nothing specific.

'So tell me some more about Nathan ... if these guys warned him off when you spoke to them at Eve Chantry's house, then why didn't you go back and tell him?'

I shook my head. 'I was mad at him.'

'Because he was fucking your girlfriend?'

'Not that he was fucking my girlfriend ... that they were so indiscreet about it.'

'Indiscreet?'

I nodded. 'I suppose I half-expected that something would happen between them, but I wished it had taken a little longer, and they'd been less exhibitionist about it, you know what I mean?'

Garrett shook his head. 'No, Mister Ford, I don't know that I *do* know what you mean. All I see is that some people apparently warned you that there would be trouble for Nathan Verney if he didn't stop seeing Linda Goldbourne, and you had plenty of time and opportunity to warn him of this, this supposed best friend of yours, and yet you said nothing, absolutely nothing. Seems to me, if you consider it in this light, then either there was no warning and there were no such men, or you and Nathan Verney were not friends at all and you wished for something to happen to him.'

'No, it wasn't that way ... they did speak to me, they did tell me to warn Nathan, but I was mad, I was upset with Nathan and Linny, and I should have told him and I didn't. That was all there was to it ... nothing else.'

'And what would have happened if you'd told Nathan about your discussion with these men?'

I shook my head. 'I don't know.'

Garrett leaned forward. He steepled his hands together

and rested his elbows on the table. 'Tell me what you think *might* have happened.'

I shrugged my shoulders. 'Hypothetically?'

Garrett nodded. 'Hypothetically.'

'Maybe he would have done something . . . maybe both of them would have done something. Maybe they wouldn't have been so obvious about the fact that they were seeing each other.'

'So if you'd said something then maybe he would be alive today . . . assuming, of course, that the men you spoke to at Eve Chantry's house really did exist, and that they were the ones who came and killed him?'

I nodded. 'Right.'

Garrett leaned back. 'How d'you feel about that?'

'I feel bad . . . worse than bad . . . guilty for not saying anything, for not telling him –'

'So hypothetically,' Garrett said, 'you could say that had you said something you might have saved his life?'

I nodded. 'Yes, I suppose so . . . possibly.'

'And the fact that you said nothing was therefore a contributory factor to his death.'

'If you look at it in that light, yes, I was responsible for his death.'

'And that was my confession,' I said, and reached for another of Father John's cigarettes.

'And you were aware that every conversation you had with Garrett was being recorded?'

'No, I was never told that anything was being recorded.'

'And the tape was spliced.'

I nodded. 'Yes, the tape was spliced. When the recording of that interview was played in court, the prosecuting attorney said –'

'We need to know that this is your voice, Mister Ford.'

I nodded.

'Yes or no, Mister Ford?'

'Yes.'

'That is unquestionably your voice?'

'Yes, it's my voice.'

'Your Honor ... request for the bailiff to play the interview section once again.'

'Granted.'

I turned to see the judge nod at the court bailiff.

The bailiff rose, he spent a few seconds rewinding the tape, and then pressed *play*.

'... he was fucking my girlfriend ... they were so indiscreet about it ... I wished they'd been less exhibitionist about it, you know what I mean? I was mad, I was upset with Nathan and Linny, and I should have told him and I didn't. I feel bad ... worse than bad ... guilty for not saying anything, for not telling him. In that light, yes, I was responsible for his death.'

'And that was considered an adequate confession?' Father John asked.

I nodded. 'A death penalty confession.'

'And the prosecution said that the tape recording had been analyzed and no signs of tampering had been found?'

'And the defense ... even the defense said the tape had been independently analyzed. "Of unquestionable integrity" was the term used, the tape was of unquestionable integrity.'

'So your defense wasn't really a defense?'

I shook my head. 'It was a joke.'

'Why didn't you change lawyers?'

'With what? I got what I was given. Either a court-appointed defense or a private lawyer. You don't get a private lawyer without serious money.'

'But the house was yours ... why not use the house as collateral?'

'The house was still tied up in all the legalities after my mother's death.'

'Convenient,' Father John said.

'Very,' I replied.

'And Linny was not permitted to make a statement or testify because she was in the State Psychiatric Hospital.'

'Yes, classified as mentally unfit to give credence to either defense or prosecution.'

'But Garrett was permitted to enter a statement that Linny Goldbourne named you as the killer?'

'Yes . . . apparently when she was found Garrett was the first person to speak to her. She told him that I had killed Nathan and attacked her.'

'How was that statement permitted as evidence to the court?'

'Because Garrett wasn't classified as mentally unfit to testify, and because there had been another police officer present when Linny had said this.'

'That would have been Jackson, Karl Jackson.'

'Right,' I said.

'And Karl Jackson confirmed that Linny Goldbourne had named you as the killer in the presence of himself and Lieutenant Garrett?'

'Yes, he testified to that.'

'And the defense didn't object.'

I leaned back and smiled, somewhat half-heartedly. 'Father John, you've got to understand that very little went on in that courtroom that made any sense at all. The public defender assigned to me was nervous about the whole thing, sweated like a pig, fidgeted with his papers, his pens, spilled water down his pants at one point and had to leave to get changed. The trial was less of a trial and more of an opportunity for as many people to say as many bullshit things as they could possibly think of, and for no-one to protest or object or imply anything was a leading question. If that was a trial, then hell I *was* guilty.'

Father John smiled. 'Careful what you say, Danny. This is all on tape, remember?'

I shook my head and sighed.

Father John reached out and closed his hand over mine. 'I'm sorry . . . I'm just amazed that all of this hasn't been chewed to pieces on appeal.'

'Because of me,' I said. 'Because I didn't want to go through it all over again. Because I didn't want my hopes raised and crushed . . .'

'And because you felt guilty for not saying anything to Nathan.'

I nodded. 'Because I felt guilty for not saying anything to Nathan.'

'And now?' Father John asked.

I leaned forward. I was tense, wound-up inside, and yet there was a wave of desperation and grief rumbling along the edges of my awareness. I could feel it there, like a shadow, a ghost of everything I should have felt over the last twelve years, but never did.

'I don't want to die,' I said, my voice a whisper. 'But it's a little too late to say that now, isn't it?'

Father John gripped my hand. He smiled as best he could.

'I'm afraid so, Danny . . . I'm afraid so.'

The wave of grief arrived.

I folded soundlessly beneath it.

THIRTY-ONE

That night, long after Father John had left, I lay in my bed and thought of the years I had spent in this cell, these four walls, and the world that lay beyond them.

Despite the absence of Frank Wallace and Cindy Giddings out of CKKL, Mr. Timmons had still left that small transistor radio playing, punctuating our existence with news from a different time and place, somewhere all of us knew we would never see again.

I recall Jimmy Carter being elected President in 1976, and twelve days later how his home town of Plains, Georgia at last ended the color bar. That brought it home to me once more that all the things we believed back then were true. Nathan had said he wouldn't see the changes that Martin Luther King fought for realized in his own lifetime. How right he was.

Before stepping down, Gerald Ford had pardoned Richard Nixon for his involvement in Watergate, the last act of a desperate man working his authority for the benefit of his compadres and co-conspirators.

We heard of Gary Gilmore, the first man executed in the States for ten years. After a lengthy campaign across the country against the return of the death penalty, he walked from his cell in Utah State to the firing squad with the words *Let's do it.*

James Earl Ray broke out of the penitentiary in Tennessee, went on the run for three days. A month later Carter gave Martin Luther King a posthumous Medal of Freedom.

And then Elvis died.

Grown men cried in their cells like it was their mother who'd gone.

Riots ensued after Leon Spinks beat Ali in February of '78, and a little-known research study showed that murder was the primary cause of death of young blacks in the United States. Regardless, in August of the following year, a fifty-mile White Rights March from Selma to Montgomery reminded the world that the things we'd believed we were resolving nearly twenty-five years before were still alive and well and living in the good ol' U.S. of A.

Nine months later five people were killed in race riots, and the National Guard was called in.

Reagan became President.

John Lennon was shot by a man with three names.

Reagan gave a million and a half dollars to investigate the murdered and missing children of Atlanta.

Someone took a shot at Reagan too.

These things, such things as we were told through that small window into the world, were simply reminders that it was crazy out there, perhaps as crazy as it was in here.

It told me that there was no such thing as true justice. That a great deal of life was a lie. Bitter, yes. Cynical, definitely. Hopeful . . . not any more.

I slept with the face of Caroline Lanafeuille floating behind my eyelids.

I was happy she was alive and well and living somewhere down in Charleston.

October 18th, a Saturday.

Outside it was raining heavily. I could hear it when I woke.

I lay for a time imagining that I was elsewhere, somewhere quiet, somewhere free from bars and guards and the promise of dying.

My imagination worked overtime but did not succeed in vanquishing the awareness of these things.

These things were certain, constant and finite. They were there when I closed my eyes, there when I opened them, there whether sleeping or waking, and they would not change.

Duty Second came down before the bell went. Told me a message had come from Father John. He would not be able to see me again for five or six days, the best part of a week. And some time after that I would move to Death Watch and I would have a week left. One hundred and sixty-eight hours. Ten thousand and eighty minutes. Just over six hundred thousand seconds. And how long would it take to count those seconds? Same amount of time it would take to live them.

It didn't seem that long.

I walked to breakfast in a quiet daze. I felt distant, disconnected, out of touch.

Someone spoke to me, another shoved past me in his hurry to eat, and these things went by like ghosts.

Dead meat walking.

For the first time in nearly twelve years I understood what Mr. West meant.

Two days later they shaved my head.

They stripped and searched my cell.

They found my wooden moth. Duty Second gave it to Mr. West who snapped it into four and kicked the pieces across the landing. I heard them rattle down the metal stairwell to the gantry below.

He came in and cornered me against the far wall of my cell.

Fucker, he said. *You dumb motherfucker. You've got twenty-two days left you piece of shit. Twenty-two days is an awful long time if you wanna make someone's life a misery. Don't fuck with me, okay?*

I didn't say a thing. A response was neither expected nor required. I got the message and Mr. West knew it.

He left then and I started putting my bed back together.

When it was done I lay down on it and counted the silences between things. There were a great many of them. I lost track eventually and fell asleep. I dreamed. I think I dreamed. A vision of myself stumbling from the edge of Lake Marion carrying my own lifeless body.

I woke with a start.

When the morning bell went I realized another one thousand four hundred minutes of my life had disappeared.

I got thirty minutes' exercise time. It was raining again but Mr. Timmons said I should go out regardless.

I did. I went out into the yard and stood looking up at the sky. The rain came down, a fall rain, fine and cool, and I appreciated the sensation on my face and hands.

I looked for God out there. I didn't see him. Figured maybe he had better things to do.

Thursday, October 23rd. I waited all day for Rousseau, but there was no sign, no word.

Hell, you don't phone, you don't write . . .

Mr. Timmons came down and told me that his wife was responding well to her physiotherapy and had lost a little more weight. I told him I was pleased for her. I lied. I didn't give a damn.

He left me then, walked back the way he'd come until I could no longer hear his footsteps on the gantry.

There seemed to be a heavy silence. More than before.

I leaned my head against the corner of my cell, stood there for nearly an hour, stood there until my head hurt bad, and then I lay down.

I think I cried myself to sleep.

I don't remember.

Maybe that was last night.

Friday.

It didn't rain, at least I didn't hear any.

Rousseau didn't come again. Not even a message. No word at all.

He'd heard what he wanted to hear, justified his own piety and innocence, played God for the dead guy down at Sumter, and now he was busy elsewhere, fooling folk into believing that something better was on the way.

Fuck him.

Fuck 'em all.

'Ford?'

I opened my eyes.

I was lying on my bed and could see through the bars behind my head.

Duty Second stood there.

'You awake, son?'

I turned over and sat up.

'Call for you . . . think it's the priest.'

Duty Second passed the belt through the bars. I put it around my waist, put my hands in the cuffs and snapped them shut.

I stepped towards the bars and turned to the right for Duty Second to check the cuff was firmly closed. I turned one hundred and eighty degrees and he checked the other.

He called down the gantry, the buzzer sounded, the door unlocked and he dragged it back.

I stepped towards him and he had me raise my right foot to put the ankle shackles on.

I shuffled noisily down the gantry after him, turned left at the end and went down the short flight to the cage.

Mr. Timmons stood inside.

He held the receiver in his hand.

Duty Second opened the cage door and I stepped towards it. As I entered and took the receiver Mr. Timmons stepped out through the other side of the cage and locked the door.

Duty Second gave me the nod and I took another step.

He closed the cage door on his side, and they each stood sentinel.

I raised the receiver to my ear.

'Daniel?'

'Yes,' I said.

'It's Father John,' the voice said unnecessarily.

'Right,' I said, my voice flat and emotionless.

'How're you doing, Daniel?'

'How the fuck d'you think I'm doing?'

There was silence for a moment.

'I'm sorry I haven't been for a few days,' Father John said. 'I have been busy –'

'Whatever,' I said. 'You stay busy, I'll stay here, we'll do fine. Anything else you wanna say?'

There was a moment's silence.

'Fine,' I said, and hung up.

I turned and kicked the bottom of the cage.

'Out,' I said.

Duty Second nodded at Mr. Timmons, and then he unlocked the cage door and let me out.

Mr. Timmons took me back to my cell.

He didn't ask me what was happening, didn't ask me anything at all.

He took the ankle shackles off, walked me into my cell, went out and locked the door behind me. He reached through the bars, unlocked each cuff in turn and waited until I handed him the belt before he opened his mouth.

'It'll be fast,' he said, which seemed the most idiotic and insensitive thing to say. 'I shouldn't think you'll feel a thing, Daniel –'

I turned, angered. 'Is that so, Mister Timmons? Is that so?'

I took a step towards the bars and glared through at him.

'Tell me the last time you spoke to someone who's done it.'

He lowered his eyes. He looked tired and defeated.

Maybe he wanted me to apologize, to understand that he was merely doing his job, that he didn't mean to upset me further.

I didn't apologize. Didn't say a thing. Didn't want to let him off the hook.

Fuck him too.

Fuck each and every one of them.

THIRTY-TWO

October 27th came and went.

Rousseau had told me the 27th would be the last day he could see me before November 11th.

My special day.

Most important day of my life.

But Rousseau didn't come. Told myself that if he came on the tenth he could turn round and go right back wherever he'd come from.

Hell, the guy would probably get some reporter to write a story about the time he'd spent with me. Make a few thousand. Donate some to the church so he didn't feel so guilty.

In a week I would move to Death Watch and begin the last seven days of my life.

I came in alone, I'd go out alone.

So be it.

There doesn't seem to be any way to prepare yourself for dying.

Dying is the great unknown, the one thing we all do that we can never tell anyone about. Perhaps here's the reason why we slow and rubberneck towards the scene of some highway smash. Perhaps we will see something; perhaps there will be some indication of what will happen to us when we go. And even those who deal with such things – the undertakers, the morticians, the coroners and executioners – know as little of this subject as everyone else. And despite their own familiarity with this closing chapter, they are no less afraid it seems.

No less afraid.

I am ready, I feel. As ready as I will ever be.

I will wait out the days until I am transferred to Death Watch, and then I will wait out the final hours before they tie me down and sedate me, before they cut loose the juice, so to speak.

Seems that before too long I will understand what happens when the lights go down for the last time.

One last thing to share with Nathan Verney.

Lyman Greeve got his harmonica today.

Within an hour I wanted to snatch it from him and hurl it out of the window and across the exercise yard.

Lyman was happy, however.

I let it be.

Didn't say a thing.

Mr. West walked down here.

He paused near the door of my cell. He paused just for a moment but I saw his face. He smiled, smiled with something dark and twisted in his eyes.

He was looking forward to November 4th. Transfer to Death Watch brought such a sense of finality. If there was an appeal, if there was to be word from the Governor or the District Attorney it usually came before the final week.

No such word had come.

I knew it wouldn't.

So did Mr. West.

And that's why he smiled.

The night of November 3rd I did not sleep. I tried, oh Lord how I tried, but sleep deserted me for someone else.

I could hear Lyman Greeve snoring. At least he wasn't

blowing his harmonica. To have Lyman Greeve's harmonica be the last sound you heard before your final week on earth would have been too much.

Grateful for small mercies.

I heard them coming as the sun rose.

I knew they would come before the bell.

They would come quietly, so as not to wake the other inmates.

I knew Mr. Timmons' footsteps, and Duty Second – whoever that was – would be behind him.

I counted those footsteps, all thirty-eight of them, and when I turned and opened my eyes and saw them looking at me through the bars I felt the wave of grief and desperation.

'Come on now, Daniel,' Mr. Timmons said. 'It's time to go.'

I lay there without moving.

Hardly dared even to breathe.

'We don't wanna come in there, Ford,' Duty Second said.

Mr. Timmons raised his hand and shook his head.

Back off, that gesture said.

Mr. Timmons squatted down on his haunches and looked through the bars at me.

Our heads were level.

'I gotta take you,' he said. 'You gotta come now or they're gonna have a medic come down here and sedate you, and then they're gonna shackle you and carry you down there . . . and that just ain't dignified, Daniel, it just ain't dignified.'

Terror gripped every atom of my being.

I was screaming inside, screaming louder than ever, but when I opened my mouth I just said *Let's do it*.

Duty Second stepped forward and passed the belt between the bars.

My hands were sweating and I struggled with it.

Mr. Timmons told Duty Second to go down and open the door.

Duty Second protested, said it was a violation of procedure, that they'd all regret it if something happened.

'Just go down and open the door,' Mr. Timmons said curtly, and Duty Second hesitated.

'Now,' Mr. Timmons said.

Duty Second went.

The buzzer sounded.

Mr. Timmons yanked the door back and stepped into my cell.

He helped me with the belt, tightened it around my waist, and then enclosed my wrists in the cuffs.

Duty Second appeared behind him and held out the ankle shackles.

'Step out,' Mr. Timmons said.

I followed him out of the cell onto the gantry.

Duty Second watched me while Mr. Timmons put on the ankle shackles.

We went side by side, Mr. Timmons to my right, Duty Second to my left.

At the end of the gantry we turned right, and as we approached the stairwell Duty Second stepped behind me as the well was too narrow for three abreast.

We went down slowly.

A funeral march.

At the bottom of the stairwell I started right, and Mr. Timmons was there ahead of me calling for the door to be unlocked.

The sounds . . . all those sounds – the buzzers, the grating of metal against metal, the clang of a door slamming into its socket, the turning of keys.

The sounds of my life it seemed.

I could feel my heart hammering in my chest, a swollen and angry fist, and yet beneath that such a sense of abject terror.

More than a decade I had waited for this point to arrive, and in all that time I had never been able to imagine the sheer horror of what I now felt.

The door came to behind me.

I turned instinctively and my view was blocked by Duty Second.

A long corridor stretched out before us.

The sound of footsteps, that was all, and the echo that came back, louder as we approached the door at the far end.

And yet, in that moment, despite everything, I knew this was nothing compared to what I would feel in seven days' time.

The door opened at the end and we passed through – Mr. Timmons first, Duty Second behind, myself in the middle.

We stood in a small office. To the right was a desk behind which sat the Administrative Officer, a small careful-looking man with an impeccably pressed uniform and shoes like black glass. Behind him and slightly to his right was the end of a narrow corridor, and down that corridor I could see the near side of the Death Watch cell.

Mr. Timmons stepped forward.

'Daniel John Ford, prisoner number 090987690.'

The Administrative Officer checked a box on a clipboard on his desk and then walked around the desk to stand near us.

He nodded at Timmons, at the Duty Second, and then stepped closer to me.

'My name is Frank Tilley,' he said. 'You call me Frank. That's the way it is down here, son. We run things slightly different from D-Block and General Populace. We run a twenty-four-hour watch, and that watch will be carried out by Mister Timmons and myself. There will never be a point during the next week when there won't be someone here to speak with you or to attend to what you need. You understand me so far?'

I said nothing.

My mind was blank.

Frank Tilley leaned forward and looked right into my eyes.

'You understanding me there, son?' he asked.

'Daniel?' Mr. Timmons prompted.

I nodded my head . . . I *think* I nodded my head.

They evidently perceived something because Frank Tilley said, 'Okay, son, good enough.'

He walked around to the other side of his desk.

'So we're gonna be here for a week, and each day at noon someone's gonna come down and take your temperature and do some basic physical checks on you. You're gonna eat a little better than you did upstairs, but nothing fancy. You need anything you let me or Mister Timmons know, and if it's within reason we'll see what we can do. You can smoke down here, and you'll get cigarettes provided.'

Frank Tilley stepped out from behind his desk again.

He leaned closer still and almost whispered to me.

'We expect there's gonna be a little difficulty here, Daniel. It's a rare man that doesn't get upset every once in a while during this last week, but I wanna let you know that there's nothing to be ashamed about; you wanna break down a little, you wanna pray out loud, something such as this, then you go ahead, son. We ain't gonna be judgin' anyone down here, 'cause we figure you've been judged already and we're here just to ensure that the letter of the law is met. Nevertheless, we don't forget you're a human being too, and you just strayed off of the line a little . . . okay?'

I nodded.

Twice.

My head was down then, didn't feel I had the strength to raise it again.

'Okay, Clarence,' Frank Tilley said.

Duty Second took my right arm, Clarence Timmons my left, and they walked me to the top of the cell corridor.

Frank Tilley went down and opened the door, and as I went down there I realized that the cell was built with bars to three sides, the wall to the back. Those bars ran to the ceiling, but they didn't disappear into the ceiling above, they met a metal plate a good six inches thick. I stepped up into the cell, and as I looked down I saw that the same metal plate was replicated for the base. The cell was a free-standing metal box, one exit and entry door, a slide at the base of the door through which could be passed food trays and other things.

I took a step further and stood in the middle of the box.

I could see a metal runner along the three facing walls about a foot off the ground. At each end of the three walls was a small red light wired into the runner.

Clarence Timmons noticed I was looking at it.

'Kick bar,' he said. 'If a prisoner grabs an officer and pulls him back against the cell bars, the officer can still activate the alarm by kicking the bar anywhere along its length. Just a safety precaution, Daniel . . .'

Clarence Timmons smiled. 'Let's do the cuffs eh, son?'

I shuffled towards him and he undid the cuffs, assisted me to remove the belt, and then knelt down to unlock the ankle shackles.

Taking the things out with him, he paused there in the cell doorway and looked at me.

'Maybe you should rest now,' he said. 'You'll find the bed here is a little less hard than the ones upstairs.'

He smiled again, smiled like he was welcoming me to Summer Camp, and then he slammed shut the cell door.

Sounded like a gunshot.

Sounded that final.

THIRTY-THREE

I don't really know how long I have been here but I already feel like someone is stealing time from me.

Frank Tilley had told me someone would come at noon to check my temperature, whatever else they do, and they came.

Ten minutes later Frank Tilley told me his shift had ended and Clarence Timmons was now coming down.

Clarence Timmons came down, no more than twenty minutes after the medic had left, and he told me it was a little after five.

Someone stole that many hours from me.

I know they did.

I think I might have heard them.

They came with soft-soled shoes, and they walked as if on eggshells, and they took some time, a couple of handfuls maybe, and then they left the way they'd come.

I called after them but they didn't hear me.

There are moments of startling lucidity.

I can close my eyes, and all I have to do is think of someone's name . . .

Caroline
Linny
Marty
Eve

. . . and their faces come to me as clear as daylight.

There are so many . . .

Sheryl Rose

Benny
Doctor Backermann
Emily Devereau

. . . and none of them know where I am.

I would like for them to know.

And then sometimes I feel that such a thing as this no-one should ever know.

Should be just between myself and God.

And Nathan Verney.

'Daniel?'

I look up.

Clarence Timmons stands there. In his hand he holds a brown paper bag, and at the bottom of it there are tiny dark spots, like there's something inside that's wet and showing through.

'My wife made this . . . a sweet apple fritter . . . you want it?'

Frank Tilley talks to me sometimes, and the feeling I get is that he is one sad and lonely man.

Yesterday, I *think* it was yesterday, he told me that he'd been to a baseball game in Charleston. He didn't say *Hey Daniel, me and my buddy Chester went to a game last Saturday* or *I took my wife to a game in Charleston last weekend*. He said *I went*, which made me think he'd gone alone.

Who goes to a baseball game alone?

Apparently Frank Tilley does.

Maybe he goes other places, places where people know who he is, and they talk about him when he's not in earshot, like *Hey, that's Frank Tilley . . . he looks after the guys down in Sumter when they're ready to fry them . . . hell, man, imagine what that kind of a job would do to you . . . sure as shit happy that I ain't Frank Tilley.*

Right now I would be happy to be Frank Tilley, even if I did go to ball games alone.

*

There's nothing down here.

I asked Frank if there was any way we could have a transistor radio, and though he smiled and looked like he understood, he told me that if he brought a radio down he would get his ass kicked from here to the Georgia state line and back.

Sorry kid, he said. *No radio.*

The third time I saw Clarence Timmons I asked him what day it was.

'Oh, you just reminded me,' he said. 'Warden's gonna come down at some point to speak with you. Can't tell you which day.'

And then he turned and walked back to his desk, and I was thinking about Warden Hadfield, and the moment was gone.

I never did find out what day it was.

Like I said before, sometimes there are moments of such intense lucidity.

I think about some of the events that I described to Father John Rousseau, and as I recall them they come back. Sometimes I close my eyes, and for a tiny moment I believe I can almost hear someone's voice.

Eve telling me about something or other, Nathan laughing as he shares a joke . . . such things as this.

Maybe the closer you get to your own death, the nearer you are to the dead.

They are somewhere, are they not?

Perhaps they are somewhere waiting for you, and as they wait they talk, and if you listen, listen real good, you can catch some vague echo of their voices.

I am not losing my mind.

Sometimes I think perhaps my mind is aware of what is about to happen, and in its unwillingness to share with me this moment of dying it is leaving early.

Like my memories are the things my mind is packing for its journey, and as it takes them out, as it folds them, I catch glimpses of those things before they are stowed forever.

Shit, maybe I *am* losing my mind.

At some point, two days, three even, Clarence came and told me that for his second shift that day he would not be there.

His wife, she had suffered a fall, nothing too serious it seemed, but he would have to drive her to the hospital for an X-ray.

I nodded.

'Daniel?'

I looked up through the bars from where I sat on the edge of my bed.

'Mister West will be coming down, just for those four hours, but I want you to say nothing to upset or aggrieve him, you understand me?'

At that my pulse slowed down, my heart too, and a feeling of intense claustrophobia pushed at the edges of my consciousness. I closed my eyes and rested my face in my hands.

'Daniel?'

I could hear Mr. Timmons but didn't want to respond.

'Daniel . . . I know you can hear me. You listen to me, son, you listen good. Mister West ain't gonna do anything. He says something to you, you use your own judgement whether you should respond or not. He ain't gonna come in there, but he may bait you, son, he may try and get you riled, but you just pay no mind . . . he's only gonna be here a coupla hours and then he'll be gone, okay?'

I didn't reply.

'I know you heard me, Daniel, so I ain't gonna repeat myself . . . but you mind what I say about this.'

I lay down.

I tugged the thin pillow out from under my head and covered my face.

Had I possessed the energy I would have cried.

I knew when he'd arrived.

I sensed the lights dim.

There was a feeling that came with him, a perception of something dark and angular, awkward facets that did not fit together without grinding and grating.

I held my breath.

'Mister Ford,' he said, his voice almost a whisper. 'How you doin' in there, son?'

I said nothing.

I was sitting on the edge of my bed, and my head was down, my eyes closed.

I heard the outer door close to and slam shut. That sound echoed forever.

'Seems to me you'd be a little lonesome there, Mister Ford ... eager for a little company, a little conversation, yes?'

Again I did not reply.

'Hey! Fucker! You fucking well look at me when I'm talking to you. You look at me right now or I'm coming in there and giving you the beating of your fucking life!'

I raised my head and opened my eyes.

Mr. West glared at me through the bars.

His face was beet red, his eyes wide, manic, like someone possessed, and when he saw I was looking at him he smiled, and stood upright.

'That's better,' he said, and his voice was once again a whisper.

'Now,' he said, 'let's talk about what's gonna be happening to you, my friend. That okay with you? You don't mind having a little chat about the next coupla days, right?'

Mr. West nodded.

'Good, fine, we'll do that.

'So come about five on Sunday they're gonna come down

here and shave your head again. Reason they do that is contact. Gotta have proper contact you see, and also if they don't shave your head then likely as not your hair will set on fire and it makes the place stink like hell. They're gonna ask you if you'll be wanting a sedative before they move you to the Procedure Room.'

Mr. West laughed.

'Don't matter what you say, boy, 'cause they don't give you a sedative, just some fucking glucose or saline or something. What the fuck would they wanna make you feel less pain for, eh? You're a killer, a fucking murderer, eye for an eye an' all that, right? So why would they be interested in saving you some pain? Shee-it, boy, it's gonna hurt. Heard that it's minutes of agony, the most agonizing pain you could ever imagine . . . and sometimes just one jolt ain't enough. Sometimes they gotta bang that sucker through you three or four times to get your heart to stop. Old guys, sure, no problem, could kill 'em plugging 'em into the wall socket . . . but a young healthy guy like you, strong heart, strong as a horse, hell wouldn't surprise me if they had to keep you running on that fucker for twenty or thirty minutes.'

He laughed again.

I tried hard to feel nothing, tried to block out his voice, but however hard I tried it seemed that the more I put my defenses up the weaker I became.

'They tell you all this shit about how it's humane, that it's instant fucking death . . . that's bullshit, son, just pure hundred percent bullshit. It's *designed* to fucking hurt, it's designed to make you feel like your brain is gonna explode all over the place . . . that's the way it's meant to be. And there's people gonna come down and they're gonna wanna watch you scream and wriggle and kick your feet, and look see as your head rocks back and forth like it's on a spring . . . and they'll love it, man, love every single second of it.'

I sought escape in my mind's eye.

I am standing on the edge of Lake Marion.

I can smell the breeze.

I hear my mother's voice.

She is calling us for dinner.

Calling both of us.

I turn and see Nathan standing there to my right.

He looks small.

He is a child.

'There's gonna be reporters, people from State Corrections, the nigger's folks –'

I must have reacted.

'Oh sure, they're gonna be there. You didn't know that? You didn't know that the dumb nigger priest and his fat wife are gonna be there? No-one told you? Hell, that's a fucking surprise isn't it? Shee-it, boy, they booked their tickets months ago . . . wanted a front row seat . . . wanted to see you kick your last little dance right up close.'

I sit up.

I lean towards the window.

I see Caroline Lanafeuille walking down the path from my house towards the road.

She turns as she reaches the end, she turns and looks up at me, and she smiles, and she blows me a kiss, and she says I love you . . .

'Everybody who's anybody's gonna be there, son . . . you're the main attraction, the real deal . . .'

Somewhere something moves.

Did I imagine it?

'Sure as hell, we ain't had us a fry-up here at Sumter for quite some time, and we ain't gonna want anyone to be missing this are we?'

Florida.

The sun is hot.

My hands are covered in fish.

Nathan is laughing at something.

I am laughing too, but I don't know why . . . and it doesn't

355

matter . . . nothing matters in the world . . . everything's gonna be fine . . . yes, everything's gonna be just fine . . .

'You listenin' to me, Ford?'

Mr. West stepped forward and looked at me close through the bars.

I felt something rising with me, something close and tight, something that told me I really had nothing to lose . . .

'You listen good now you fucked-up piece of shit. You hear what I'm saying now 'cause this is the end of your pathetic miserable life we're talking about here.'

There is a wave inside me, a wave of hate and anger and the intense desire to smash something, to smash some-*one . . .*

'Seems to me maybe there isn't enough to talk about . . . thirty-six years old, right? Thirty-six years wanderin' round accomplishing absolutely nothing. I'm right, ain't I?'

The wave builds, gonna break somewhere, gonna break against the shore and come crashing across the beach, and I can hear it, hear it inside my head, hear the sound of that wave filling my ears, filling my entire body . . .

'And now you're gonna get yourself fried come Monday for the only worthwhile thing you ever did . . . only thing you ever did that was worth a damned thing, eh Ford? Killed yourself a stupid fucking nigger.'

I went across the short space between myself and the bars faster than I could ever have imagined possible.

But Mr. West anticipated everything, knew how far to push, knew when I would snap, saw me coming as if I was in slow motion.

Even as I reached the bars his hand came through and grabbed the back of my head and pulled my face against the bars with a sudden jerk.

His other hand reached through and gripped my shirt around the waist. I was pinned up against the cold metal. It felt like he was trying to pull me right through the four-inch gaps.

I could feel his breath against my face.

It was cold.

There was no warmth inside.

Just the sound of his voice.

'You're fucked, Ford. You're just fucked, and there sure as shit ain't anyone in the world who gives a rat's ass about you and your pathetic little life. Your life is worth nothing ... less than nothing, and as far as I'm concerned they should just take you out and drop you off of D-Block into the yard and save the expense of the fucking electricity –'

I could feel the pressure of his fist against the middle of my body.

'And your life was *never* worth anything,' he hissed. 'You were just there, could've been anyone ... just anyone at all. You an' your dumb nigger friend gettin' involved with people who shouldn't have taken a piss on you if you'd been on fire.'

My eyes were wide.

I thought of Robert Schembri, what he'd said about West and Goldbourne.

West read my thoughts.

'Easy to put together, eh? You got fucked, fucked so bad it's gonna kill you.'

He smiled, an expression of heartfelt personal pleasure.

The hands suddenly released me and I fell back, my head missing the edge of the bed by mere inches.

I didn't see what happened for a few seconds.

There was silence, seemingly endless, and in among the silence there were waves of red and gray, something turquoise that seemed to burst silently out along the horizon of my consciousness.

I thought I heard footsteps. A door slammed. For a while there was nothing at all.

And then there was a voice.

Stay there, son, I got someone coming down to help you.

I did.

I stayed right where I was.

A little while later I felt someone helping me up, laying me down on the bed, and for a time there was the murmur of voices somewhere beyond the edges of my immediate perception.

I couldn't hear what they said.

I didn't care what they were saying.

I closed my eyes.

THIRTY-FOUR

'You wanna pray with me, son?'

I turned at the sound of Clarence Timmons' voice.

He is seated there beyond the bars, has pulled a chair up close and is looking through them at me as I lie there on the bed.

He is smiling.

'I heard you had some trouble with Mister West,' he said. 'I'm sorry, Daniel, sorry I wasn't here. I had to take my wife . . . and if it's any consolation she's gonna be fine.'

It wasn't. No consolation at all.

I moved my head and tried to smile anyway.

'I know it's tough, Daniel –'

Fuck you do.

'– but I want you to know that there's folks who believe in the basic goodness of people too, and that there's a better place in the end. So pray with me a while, okay?'

I didn't respond; I turned over and looked at the wall behind me. The side of my face was bruised and swollen. My tongue felt too big for my mouth.

'Our Father, who art in Heaven –'

Hell is in my brain.

'Thy kingdom come –'

My will is gone.

'– on earth as it is in Heaven. Give us this day –'

The day we're dead.

'– and forgive us our trespasses –'

As you just leave those who trespass against us.

And let them walk the face of the earth while you kill the innocent and the lonely and the weak and the defenseless, you Almighty son-of-a-bitch . . .

'Shut up! Shut the fuck up! Leave me alone for God's sake!'

I started to cry.

Mr. Timmons didn't say a thing.

He rose from his chair, lifted it quietly, and returned to his desk at the end of the corridor.

He didn't pray with me again.

Food came later.

The food was better down here.

Why was the food better down here?

Wanted to remind you what you were going to be missing? Wanted to do everything they could to ensure you held your strength up? Or was it that they felt sorry for you?

Fuck knows.

Fuck knows and who gives a shit.

I ate the stuff.

All of it.

And then I chain-smoked even though I knew Clarence Timmons didn't smoke and it would bother him.

Fuck him.

And his prayers.

Fuck everything.

I had been asleep, for how long I didn't know, but when I woke Clarence Timmons was gone and Frank Tilley was there.

I wanted to ask him what day it was, even the time, but I didn't.

Because I decided I didn't want to know. That way I could make believe I still had a week, or six days, or five. I knew I didn't have that much. I didn't want to know how much less.

I thought of John Rousseau.

I asked Frank where he was.

'Don't know, son ... don't know much about his comings and goings. Why?'

I told Frank that Father John Rousseau and I had spent many hours together for some weeks, that he said he would see me back on October 27th, that I missed talking to him.

Frank Tilley assumed an expression of philosophical resignation, and he said, 'Just because he's a priest, Daniel, don't mean that he's necessarily any more reliable than anyone else. Wouldn't get your hopes up too high, you know? If he comes he comes, if he doesn't he doesn't.'

He waited for me to respond.

I didn't. I had already accepted the fact I would never see Rousseau again. If he was a representative of God, then either God needed to be more selective about his staff, or God was in on the joke and loving it.

I forgot about it, tried to sleep, couldn't, and for some time I lay there looking at the ceiling wondering if it would be tomorrow that I would die.

They came a little later, two men in white tunic-tops. They brought an electric razor, a towel, a plastic bowl half-filled with water. They rested the bowl on the floor outside the cell, and the first one, the taller one, looked at me through the bars.

'I gotta shave your head,' he said. 'I know that it's fucked up, I know this is possibly the worst that it's ever gonna get, but I still gotta come in there and shave your head. You either co-operate and it's done in five minutes, or we have to call Medical and they come down and stick a tranquilizer in your ass and you go down like a lead weight ... how's it gonna be?'

'I co-operate,' I said.

'Good enough,' the man replied, and he nodded to Frank Tilley to come open up the door.

My hair was already very short, shorter than it had ever been, but they ran that thing over until I could feel my skull vibrating. It was not an unpleasant sensation, but beneath it was the awareness of why it was being done.

To get good contact.

When they'd gone I sat there on the edge of my bed with my hands on my head, and realized that the last time I'd had no hair was when I was born.

Go out as you came in.

Bring nothing with you, take nothing away.

I didn't eat later, but I puked on the food tray.

'No word from Rousseau?' I asked Clarence Timmons the next time I saw him.

Clarence shook his head.

'Fucker,' I whispered.

A while later Clarence asked me some questions.

Anyone you want to call?

No.

Anyone you want to be informed?

No, there's no-one.

And your . . . your remains, Daniel . . . you understand that a cremation will take place, and the ashes are buried here within the confines of the Penitentiary?

Flush 'em, Mr. Timmons . . . may as well just fucking well flush 'em down the john . . .

We speak of prescience, premonition, omens and portents, patterns in sand and waves, and the way the moon turns half its face towards you and tells you the future. There are dreams and nightmares, the lines in your hand and the wrinkles in your face, the discolorations in your eyes and remnants in your teacup after you've drunk the last drop. There are soothsayers and mind-readers and fortune-tellers, and the seventh daughter of the seventh daughter through a Romany line that runs all the way back to the old country.

There are all these things.

And then there is intuition.

Gut feelings.

And these things tell me I *will* die. I have never been more certain of anything. And I have never been more uncertain about what comes later.

What lies beyond?

What comes *afterwards*.

The walls are plain. There is no decoration. Upon those walls I can see all the images of my life. Everything that came before.

Sometimes I smell something familiar, and realize that this is the smell of myself. My own bodily scent. My own physical *being*. I am the one person I have never been without. And I think of things I should have said and done. Like my father once told me: *Folks never really regret what they've done, only what they didn't do.*

I didn't say anything.

Not to Linny Goldbourne – because of my envy, because of my pride, because of my own conceit and rightness. And she found herself lost somewhere within the system, much the same as me. The State would not be killing Linny Goldbourne, at least not physically.

And I said nothing to Nathan.

And he *was* killed.

So I should die too, right?

Father John Rousseau would have been all too quick to justify the universal balance in all things, wouldn't he?

If he were here.

But he is not.

Fucker.

*

Somehow I knew.

I *knew* the time had arrived.

I was sleeping, and I woke with a jolt.

And I *knew*.

A week had gone.

So fast.

Like a breath.

Like a heartbeat.

I lay on my side facing the back wall, and even as I heard sounds behind me there were other sounds as well. Sounds inside sounds. Sounds beneath sounds.

Somewhere I heard a child laughing and realized it was . . . *me, standing there on the front path watching a dog chase a cat, and the dog was so fat, and the cat was so fast, and the cat seemed to be laughing at the dog because it knew a great fat dog like that could never catch him* . . .

I smiled.

There were tears in my eyes.

'Ford?'

It was Mr. West's voice.

Mr. West had come to take me. This was my perfect justice.

I didn't move.

Didn't dare to breathe.

Play dead and they'll leave you alone.

'Ford . . . you gotta get up, you little cocksucker.'

And then, with such a sense of satisfaction in his tone, 'It's happy hour, you little fuck . . .'

I heard the key in the lock.

'Sit upright, sit still, and then don't fuckin' move 'til I tell you.'

I started to move and his hands were under my arms, under my shoulders, and I was being hoisted like a dead animal. I was hauled to the edge of the bed, and then Mr. West shackled my feet, put the belt around my waist, put my wrists in the cuffs and pulled me upright . . .

And then we were walking . . .

I was crying.

I know that.

We came out of the cell and crossed to the end of the corridor. We paused while the door was unlocked, and then we were moving again . . . and somewhere inside myself I resigned everything to some other force, some other power, and I hoped that there *was* a God, and I tried to believe . . .

I tried so hard to believe.

I asked for a sign.

I was a dead weight.

Dead meat.

We reached the end of the corridor, each footstep a labored and impossible movement, and each time I slowed Mr. West was there behind me, his arm, his hand impelling me forward . . .

And with each footstep there seemed to be a thousand heartbeats, and within each heartbeat a thousand memories, and within each memory a million reasons I didn't want to die . . .

'Mister West . . . Mister West, I don't wanna die . . .'

I heard my own voice from a distance.

I was a mile beyond here, a mile again beyond that.

'Mister West . . .'

'Too fucking late for that now, asshole . . . just too fucking late.'

I heard him.

I heard everything.

I heard my own heart and thought it would stop any moment.

Mr. West was now beside me. He indicated right.

'This way,' he said.

I glanced back at him. He was expressionless, implacable.

We went through a second and third door, and then down a flight of stairs.

I sensed we were heading towards the rear of D-Block.

How long now? I seemed to remember asking.

Perhaps I just thought it.

Mr. West looked back at me, but said nothing.

My heart was thundering in my chest, my pulse was racing. My hands, my legs, my entire body was a river of sweat, and yet I was chilled to the bone.

We passed through a door at the base of the stairs, and the light was brilliant.

I was dazed for a second, dazed into blindness, and even as I instinctively raised my hands and could not, even as I tried to turn and see where I was, I heard the sound of a car engine.

I turned to my right, and even in that moment I knew the end of my life was closing up against me.

Warden Hadfield stood there, immobile, his hands folded together like origami in front of him. His face was quiet, expressionless almost, and then there was something in his eyes, something warm . . . *It's okay, Daniel*, he mouthed.

I *knew* he wasn't there. I knew without doubt that my mind had slipped its moorings, and was now playing games, merging the present with past memory. I *knew* I was hallucinating, for beside him stood Father Rousseau, and Father Rousseau smiled understandingly, and beside Father Rousseau stood Caroline . . . Caroline Lanafeuille . . . and I believed perhaps she was my imaginary angel, sent to guide me out of this dark place . . .

I looked for Nathan, for my mother and father. I looked for Eve Chantry and Larry James, for the boys that became men in some desolate waterlogged field in a country we had never heard of before . . .

But they were not there, none of them . . . and how I longed to see someone with whom I could share what I was feeling.

I wanted to say something but Mr. West carried me forward, carried me punctually, precisely, effortlessly, to my death.

My knees gave.

'Daniel.'

Another voice.

Mr. Timmons.

His hand beneath my arm, holding me up.

Another hand on my shoulder, someone guiding me, and then they were telling me to duck my head. I could feel them bearing me up, and I was sitting without being aware of where I was sitting or why.

'Mister Timmons!' I shouted, and even as I heard my own voice it was the sound of a terrified and desperate child. 'Mister. Timmons!'

'Quieten down now, Ford,' Mr. West said.

'You told him?' I heard Clarence Timmons ask. 'You told him where we're going?'

'Sure did,' Mr. West replied. 'Sure I told him.'

'Told me?' I asked, my voice a painful twisted sound. 'Told me what?'

A door slammed.

I was inside a vehicle.

The bright light had come from windows high up in the wall.

I was seated in the back of a car.

The car was moving.

Mr. West sat facing me, smiling, smiling like I'd never seen anyone smile.

'Time's up, little man,' he whispered. 'Special arrangement for you, son, special arrangement altogether. Little trouble with the generators back there so we're takin' you someplace else to finish up. Won't take long, twenty, thirty minutes 'til we arrive ... an' that gives us a little more sharing time, don'tcha think?'

I think I pissed myself.

'Ain't so full of your self-righteous bullshit now, eh kid?' West hissed.

He leaned forward and gripped me around the throat

with his right hand. He leaned closer still, and when he spoke I could feel the dampness of his words against my skin. There was a smell there, something fetid and rotten, something age-old and rank from the very deepest of Florida swamps.

'You figure it gets easier here, son?' he asked. 'You figure we're in for a little ride and then they plug you in an' we's all done for the night. I think not. You have no fucking idea how much this is gonna hurt, no idea at all. No-one knows how much it hurts ... hell, we ain't ever had a chance to ask anyone, have we?'

West gave his coarse laugh.

He said other things – dark and hideous things – and somewhere within the beating of my heart, within the rumbling of the vehicle and the throbbing of the engine, I think consciousness slipped away.

I could see Caroline's face.

We should ... you know, we should ... before I leave ...

And then her face was a pattern in the wing of a moth, and then there was a flame, a brief rush of color.

... and moths are attracted to light because they wish to be seen, to have their own magical beauty recognized ...

I could hear my mother's voice calling me from the bottom of the stairwell.

Dan-ny! Dan-ny! Daaaa-ny!

And then there was a sensation like falling backwards, backwards in slow-motion ...

I felt a sharp pain in my side.

I opened my eyes.

'Get it together, shit-for-brains,' Mr. West hissed. 'You ain't passing out on me now, you fuck!'

I closed my eyes again, couldn't help it.

Felt like something dark and cool was dragging me inside itself.

I saw Eve Chantry.

... so she went out on her own, took that little boat out across the water one morning ...

Another pain in my side, sharper, harder, and then Mr. West brought his hand up and slapped me hard across the face.

'What the fu –'

His hand gripped my throat. His face was in mine. Closer than I imagined it could be.

'What the fuck? Is that what you were gonna say? What the fuck? Is that all you have to say for yourself in the last minutes of your worthless piece of shit life? I'll tell you what the fuck, Ford. I'll tell you the truth, right here and now. We're gonna be getting someplace real soon, and then they're gonna walk you down a long corridor, and that corridor will go on forever, feels like it will never end . . . and about halfway down you're gonna realize that there ain't no going back . . . and that's when you start to lose the plot completely. Guys tell me that you lose control of your muscles, can't walk properly, piss yourself –'

I am not hearing him.

I remember standing as a child with my fingers in my ears . . .

I can't hear you! I can't hear you!

I could feel his breath – cold and damp – against my face. I felt as if it was freezing against my skin.

Images flooded up towards me like a kaleidoscope.

Serpent Mike . . . is the Vietcong like King Kong?

My breath came short and fast as he gripped my throat . . . like he wanted his fingers to meet through my jugular.

Nathan's face?

Nathan was saying something.

Guilty is as guilty does . . . Dagnabbit Luke, fetch a rope . . .

'. . . feel like your tongue is swelled in your mouth, swelled up and choking you . . . and you wish to hell you would choke to death right there on your feet 'cause anything has to be better than frying alive, boiling in your own blood and bodily fluids, don'tcha think?'

I closed my eyes.

Mr. West slapped me again.

'Wake the fuck up, you asshole! Wake the fuck up!'

I tried to open my eyes. Couldn't.

I imagined John Rousseau was sitting facing me.

I believe there are still Cheyenne Dog Soldiers in the Oxbow . . . believe that Elvis is alive and well . . . I believe that they never really went to the moon . . .

I could feel Mr. West's fingers poking at my eyelids, forcing me to look right at him . . . and I did . . . I opened my eyes and I looked right back at him. His eyes were dark and black and soulless.

Like the deer I saw at the bend in the road near Eve Chantry's house a million and a half lifetimes before.

This is the candlemoth.

Hell of a thing, Mister Ford.

I could hear Jack Chantry's voice as he staggered from the side of the lake, his daughter's lifeless body in his arms . . .

. . . sounded like his soul had been wrenched from his body . . .

Hell of a thing, Mrs. Chantry.

I could hear the blackness coming. Black and gray with scarlet waves in between, and there was a sound like a rushing storm coming at me from left field . . .

And then there was nothing.

I was lifted from the car.

I heard Clarence Timmons' voice. He was speaking to Mr. West.

'You told him where we were coming and why?' Timmons asked him.

'Sure I did,' West replied sharply. 'I told you once already.'

Clarence Timmons came forward. His face was sympathetic and understanding. He reached towards me and helped me to stand. He started walking me, slowly, carefully, and before I knew it we were entering the mouth of some high-ceilinged corridor.

I didn't know where I was, and even as I turned to open my mouth, to ask something, to ask *anything*, Mr. Timmons smiled and nodded and indicated forward.

Why did he smile?

Was he pleased he would no longer have to speak with me?

Was he upset because I didn't pray with him, that I had now demonstrated my lack of faith, my ungodliness, and thus had given reason enough to die?

I tried to open my mouth again, but my lips were stuck together.

I stumbled forward, I lost my balance for a moment, but there were hands to catch me, so many hands . . . as if no-one wanted me to lose it now, to lose it in the most significant moment of my life.

The moment of my death.

Even as I staggered forward, breathless, disorientated, I could imagine them holding me down, the cool hard surface of the chair, the electrodes they would stick to my scalp, the smell of the cloth as they placed a black hood over my head . . .

So your eyes don't explode all over your chest and upset folks too much . . .

And then the waiting.

Seconds becoming minutes.

Minutes becoming hours.

Somewhere the sound of a ticking clock.

No-one daring to move for fear of breaking the breathless and horrifying tension.

And feeling a cool bead of sweat escaping from my forehead, running down my nose.

The sensation . . . possibly the last sensation I would ever feel . . .

Until the pain came.

Like lightning.

Like fire ripping through my body.

Like a knife so great it would pierce your skull and run right through your frame until you were suspended upon it like a marionette.

And wishing you would choke to death as everything inside you rushed upwards in some vain attempt to escape the sheer tidal wave of agony . . .

And screaming . . .

And hearing nothing . . .

Because the sound is inside your head.

Because you died already, but no-one knows it, and they keep running that generator as the lights dim . . . and outside the gate the protesters and life campaigners wait and listen and realize that yet again there was no point in being there at all . . .

'Cause Daniel Ford is dead.

Deader 'an Elvis.

I gave up then.

In that final moment as we reached the end of the corridor I gave up.

Consigned myself to fate and destiny and the will of God.

We came through the door at the end. We came through it as if surfacing from water, breath gasping, a burning fist of terror inside me, and that fist enclosing my heart and threatening to squeeze every last drop of blood between its fingers . . .

My legs didn't work. Nothing worked. Every muscle like Jell-O, my arms like worn-out elastic, limp and lifeless.

I closed my eyes. I didn't want to see the Procedure Room ahead of me, the steel doors, the porthole windows, the chair where my last dying wish would fail to rescue me. The patient and expressionless men whose God-given task it was to burn me alive. And knowing that the letter of the law *must* have been seen to be done for me to be here at all, they would rest easy in their certainty that what the Bible said was in fact the word of God. An eye for an eye . . .

A smell filled my nostrils. It was unmistakable. I couldn't have described it, but it was there – the realest thing of all. Like the dust that gathers on books, like wooden floors and vaulted ceilings, and a thousand years of precedents.

We came through the door, and then there were two police officers, one on each side of me, helping me as I stumbled along an aisle between two banks of chairs . . .

Is this where they will sit? Is this where Nathan's mother and father will sit to watch the show?

I saw my feet dragging along as if by themselves, each step a motion that required the greatest effort. I watched my feet because I couldn't look up . . . couldn't bear to see the end coming, knowing that now – now at last – there was nothing that could be done . . .

And with my bright orange overalls, my hands and feet shackled, my shaved head, I felt like some demented clown.

I was almost carried the last few yards, and then I was being directed to sit.

I squeezed my eyes tight.

I opened my mouth to scream, but only silence issued forth.

I waited for the hands, the electrodes, the cotton sack they would place over my head . . .

The sounds of breathing, my own and others', the smell of my sweat escaping before it became steam . . .

The sensation of time stretching out before me, every second becoming a minute, every minute becoming an hour . . . my entire life now encapsulated within a single explosive heartbeat that would signify the end of all that I had ever been, all that I could have become . . .

Oh God, oh God, oh God . . . not like this . . . not like this . . . any other way than this . . .

There was a voice.

'Open your eyes, Mister Ford.'

It was a new voice, a voice I had not heard before. I didn't wish to comply. I didn't want to see the faces of the men who would do this to me.

'Open your eyes please, Mister Ford,' the voice repeated.

I shook my head.

'Mister Ford,' the voice demanded, curt and authoritarian.

My eyes opened involuntarily. I cursed them. I wished I were blind.

The light dazzled me. Stunned me. For a moment I could gain no bearings, and then as colors and shapes swam into view I saw a wide table ahead of me, another twenty feet ahead of me a witness box, to the right and adjacent an elevated podium, a desk upon it, and upon the desk a decanter of water and an upended glass.

The police officers sat behind me.

I tried to turn, almost fell as my ankle shackles twisted around my feet, and then there were people coming, the sound of voices, a uniformed bailiff appearing from a door behind the podium.

I wondered if I was dreaming.

I wondered if I was already dead, waiting for my final judgement.

The bailiff shuffled some papers ahead of him and stood up.

'All rise,' he commanded.

I tried to stand up, I felt sick, dizzy, and then one of the police officers was again behind me, assisting me to rise.

I stood uneasily, awkwardly, like a child learning to balance.

I thought of a small colored girl, no more than five or six, her hair tied up in wiry pigtails with bright bows at the ends, as if she wore some strange exotic flowers with sunshine yellow petals and black stems ... down there along Nine Mile Road she was going, tears running down her face, her eyes wide and hopeless ...

And in that moment I wondered if this was the last thought I would ever have . . . the Killing of the King . . .

'All rise,' the bailiff commanded again. 'South Carolina State Appellate Court is in session, the honorable Judge Thomas J. Cotton presiding.'

From the same door through which the bailiff had appeared the Judge came. A tall man, imposing, distinguished, his bearing immaculate and refined. He walked across the back of the podium and sat down.

He raised his gavel and banged it once.

'Let's make this fast. It's early, I'm not supposed to be here. Who's up first?'

I heard footsteps behind me. I tried to turn and couldn't.

Someone passed me and walked towards the witness box.

I watched him go.

The bailiff stepped forward to give the oath.

The man reached the witness box, took one step up and turned.

Then I *knew* I was dreaming.

It was Father John.

He was not wearing his collar.

I tried to stand.

A police officer appeared over my left shoulder, his hand on my arm, and he brought me down into the chair once more.

I could hear the bailiff swearing in the oath.

'Name?'

'Frank Stroud.'

The Judge turned and looked at him. 'Mister Stroud,' he said, smiling. 'A pleasure to see you again.'

I looked at Father John. He looked back at me. His face was expressionless, implacable.

'But –' I started, my voice weak and strained. 'Father John . . .'

The Judge nodded at one of the police officers and I was told once again to sit still, to quieten down.

'Well, this is a better morning than I anticipated,' the Judge said. 'Well, despite the fact that we all know you very well, please give your occupation for the Court stenographer.'

'South Carolina Federal Court Special Investigator.'

'And what exciting revelations have you today, Mister Stroud?' the Judge asked. 'I understand that you have an assistant who will be giving evidence, and also some witnesses.'

'Yes, Your Honor. I have an assistant who will outline the facts of this case, and then statements from three witnesses.'

My heart stopped.

I started to cry.

I tried to turn, tried to see anyone – Mr. West, Mr. Timmons . . .

You told him where we were coming and why?

I sensed someone behind me.

Again I tried to turn.

Again I failed.

A hand on my shoulder.

I smelled perfume.

'Sit still,' a voice said.

Her voice.

Caroline . . .

A voice from someplace a thousand years before . . . and within that voice was everything I could ever remember from home.

The tears rushed from me like a wave, running down my face.

I could barely catch my breath.

'Bailiff, please see to the appellant, give him a glass of water or something,' the Judge said.

The Judge turned once more to Father John, a man he kept calling Frank Stroud. 'And your witness statements?'

Stroud nodded. 'Retired Sergeant Karl Jackson of the Greenleaf City Police Department, an Audio Forensics expert from the Charleston FBI office, and a Miss Linda Goldbourne.'

And after that name, and after Caroline Lanafeuille sat down beside me, I heard little else.

There were voices, people's faces, names and dates and questions. Endless questions.

And when Linny came down there, when she walked past me, and when I saw the expression on her face – an expression of such pain and sympathy and compassion and fear – I felt a sound escaping from my lips.

Uuuhhh . . .

A sound like Jack Chantry must have made as he kneeled in the dirt with his daughter in his arms.

It all came back.

Everything.

Every sound, every color, every emotion and thought and broken hope. Everything.

And there was silence in my head.

I stayed seated for some hollow eternity.

I felt nothing.

Every once in a while there was a rushing sound inside my head, like someone had let the sea loose and it was coming to take me.

At one point I thought I would faint, and as I pitched forward towards the table, one of the policemen was there behind me, and I could hear his voice, gentle, almost comforting, saying something that I cannot now recall.

And I sensed *her* beside me . . . my Caroline . . . and it was all I could do to restrain myself from turning to face her . . . I wanted to see her face, wanted to so much, but I could not – dared not – for in that moment I believed that if I saw her

377

face I would wake and find that all this was nothing but a cruel dream.

And then more people, people saying things I couldn't even begin to understand. And time was unravelling around me, and there were voices within that time, voices from my past, names and moments and memories I had quite forgotten.

And all the while *she* was there beside me.

At one point she reached out and closed her hand over mine. A sensation like electricity, but slow and gentle, passed through me.

And then there was a commotion to my right, and I saw the bailiff standing, and he turned to the Judge, and the Judge leaned forward, and he said:

'Appears to me, Mister Ford, that you have been the victim of a complex and involved conspiracy. If the technical information given about your taped confession presented here by Mister Stroud's expert witness, combined with the testimony regarding the actions taken by Richard Goldbourne to have his daughter indefinitely incarcerated in the State Psychiatric Hospital, are in fact true . . . well, if these things prove to have even a shred of credibility, I would be hard pushed to find any judge who would not throw this conviction out.

'Stay of execution granted.

'Appeal granted.'

The gavel came down.

I could hear myself crying, and then making that sound once more . . .

Uuuhhh . . .

I think I pissed myself again.

THIRTY-FIVE

Four months later.

Reverend Verney stands in the hallway of his house. From where he stands he can see the TV in the front room. He can see his wife as she watches it.

A pretty blonde girl appears on the screen.

She holds a microphone.

Behind her Reverend Verney can see a Penitentiary building.

The pretty blonde girl speaks.

'In yet another revelation today, the South Carolina State Appellate Court ruled that Daniel Ford, the Sumter Penitentiary Death Row inmate found guilty in 1971 of the murder of Nathan Verney, was tried unconstitutionally and was the victim of a premeditated conspiracy. South Carolina District Attorney Robert Moriera today issued a subpoena for ex-Greenleaf City P.D. Lieutenant Michael Garrett after testimony forwarded by retired P.D. Sergeant Karl Jackson revealed that Garrett was involved in the conspiracy. In return for his testimony, Sergeant Jackson is said to have been granted immunity from prosecution.

'Special Investigator Frank Stroud, a man who earned his reputation in the early '70s when he was involved in the failed attempt to prosecute Congressman Richard Goldbourne for complicity in the assassination of Robert Kennedy, said today that he was overjoyed at the outcome of the appeal, and stressed the importance of reviewing the death penalty and its consequences in South Carolina.

'Perhaps the most astonishing aspect of this case was that

of Linda Goldbourne, daughter of Richard Goldbourne who, prior to his death, had been a leading political figure in the State. Information revealed during the appeal indicated that Linda Goldbourne had been incarcerated in South Carolina State Psychiatric Hospital by her father for nearly twelve years, in fact the same length of time Daniel Ford was himself imprisoned.

'Having been classified as mentally unfit to give testimony at Ford's original trial in the early '70s, Miss Goldbourne's legal and personal affairs were managed exclusively by her father. In order to prevent her from appearing before the court or making a statement to the police, Richard Goldbourne continued to deny his daughter access to any visitors except himself and certain immediate family members. With his death, Linda Goldbourne was interviewed by Special Prosecutor Stroud and the full facts of the original killing were made available.

'Though District Attorney Moriera made it clear that convictions were unlikely due to the death of Richard Goldbourne, he still emphasized his gratitude to Special Prosecutor Stroud in uncovering this dramatic miscarriage of justice.

'And now, leaving Daniel Ford somewhere in South Carolina celebrating his release after twelve years of imprisonment, and his rescue just two days before his date of execution, this is Cindy Giddings for NBC News returning you to the studio . . .'

Mrs. Verney stands and turns.

There are tears in her eyes.

She reaches out her hands and her husband walks towards her.

His huge presence engulfs her, and she buries her face in his shirt.

'Praise the Lord,' he whispers. 'Praise the Lord . . .'

No-one had told me what was happening. Father John said

he wished to avoid any possibility of false hope being given.

He figured I was more likely to talk to a priest than a Federal investigator. So he changed his profession, and he changed his name.

And Linny Goldbourne had been the one to start all of this. After her father's death she spoke freely. Stroud had been there to listen to her, just as he had listened to me. And if he listened because he wanted to bring Richard Goldbourne down any way he could it didn't matter. The fact was that he listened, and he listened good. Linny told him she didn't know who had killed Nathan, had never seen them before herself, but she did know one thing.

I had not murdered him.

I am sitting in a diner somewhere in Charleston.

Opposite me is Caroline Lanafeuille.

She is beautiful. Her hair is multi-hued between amber and ochre and straw. And then there is the way she tilts her head and half-smiles.

'And so she'll return home,' she is saying, but I am not really paying much attention. I am watching her lips move. I am thinking that once there was a time when I had kissed those lips. A time that now seems a hundred lifetimes ago. A life that I believe now could never have been mine.

'And seeing as her mother's still alive, and the family home is more than sufficient for her needs, I think Linny will be fine. It will take time . . . like with you, Danny.'

She reaches out and takes my hand. She smiles. 'But I think she will be fine.'

I smile. Sometimes I feel like crying, but now it is different.

'Thank you,' I say, I think for the hundred thousandth time.

She nods.

A waitress appears to my right.

'You folks hungry?' she asks.

'Starving,' Caroline says. 'Can you make some eggs and rye toast?'

The girl, whose badge says Charlene, says *Sure we can make eggs and rye toast.*

And then Charlene turns to me, and she smiles, and she asks me what I want.

I look up at her. I want to hug her. 'You have a baked ham sandwich?'

Charlene smiles again. She has the whitest teeth of anyone I've seen.

'Sure we have baked ham,' she says. 'Honey, we have the finest baked ham this side of the Georgia state line.'

I start to laugh.

Caroline frowns.

Charlene starts laughing too, but she doesn't know why.

Frank Stroud did not lose his job for impersonating a priest.

He made me believe such a thing was possible, but he was joking.

He seemed to take it all in his stride, like he didn't even need me to tell him thank you.

After the appeal was over, after my story was forgotten news, I saw him on TV. He was saying something about corruption in some police precinct somewhere.

He was like that, it seemed. Always fighting something.

I will never forget him.

She ate her eggs the same way she always had.

We could have been in Benny's. We could have been on the verandah enjoying the smell of my mother's fried chicken cooking.

I asked her why; why did she come to see me after so many years?

She just smiled. She just smiled and said *Because* . . .

I asked her also why she left the way she did, what it was

that her father did that prompted their sudden departure from Greenleaf all those years ago.

She was quiet for a time, and then she said that there were things that happened back then that she didn't understand, but she felt it had something to do with people he was involved with. He had been a doctor, a good one, but there were people who came to him for help late at night, or the early hours of the morning sometimes, and she believed that those people were connected to another part of his life that he had no wish to share with her.

She had thought about pursuing this, discovering the truth of what had happened, but she'd been scared to look, scared to touch a wound that was almost healed.

And then she smiled once more, and laughed gently, and we didn't speak of it again.

'I would like to see you again,' I said.

'I understand,' Caroline said.

I leaned forward imperceptibly. There was something in her expression, something there back of her eyes . . . a word, a sound . . . something . . .

I felt my heart close up like a child's fist, tight and desperate, a futile response.

'I have a life, Daniel –'

She looked at me, looked right through me perhaps.

I felt transparent.

I heard nothing but the sound of my own heart, beating frantically like the wings of a moth.

'I have a life,' she said, repeating it as if to convince herself. 'What happened between us . . . we were kids, nothing more than kids . . . you know that, right?'

I sensed a fragment of desperation in her tone, as if once again she was saying these things merely to convince herself that she was right.

'I have a job,' she went on, 'and I have my own house and a car and a dog . . .'

She paused, she looked right at me. There was something

so direct in her unflinching gaze that I was momentarily unnerved.

'And a husband,' she said. 'I have my life . . .'

She glanced away. I could see tears welling in the corners of her eyes.

'Frank came to see me . . . he told me about Linny, how her father had died and she wanted to give evidence about what had happened. He told me she had tried again and again to send some message out but her father had always been there. He told me what he was doing and why . . . and believe me, I wanted to believe you were innocent; all these years I really wanted to believe you were innocent . . . and now I know you are I feel like I have attained some sense of closure . . .'

She reached towards me and closed her hand over mine.

'But I can't see you again. You have to go forward, Daniel, but I can't go backwards to meet you, you understand?'

I did not, but I nodded as if I did, perhaps in an effort to make myself believe I understood her, believe that she was right.

'I wanted to see you again,' she whispered. 'I thought of you often, more than often, but I could never bring myself to come see you in that place . . . the thought of you dying . . .'

She turned away, just for a moment she turned away.

'I wanted to make sure you were okay . . . I wanted to tell you that whatever anyone might have said, you were the first.'

I looked up at her.

She smiled with that same tilt to the side, her hair falling in slow-motion.

'Always the first. And I did love you, loved you the only way I knew how back then . . . but I have to leave you here to find your own way.'

She left the rest of her eggs and rye toast.

I watched her rise. I watched her edge sideways from behind the table. I watched her stand and gather her things, reach towards me and touch the side of my face.

I could smell her perfume even after I could no longer see her.

And though I heard the sound of her car I did not turn and look through the window to watch her disappear.

I did not let her go; I was merely bound by honor to release her.

And released she was . . . like a moth, in that last hair's-breadth of silence before the flame at last consumes.

And there were so many questions I had wanted to ask her.

I felt a breeze creep in through the diner exit, a breeze that seemed to close in around my table and occupy the seat where Caroline had been only moments before, and I wondered if I would ever have had the courage to ask those questions.

She had come and gone so quickly.

Just like before.

I stared at the plate ahead of me.

You have to make your own way now, Daniel . . .

I questioned her reasoning and motivation for coming at all.

. . . attain some sense of closure . . .

What had Frank Stroud told her?

I believed I would never ask him.

I believed he would perhaps tell me the same thing: that I had to find my own way.

So I let her go without a struggle.

And as the sound of her car faded into nothing I told myself that I *had* let her go.

Time would tell.

I believe I will see him again, my brother.

He will hold his head high.

As will I.

And this time, when we walk together, we will not take separate paths.

We will walk side-by-side, as we always did . . . if not in body, then surely in spirit.

Sometimes I ask myself about my own life. By almost anyone's standards I am still a young man, a man who has seen twelve years of his life folded away quietly somewhere in the zone of forgetting.

Sometimes I try to tell myself that those twelve years were part of my growing up, part of the necessary steps I had to take in order to become an adult.

I watch people around me – in the street, the mall, the tidy lives of those who spend their daylight hours confined within some office somewhere – and I see how they take those hours and days and months for granted.

To do such a thing scares me.

People sometimes ask me about myself, just in passing you know, like at the bus station, waiting somewhere for something one has to wait for, and I smile, I make small talk, and I tell little white lies. Not because I am ashamed, for I know, have always known, that killing a man was never within me. That's why I didn't go to war. But people are prejudiced and judgemental, and their own past experiences have served to darken their thoughts and expectations. Like they expect the worst. Like they are indoctrinated into thinking that it's always best to believe the worst . . . for in that way you can rarely be caught out.

Truth is, I am not trying to catch anyone, but then again I wouldn't expect them to know that. I am a stranger, just like everyone else who passes in the street, and it seems a shame that these days one cannot smile at a child, an adult even, and not be received with some air of suspicion.

I will find work. I was never afraid of it, and it will come my way, but for now, just for a little while, I will take the time to look at the world once more. To try and see it for what it truly is. I forgot how it was, and I find myself in a position where I am learning all over again. There is a certain magic in the process, like sight returning to the blind, hearing to a deaf man, but there is, equally, pain in my recognition that as we have advanced in so many ways, we have also walked backwards.

And the house where I was once a child still stands. It is damp. The windows are broken. The screen door hangs from its hinges and leans out across the front steps like a drunk. When you stand on those steps you can feel your weight threatening the very fabric of the structure.

But still, I went down there.

Went inside.

I was alone, it was quiet as a cemetery, and once inside I moved slowly, carefully, walking on eggshells. Once again I stood in the hallway looking through into the kitchen where almost every childhood meal had been eaten, where Nathan and I had hidden from the world when we returned from Florida. I turned and stood in the same doorway where I had watched Nathan and Linny, where I had believed my trust violated, where I had recognized my own inability to control the significant aspects of my life.

I shed some tears. For Nathan. For Linny. For myself.

I think of her even now – Linny Goldbourne – and I imagine her somewhere in South Carolina, coping with her own healing process, and though I could pick up a phone and hear the sound of her voice within a heartbeat, I do not wish to.

I believe also that she does not wish to speak with me, because each of us would remind the other of a part of our lives that is now gone. Not forgotten, just gone. A part that is better gone.

What happened, happened.

We should each let it go.

The first time I returned home I did not go upstairs. I told myself that it was dangerous, that perhaps the stairs were unsafe. That was not the truth.

So I went back, and I steeled myself, and I went up there like a ghost from my own past and stood there on the upper landing and looked in through the door of my bedroom.

I left with the candlemoth, clutching that small wooden frame, the glass intact, the creature behind still perfectly preserved.

I hung it above the narrow bed in a room on the outskirts of Charleston, a room I call home for now.

I will sell the house, and I will eventually decide what to do and where to go.

For now it doesn't matter.

I have time.

I had time at Charleston, time at Sumter.

Now I have a different kind of time.

Like each day is a new thing, and I want for it to mean something.

I ask myself what life is, what does it mean? Perhaps nothing more than a story, and each story different and rare and pronounced with its own voice. Some lives rich and heady, tales told with such fervor and passion one is lost in the language of the telling. Other lives racing forward with such power one would be carried along by the sheer momentum of events, and care not how they had been told. Or what language had been used. Just that they were, and you were there to hear about them.

I believed – once upon an age ago – that I would perhaps have such a life.

And then I lost my belief.

And then it was recovered.

And one day, *some* day, I will have a son.

I *know* this.

I will call him Nathan.

I believe that would be fitting.

And when I say his name, and when he looks at me with love in his eyes, I will be reminded of baked ham sandwiches wrapped in linen.

Of a fish in Eve Chantry's mailbox.

Of the breeze off of Lake Marion, of summer mimosa down near Nine Mile Road, and the scent of something like pecan pie and vanilla soda all wrapped up in a basket of new-mown grass.

Reminded of the feeling that came with them, a feeling of warmth and security and everything that was childhood in South Carolina.

Reminded of all those early years, the bruises and tears, the passion and promise of growing up, the pains we suffered in our naïveté as we looked at the world with awe. And like gourds we were, and how the world rushed in to fill us to bursting ... the sound and the fury ... the thunder of life ...

All these things ... all these things I will remember.

But most of all, more important than everything else, I will remember the boy with whom I shared them.

He gave his life, not for nothing I know, but still he gave it.

And yet, in giving his life, I somehow regained mine.

And I am grateful.

EPILOGUE

I stand in a market somewhere. Absent-mindedly I glance towards the fruit – watermelons and quinces, pomegranates, other such alien things. I feel a moment of fear, of desperation. I want to say something, anything perhaps, but the aisle is empty. I want to call out, to hear someone's voice in return . . .

Hey there!

What?

You heard about the cell search?

What cell search?

Timmons said there was gonna be a cell search.

There is tension in my chest, tears in my eyes, and stepping to the side of the aisle I lean heavily against the fruit stand. I look down at my feet. I am standing on a single sheet of newspaper. I kick it away, but it sticks to the sole of my shoe. I balance myself awkwardly and lean down to pull it free.

I turn the paper over.

I stop.

I wipe my eyes and look again.

I see the face of Mr. West and am struck by such a sense of terror and anguish I can barely breathe.

I run from the market, people watching me fly through the aisles. Perhaps I stole something, they think.

Thirty yards down the street I stop. I am breathing heavily, painfully. In my hand I clutch the dirty sheet of newspaper. I look again. No hallucination: Mr. West's face stares back at me. Deadlight eyes.

WARDER MURDERED.

I lean against a streetlight. I feel dizzy, nauseous.

Sumter Federal Penitentiary Warder Harlon West, a thirty-year veteran of the Detention Service, was murdered last night in a brutal attack.

My mind reels. I see colors that cannot be there.

Death Row inmate Lyman Greeve, due to be executed in the New Year, assaulted West and held him to the ground. With the metal casing of a cheap harmonica Greeve stabbed West repeatedly in the throat.

I start to cry, the tears run down my face. People are watching me. I don't care.

One of Harlon West's colleagues and fellow warders, Clarence Timmons, was quoted as saying that every attempt had been made to reach West before Greeve killed him, but 'the man was wild, he just got away from us . . . and before we could do a thing Mister West was beyond rescue.'

I start to laugh. Now folks are really watching.

Warden of Sumter Federal Penitentiary John Hadfield stated that Harlon West was a long-serving and dedicated member of the Detention staff and would be sorely missed by his colleagues.

I hold the newspaper in the air. I wave it like a flag. I believe in karma. I believe there is a God.

I believe Lyman Greeve will go to his death a great deal more satisfied than if he'd learned 'My Darling Clementine' . . .

And I believe that Nathan – perhaps more than anyone – would have appreciated that.